"An action-packed, globe-trotting thriller!"

King David's lyre wields a great and terrible power. With it, David raised thunderstorms, controlled the beasts of land and sky, and conquered a kingdom. Until it drove him mad. Now, a power-hungry cult leader seeks to harness its power to bring the world to its knees, and it's up to former Navy SEALs turned treasure hunters, Dane Maddock and Bones Bonebrake, to find the lyre before it falls into the hands of the minions of Prester John.

The modern world meets an ancient power in the globe-trotting adventure, BAAL!

Classic adventure for the modern reader! Fans of Indiana Jones, Doc Savage, and National Treasure will love Dane Maddock!

Praise for David Wood and The Dane Maddock Adventures!

"With the thoroughly enjoyable way Mr. Wood has mixed speculative history with our modern-day pursuit of truth, he has created a story that thrills and makes one think beyond the boundaries of mere fiction and enter the world of 'why not'?" David Lynn Golemon, Author of the *Event Group* series

"What an adventure! A great read that provides lots of action, and thoughtful insight as well, into strange realms that are sometimes best left unexplored." Paul Kemprecos, author of *Cool Blue Tomb* and the *NUMA Files*

"Dane and Bones.... Together they're unstoppable. Rip roaring action from start to finish. Wit and humor throughout. Just one question - how soon until the next one? Because I can't wait." Graham Brown, author of *Shadows of the Midnight Sun*

"A page-turning yarn blending high action, Biblical speculation, ancient secrets, and nasty creatures. Indiana Jones better watch his back!" Jeremy Robinson, author of *SecondWorld*

"Let there be no confusion: David Wood is the next Clive Cussler. Once you start reading, you won't be able to stop until the last mystery plays out in the final line." Edward G. Talbot, author of *2012: The Fifth World*

"A twisty tale of adventure and intrigue that never lets up and never lets go!" Robert Masello, author of *The Einstein Prophecy*

"I like my thrillers with lots of explosions, global locations, and a mystery where I learn something new. Wood delivers! Recommended as a fast paced, kick ass read." J.F. Penn, author of *Desecration*

BAAL

A DANE MADDOCK ADVENTURE

DAVID WOOD
C.B. MATSON

ADRENALINE PRESS

BOOKS BY DAVID WOOD

THE DANE MADDOCK ADVENTURES
Blue Descent
Dourado
Cibola
Quest
Icefall
Buccaneer
Atlantis
Ark
Xibalba
Loch
Solomon Key
Contest
Serpent
Eden Quest

DANE AND BONES ORIGINS
Freedom
Hell Ship
Splashdown
Dead Ice
Liberty
Electra
Amber
Justice
Treasure of the Dead
Bloodstorm

DANE MADDOCK UNIVERSE
Berserk
Maug
Elementals
Cavern

Devil's Face
Herald
Brainwash
The Tomb
Shasta
Legends
Golden Dragon
Emerald Dragon
Baal
Destination: Rio
Destination: Luxor
Destination: Sofia

BONES BONEBRAKE ADVENTURES
Primitive
The Book of Bones
Skin and Bones
Lost City
Alamo Gold
Lair of the Swamp With

BROCK STONE ADVENTURES
Arena of Souls
Track of the Beast
Curse of the Pharaoh

MYRMIDON FILES (WITH SEAN ELLIS)
Destiny
Mystic

JADE IHARA ADVENTURES (WITH SEAN ELLIS)
Oracle
Changeling
Exile

JAKE CROWLEY ADVENTURES WITH ALAN BAXTER
Sanctum
Blood Codex
Anubis Key
Revenant

SAM ASTON INVESTIGATIONS (WITH ALAN BAXTER)
Primordial
Overlord
Crocalypse

STAND-ALONE NOVELS
Into the Woods (with David S. Wood)
The Zombie-Driven Life
You Suck
Callsign: Queen (with Jeremy Robinson)
Dark Rite (with Alan Baxter)

WRITING AS FINN GRAY
Aquaria Falling
Aquaria Burning
The Gate

WRITING AS DAVID DEBORD

THE ABSENT GODS TRILOGY
The Silver Serpent
Keeper of the Mists
The Gates of Iron

The Impostor Prince (with Ryan A. Span)
Neptune's Key

Baal- ©2023 by David Wood

The Dane Maddock Adventures™

Published by Adrenaline Press
www.adrenaline.press

Adrenaline Press is an imprint of Gryphonwood Press
www.gryphonwoodpress.com

Prologue

Niki elbowed Ezio awake when Loizos emerged into daylight. A shovel in his hand and a bag on his shoulder, the old man paused to scan the surrounding hills. Niki hunkered a little lower in the bushes. "See, I told you he finds treasure here."

A few years younger, little Ezio peeked between the leaves. "Father said Loizos will kill us if he catches us again."

"That is why he must not catch us. This time we wait until he meets with the German before we search the cave."

Sage beyond his years, Ezio pulled a wry smile and nodded. "Loizos harvests the old things and sells them to the French, the Germans, whoever has the drachma to pay him."

"It's garbage," Niki said, "broken pots and bits of bronze that nobody uses."

"They say he finds gold too. I wonder where he hides it."

"Someday I will find out. Then father won't have to labor in the vineyards and mother won't have to take in lodgers."

Niki froze when old Loizos stopped at the crest of an adjacent rise and once more scanned Ithaka's rugged hillsides. Legendary home of Odysseus, the island's fame far exceeded its size or importance. Niki could never understand why visitors stopped at such an isolated place. Yet every few weeks a steamship or coastal trading sloop would anchor off to deliver foreigners to their little harbor. Even now, Heinrich Schliemann was encamped at Niki's house, eating his mother's souvlaki and sorting through the trash Loizos and others had brought him.

The old man took one last look back at his cave and continued toward town. Niki dragged Ezio to his feet. "Follow him. Make sure he meets with Schliemann." Niki glanced both directions, looked his little brother in the eye. "If he comes back, run as fast as you can to warn me."

Ezio nodded and slipped off through the brush. Niki hoped the boy was too scared or too cautious to get caught. He turned to the cave entrance. *In there somewhere, Loizos keeps his treasure.* Niki drew a candle from his shirt pocket and a tin of sulfur matches he had filched from his mother's kitchen. Most Greek islanders held a superstitious fear of Ithaka's caves, but Niki had explored several of them. The old man had caught him once, emerging with a broken pot in hand. He could still feel the welts on his back from that encounter.

Niki turned sideways at the entrance and slid between rough limestone walls. A quick glance back. *Maybe the stories are true—maybe the old gods still live beneath the earth.* His candle flickered briefly, and he shivered in the cool air. A moment passed before the dream of hidden gold pushed aside his dread.

The passage he followed led straight into the hillside. On occasion, Niki waded through pools of standing water or climbed over heaps of broken rock. He looked for side passages but found none. The cave ended in a forbidding pile of rock. The boy held his candle up and examined the barrier. He almost missed the shadow, the dark opening near the top.

Niki scrambled through and found himself in a circular chamber. He paused in awe at the precise stone walls, the blue tiled ceiling and the symmetric mosaic floor. Picking his way through the broken stones, he almost missed the black pit at the center of the floor. A casually thrown rock clacked and rattled into the dark hole until the sound died away. Niki paused in fascination before another feature caught his eye. A wooden chest stood against one wall. Bigger than one of Schliemann's steamer trunks, its lid bore a massive iron lock.

Yanking, kicking, shaking the lock did nothing. He searched for a pry bar. A pick or even a hammer would do. Niki pawed through heaps of broken wood, ancient pottery, and bits of marble. *There must be something here to bash it open.* The best he could find was a slender stick a little longer than his forearm.

He jammed it between the lock and the chest and pried with all his strength. Nothing moved. He tried again, pulling until the stick slipped from his hands and he nearly staggered back into the yawning pit. Niki recoiled, frightened at first, then infuriated. He raged in frustration. Waving the stick about, he struck the lid and yelled, "Open!"

With a quiet *snick*, the lock fell to the floor. Niki stared in disbelief. When nothing further happened, he crept closer. Loizos would know. He would certainly see that someone had broken his lock, but the boy planned to be well away before the old man returned. He pushed the lid open and gazed inside.

Niki wasn't sure how long he had stood there, his jaw agape, but he knew that the bags of gold shining beneath his candle represented more wealth than the entire island of Ithaka could boast. *One bag, he will not miss one bag.* Niki chose a sack of coins, almost more than he could lift. As he started to heave it from the chest, he heard the clatter of stones behind him.

Ezio called down, "Hey what are you doing?"

"Nothing. What do you want? You should be watching Loizos."

His little brother scrambled down. "Old Loizos and the German have started their second bottle of ouzo. We won't see him for a while." Ezio moved closer. "That chest—*Mother of God*—all that gold!"

"Do you want it? Do you think it is yours?" Niki pointed the stick at him. "I found it. The gold is mine—now get back."

Ezio stepped backward, then took another step. Niki glowered at him, then gasped in horror. "No. Stop, stop, *stop*."

Too late, little Ezio took one last step. His foot hovered over nothingness. His arms flailed as he fell shrieking into the pit. Niki rushed to the edge. The boy's cries echoed back, dying away without ever coming to an end.

Niki stumbled back, *my brother, my only brother.* He thought of his parents, their grief. *I can never look at them again—never go home.* Again, he peered into the chest. All that gold—he did not need to go back. He could run away and never have to explain. *Loizos will be blamed, not me.* Digging through the treasure, he found a leather purse stuffed with modern coins. He tied it to his belt and hefted a manageable sack of ancient gold.

The small candle had burned to a stub. It flickered and guttered, throwing wild shadows against the stone walls. Niki shuddered and closed the lid—*time to go*. One last look around, he picked up the stick and shoved it in his belt. *It might be useful for fending off stray dogs.* He dragged his sack of gold up the heap of broken rock and worked his way out into daylight.

Evening had arrived. Niki knew he would be expected home soon. For a moment, he considered returning—confessing all. He shook his head, *impossible*. A whistle sounded from the harbor. The last ferry for the mainland, if he ran, he could make it. Wishing for a moment he had never followed Loizos, had never entered the dark tunnel, he touched the stick at his belt. *Somehow, if I could only make it disappear.* The earth trembled. A cloud of dust arose from the hillside. Niki took one last look back and ran for the harbor.

1

Gravel crunched under the Bronco's big tires as Dane Maddock pulled into the marina parking lot. He spotted a familiar pickup, a blue Ram belonging to his friend Bones Bonebrake, near the local eatery, Toni's Dockside Bar and Grill. Maddock wheeled around to park in back where dumpsters and abandoned boat trailers competed for space. The kitchen entrance hung half-open, as it usually did. He slipped inside.

Fifteen minutes earlier, his phone had buzzed with a text, "Need some advice." The message came from Corey Dean, resident tech whiz and a longtime member of Maddock's treasure-hunting crew. Maddock shook his head. *Corey never asks for help. If Bones is involved, it likely means trouble.*

Maddock smiled at Toni as he passed the bar. Tall, wavy black hair, she wore cutoffs and a white shirt knotted at the waist. Toni grinned back and handed him a Corona. He spotted Bones and Corey out on the deck—a third figure sat with them. Maddock pulled up a chair. "First, I want to hear the good news."

Bones sprawled back and swigged his beer. "Good news is, Corey's got himself a new girlfriend."

The young woman next to Corey shot him a side-eye. She was petite and dark, with hair cut short. An unruly black tuft hung over her forehead. Corey glanced at her and blushed. "We're friends, okay? We haven't talked about that girlfriend-boyfriend thing."

"I've got a feeling there's bad news too. What's up?"

"This." Corey set a smooth black stick on the table. "She doesn't think I should keep it."

"I didn't say that. I said it could be dangerous. Just don't carry it around everywhere."

Before Maddock could answer, Toni strolled up with an order of nachos for Bones. She glanced down at the stick and picked it up. "This looks interesting…"

In one fluid movement, the young woman leaped to the

table, grabbed it away from her, and gave Toni a hard shove. Toni fell and rolled into a crouch. The girl raised her stick as if to strike, but Maddock plucked it from her hands and stepped back. She spun to face him and assumed a martial stance. In an instant, Toni tackled her to the ground, twisting her arm into a painful hold.

"Tell your little friend here to stop trying to cripple me," Toni said through gritted teeth, "or I'll dislocate her shoulder."

Corey sat frozen in astonishment through the scuffle. He jumped up. "Please. just don't hurt her."

Toni's left eye had nearly swollen shut. She shot him a glare from her right. "You could have warned me she was a kung-fu fighter."

"Toni has a point there," Bones said. "You could have warned us."

Toni rolled her good eye at him. "I didn't see you helping any."

Maddock held up the shiny black stick. A little longer than his forearm, it tapered from the thickness of a boathook to the diameter of a decent cigar. He ran a finger over the carved spiral that wrapped it from one end to the other. "Why is this worth fighting over?"

Corey eased past the two on the ground. "Because I need it. Can I have it back?"

"Will one of you big lummoxes shut up and help?" Toni grunted and punched her captive in the side of the face. "Just give it up already, girl."

Maddock kept the stick. "You can let her up. I think I have what she wants."

Toni let go and jumped back. She had learned to fight *capoeira* style in her native Jamaica and few people messed with her—none tried it twice. However, to Maddock she looked pretty well trashed.

The young woman on the ground did a forward roll and flipped to her feet. Goth makeup and blood-streaked her face like poorly applied camo. Her eyes flicked between the four of them, rested a moment on Corey, then focused on Maddock.

"Give me the staff and no one else gets hurt."

Maddock met her eye. "How about you sit down and we talk this over?"

"How about I let you keep your front teeth?"

He sized her up and figured she wasn't one to blindly fly at him. "You think to come in low. Maybe take me by the ankles, cripple a knee when I go down." He grasped the stick about a third of the way up. "You won't get that far with a broken skull."

Corey stepped forward, arms out, palms up. "Jeez Zoya, what in hell are you doing? These guys don't fool around."

She turned to him. Her shoulders slumped and she shook her head. "Sorry Gingerbread, I don't know what came over me. It's that staff—I told you it was dangerous."

Bones set an empty bottle back on the table. "Yeah, so you just clobbered our friend?"

"Seeing her touch it, something snapped. I'm sorry, I really am."

Toni hadn't relaxed from her defensive posture. "You can get the hell out of my place, right now. Don't even think about coming back."

Zoya looked at Toni, then back at Corey. "If you're smart, you'll lock that thing up and throw away the key," she backed toward the parking lot, "and you can forget about tomorrow."

Bones watched her go. "She's got the personality of a Florida short-eared bobcat, and you're hanging with her? What the hell, dude?"

"Yeah, we've been seeing each other. Is that okay?"

"Not okay when she tries to kill Toni—and spills my beer." Bones shook his head. "And she calls you Gingerbread. That's cute."

"Because my hair…never mind."

Corey insisted on caring for Toni. Bones fished two Coronas from the cooler and made a pair of check marks next to his name. Maddock pulled up a chair and sat. "I think we owe her for a lot more than a couple of beers." He glanced over at Toni and Corey. "So, what just happened?"

"Same as you, I got Corey's text so I came right over. Not

that I need an excuse to have a cold one." Bones draped his lanky form across a chair and tipped back his beer. "He and the goth chick were whispering about some con game. They shut up when I sat down. We had been talking about crap like the weather and the Miami Dolphins until you cruised over."

Maddock set the tapered black stick on the table. "And this?"

"Corey had it on his lap. Toni picked it up, the goth chick went all psycho." Bones took another swallow of beer. "What do you think of Corey's little playmate?"

"She's a bit… temperamental, isn't she?"

"That's an understatement." Bones sighed. "Shouldn't be surprised. Crazy is smack in the middle of Corey's wheelhouse."

Maddock watched his friend daub antiseptic on Toni's eye. She nodded when he'd finished and wagged her head towards their table. Corey shambled over.

"I guess I should apologize for Zoya. Can I have my staff back now?"

Maddock frowned. "First, explain to me what's going on."

Corey slumped into a chair and buried his face in his hands. "I wish I knew. I thought… I thought she was into me or something." He looked up. "Zoya—that's her name—she plays an assassin character online. She's really good, too. Was anyway. I'll probably never see her again."

"Man, you sure have got a way with women," Bones didn't name Sally, Corey's previous girlfriend. Nor did he mention how she had died, but it was on all of their minds.

Corey hung his head. "Sally dumped me for Willis. Now Zoya's dumped me because of that thing."

Toni wandered over with a bottle of IPA for Corey and sparkling water for herself. "And what does your little dynamite stick drink, nitro?"

"Ouzo." Corey blushed slightly. "I don't know where she picked up the taste."

"Probably reform school. That little harpy learned to fight somewhere. I've never seen anything like it."

"Krav-Maga?" Bones said. "Like the Israeli Mossad?"

"Krav on meth maybe. Where in hell did you find her?"

"He bought her online," Bones said.

"I *met* her online. We play in the same world sometimes."

Toni cocked her head. "World?"

"Dragon Apocalypse. There's these different worlds…" Corey looked around. "You wouldn't understand."

Maddock held up the stick. "It's just games, computer games. It's not real, Corey. Why the hell were you fighting over this thing?"

"Because I found it and it's mine."

"It was me that got hit," Toni said, "but it's you that sounds loopy."

Maddock hefted the stick and ran his hand along its spiral pattern. Strangely attractive, it possessed an innate beauty he couldn't identify. "Where Corey? Where did this come from?"

"Estate sale. You know, people get old and come down here to die. This one, the old guy was a musicologist or something. Had a bunch of rare stuff. Too rich for me, but then I spotted this staff sticking out of a pile of chair legs and all." He took a careful sip of his IPA and looked around. "I gave them five bucks for it and split."

Bones got up and pulled another beer from the cooler. Maddock shook his head. *Corey isn't telling the whole story.* Toni didn't buy it either. "Did that little hellcat come with it?"

"No. We met later. I put pictures online and she left some comments. Seems we both played Dragon Apocalypse."

Bones flopped down on his chair again. "Pics of your tiny package?"

"No, genius. Pictures of the staff. Maddock, now will you give it back to me?"

"Still nope. Not until you tell me why you wanted it in the first place."

Corey looked down and didn't say anything. Bones tipped his bottle back and swallowed half its contents. "I think our gear-geek is blushing. Out with it buddy. This is Toni's—we don't keep secrets around here."

Corey kept his head down. "I'm going LARPing in Atlanta

tomorrow."

Bones shot up straight and slammed the bottle down. "That's illegal in Georgia. They'll arrest you and put you in a tank full of perverts."

"Relax Bones." Maddock handed the stick to Corey. "It's Live Action Role-Playing, LARPing. Kind of like Civil War re-enactment, but without the guns."

"I'm hating it already."

Madock said, "Come on Bones, it's *Hot-Lanta*, women in skimpy costumes, what's there to hate?"

Corey held the staff by the thick end and sighted down at Bones. "You ought to come with me. You might see something you like."

"What, a whole room full of whacked-out psycho chicks?"

"It's Dragon Con weekend. The entire convention center will be filled. I know a guy that could get you in. I've got my wizard costume and my magic staff. You could go as an orc—you look just like one. And you Maddock, you could be Captain Midnight, really the best ever." Corey stood up, waved the staff over his head, and pointed it at Toni. "You could be Wonder..." He stopped and looked around the table. Silence.

Toni drained her sparkling water, stood, glanced at Maddock. "Should I be concerned?"

Maddock grinned. "Corey likes what he likes. I don't think it would be your scene.

"That leaves the two of you." Corey waved his wizard's staff between them.

"Only if you can get Bones to go dressed as an orc."

"How about I go in blue jeans as a big Cherokee with a bad attitude?"

Corey whooped. "Road trip! I got shotgun."

Maddock shook his head. "Nope. I get shotgun because you are going to drive."

"He's buying gas too," Bones said, "and he's paying for the hotel. And there had better be a lot of hot women."

Corey ran a hand through his red hair. "For a brief moment, I thought this was going to be fun."

2

Bones bent over and poked around in the little refrigerator. "What kind of hotel room doesn't have a mini bar?"

"It's not the luxury suite. This is the best I could get us on short notice."

"At least it's got snacks."

Corey looked back at Bones. "Hey, don't open... nooo, those chips cost like five bucks a bag."

"Good thing you're paying...Gingerbread." Bones tipped the bag back and poured half its contents into his mouth.

"I didn't bring you all the way here just to pillage the snack basket."

Maddock tossed his backpack on a green couch. "I claim this bunk for my own. You two can fight over whatever other bedding you can find."

Bones offered him the bag. "Trade you for the couch?"

"Maybe later."

"This sucks." Corey flopped in a matching green armchair. "I was counting on Zoya to come with me." He looked up at Maddock. "I suppose putting up with you two clowns is better than being here alone."

"You sure know how to make a guy feel welcome." Bones flicked the TV on and off, prowled the room once more for hidden amenities, then headed for the door. "I'll pick us up a six or two. Right back."

Corey watched him go. "This is gonna suck, isn't it?"

They had driven all night. Corey made it until about two a.m. When he nearly put them in a ditch, Maddock took over. Bones had slept the entire way. Maddock wasn't sure why he had agreed to go, or what they were supposed to do. *But hey, Atlanta right? Can't be all bad.* "It won't suck if we don't let it suck."

Corey pulled out a slender notebook computer. Spray-painted pink, it was covered with anime stickers. Maddock looked twice. "What the everlasting hell?"

"Yeah..." Corey's fingers flew across the keyboard. "...it was hers. Some weird little guy gave it to me. Said she wanted me to have it."

"Little guy?" Maddock asked. "Slender, well dressed, maybe called you '*petal*' or something like that?"

"That's him...kinda creepy. You know him?"

Maddock didn't believe in ghosts, but suddenly he felt a chill. "Yeah, he was a friend of Sally's. Called himself Uzi, but it was all crap."

Corey's fingers stopped and he hung his head. "I still think of her, a lot. Why—I know she's dead—but why couldn't she tell me about the cancer?"

"There's a lot Sally never told us, a lot we'll never know about her."

Corey nodded. "This Uzi guy, he's the one you followed to Mt. Shasta, right?"

"That's the one. Slimy as hell, he works for an organization that's so secret, even Tam Broderick and her Myrmidons couldn't find out much about him." Maddock shook his head. "Watch out for that guy. If he gave you Sally's computer, it was for reasons of his own." Corey refocused on the notebook. Maddock watched him scroll down a web page. "What are you looking for?"

"Our entry badges. Says we pick them up at the Hyatt ballroom. And here's the program. Check it out."

Maddock read over Corey's shoulder. Video gaming, costume contests, exhibits, vendors. "What's this HEMA thing?"

"Historical European martial arts. It's mostly sword fighting but there's hand-to-hand as well."

"Bones might like that."

The man in question chose that moment to shove his way through the door. He gutted the racks from the little refrigerator and crammed a case of beer in their place. "Do you know what's loose on the street? Every super-hero babe ever spawned is out there strutting it in a bikini and cape."

Corey grinned. "I knew you'd find something to like."

"I always find…" Bones stopped and stared at the table. "Is that what I think it is?"

"Sally wanted me to have it."

Maddock added, "You mean *Uzi* wanted you to have it."

"That little rodent? Knowing Uzi, he planted a bug in it."

"No way," Corey said. "Why would anyone want to track me?"

Bones paced around the room. "Still, I've got a creepy feeling this trip ain't gonna turn out the way you expect."

"Get togged up and we'll go find out."

Maddock looked at Bones. "You brought your orc costume, right?"

"You were supposed to bring the costumes."

"That's fine," Corey said. "You both can look like tourists if you want, but I'm playing this one for all its worth."

Bones smirked at him while he dressed. "Corey Potter, the Wizard of Odd."

Corey straightened and put a monocle in his eye. He wore a silk smoking jacket, a white cravat, and a low-crowned top hat. "Steam-punk wizard. Now where's my staff?"

"Damn, buddy! You'd look convincing, but the jeans and sneaks give you away."

"I just need to blend in, not win a contest." Corey dug the staff out of his pack and tucked it under his arm. "Now you see it…" He flipped the staff in his hand. It disappeared. "Now you don't."

"Hey," Bones said, "I dare you to do that again."

"Don't have to." With a flourish, the staff popped into view and spun between his fingers.

Maddock said, "Are you sure you want to parade that stick around after what happened yesterday?"

"Parading around is what I bought it for—every wizard needs a wand." Corey held it out and admired it. "The thing does have kind of a magical appeal, don't you think?"

Bones fished a can of beer from the fridge and tossed it to Maddock. He took another one, popped it open, and kicked the door shut. "Let's see you conjure one for yourself."

Corey waved the wand in the air and pointed it at the fridge. "*Magico-magico, open!*"

The door clicked and hung two inches open. Bones stared at it a moment. "I want to see you... No, actually, I don't."

Corey retrieved his own beer and raised it. "To a kick-ass Dragon Con."

Raising his beer can, Maddock turned to Bones. "Come on, let's go check this thing out. Maybe you'll hook up with Pneumatic Lass."

An hour later, all three were registered and badged. Bones glared about over the heads of the other attendees. "I think I've been dragged and conned into a geek show. They got any food in here besides Froot-Loops?"

A bit hungry himself, Maddock followed Bones as he sniffed around for a snack bar. A few outlandish costumes passed by, but most attendees wore street clothes. A big guy, fuzzy red beard, wart on his right cheek glanced their way. He slipped behind a booth and disappeared. It wouldn't have mattered, if this hadn't been the third time he'd walked by.

I'm getting paranoid. Maddock watched the crowd and tried to memorize faces. Corey rattled on about the upcoming events. Bones walked faster, pretending to ignore him. They passed a row of gamers intent on some contest. Corey said, "Hold up a moment, I want to watch some of this."

Bones stopped and squinted at the array of giant video screens. Slouched forward, scowl across his face, he looked more than ever like an orc. "What are they doing?"

"They're on Twitch. It's a prelim for tomorrow's games."

"Let me know when we get to *twerk*. Then I'll be interested."

Bones pushed on without further comment. Maddock hung behind while Corey followed. A little guy at the last console, short, dark beard, salt-and-pepper hair, turned to watch Corey leave. The character he'd been playing collapsed in a heap of blood and flailing limbs. The word *Fatality* flashed briefly on the screen. It didn't seem to bother the player.

Maddock stayed a few dozen paces behind Bones. He was easy to follow. Corey had to be down there in the crowd somewhere. Outside on the street, Red-Beard flashed by the window. *Likely a coincidence... or not.* Maddock didn't see the Twitch guy again. At least not until they'd found a café and ordered lunch. Back turned, same salt-and-pepper hair. *Could be the guy.* Maddock watched him walk away. "You weren't expecting to meet anyone here, were you, Corey?"

"No. Why?"

Bones answered. "Because we're being tailed."

Maddock grinned. "So, you're looking for tails now instead of tail?"

"Screw you, Maddock. I know you spotted Beardo. Did you see the pixie?"

"Nope, but Twitch just walked out of here."

"What the hell are you guys talking about?"

Bones punched Corey in the arm. "You, little buddy. You're a celeb... sort of."

"Alright," Maddock said, "where's the pixie. I missed that one."

"Don't turn around. She's in the corner, back by the kitchen door."

Corey glanced up without moving his head. "Blond wig, pointed ears, gauzy dress, skin like fence paint, and glittery wings."

Maddock wanted to look but knew better. "Sounds like your ex."

"What, Zoya? She's not..." Corey glanced up again. "No way. This girl is taller and skinnier. She looks albino. Not my type."

Bones grunted and sniffed his sandwich. "Smells like Teen Spirit."

"Get out! She's not my type."

"Damaged nerd chick." Bones took a bite and spit out a pickle chip. "You are thinking about going over there, Wiz man."

"I am not." Corey blushed and looked down at the table.

"Not now, anyway. I saw her at the reception desk. Thought she worked here or something."

"So, what's with this Twerk guy?"

"Twitch. He lost interest in the game as soon as you two walked by."

Bones grinned at Corey. "You still got it, buddy."

Maddock finished his slice of soggy pizza. "I don't know what he's got, but some folks here seem interested."

Corey laid his wizard's staff on the table. "It could only be this."

"Got to be…" Bones shoved the rest of the sandwich in his mouth, wiped his face, and belched. "…after all, your little fuzz-ball battled Toni over it."

Maddock checked the time. "Speaking of battles, I think the HEMA demonstrations are starting about now."

"As in hema-*globin*?" Bones cocked his head. "I like blood sports."

Corey said, "Historical European…"

"…Martial Arts." Bones finished for him. "Yeah, LARPing with bruises. Should be fun."

Maddock stood and pushed Corey in front of him. "Which way, wizard?"

Corey stepped outside, looked both directions, and nodded to his right. "Through the park and two blocks down."

When they finally shouldered into the crowded arena, Maddock heard the clatter of wooden blades and grunts of the contestants. Corey wormed toward the action. Bones followed, a human snowplow. Maddock filled in behind, looking for familiar faces. The initial rounds had finished by the time they reached the front. A fresh pair of contestants scrambled up to the raised dais. They both wore padded armor, one in black with a coal-scuttle helmet. His opponent was dressed in white with a full-length red cross, front and back.

Bones nudged Corey. "Who's the Templar dude? I think he's even taller than me."

"Calls himself Prester John. He's here every year and usually wins."

Maddock sized up the pair. Bones was right, the fighter in black was a bear of a man, but Prester John was half a head taller and broad across the shoulders. "Think you could take him, Bones?"

"You know I could, little brother. As long as we didn't have to use swords."

"Well, I think that's the whole point," Corey said. "Get it? Swords—the point?"

Bones squinted down at him. "Since when was I talking to you, halfling?"

"You say you don't like nerd stuff, but then you use a term straight out of Tolkien?" Corey laughed. "You're such a fraud."

"Check this out, guys," Maddock said.

A tall girl, all in white, floated across the dais. She wore diaphanous fairy wings and held two wooden swords in her outstretched hands. Bones straightened. "It's our freaking pixie from the café."

Corey said, "Her legs look weird."

Maddock couldn't tell. The pixie's dress draped almost to her shoes. She bowed and let each contestant choose a sword. Bowing again, she stepped back and dropped a red handkerchief. The fight began without further ceremony. Maddock had seen similar demonstrations, using knives. The tactics were the same, get inside your opponent's guard and strike a fatal blow. Corey had explained that a judge scored points and decided the outcome. If either of the fighters fell off the platform, the bout was over.

Maddock watched them spar, lunging, feinting, testing each other's guard. Prester John didn't seem in any hurry to engage with the guy in black. The whole match looked strange. No one yelled or jeered. None of the raucous jostling he'd seen at cage fights and other unsanctioned brawls he'd attended. Bones seemed to think the same way.

"How long until someone draws blood?"

Corey shook his head. "It doesn't work that way. The swords are heavy wood without an edge. They're fighting for honor and style."

"Then I don't get the point, after all."

Prester John had gone on the offensive. Maddock watched his moves, smooth, confident, almost choreographed. Step forward, swing, parry, turn, and again. A routine designed to tire his opponent. He grabbed Bones's arm. "Will you two shut up. It's about to end. Watch."

As he spoke, Prester John laid into the man in black, striking blow after blow at the shoulders and chest. The judge stood and blew a whistle, but by that time, the man's coal-scuttle helmet rolled across the dais, its owner crouched on the mat with his arms across his face.

A touch on Maddock's shoulder, a rich contralto voice, "Think you could take him?"

He spun around to face a short woman, a few pounds past voluptuous. "Judith Moon, the flying geologist. What in holy hell are you doing here?"

3

"That's *June* to you, big fella. And I was going to ask *you* the same thing."

Bones had already turned and done his double-take. "Sister, you are one long way from Tipperary or wherever it was you were supposed to be."

"Tambacounda. Already got back. Got me another mission if I can ever get out of this crazy place."

Maddock glanced about the crowd, no other familiar faces at the moment. "Unless you've acquired a sudden passion for Dungeons and Dragons, I can't imagine…"

June pointed to the dais. "There, the white knight up there is my current boss."

Bones flicked his eyes to the tall figure still gloating over his fallen opponent. "Holy crap, Junie Moon, you sure know how to pick 'em."

"Well, this one picked me. Called me up—asked if I was the one responsible for that debacle out in northern Cal. Responsible, hah! Like I caused it or something. But his money is good." She looked over her shoulder, "his retainer was a butt-load of cash. Considering my butt, that means a whole bunch."

Corey spoke up. "You work for Prester John?"

"Well finally someone I can talk to without straining my neck. Yeah, I work for the Kingdom of Prester John Missions, Incorporated. Spreading good food and the Good Word across the world. Or that's their story, anyway."

"Doesn't sound much like geology to me," Maddock said.

"Well, the oil patch took a dump last year and now geologists are flipping burgers and glad for the work. These days it's flying that pays my bills."

Prester John stopped bowing to the audience and waved at June—or maybe it was at all of them. Maddock couldn't tell. June waved back. "He asked about you three as well." She fingered the lapels on Corey's jacket. "I'm guessing our magician's assistant here is the intriguing Doctor Denarius."

"I'm supposed to be a steam-punk wizard." Corey stopped and squinted. "Where did you hear that name?"

"Didn't you know? Preacher owns the Dragon Apocalypse franchise. He seems to know you. Mentioned you a few times."

Bones glanced over his shoulder. "Oh crap. He's headed this way."

Maddock turned in time to see the tall figure in Templar garb striding toward them. Blond hair, short curly beard, he held his helmet under his left arm and extended a hand. "You must be the renowned Dane Maddock."

"Yes, that would be me, but I'm not sure we've met." Maddock shook the proffered hand.

Without missing a beat, the man turned to Bones and looked him up and down. "And you, you've got to be the biggest darn Indian I've ever seen. Cherokee, right? I'm known as Prester John to my friends and followers, but Sister Judith would have told you that by now. I hope you haven't tempted my faithful pilot into more iniquity. I need her services."

Maddock patted his wallet and counted his fingers. "I'm not sure there is any new iniquity that we could tempt June with, Mr. John."

"Just Preacher, just Preacher, my son. In the old tongues, prester meant preacher, you know. Long ago, John the Preacher brought the Holy Word to the heathen. He was famous, you know." Prester John tilted his head back and stared up at the ceiling. "I try, Lord you know I try."

With that, he stalked off. Bones rubbed his chin and smirked at June. "Oh, yeah. That dude's a whole barn full of hoot-owls wearing a suit and walking around."

"Well his suit's got pockets fulla money, so unless you boys are going to make me a better offer, I'm flying with the hoot-owls." June quirked an eyebrow.

Something odd about their encounter—Maddock couldn't make it add up. "He looked at Corey a few times, but never spoke to him. Why?"

June scratched her head. "Corey? Oh, I get it, aka Doctor Denarius of Dragon Apocalypse fame."

"Player name, yeah," Corey said. "There are thousands, hundreds of thousands of players. Why me?"

Maddock scanned for Beardo or Twitch, but saw neither of them. He turned back to Corey. "He knows something about Bones and me. He might have looked you up too."

"It's freaking creepy." Bones had been scanning the room as well. "We show up here on a whim and everyone acts like they expected us. June, you been spreading the word?"

"Not me. The guy seemed to know who you were before he even called me."

"If this Prester John has access to the Dragon Apocalypse servers," Corey said, "then he could have looked up my personal info. He could have tapped into my online chat log. Anyone with access to that would know I was coming to Dragon Con."

"Still doesn't explain why he knew who we are, or that we came with you," Maddock said.

June looked both directions and lowered her voice. "How 'bout we blow this freak show—no offense, magic man—and go out to the airport. I want to show you my baby. Besides, the Preach dumped me here and I need a lift."

"This child wouldn't have a name now, would he?"

"Hercules, mighty Hercules."

Maddock groaned. "Really? You are flying a C-130? You do have a weakness for antique aircraft."

"That's C-130 J, as in jackpot. Latest model, repossessed from a Middle Eastern nabob—to remain unnamed. Got all the latest avionics. Got extended range. I can take off from anywhere with twenty tons of food and relief aid. It's the bomb. I'm tellin' ya, the Preach is crawling with cash and doesn't mind spending it."

Corey interrupted. "Mind if I hang out here? I'd like to get in on some of the gaming action."

The crowd had started to thin. Maddock scanned their faces for anyone taking undue interest in his little group. Bones shook his head. Maddock had to agree. "Too much hinky business going on lately. We should stick together."

"I've been coming to Dragon Con for five years now.

Nothing is going to happen."

Bones said, "Just maintain a little situational awareness, buddy. Stay with friendly crowds and bail if things go sideways."

Corey grinned. "Yes mom. If you guys need me, I'll be kicking some butt over at the Dragon Apocalypse booth." He tossed Maddock a set of keys. "Don't wreck my car."

Maddock watched him go, top hat pulled down at a rakish angle, swagger in his step, staff tucked into his belt. "I still don't like it."

June's *baby* was everything she'd said it was. New, clean, digital avionics, a ghost of Arabic script still clung to its gleaming aluminum tail, the only vestige of its former owners. Along its fuselage, *Kingdom of Prester John Missions* blazed in blue and gold letters. Maddock mentioned the absence of a cross or other Christian symbology.

"Yeah, the Preach is pretty cautious about looking too evangelical, especially flying into the Middle East and parts of Africa like he does."

Bones walked up the tail ramp and peeked into the spartan cargo bay. "You mean he rides this thing all the way to Baghdad?"

"No…and no, Gomer. We don't do Iraq and no, he doesn't ride with me." She pointed out a sleek little Gulfstream parked next to a white Quonset building. "He rides that."

Bones whistled under his breath. "Sweet. Maybe I should learn to be more charitable."

"Yeah, it'd take a heap of learning to figure where his money comes from, but we do deliver a lot of food."

"So where next, angel of mercy?"

"Northern Ethiopia, if I can ever get my ass outa here. We're supposed to pick up a load of farm equipment before we leave, but I haven't seen it yet."

June showed off the gear. "Navigation antennas right above the flight deck, and look, cargo 'chutes for when we can't land. We've got dual load-master controls, one forward, one aft. I just drop the ramp, hit the launcher, and whoosh, out it goes."

"Got 'chutes for the crew as well?"

"Don't expect to need them, but we do have life rafts."

Bones peeked through a small window. "I don't suppose this thing is armed?"

"Nope. We only fly missions of mercy out in Preacher land." June looked over her shoulder and lowered her voice. "But I still carry my forty-four magnum and a K-Bar knife on my hip. A girl can't be too careful traveling where we do."

June took them on a tour of the flight deck. "We've got this whiz-bang autopilot. Artificial intelligence or something, but I swear it could fly this ship by itself."

She planted herself in the left-hand seat. "This baby's got a two-person flight station including four multifunctional LCD panels and two holographic head-up displays."

Bones looked around. "Yeah, but does it have a fridge?"

"Fridge, microwave, coffeemaker…everything a gal could need," she rolled her eyes at him, "except a big, strong hombre like you."

Maddock mumbled under his breath, "Be careful what you wish for."

June led them back out through the tail ramp. Maddock pointed his thumb at the Gulfstream parked across the tarmac. "Your boss is taking his yacht out there too? Rather dangerous country for a nice little rig like that."

"Piloting it, no less. Regular Howard Hughes, he is."

"And how about you?" Bones jerked his head toward the massive C-130. "You got a crew, or you going full Charles Lindbergh on us?"

"Why not Amelia Earhart?" June flashed a grin.

"I like pilots who actually make it to their destination. Besides, I've got some bad memories connected to Earhart."

June fixed him with a speculative look, but Bones didn't elaborate. Finally, she shrugged. "I've got a crew." She started off toward a low-arched Quonset building. "Come on, I'll introduce you around."

A string of cloud shadows fled across the taxiway as they walked. Maddock looked up at the blue sky and wondered what it would be like landing in the desert of northern Ethiopia. June seemed content with her role as transport pilot. He suspected that she missed her time flying military missions.

Bones stretched his legs for the last few yards and held the door for June. She snorted as she walked through. "People, I want to introduce a couple of the worst rogues you are ever likely to encounter."

Three faces turned as Maddock walked in behind her. A tall woman stepped forward and held out a hand. "Hi, I'm Margo, June's copilot and general mechanic."

Strawberry blond hair cropped short, cargo pants, olive drab tank top, Maddock reached out, but Bones stepped between them and took her hand. "Pleasure to meet you, ma'am. I'm Bones Bonebrake. My friends just call me…"

"Yeah, I know—Bones." She grinned at him. "June told me *all* about you."

"Bunch of lies, I'm sure."

Margo leaned to one side. "And you would be Mr. Dane Maddock."

He smiled back and nodded. "Our reputation seems to have preceded us. June, have you been making up stories?"

"What, you mean earthquakes and volcanos and caves and stuff? Are you saying none of that happened? I know what I saw."

Margo nodded. "Yes, and you do like to talk." She glanced between Bones and Maddock. "But there's more talk going around than just June. The Preacher says you two had something to do with that accident out in California."

Maddock chewed his lip and Bones lost his grin. "Seems this Prester John knows a lot about us."

"The Preach does his homework." June pointed out two other men, standing next to a stack of shipping crates. "And that's Pete and Repeat. I don't speak Russian or I'd introduce you."

Margo rolled her eyes. "Actually, it's Pyotr and Paheliyan, but June can't pronounce their names and they don't speak English anyway."

Bones jerked a thumb over his shoulder and said, "So who's

the lucky dude flying shotgun for your boss?"

"That would be Reznik," June said. "He's still in town with the Preach."

Maddock nodded. "It's time we got back to town ourselves."

Bones thumped June on the shoulder. "You be careful out there miss volcano lady. I don't want to read about you in the news."

"Yeah, sure big guy. Like you're ever gonna do the same."

June let them out through a security gate and waved as Maddock swung Corey's Prius out of the parking lot. He glanced over his shoulder at the hulking C-130 beyond the chain-link fence. "I wonder what our Junie Moon has gotten herself into?"

Bones crouched in the passenger seat, knees under his chin. "I'm more worried about Corey wandering around with that ugly stick under his arm."

Maddock had similar thoughts. Although Corey Dean wasn't a former SEAL or trained in special ops, he'd been a member of their treasure-hunting team since its formation. Corey had held his own in some tough situations, despite his nerdish tendencies. Maddock glanced at Bones, bent over, struggling with the seat adjustment bar. "That's as far back as it goes. Believe me, I tried."

Bones stared out the window. "Think they've got any fried chicken in this burg?"

"Might have peach cobbler too. Let's find out."

Corey hadn't returned to the room when they let themselves in. Maddock called, but his mobile rang straight to voicemail. Bones wasted no time heading for the fridge. Maddock caught the beer he tossed and cracked the top, slurping suds as they foamed up around the rim. "I'll say this town does have some decent food."

"Look, got we get Netflix on the tube too…"

"Be my guest. I'm hitting the gym to work off some of those carbs."

Down in the hotel basement, the little indoor pool sat dark

and empty. Maddock pushed through an adjacent door and checked out the gym. Also dark—he switched on a light. Cycles, ellipticals, and treadmills stood against one wall. Maddock found a treadmill that looked like it still worked and dropped his beer can in the water bottle rack. He had just launched into an easy jog when his pocket buzzed. "Yeah, Bones…"

"We got trouble buddy, better get back up here."

4

Trouble crouched in a corner, a raggedy elf that looked like she'd lost a fight with Godzilla. One broken leg jutted out beneath her torn skirt at an impossible angle. She held the other leg in her hands like a baseball bat. The pixie from that morning, her glittery wings and long white wig were gone. Blood-smeared white makeup ran down her face and dripped from her chin. Bones stood in the other corner, fists at his sides.

Maddock took a half second to scan the room. "Holy crap, Bones. Did you do that?"

His friend just shook his head. "Look at her again, buddy."

Stilts, he'd thought they were legs. She held nothing more than a shoe on a stocking-covered stick. Upright then, not crouched. Short dark stubble, he recognized her defensive stance. "You—what in hell are you doing here?"

"Do you know where your little friend is, Dane God-Almighty Maddock? Well, if you don't, he's probably dead by now."

Maddock stepped through the doorway. "Zoya isn't it? You can take off those ridiculous stilts and sit down."

Bones shot him a glance. Maddock shook his head. "Stand down Bones. She wouldn't have come to us if she didn't need our help."

"She busted in through the door."

"It wasn't locked, you big lummox."

Bones clenched his fists again, but Maddock ignored him. "Zoya, you look thirsty. Would you like a beer?"

"You're both sitting here drinking beer while your friend is out getting himself murdered?"

"We're going to drink beer and talk. When we figure out what happened then we'll do something about it."

He watched her expression. Hostility gave way to resignation. Maddock nodded. "That's better. Bones, I'm going to get our guest a can of beer, why don't you find her a washcloth and towel."

Maddock dug out a can for each of them while Zoya daubed a wet washcloth to her forehead. With most of the blood and makeup wiped off, she dumped the towel on the floor and bent to unbuckle the remaining stilt. "Stupid costume. Did either of you two mouth-breathers ever have to fight on stilts—in a dress…huh? You got any scissors?"

Maddock took out his pocket knife and set it on the bed. "Best I can do."

Zoya snatched it up and hacked most of the dress off, well above her knees. She glared at the two of them. "What're you looking at?"

Bones snorted. "Tinkerbell dragged ass-first through a thrashing machine, that's what."

"Well, I bet you never had Tinkerbell carve her initials on your…"

"Just sit down and drink your beer, Zoya." Maddock took the couch and opened his can.

The young woman settled into the green armchair, her legs tucked beneath her. Maddock nodded. "Good. Now, tell us everything that happened."

"Some friends you two are. You just left him and now he got jumped and dragged off and I don't know where he is."

"When, Zoya? How long ago?"

"Maybe two hours, maybe more. You weren't here. I tried to stop them, but the big guy had a sword, I mean a real sword, and there were those other guys, especially that little weaselly one."

Bones sat up. "What big guy? Who were they?"

She crossed her arms, settled back, and glowered at him. "You know who I mean. I think he's a friend of yours."

Maddock closed his eyes. "Not Prester John."

"Well, who else?"

Bones shook his head. "I don't buy it. You're saying this Prester John dude mugged and kidnapped Corey in broad daylight and nobody but you noticed?"

"I wasn't there, okay? Maybe they caught him in an alley or something."

"So now you're saying you weren't there, but you tried to stop them anyway?"

"Well later, stupid...of course. I saw the big jerk standing outside the conference hall and told him I knew what he did. The guy got all pissed off and one of his creepos tried to pull me away. I dislocated his arm—that's when it started."

Maddock took a deep breath and said, "What started, Zoya?"

"The fight, of course, that is, until asshat pulls out this sword, and then I knew it wasn't gonna work out for me—or Corey, so I split."

"And besides the broken arm, was anyone else hurt?"

"Look at me. You mean besides me? Well, that other creep, he was laying on the sidewalk bleeding and all."

Bones looked at Maddock. "Any of this add up to you?"

"It might." He turned to Zoya. "Those guys with Prester John, did one of them have red hair and a wart on his cheek?"

Zoya looked around the room and finally discovered her beer. She took a swallow. "His beard could have been red. Didn't see a wart, but I was kind of busy."

Bones closed his eyes. "Beardo, I knew it. We never should have let Corey out of our sight."

Maddock wasn't sure. "So how do you know this Prester John did anything to Corey?"

Zoya took another long swig of her beer and flashed her eyes between Maddock and Bones. "You two apes must be even stupider than I thought. The weaselly dude and his buddy, have been following you clowns all over downtown Atlanta."

Bones pulled a face. "Crap. Beardo and Twitch, yeah, we saw them. We warned Corey too. What makes you think he's dead?"

"Why would they keep him alive once they'd ripped him off? They got his relic, no use packing extra baggage."

"I think you mean his staff, the one you two were fighting over." Maddock leaned forward. "Now tell me, what kind of *relic* would that be, and why is it so important?"

"Gotta go." She glanced at the door and then through the

window.

Maddock held up a hand. "Wait a minute before you go flying out of here, why did you even come to us?"

"I thought you might want to help your friend. Guess I was wrong."

"There's something else—what is it?"

Zoya stood and peered out the window. "I gotta split."

Bones looked over her shoulder. "Cops. How did they know you were here?"

"Your dick-head friend must have told them."

Maddock heard footsteps and a radio crackle from the hall. *Trust her?* He pinched his eyes shut for a moment. "In the closet. Now!"

A heavy knock on the door, Maddock didn't look back as he stepped over to open it. Two Atlanta city policemen stood in the doorway. The hotel manager shuffled nervously behind them. "How can I help you, officers?"

There had been an assault, injuries, the attempted theft of a valuable sword. Maddock agreed to let them look around. The manager followed them in. Bones glanced over but didn't move from the couch. One officer stood near the door, hand on his gun. The other checked out the bathroom, under the bed, behind the drapes—he stepped over to the closet and threw it open.

Nothing. A few blankets sat on a shelf above a row of empty hangers. Maddock nodded. "I told you, there is no one else here."

"So, what are those things there on the bed?"

Maddock winced. *The stilts.* Bones stood and picked them up. "These? They're part of his costume. We're going larfing, or morping, or something tonight."

The other officer snickered, rolled his eyes. "Come on Jones. Unless you're interested?"

"Screw you, Mannix."

The manager stayed behind when the policemen left. "I don't tolerate trouble here. The rule is no cops. You can all clear out now—I want you gone by the time I come back."

Bones waited until the door shut before saying, "Ollie, ollie, oxen free."

Maddock looked around. "Where…"

Two stacks of blankets tumbled to the floor and Zoya uncurled from the closet shelf. "You couldn't just get rid of them—you had to stand and chat."

Maddock eyed the shelf as she swung down. "How the hell did you squeeze in back there?"

"I worked for a stage magician."

"Let me guess," Bones said, "you were the rabbit."

Zoya marched up to him and stood looking straight at his pecs. "You're too heavy to carry, so I'll let you walk out of here this time."

Maddock hoped neither of them would do something stupid and concentrated on the problem at hand. He tried Corey's mobile again with no results. He thought of just calling the cops and letting them handle the woman. *But she's our only connection with Corey…at the moment.*

The banter escalated in the background. Maddock heard a new edge to his friend's voice. He spun around. "Bones, stand down and get ready to move out."

"*Jawohl mein Kommandant.*"

"You too, Zoya. Sit—drink your beer."

"Hell I will. I already have to piss like a pregnant cow."

"Lovely." Maddock closed his eyes. "Just take care of business, people."

"Don't we have a bigger problem?" Bones said. "Like getting Smurfette past the front desk."

The bathroom door had closed. Maddock was glad to know their guest was taking care of business as requested. "Be careful Bones. She was a handful for Toni, and she seems to have disabled two guys this afternoon. I don't want anyone else getting hurt."

"Do you really think…?"

"Not just you. I'd rather keep her in one piece as well. At least until we get her out of here."

The hotel record would show that Mr. Maddock, Mr.

Bonebrake, and Mr. Corey Dean checked out at seven-thirty that evening. Mr. Dean wore a pair of baggy trousers, rolled up at the cuff, a knit cap, pulled low across his forehead, and a gray hoodie that dangled halfway to his knees. He said nothing as they pushed through the rotating door and stepped out onto the sidewalk.

Maddock turned to the ersatz Mr. Dean. "You have someplace to stay, I presume?"

Zoya scowled up at him. "You wish. I was planning on crashing with Corey but now he's dead and you two galoots got us tossed out of our flop."

Bones leaned forward. "I seem to remember that it was you..."

"Enough—" Maddock slung his pack over one shoulder. "We give Corey a little more time to show up on his own, then we tear this town apart."

"Yeah, maybe starting with the airport," Bones said. He nodded toward a coffee shop across the street. "We could watch the entrance from there."

Maddock jaywalked to the door and held it open for the others. Zoya pulled up short. Just inside. Corey sat huddled in a corner booth looking almost as battered as Zoya had. Bones dashed over. "What the hell, man?"

Zoya bolted for the exit, but Maddock blocked her way. "Try me if you must, but you're going to face him now and I want some answers."

She crouched back on one foot and looked past him. *Going for my eyes this time.* Maddock didn't doubt she could do some damage, but he stood his ground. Corey called from across the room, "Zoya—is that you?"

Zoya slumped and turned. "Well, it's not your bleeding mother." She walked over and sat next to him. "Here's your pack, I rescued it."

Bones can chaperone. While the barista busied himself with their coffee, Maddock checked the back, fire exit, restrooms, and an unlocked supply closet. When he returned, Corey was already into his narrative. "...I was doing great. We were down to three teams and our tanks had just about cleaned up on their rangers. I'd maybe been playing for a couple of hours and had to go for a bio…"

Bones grunted. "What? Like a facial or something?"

"Bio," Corey said. "A *biological*, a bathroom break, of course."

"Rookie mistake," Zoya said. "You dehydrate before the game starts."

"It was just a warmup for tomorrow." He shook his head. "What? Why do you care anyway? It doesn't matter."

"And that's when they grabbed you."

"Yeah, jammed a rag in my face, smelled like crappy bananas or something. I fought for a couple of minutes—next thing, I wake up in the back of a car with this big hairy dude."

Maddock leaned across the table. "Red beard? Wart on his cheek?"

"Yeah, I think we saw him this morning."

Zoya took a gulp of coffee and smirked at Maddock. "I told you. It was the Preacher's goons." She turned back to Corey. "So how come you're sitting here and not dead?"

Corey wiggled around in the booth and put both hands on the table. "Look at my wrists. They tied my hands. If they were gonna kill me, they would have done it as soon as I was in the car and not bothered. What I don't get, is why?"

"It was that damned stick," Bones said. "Well good riddance. Can we go home now?"

"If all they wanted was the staff, then why bother to grab me at all? Just leave me in the puddles on the restroom floor."

"I don't give a crap. Can we go home now?"

Maddock shook his head. "Not until I get a lot more answers. For instance, why didn't you just come up to the room and tell us what happened?"

"The place is crawling with cops, that's why. I thought they were looking for me."

"They left about a half hour ago. Besides, they were looking for Zoya, not you."

"They didn't all leave. Or did you miss the gray sedan?"

Bones uncoiled from his chair and went to the coffee shop window. "Two cops—just sitting there."

"Not cops, goons. They're waiting for me," Zoya squinted at Corey, "or you, or both of us. You should be dead. How did you get away?"

"Now that was the weird thing." Corey rubbed his wrists. "They'd tied me with nylon cord, did a sloppy job. I'd worked it loose after about five minutes, thinking maybe I could bolt out the door at the next stoplight. So, the big guy…"

"The Preacher?" Bones interrupted.

"No, the bearded guy, he's sitting next to me, fussing with the staff. I'm all, *no way I let him keep that.* Don't know why I care so much but it's in my head, so I wait until he's not paying attention." Corey sneaked a glance at Zoya. "Next moment, I'm grabbing that thing. We're like headed up this freeway on-ramp and he's like, all yanking on the staff and smacking me in the face and I try the door."

"Let me guess," Zoya said. "Kiddy locks."

"Yeah, no crap. It won't open. So, I'm holding the staff and yelling, 'Open, you stupid door,' and pow, it opens just as the driver slams on his brakes, and I let go, fly out into the bushes and weeds and stuff. Then I run like hell."

Zoya closed her eyes. "Without the relic—damn!"

"Yeah." Corey looked around at all of them. "Now I kind of miss it. Like a part of me is gone. Like an amputation."

Zoya's eyes were still shut. "This is bad. Really bad."

"Then we leave now," Bones said. "We're out half a case of beer, a pair of stilts, and a chair leg. I say we cut our losses and go."

"I lost my hat too—it was a good hat."

"You lost more than that," Zoya said. "When you lost that stick Gandalf, you lost a piece of your *atman,* your inner self." She went nose-to-nose with Corey and hissed, "*Your… soul…*"

5

Bones had circled the shop interior and returned to the table. He swallowed some of the lukewarm coffee, made a face, and said, "Man, you sound crazier than that Preacher dude. How are we supposed to get out of here without being seen?"

Maddock lowered his voice and nodded at Bones. "So, who's their spotter?"

"Nine o'clock, three tables over. Tall dude pretending to read a book. He came in right after us…" Bones twitched his head.

"That means at least two outside and one behind us. See any metal?"

"No, but I'd be surprised if they weren't packing this time. If there's a back door. You can bet they've got it covered."

"We go out the front then, but first a minor detour."

"What if I just take out their bookworm?" Zoya said.

Maddock shook his head and stood. "No more mayhem, no more cops. Grab your gear people, and follow me—hustle, hustle."

He shepherded them all to the back, pushing Bones, Zoya, and Corey into the supply closet. They managed to slip around the corner while Bookworm struggled to his feet. Maddock kicked the fire door open. When the alarm went off, he jammed into the cramped darkness with the others.

"That better not be your hand…"

"Is that a mop handle, or are you glad to see me?"

"For God's sake Bones…"

"Will all of you just shut up?"

Maddock heard the alarm clang and feet rattle past. He clutched the door handle, but no one tried to open it. A few moments later, the alarm stopped. Maddock cracked the door. A tall kid in a striped shirt and apron stood staring back at him. A finger to the lips and a twenty silenced whatever the kid was about to say. With no sign of Bookworm, Bones peered out the front window. "All clear for now."

"Go, go… the parking garage is two blocks down. Don't take the elevator."

Bones led the way with six-foot strides. Zoya sprinted right behind him. Maddock followed Corey, watching their six o'clock for pursuit. When they made the garage, he paused in the shadow of the overhang. A little traffic, a few disinterested pedestrians. Nothing else moved. He took the stairs two at a time.

Rounding a turn, one flight from the top, he ran into Bones and the others, headed down. "Atlanta cops on the next level. Got Corey's wheels all staked out."

"Crap. Good thing we didn't…"

"…take the elevator. Yeah, what now boss?"

Corey broke in. "We go underground."

Zoya nodded. "Exactly, the Atlanta Underground. I have to stop and get some stuff. Besides, I know a guy there you should talk to."

Maddock looked over at Bones. "One last thrilling Atlanta adventure?"

"Why not, this day just keeps getting crappier and crappier."

Still toting his pack, Maddock led them out a service door and down a side alley. Six blocks over, they hit the Five Points metro station.

"Down here," Zoya said. She wormed through the crowd and took an escalator.

Maddock followed, halted at the bottom. A large sign read, *Underground*. It hung over a boarded-up opening. "Looks like your secret hideout is closed for repairs."

Zoya didn't stop. She continued to a door marked with a stylized electrical spark and multiple danger signs. In a single motion, she carded the lock and gestured inside.

"Oh, great," Bones said. "I always wanted to be on the evening news."

Maddock fished a mini flashlight from his pack and lit up the interior. Rows of obsolete electrical panels sat in dusty silence behind metal cages. Zoya pushed Corey in and followed, dragging Bones by the shirttail. "Get in here you dumb oaf, before someone asks questions."

Corey took out a flashlight as well. He panned it along the ancient wires and equipment. "A side-quest. Totally awesome!"

Near the back of the compartment, a bundle of cables passed through an opening in the floor. Maddock looked down at a ladder. It disappeared into the darkness below. Bones peered over his shoulder. "Freaking Dungeons and Dragons—only Corey could find something like this."

Zoya said, "We have to do a little climbing. You first, big guy."

Maddock let his friend descend a few rungs before he started down. They passed two landings before stepping off into a low tunnel. A few hundred yards away, a dim yellow light reflected off the damp walls. Corey swung down behind Maddock. Zoya landed with a thump. "You going to stand here all day?"

Bones folded his arms and didn't move. Maddock looked back. "What's in the tunnel behind us?"

"It doesn't matter. We're not going that way."

"It matters," Bones said. "I don't like the setup here at all."

Zoya rolled her eyes at him. "These were service tunnels for the railroad back in the early nineteen-hundreds. Steam, water, hell I don't know. Okay?"

"And there?" Maddock nodded toward the yellow light.

"Friends. Sometimes I stay with them. I left my stuff there."

Bones looked up the ladder. "Why don't we let ourselves out. You can go stay with your friends and we'll just toddle on back to Key West."

"No." Corey held up his hands. "You don't walk away from a side quest. It's bad mojo, man. It's a three-point hit on your rep score."

Maddock bit back a groan. *This was what I was afraid of, Corey in gaming mode.* He knew it was going to get old before it got better. *If Bones picks up on it, I may have to kill them both.* He glanced at his friend. Bones slipped a compact Glock nine-millimeter from his pack and made a show of stuffing it in his back pocket. "Lead on."

Zoya said nothing and started toward the light. Corey followed. Maddock signed for Bones to go ahead, his flashlight swinging arcs behind him. Anyone hiding in the darkness would have a clear shot if they wanted to take it. Maddock didn't like thinking about their chances in a firefight.

The light had been a single bulb hanging outside a gray steel door. Zoya pushed through without looking back. Maddock took a final glance behind them and slipped in with the others. Mismatched cubicles, tables, chairs, and flickering monitors filled the room. Bundled cables hung from the ceiling and draped into the banks of computer blades that decorated every vacant corner of the space.

Corey stood speechless. Bones said, "I think you just swallowed the red pill, Neo."

"It's not the Matrix," Zoya said. "Day traders and a bunch of guys mining crypto, that's all. Come on."

Up a short flight of stairs, she led them to a darkened room. Maddock could see rows and stacks of plywood crates. Zoya hustled ahead, weaving her way toward what looked like a lighted storefront. "Welcome to Lazar's Emporium."

Lazar in person sat like Aladdin in his cave of wonders. Glittering piles of rare antiques, pottery, sculpture, and jewelry sat perched like stadium seats, radiating from where he sat. On the walls, Maddock saw frame after frame of classic and modern art, all hung in random order.

The man stood when Zoya entered. "What have you brought me, my little wren?"

She pointed to Corey. "Well, if he hadn't gone and lost it, I'd have brought you the relic."

Maddock stepped forward. "That's the third time you've used that term. What kind of relic do you think that stick was, anyway?"

Lazar stood less than six feet tall, but he looked to weigh over three hundred pounds. Wearing a baggy silk jacket and loose pants, he would have been well-dressed a century earlier. "And you must be the Mr. Dane Maddock I've heard so much about."

"Yes. I seem to be famous in all the wrong places. I assume I'm speaking with—" he gazed about at the piles of treasure, "—Mr. Lazar?"

The man bowed. "Lazar Dnevnic, purveyor of the unusual."

"Hey, look at this." Bones pointed to an enormous bronze dagger sitting by itself in a glass case. "Isn't that part of the treasure we brought up from…"

"You are very perceptive…Mr. Bonebrake, yes?" Lazar smiled. "Late bronze age I believe, almost unheard of in that condition. And no, you will not get it back. I have a customer eager to buy it for twice what the lot of you are worth."

Maddock inspected the blade. Almost eighteen inches long, it was more a sword than a dagger. He hadn't wanted to sell the thing. *But crap, we were almost broke at the time.* A few bits of antique jewelry looked familiar as well. "I see you have pieces from the *Santa Lucia* wreck."

"True, Mr. Maddock. Some of your more *interesting* finds have passed through my hands."

"Yeah, but these dolts fumbled the last one." Zoya glared up at Maddock. "You were supposed to be guarding him, not joyriding all over."

Bones stepped between them. "Okay, out with it. What's the big deal about that stick of firewood Corey's been waving around?"

Lazar's eyebrows shot up. "You don't know? Darling Zoya, you didn't tell them?"

"I wanted it to be a surprise."

Bones folded his arms. "You wanted it for yourself."

Corey stood stricken. "I… I would have given it to you. I was going to, after Dragon Con. You just never gave me the chance."

"Well, it's too late now, Gingerbread. That dragon has flown."

"I'm still not hearing answers," Maddock said. "What was that thing?"

Lazar rummaged through an ancient desk, littered with books and papers. He pulled out a wrinkled parchment fragment and held it up. "This. At least a portion."

Maddock inspected a crude drawing of a figure playing some kind of stringed instrument. "A harp?"

"A *kithara*, to be precise, a Greek lyre. You had one arm of it…fashioned from the horn of an extinct species of Egyptian oryx."

"And you know this, how?"

Lazar turned to Corey. "I believe you attended the disposition of the late Dr. Humphery Bartholemew's estate, correct?"

"I guess. I didn't dispose of anything, but I bought my wizard's staff from a bunch of old junk they had for sale."

"I've been trying to track down *your staff* for years. It only recently came to my attention that Bartholemew had acquired it. By the time I found out, it was too late." Lazar closed his eyes. "Now tell me honestly, of all the treasures that man had collected, why did you choose this particular item?"

Corey looked down and rubbed his chin. "I needed a staff for my costume and there it was. The right size, the right shape—it kind of called to me."

"*It called to you.* That's what I feared most. This particular artifact was discovered by a group of amateur archeologists in the late nineteenth century. More looters, I fear than archeologists—not that you three would know the difference." Lazar resumed his seat at the center of his trove. "One by one, they all met with a bad end."

"Meaning what?" Bones said. "It's cursed?"

"Meaning it has a history. According to my research, this *staff* as you call it, was a part of the ancient kithara belonging to Orpheus himself."

"That Greek guy who invented music?"

"He didn't invent music, so much as harness its power as a source of influence. He used it to control people, animals, even the weather."

"That would make him a god, almost," Maddock said.

"Indeed. Of course, the Maenads became jealous." At Bones's quizzical look, Lazar interrupted himself. "The Maenads, the insane female worshippers of Dionysus. They fell on poor Orpheus while he was sleeping. Ripped him to shreds I'm afraid. In their fury, they dismantled his sacred instrument and scattered its parts across the Aegean islands."

Bones squinted at Zoya. "Good thing I don't play the harp."

Maddock said, "Why didn't these Maenads just smash or burn the thing?"

"Well, that's where the story gets interesting. It seems they didn't dare. Orpheus's lyre possessed some power of its own. They dismantled it and hid the parts, but that's as far as they would go."

Corey's eyes focused on someplace far away. "I was holding a real magical wand…"

Lazar shook his head. "It's all Greek fable, tales to entertain children. Still, I have heard stranger things. Now please tell me, young man, you didn't really try to use it, did you?"

"Well, it got him a beer," Bones said.

"It did not. You just didn't close the fridge all the way."

"I pushed it shut. The door has a magnetic strip—no way it wasn't closed."

"Forget the stupid beer," Zoya said. "You pointed that stick at a car door and commanded it to open."

Lazar had steepled his fingers beneath his chin and once more closed his eyes. "I presume it opened?"

"Yeah, or so he says. Up a freeway ramp with the locks on, no less."

"Well Mr. Corey Dean, for your sake, I pray you recover your relic."

Maddock hesitated, pushing something deep in his pocket. "I take it the wand was valuable then?"

Lazar spread his arms and looked around. "To certain buyers, a part of the Orpheus lyre would be worth more than everything in here, more than all the crypto mined next door, more than you could possibly imagine."

Bones nodded and rolled his eyes. "I feel your pain, man."

"I'm afraid it's gone," Corey said. "Other than the obvious, why should that matter to me?"

"I've handled artifacts like yours in the past. Talismans, amulets, charms, fetishes, call them what you will, it's all the same. Like the genie, the *djinn* in the lamp, each item imprisons an entity. If you use it, it will bond you, eventually come to own you.

"Find the lyre fragment. You must learn the entity's name. Only then can you abjure your connection to it," Lazar closed his eyes, "and pray that it frees you."

"How…" Corey slouched. "How am I supposed to do that?"

"I truly have no idea."

6

Their conversation with Lazar ended as quickly as it had started. The man bent to his paperwork and bid them a good day. While Zoya packed her belongings, Bones prowled between the shadowy stacks of crates and trunks. On returning, he looked over his shoulder and shook his head. "I don't know what half this stuff is, but it smells like munitions. I don't think Zoya's play-pal is being straight with us."

Maddock nodded. What started out as a weekend joyride had turned serious the moment they arrived in Atlanta. "I've got a bad feeling about this place. Grab Corey and his girl. We need to bail."

They had just about returned to the ladder, Zoya leading the way and Maddock scanning front and back. The faintest flick of the shadows and he turned. Someone had doused the light behind them. "Everybody hit the floor!"

He'd just done so himself when a volley of shots whined and sizzled about their heads. Corey had thought to kill his flashlight. Zoya whispered, "Quick up the ladder."

"No, that's what they want. They'll be waiting for us at the top."

Three muzzle flashes and another scatter of bullets ricocheted off the walls and spun into the darkness behind them. Maddock set his flashlight on the fourth ladder rung and flicked it on. Another volley of flashes. Maddock returned two shots but knew he had little chance of doing more than keeping their heads down.

Bones crawled up. "Think they have night vision?"

"Could be. Won't do much good with that light in their face. Ideas?"

"Crawl back there and bushwhack them?"

"If someone comes down the shaft, we'd be screwed." Maddock looked over his shoulder. "They expect us to climb the ladder, we've got to take our chances on the tunnel."

Maddock crouched low and scuttled down past the ladder.

There was just enough reflected glow to make out the damp brick walls and cement floor. A few random shots sizzled off the ceiling overhead and whined past his ear. He kept going.

Twenty yards farther, Maddock froze. Before him stretched an abyss of darkness. He felt someone at his back. "Corey? Give me your light."

Pinching the beam between his fingers, Maddock panned an enormous empty chamber. Rusting pipes, scrap metal, and vacant concrete slabs filled the floor. He picked his way down a crumbling brick stairway. Bones hissed, "What the hell is this place?"

"Steam generation plant from the past century, I would guess." Maddock paused at the bottom to let the others catch up. "There's got to be a ventilation shaft here somewhere."

A soft clatter echoed from the tunnel above. Maddock killed the light. Quiet, pitch black, he was just getting oriented when a blinding white glare caught him in the face. A glimpse of pistol barrel, its muzzle the size of a sewer main, then a smack like a side of beef falling from the back of a truck. The light went skittering. Bones snatched it up. "Looked like you needed a little intervention there, buddy."

Maddock wasn't listening. He had a knee on the man's chest and a hand on the pistol. "Bones, give me some light here."

His friend held a hand over the flashlight lens and let a few narrow beams fall on the man's face. "I think I know this guy."

"Repeat."

"I think I know… Huh?"

"It's Repeat from the Preacher's warehouse. Looks like you cold-cocked him good."

Corey knelt next to them. "It's who?"

"One of Prester John's minions. We saw him at the airport this afternoon."

Maddock eased his knee off the unconscious man and checked him for other weapons. "No goggles. He was supposed to catch us in the shaft. Couldn't wait, I guess."

Bones made a quick sweep of the tunnel. "Crap! Where's Zoya?"

"Here." She dropped from an unseen perch and crouched next to the tiny glow of Bones's flashlight. "I wanted to make sure there were no others. What do we do with him?"

"Leave him here. It's time we scram."

In one corner of the chamber, Maddock found a rusted iron ladder bolted to the wall. Bones started to climb. Signaling Corey and Zoya to follow, Maddock waited. Muffled voices echoed back up the tunnel, he grabbed an iron rung and scrambled up. "Go, go."

The others needed no encouragement. Bones kicked open a rotting wooden hatch and they slipped into the outer hall. A few weary commuters filed past without giving a second look. Bones glanced at the escalator. "Where to, boss?"

Maddock had made up his mind as they climbed the shaft. "I'm tired of running from these guys. We go back to the airport and have a talk with this Prester John. I don't care what June says. I'll camp in his flying limo if that's what it takes."

"And the car?"

"Leave the car. We'll get it when we return." Maddock nodded toward the subway entrance. "This way, and hustle."

They jumped the Metropolitan Atlanta Rapid Transit train heading south. The four of them stood for a few stops before the crowd cleared enough that they could commandeer the back end of their car. Bones checked the route map over their heads, scanned the remaining few passengers, and then turned to Zoya. "Why are you even still here?"

She glared back at him. "You goons screwed things up the first time. I'm coming along to see that you don't do it again."

Corey had been sitting quietly, staring at his feet. He looked up and said, "Who's side do you think she's on?"

"Well, that's what I'm trying to figure out."

"No, not Zoya, your friend June. She's the one working for Prester John. She's the one who lured you away for the afternoon. What happens when we confront her?"

Maddock had been thinking along the same lines. It seemed awfully convenient, June in Atlanta when they arrived, Zoya too. *Had they known Corey would be here?* Something else didn't add up. "They got the staff. What more do they want—and why are they shooting at us?"

"And why did they miss?" Bones said. "They had goggles and guns. They could have ambushed us any time. We'd have been dead meat."

Maddock had been watching Zoya during the exchange. *The young woman knew a lot more than she let on.* "And how did they know where we were?"

In one fluid movement, she leaped from the floor and stood on the seat. "Just say it. The two of you—you think I set you up? You think this is all my doing? Are you nuts? They were shooting at me, too. I could have stayed with Lazar. You wanted me to, but I didn't and here I am with a bunch of thugs, running from a bunch of thugs and cops and God knows who else."

Corey and Bones had jumped to their feet, but Maddock stayed put. "Sit down, all of you. You too, Zoya."

He waited until they'd settled back. Feet still on the plastic seat, Zoya squatted on her haunches, balancing effortlessly as the train accelerated and braked. Maddock figured it was the best he was going to get. "Not you, your friend Lazar. How well do you know him?"

She glared at all of them. "We do business sometimes."

"Be more specific."

"He trades antiquities. Sometimes I get a finder's fee."

"Back in his warehouse there," Bones said. "That sure didn't look my gramma's attic."

"He might trade other stuff too. I don't know about that."

Corey said, "You could have told me all of this when we first met. I liked you, Zoya, maybe I still do. I just don't understand."

She dropped her eyes for a moment. "Nobody does, so don't even try."

Maddock glanced at the station they were leaving. The airport would be next. "We will have to cab it around to the private terminal. In answer to your question, Corey, I just don't know where June figures into all this, but we're about to find out."

The cab dropped them across from the darkened Quonset building. Bones grumbled as he got out. Zoya hung back in the shadows. Corey looked around and said, "I wish we had someplace to stash our gear."

Maddock shook his head. "I don't know what's going to happen next, but we've got to stay mobile."

They crossed the median and descended an embankment. A single yellow lamp glowed from a pole next to the security gate. Bones scanned the darkened tarmac, "Looks like they all split."

Maddock peered through the fence. "Nope. Lights moving out on the taxiway."

Corey walked over to the gate. "One problem, gents—how do we get in?"

Zoya glided out of the shadows next to him. "Leave that to me."

She leaped halfway up the fence and sprung to the light pole. Hands and feet, she climbed the pole and dove over the wire, into the darkness. Maddock was sure she had broken her neck. She reappeared behind the security gate and swung it open. "Easy as that."

"Let me guess," Bones said. "You worked for a circus too."

"*Angampora*, it's a way of life."

"Anga—what?"

"Quiet, all of you," Maddock hissed. "We need to maintain the initiative."

Beyond the yellow pool of light, the steel Quonset crouched in darkness. Maddock waited in the shadows and watched a pair of forklifts shuttling back and forth to the bulky C-130. Corey sidled up next to him. "So that's June's baby," He whispered. "I wonder what they're loading?"

"Relief supplies, or so they say." Maddock inched forward and leaned around the building. "Crap on a stick, it's gone!"

"Shhh… what?" Bones said.

Maddock pulled back. "The Gulfstream. Bastard flew the coop."

Bones peeked around. "Damn. What now?"

Maddock hunkered down in the shadows. "Circle up—you too, Zoya. We've got decisions to make."

The young woman materialized. "Day late, huh?"

"Maybe not. How bad do we want this guy?"

"He went gunning for you, doofus. Do you think he'll stop?"

Corey said, "I think it was me he was gunning for. He can't use the staff while it's bonded to me."

"Nuts," Maddock shook his head, "Lazar said it was all fairytales anyway."

"You think." Zoya looked at each of them. "Lazar has his own agenda—you should have figured that. They need Corey, if not alive, then at least dead. You know what else they need?"

Maddock let her talk as he mulled over the risks. When no one answered, she continued. "They need the rest of the Orpheus lyre."

Bones sat somewhat apart, his arms crossed. "Crap, it's got to be over three thousand years old, if it ever existed. Good luck with that."

"Maybe, but Prester John is going to look for it and I happen to know where he'll start."

Bones grunted and shook his head. "Yeah, right."

Zoya stood and pointed her finger at him. "Up 'til now, you've been wrong and I've been right, Gomer."

"Keep it down."

"I don't give a rat's ass who hears me. I'm telling *you*, I know where they are going. It'll be a modern-day odyssey."

Maddock said, "I think I know as well. Just give us a chance here."

Zoya settled back on her haunches. Corey glanced between them. When no one else spoke, he said, "You've got something in mind, skipper?"

"What if we follow the Preacher?"

"Not sure I like where you're going with this," Bones said.

"They are almost done loading. June will be cranking up the engines in a few minutes."

Maddock gazed out at the C-130 squatting in its own pool

of light and patted the folded lump in his pocket. *It's go now or go home.* He turned to the others and explained his plan.

7

Corey had been on board with the plan from the beginning. Bones was a harder sell. "I did not sign up for this tour, and I've got better things to do than getting dead or arrested or both."

Zoya had said nothing, but simply disappeared. When the forklift shuttle ended and the fuel truck pulled away, Maddock gave the high sign, grabbed his gear, and dashed across the pavement. The second engine had started by the time they reached the tail ramp. They had scuttled up and lost themselves among the boxes. Maddock was not surprised to find Zoya there before them, nestled behind a large crate.

Pete and Repeat gave the load one last check and made their way forward. Maddock was tempted to neutralize them before they even took off. *Not until I know June's part in all this.* The tail ramp closed and the starboard engine spun up.

Maddock wedged himself into a crevice. Zoya had done the same, curled up like a cat in a cardboard box. June hit the brakes, and everything shifted a few centimeters forward. The other two turbines whined into life. The plane shook as she ran up all four engines and tested them. Moments later the cargo shifted back, and Maddock felt the surge of acceleration. Settling into his own hiding place, he used his pack for a pillow. Like those Bones and Corey carried, it was military issue, waterproof and nearly indestructible—*just not terribly comfortable.*

He awakened amidst the usual creaks and grumbles of a cargo plane in flight. His watch said twelve-thirty. *About two and a half hours, enough sleep for now.* By the red interior lights, he could make out Zoya where she lay curled against a crate.

Maddock eased from behind a stack of boxes and followed a narrow aisle forward. A heavy bulkhead divided the crew compartment from the cargo bay. He peered past a hanging curtain. Dark. By a trail of red lights, he made out more curtains on either side of a central aisle. Nothing moved. He figured June would still be on the flight deck. Maddock padded forward and cracked open the door. June sat in the left-hand seat, headphones on, running through an instrument check. The copilot's chair was empty. He sidled forward and settled himself in.

"Glad to see you could make it." June didn't look up from her panel. "I was worried for a while."

"So was I. Your ground crew had other plans. How did you know I was on board?"

June touched the screen and tapped an icon. Four images zoomed up. In the lower-left box, Maddock watched the three of them sneak up the ramp. "Told you I had the latest tech."

He watched it cycle again, himself and Corey. Bones followed with his head on a swivel. "You've got a camera on every hatch?"

"Yup. Gotta keep an eye on the Brothers Karamazov. Never know when one of 'em is gonna stick a knife in my back."

"They were shooting at us earlier." In the upper box, a video showed the two climbing onboard. Maddock pointed. "Stop it there. That guy—Bones conked him good. We left him unconscious in Atlanta. How…?"

"Meth. They're both tweakers."

"Great. What about your friend Margo?"

"She's… she's a different part of the operation."

"So…what about you, June? Who are you really working for?"

"I don't know. Really, I don't. You remember that little guy?"

"Little guy… little guy?" Maddock scratched his head. "Oh crap, Uzi? Mr. Secret Agent Man? You've got to be kidding."

"Afraid I'm not. He hooked me up with this gig, no instructions, no warnings, no get-outa-jail-free card, nothing. Pay is good and a gal's gotta eat."

"Any idea what you're hauling back there?"

"Farm equipment, beans, rice, tinned meat. That's what the manifest says."

"Yeah, right. So where are we going fly-girl?"

"I was about to ask you the same thing. Why'd you tag

along?"

"I need to catch up with your boss and finish a conversation we had."

"Too bad I'm not gonna see him for a while. In about two hours we stop at Gander to refuel, then on to Shannon, and from there to Istanbul. The Preach flies directly to Athens. Not sure when he intends to meet us."

"Any chance of Pete and Repeat wandering aft of the bulkhead?"

June shook her head. "They'll be out until we reach Turkey. You better think of something by then, 'cause they'll be all shot up and bouncing around like ferrets in a rabbit hutch."

"In that case, I'll head back to steerage and try to get some sleep. Tell Margo that Bones said hi."

The C-130 touched down without a bump. Maddock would have slept right through it if the roar of four reversed props hadn't roused him. They taxied across the apron, suspension squealing over every seam in the pavement. Bones' head popped above the shipping crates. Palms down, Maddock signed for him to stay put.

Fuel hoses clunked and rattled outside once they'd rolled to a stop. He heard tractors growling by. The curtain separated and June stepped through. "Coast is clear, boys."

Maddock put a finger to his lips and shook his head at Zoya. Bones had materialized from the other side of the narrow aisle, Corey in his wake. "You knew?"

"Your boss came visiting."

"I filled her in on the three of us." Maddock held up three fingers and nodded. "Where's Margo?"

"Up forward, directing traffic and filling out paperwork. She knows."

Bones ducked his head. "And?"

"She's not gonna say anything, if that's what you mean. It's my ground crew that you've got to worry about."

"Would they sleep through an unscheduled landing?"

"What, Athens? You're nuts."

"Maybe someplace on the western side, away from

Athens."

"Not gonna happen. Preach would know before our wheels touched pavement."

"Let me think about this. Who's flying the Atlantic?"

"Margo has first watch, four hours. I'll land us at Shannon. From there,

it's over the Alps, down the Adriatic, and across Greece. We land in Istanbul late tonight. You guys sleep okay?"

Bones grinned at her. "Like on a cloud, Ms. Junie Moon."

"Well, get what rest you can. We'll figure out how to handle the Preacher's thugs when we get closer to Ataturk Airport. Maybe I'll just open the tail ramp and jettison the excess trash."

Maddock caught his breath. June gave him a quizzical look. "Just kidding big guy, right? Even Pete and Repeat would eventually be missed."

She turned to leave, then paused. "I don't like this business any better than you do, cowboy, but your friend was quite persuasive."

"I don't know who the hell that guy is, but he's not my friend. He stole someone we cared about. He manipulated all of us. Uzi is no better than your boss. Go back and fly this plane."

June retreated through the curtains and Zoya uncoiled from behind a web of lashings. "Were you ashamed to introduce me, or am I just excess cargo?"

"Nobody knows you're back here," Maddock said. "Not June, not Margo, nobody. Let's keep it that way for now. So how did you sneak on board without June's cameras catching you?"

"Easy, I snatched an orange vest. Four cargo riggers walk on, three walk off. I'm using the vest for a pillow."

"What's this with those two goons?" Corey said.

"Pete and Repeat are up forward sleeping off a meth high. June thinks they'll be crashed out until Istanbul."

"What do you think?" Bones said.

"Same thing you're thinking. We assume nothing."

Zoya looked up at the curtain. "I could just go…"

"Forget that. I may have a better idea. First, we take inventory. Anyone happen to bring a passport?"

"Atlanta is a little weird," Bones said. "But I didn't figure on needing one."

Corey shook his head. Zoya pinched out a smirk. "Never leave home without it."

"Well, that'll put you on point if we have to deal with officials. The rest of us will go rogue."

Bones smirked. "Works for me, I'm already going commando."

Maddock gave his head a small shake. "Okay, we're packing two Glocks. How much ammo you got?"

"I've got a half mag in the grip plus a spare. You?"

Maddock nodded. "About the same. Corey, you packing anything?"

"I've got the hottest pink notepad computer outside of the NSA."

Maddock grabbed the edge of a box as the plane lurched backward. He heard one engine whine to life and then another. "Get some sleep, people. We're going to be busy in the next few hours."

As Maddock settled into his corner, Zoya peeked from her hiding place. "What am I missing?"

"A long, messy, and unbelievable story. Don't worry about it. I've got a question—by chance, was Corey's staff found on the island of Ithaca?"

"You couldn't possibly know. How?"

"Never mind how. You said yesterday that you knew where the Preacher would be going. He's landing in Athens, but that's not his final destination, is it?"

"I don't know what you're talking about."

"Yes, you do. He's going back to the site where Corey's staff was found, isn't he?"

Zoya crossed her arms and looked aft. She turned and looked forward at the curtain separating them from the crew compartment. Licking her lips, she faced Maddock. "The cave of Loizos, on Ithaca. It collapsed some time ago—you can't get in there."

"And twenty-four hundred years ago, a portion of the roof

caved in, just about the time the Maenads dismantled the Orpheus lyre, right?"

"Kithara—Orpheus played the kithara." She glared at him. "How does a lunkhead like you know something like that?"

Maddock smirked. "I'm kind of a history nerd. Bones gives me a lot of crap about it. Makes sense that Prester John studied from the same book."

"Yeah—well, no. I don't know for sure where the Preacher is headed, but Lazar once told me where the relic had been found, so I'm guessing…"

"He's looking for more parts."

"That means he's not going to be in Istanbul for a while," Zoya said, "and you children are all flying rogue commando or whatever, which means you're not flying back to Greece any time soon." She gave Maddock a sour look. "This is stupid. I never should have come."

"You still like Corey, don't you…"

Zoya curled back into her hiding place. "I didn't say that, and you better not say it either."

At Shannon, Maddock waited until he heard the fuel truck pull away and felt the bump of a tug connecting to the nose wheel. He crouched in the shadows while the plane rolled from the fueling apron to the taxiway. Save for the lurch and sway of the fuselage, nothing moved. He watched the curtain for other visitors. It hung closed while the props spun up and the concrete runway fell away beneath their wheels. Satisfied that they weren't about to receive another visitor, Maddock worked his way aft.

He panned his flashlight across the cargo chutes secured to the overhead. Bundles of web mesh and coils of rope hung lashed to the wall. *June is not going to like this.* Maddock figured his own crew would not be too enthusiastic either. *Better to do and beg forgiveness than ask and be denied.* He got to work.

8

Three hours later, he tied off the webbing and checked the rope laid out like a hose in the back of a firetruck. Maddock looked at his watch. *We ought to be crossing the Adriatic by now*. He slipped past the crew's quarters and stepped onto the flight deck. Margo turned around. "I wondered if one of you would show up."

"And June?"

"I'm letting her sleep before we land in Istanbul and all hell breaks loose."

Taking care not to bump any of the controls, Maddock settled into the right-hand seat. "You called the Preacher already?"

"No, but when his little minions realize we have stowaways, it's not going to be pretty. You have Turkish visas, I presume?"

Maddock let the C-130 drone along on its autopilot while Margo watched him for a reaction. "What if there are no stowaways?"

"We're not landing if that's what you're thinking."

He pointed to a digital map on the console between them. "You mind?"

When Margo shrugged, he used the trackball and controller to zoom in on a stretch of Greek coastline. "Take us a little farther south before you turn east, descend below six thousand feet and depressurize. I'll do the rest."

"No way."

Maddock pulled out his Glock. "I can depressurize this plane right now and you'll have to take us down. I'd rather not."

The woman's eyes opened, and her mouth dropped. A half minute passed before she croaked out, "You... you wouldn't. You wouldn't dare."

"I've already been in a shooting war with your little friends back there. This would just be icing on the cake."

Margo's left hand crept up toward a button on the yoke. Maddock shook his head. "Nope, don't do that either or you'll give me no option. Just start your descent now, nice and slow. No use alarming anyone. We'll hit six thousand by the time we've reached the drop zone."

"Drop zone—are you going to fly? Or did you bring your own parachutes..."

Maddock nodded and watched their blue flight path crawl south along the Greek coastline. Margo cut power and let the altimeter crawl down. "Fifty-five hundred feet at the location you chose. Hope you're a good swimmer."

"Navy SEALS ma'am. Good as they come."

Maddock waved his pistol around as he talked, hoping to look crazy enough to use it. *June would have called my bluff, probably pulled out her own monster forty-four.*

They had passed below a layer of clouds when the gray outline of Kefalonia bulked up on the horizon. Farther east, a tiny smudge betrayed the island of Ithaka. Maddock eyed the altimeter and said, "Change course to one-seven-zero degrees and hold altitude."

"There's duct tape in the box under your seat," Margo said. "Use it, because no way I want the Preach thinking I cooperated."

Maddock checked their course and airspeed once more. *One hundred and sixty-five knots, the woman knows what she's doing.* He did a quick estimate of time-to-target as he taped Margo's arms and legs. Maddock checked his watch again. *Five-minute window, starting now.*

Striding aft, he blew through the curtains and ran to the tail ramp. The loadmaster's station clung to a stanchion. He flipped a toggle and lit it up. Checking internal pressure, Maddock raised a plastic cover and pulled the ramp lever down.

Hydraulics growled. Bones leaped from his hiding place. "What the bloody hell?"

"Pack everything up and tie it tight. We're going swimming."

The slipstream thrummed and roared as the cargo ramp descended. Sky, clouds, and then the sparkling Adriatic appeared before them. Corey gaped at the view for a moment. "You're insane. I'm not going out there."

Bones said, "For once I'm with the little guy. Who authorized this?"

"I did." Maddock checked his watch. "You've got two minutes and thirty-seven seconds before jump time—hustle, men."

Zoya had vaulted to the top of a plywood crate. She glared down at them. "No way, just no freaking way. This trip was an idiotic stunt in the first place. I'm staying put."

Corey said, "If she's staying, I'm staying too."

Zoya leaped down and grabbed Corey's arm. "They will catch you in Istanbul. That dick-head Preacher will have you killed so he can use the wand."

"He'll kill you too."

"No one catches me. I've got my orange vest. I walked on— I'll walk off."

"So what? You want me to jump out here and go splatter?"

Zoya kissed him on the lips. "Go, you stupid jackass or I'll kick you out the back myself."

"Saddle up people," Maddock said. "Launch in fifty-three seconds. There's harness and carabiners on the payload. Strap in."

While the others slept, Maddock had knotted lengths of webbing into step-in climbing harnesses. Bones had already hiked one around his waist. "Looks pretty mickey-mouse to me, boss. You sure about this?"

"Clip yourself to the cargo net and hold on tight. You too Corey, we go in forty."

Maddock had pulled his own harness up, the carabiner hanging from his waist. Corey snapped himself in and turned to look at Zoya. She had disappeared.

In her place, June came storming into the cargo compartment. "Are you all bat-shit *crazy*?"

Maddock slammed the red cargo chute launch button. A small report, a brief puff of smoke, and a package went sailing over his head and out the cargo door. Behind it, the loops of rope whined and sizzled. Maddock leaped for the cargo netting and groped for his carabiner. Lost, somewhere in the tangle at his feet—he reached down just as the rope pulled tight.

Left arm looped through the net, it yanked him from his feet and whisked him out the back. His shoulder screaming in pain, Maddock felt the heavy straps slip past his forearm. In desperation, he clutched the webbing, losing his grip, swinging wildly, grabbing as the sky and sea rotated in mad gyrations.

Corey screamed like it was his first roller-coaster ride. The payload flying with them spun and bashed at Maddock's side. Twice the size of an oil drum, it slammed back and forth, crushing his fingers before threatening to shake him off. As his battered hands slipped from the netting, Maddock heard Bones yell.

His flailing arms grabbed nothing but air. The sky spun away, the harness jerked tight, and Maddock dangled head-down like a trapeze artist. Bones called from above. "Next time, buckle up, buddy."

Somehow, his friend had snagged the wayward carabiner and clipped it to the cargo net. Maddock reached up and clasped Bones's outstretched hand. "Thanks, man. My timing was a little off."

"It's okay. I need you around to explain what the hell we're doing."

Their parachute rotated slowly, bringing the big cargo plane into view. June had already started closing the tail ramp. As Maddock watched, the engines trailed a whisp of gray smoke as she powered them up and banked hard to port. "Sure wasting no time on our account."

Corey just stared after the retreating plane. "I think she actually likes me…"

Bones shook his head. "Dude, I think you just kissed the hornet's nest."

"It's kicked—kicked the hornet's nest." Maddock let out a frustrated huff. "Doesn't matter, I'll probably never see her again…" he looked down at the waves, "…because we'll all be dead pretty soon."

Bones knocked on the large plastic cylinder that hung between them. "Not if this is what I think it is."

"It is," Maddock said. "Unsnap before we hit the water."

They clung to the netting as the chute dragged them along the surface. The canopy collapsed into a gray heap and Maddock grabbed the rope. With Bones and Corey dragging on the line, they managed to secure the trailing wads of fabric. Corey clung to a rope handle bolted to the container. "Now what?"

"Now swim clear," Bones said. "May I do the honors?"

Maddock nodded and Bones pulled on a recessed lever. With a loud crack, the container split open and erupted mounds of bulging fabric. The apparition hissed and thumped as it expanded into an elongated raft. "Behold," he said. "Your luxury accommodations await."

Corey grabbed a strap and slung his pack over the side. Maddock did the same. Moments later Bones hit the surface, spluttering and cursing. "You didn't say it was the freaking Titanic."

Maddock crawled over the side. "Ten- or twelve-person capacity—and made to travel. Grab the 'chute and webbing, I don't want to leave anything out here to show we landed."

Corey scanned the horizon. "Do you think anyone saw us come down?"

"You can count on it. We need to be good and gone before they come looking."

Maddock took inventory, paddles, a collapsible mast, and a small triangular sail. With the bundle of netting and parachute secure, he and Corey erected the mast. Bones flopped over the side. "Not leaving without me, were you?"

Maddock pointed toward a hazy landmass on the horizon. "That's about ten miles off. If you start swimming now, you could probably make it before dark."

"Probably beat this tub, if that's where you're headed."

Corey worked out the simple rigging and hung the sail. He fitted a paddle into a bracket on the stern and headed their raft downwind. "Where away Cap'n?"

"Ithaka, the fabled Isle of Odysseus."

"And why there?"

Bones began paddling. "Yeah, not my first choice. Why not Capri? Or wait, I heard of this island where the women don't even know what clothing looks like."

Maddock picked up a paddle and started on the other side. "Because Corey's little sweetheart gave it away when she mentioned the Odyssey. Almost a hundred years ago, they found a bunch of stuff that's been hidden in a cave since the time of Odysseus. The locals say it proves Homer's story was real."

Bones paddled in silence for several minutes before speaking again. "What makes you think we're gonna catch the Preacher there?"

"If you were looking for the rest of the Orpheus lyre, where would you start?"

Bones didn't say much after that. Their sail flapped. Corey crawled forward and adjusted the forestay. With the wind off their stern quarter, their raft plowed across the waves at a decent clip. A few miles behind them, Maddock saw a helicopter circle their landing site. He doubled down on paddling.

They had sailed and paddled almost five hours after inflating the raft. By late afternoon they entered a narrow strait between the island of Kefalonia and Ithaka. Maddock had them hug the shoreline, hoping they looked more like snorkelers or fishermen than refugees. On nearing land, Corey had dug into his pack and come up with his cellphone. "I got bars."

Bones grumbled, "Yeah, and I got a backache. How 'bout we trade?"

"Oars up," Maddock said. "We're making good enough time under sail. Corey, you wouldn't happen to have the Airbnb app on your phone?"

"Looking at it right now boss. Where we going?"

"Town of Stavros. First, find me the priciest villa in the area."

Corey whistled. "Sure don't have that kind of dough. Can't we rough it a bit?"

"Not for us. For the Preacher. I want to know where he might be headed."

"Only one place, big villa, pool, view, it looks posh."

"Now what's in our range?"

"Bingo!" Corey held up his phone—it showed a modest two-story building. "A little north of town, but look here, less than a hundred yards from the Archeological Museum."

They had swung into a little cove and run up on the wet sandy beach. A row of yacht tenders, kayaks, and fishing boats sat well above the line of seaweed that marked high water. They dragged their craft up and parked it between two zodiacs. Maddock walked around and inspected their little orange inflatable. "Almost looks like it belongs. Hopefully no one eyes it too closely."

The road had climbed from the small harbor near where they landed, up the brushy hillside to the town of Stavros. Maddock led the way. "I've always wanted to visit the home of wily Odysseus."

"Your patron saint or something?" Bones said.

"Something like that. Dad was fascinated by the story. He'd read to me from the Odessey—skipped over the boring parts."

Corey puffed along behind. "That's all nice. But do either of you ever get hungry?"

Bones grinned back at him. "I could eat something."

"You ate a whole chicken and half a pie last night," Maddock said.

"That was last night."

Maddock waited at the top. "I'm sure we'll find a *taverna* in town. How far to the hotel?

Behind them, the sun had settled over the isle of Kefalonia, glowing orange in the evening haze. Corey checked the map on his phone. "About fifteen minutes—and look, there's a taverna just up the street."

"What we really need is around that corner and two blocks down." Maddock had his own phone out.

Bones gave a wistful look back. "I could wait for you there."

Maddock dragged him along. Two blocks later he said,

"ATM—everybody, cards out. I need you to withdraw your max."

9

"Well, it's not the Ritz, but it beats that flop we had in Atlanta." Bones stood on a balcony and gazed out over the western Ionian Sea. A cool evening breeze blew off the water, and a full moon had just cleared the eastern horizon. "Your pal Odysseus was an idiot to ever leave."

Night had fallen when they finally arrived at their lodging. A couple of large euro notes had served in lieu of passports.

Two bedrooms and a couch, a clean spacious bathroom, comfortable chairs. Maddock agreed with Bones. It was far better than Atlanta. Corey grinned at the two of them. "Yay! We've completed our mission and leveled up." He picked up a large green bottle with a screw-on cap. "And look, this was in our loot-bag. Zoya's fav, ouzo!"

Maddock snatched it away. "No, nope. If Prester John and his minions are lurking around, we've got to stay sharp."

Bones and Corey exchanged looks. "I'd vote we tie him to the mast," Bones said.

"It's not a vote. We get some rest and start early tomorrow."

Early meant five a.m. to Maddock. He jogged past the museum and back into town. Corey and Bones were up when he returned. Maddock retrieved his pistol from the pack and clipped it to his belt. With his shirt untucked, he checked his reflection. The slim plastic holster made only a minor lump at his side. "Armor up, Bones. I'd rather have it and not need it than need it and not have it."

As the sky lightened, they walked to the taverna for coffee. The proprietor poured them each a small cup from a brass pot. Bones downed his in one swallow and made a face. "Takes the rust off a battleship's butt."

Maddock ignored his friend and watched the street traffic. Bones thumped his shoulder and ordered another coffee. "You look wound up tight—what's bugging you?"

"I'm wondering if Prester John knows we're here."

"Nah, how…" Bones paused a moment. "Not unless…"

"Yeah, not unless June or Margo ratted us out. He's smart enough to figure where we'd come ashore." Maddock turned to Corey. "Where did you say that villa was?"

"Passed it last night. I didn't see anything moving."

"Well, I need you to sit on it. Stay out of sight."

"We're gonna split up?" Bones said. "Like in the horror flicks just before the cute chick gets offed?"

"Fresh out of cute chicks so we're safe. Besides, anyone nosing around will be looking for three of us together." Maddock touched the screen on his mobile and showed it to Bones. "Here, I need you to check this out."

Bones stared at it a moment and scrolled down. "Cave of…" He squinted. "Of Loizos?"

"Yeah, it's down past the beach. That's where they claim to have found a bunch of artifacts, including stuff from Odysseus."

"You think Corey's stick came from there?"

"I'll bet the Preacher thinks so. You need to camp on it. Stay invisible."

"Maybe I ought to check it out, see if there's more…"

"There isn't, so don't risk going inside. We just need to know who else is interested. Stay in touch by text. I'll meet you both at the hotel about thirteen hundred."

Maddock watched them leave the taverna in opposite directions. He hoped Corey could wait it out without getting distracted or giving himself away. Of Bones, he had no doubts. He'd follow a goat track around to the north and come at the cave from the brushy hills above. With Bones on the hunt, they'd never see him.

The proprietor came by—Maddock took another cup of coffee. More people passed on the sidewalk, mostly shopkeepers and service workers hustling to start their day. Across the street, he caught a momentary glimpse of a small man in a neat gray suit. He wore a matching hat over his slicked-back. *Crap! If I didn't know better, that could have been Uzi.* Before Maddock could focus, he was gone. *Time I was gone as well.* He paid the bill and fell in behind a gang of carpenters headed out of town.

He fell out as they passed his lodging, checked his six, and ducked inside. Maddock couldn't get over the feeling that he was being watched. Up in their rooms, he poked about, noting the placement of a few items. Nothing definitive, everything was just about where they'd left it. Beds still unmade, towels still on the floor, he looked again. The ouzo—after he'd relieved Corey of the bottle, Maddock had set it with the label facing the wall. It faced the room now.

He examined their gear more carefully. Nothing had been disturbed. Corey's little pink notepad computer was still zipped in its waterproof case. Bones's pack still sat undisturbed beside his bed. Maddock closed everything up. *Why the ouzo bottle?* If Zoya had been around, he'd have suspected her. He stepped onto the balcony and scanned the surrounding terrain. Olive groves covered the hillsides. A few houses, chickens wandered in their backyard gardens. A jitney bus passed on the street. He checked his watch. *The museum opens in a few minutes.*

Maddock slipped out the back door, crossed a small courtyard, and found a narrow trail through the brush and olive trees. Scattered trash and a line of small footprints showed it to be the haunt of local kids. He followed the trail north, parallel to the road, until he found himself facing the yellow museum walls. Maddock slipped around the far end and worked his way back toward the parking lot. He loitered behind a dumpster and watched the entrance. About five minutes later, a van arrived and discharged a half-dozen tourists. Maddock followed them in.

The artifacts were well arranged, showing the progress of ancient Greek civilization from Mycenaean times to the rise of Byzantium. Near the back, Maddock stopped to admire an illuminated diorama of bronze and ceramic objects found in the Cave of Loizos. A slender, middle-aged man with a black moustache approached. "You are interested in our Odysseus, yes?"

Maddock nodded. "Are there any other artifacts that could have been his?"

The man closed his eyes. "Schliemann comes and he digs. He digs in many places. Who knows what he takes. It is one hundred years, there are wars, things get lost. We were left with a few small treasures, yes?"

"Schliemann, the discoverer of Troy? He was here?"

"Yes, here. He is mad to find his Ulysses, our Odysseus. Where else does he start?"

"But this cave, Mister…?"

"*Keerie*… it is our word. I am Keerie Demou," the man held out his hand, "archeological docent."

Maddock shook his hand. "I am… um, Captain Mannix."

"Ah! A seafarer by your look. Welcome Captain. No wonder is your interest in our Odysseus. You should call me Demou, just Demou."

"This cave of Loizos…?"

"Loizos, *ha*. He says he is a farmer. He is a hunter after antiquities. He sells them to the English, the Germans," Demou made a spitting sound, "even the French, he sells them."

The docent looked over his shoulders, as if fearing they might be overheard. "You are an honest man, so I tell you a secret. This cave, the one with the sign and the path that the tourists all take, is a ruse. Our island, she is filled with caves. For Loizos, they are his olive trees, his farm. He steals from all of them."

"You talk as if he were alive."

"No, you must excuse my English. Loizos, he meets Schlieman and then dies. It is over a hundred years ago." Demou pointed out a small leather-bound book. "It is the German's field notes. They tell of a conversation. Loizos finds something exciting and boom, the next day he is dead."

Maddock looked at the unremarkable brown volume. It sat alongside a corroded bronze dagger in a glass case. "I don't suppose you have an English translation of this?"

Demou gave him a sideways glance. "You do not think to look for this thing, I hope? It is no use anyway—Schliemann writes that he does not know what Loizos finds or where he finds it. Still, he leaves Greece the next day."

Maddock shook his head. "I'm not here to dig. I'm sure your Loizos and the others were most thorough."

The docent sighed and nodded. "Too thorough. They leave us only scraps. Enjoy your visit, captain. If you have any questions, my office is always open."

He continued to browse the exhibits after Demou left. A few minutes later, he sensed a presence behind him. Maddock didn't turn. The distorted reflection from the glass case told him all he needed to know. "Should I be surprised to find you here, Mr. Dane Maddock?"

"I might ask the same, Mr. Prester John. You must have an interest in Homerian epics."

"Only in the victories of Yahweh. It was Him, you know, who cast down the walls of Troy, not Zeus. It was God Almighty who scourged the fornicators and idolators from that land."

"And here I thought it was Odysseus and his wooden horse. Besides, wasn't Zeus on the side of Priam?"

Prester John put a hand on his shoulder. "You should study the holy works, my son. You should lead your followers on the road to truth and pay no attention to the Great Whore and her sycophants."

The hand tightened. Maddock spun away. "Why did your men attack us?"

"I have no idea what you are talking about."

"They assaulted my friend and kidnapped him. They came after us at the café, and they fired on us at the Atlanta metro station—or was that someone else?"

"Truly, you must be imagining things. Ask your companions. Where are they, by the way?"

Maddock looked around in mock surprise. "Why, I don't know. They must have left without my permission. And what about yours?" He nodded toward two men pretending to study a battered marble statue. "Over there, they seem familiar."

"Yes, my pilot and his assistant. They were assaulted in Atlanta as well. One cannot be too careful in a strange city. You should take that advice." He glanced at his watch. "I have business to attend. Enjoy your stay, Mr. Maddock. Oh, and one more thing, don't stow away on my aircraft again. I would hate to see anyone else get hurt."

Prester John joined the other two and headed for the entrance. Just before stepping out the door, one of them, the one with a beard and a bandaged head, turned and scowled. Maddock ignored him and stared at a row of terracotta plates. It didn't make sense that the Preacher would have found them so quickly. *June?* He thought it more likely Margo had reported them. Either that, or one of the tweakers woke up. *They would have had to explain the missing raft.* He wondered what the Preacher's next move would be. *He's probably made it by now.*

Maddock pulled out his phone and texted both Corey and Bones. Four periods, Morse for the letter H, *get home.* He started to leave when he gave one of the plates a second glance. It looked familiar. He leaned closer, then stepped over to the small gift shop near the entrance. Demou smiled across the counter at him. "Did you see interesting things?"

"That row of plates, you wouldn't happen to have a picture, would you?"

The docent reached beneath the counter and pulled out a flat box. "You like placemats, yes?"

Maddock opened the box and slid out six laminated pictures. Mycenean bronze tripods, a bronze knife, two small statues, he stopped. The last three placemats were sharp, professional photos of the plates. "The perfect gift for my nephews. I'll take it."

He hustled back to their lodgings, set the ouzo on the floor, and spread three of the placemats on the table. From the bottom corner of his pack, he fished out a folded scrap of parchment and compared it with the placemat images. Maddock scratched his head and rotated the parchment. He shuffled the placemats, took out a knife, and cut a strip off two of them, and pushed them together. Ten minutes later, Bones walked in. "Saw nothing but seagulls. Why'd you sound the retreat?"

"Had a visit from the Preacher man."

"What, here? How the hell did that happen?"

"At the museum. He found me. Oh, and someone was here in the room too—left a subtle calling card. We've been made."

"Crap, crap, *crap*! It was supposed to be the other way around." Bones glanced down at the table. "You taking up scrapbooking or something?"

"It's time I let you in on a little secret." Maddock handed Bones the scrap of parchment. "I lifted this from Zoya's friend, Lazar. It shows more than just a picture of a lyre."

"Kithara," Bones said, "remember, it's a kithara, not a lyre." He examined the scrap. "A gal with her boobs hanging out and a bunch of squiggly lines, I don't see much else."

"Align the lyre… kithara, whatever, align it with the one on those plates."

"I still don't see it. Lots of skin, though. They must have liked eating off plates with naked women on them."

"I'm thinking those are libation plates and the women are maenads—same crazies that shredded old Orpheus. But look at the overall pattern."

Bones squinted and rubbed his chin. "Seems oddly familiar, but I still don't get it."

"I didn't either until I remembered this." Maddock unfolded a tourist brochure he'd found in their room. "Do you see it yet?"

A map of Greece covered the entire back of the brochure. Bones compared them. "It's a map. Lazar's parchment was part of a map. Wait a minute," he pulled out his phone, "I want to get some pics."

"Yes, and look, there are four parts to the lyre—the two arms, the sound box, and the crossbar with string-winders. Our lady here on the parchment is holding her instrument by the left arm. The other three are holding theirs by the different parts."

"And you think these plates are a map of…?"

Maddock nodded. "…the other three parts of Orpheus's lyre."

"Has Corey seen this?" Bones looked around. "Where is our little dragon slayer, anyway?"

"I don't know. He should have been back before you. The Preacher seemed awful smug. I hope Corey hasn't gone and done something stupid."

"You mean…" Bones stepped out on their balcony to look around. "…like getting nabbed again?"

"Or standing out in plain sight, yeah."

"Screw you, Maddock. Maybe Thumbelina was right—you never should have left him by himself. So, what do we do now?"

Maddock bowed his head in thought. *Crap! So preoccupied with finding the damned relics.* "I've got a feeling we might have to bug out quick. Let's load up the gear and be ready to boogie."

Maddock collected Corey's belongings and padded his notebook computer with their extra clothing. Bones policed up what little was left and shoved it in his own pack. Arriving at their table, he hefted the bottle of ouzo. "Bottoms up?"

"Forget about it." Maddock thought for a moment. "Wait, stuff it in with Corey's gear. He wanted it—he can lug it."

"He can't lug it if the Preach has him. The little guy probably walked right up and rang the doorbell."

"Pretend for a minute he's smarter than that. What if he sees them staking this place out, where does he go?"

"Not the boat. Too obvious."

"Not the taverna either, same problem. Say he's really, really smart. What then?"

"You mean like me?" Bones said, "Because me, I'd just stay as close to Preacher's luxury villa as I could. I'd hide right in his own backyard."

Maddock nodded. "Then here's what we do…"

10

They had waited until evening and taken up positions just outside a comfortable-looking house perched a few hundred yards below the road. Maddock crept down the hillside until he was close enough to spot Prester John inside. Bones moved like a shadow through the underbrush, circling the house. He settled next to where Maddock crouched. "No sign of Corey. I wonder if he's even here."

"He's here."

"Well if he is, he's wearing some kind of magic invisibility suit, because I haven't seen him anywhere around."

Maddock winced. "Corey may be smart, but I just realized, he's also an idiot."

In response to Bones's questioning look, Maddock said, "No more talk, we just have to wait him out."

Bones settled behind a rock, keeping an eye on the villa entrance. Maddock low-crawled to the edge of a concrete patio. Fifty feet away, the moon reflected off a glass sliding door. He settled into the grass and watched. *What if I'm wrong?* It didn't seem likely. *If they'd grabbed Corey,* he thought, *wouldn't they have pulled up and left?*

The moon had arced about fifteen degrees across the sky before Maddock noticed a dark line grow and widen along one edge of the sliding door. A slender shadow emerged, carrying a staff. It hesitated a moment before sprinting for the bushes. Maddock jumped up and raced after. A moment later, he heard Bones grunt followed by a soft squeal of anger. Two figures rolled on the ground.

Maddock charged in and pulled the smaller figure by the arm. "What the devil are you doing, Corey?"

He was rewarded with a jab to the solar plexus that knocked him to his back. Rolling away, he felt the draft of something passing inches from his ear. Another squeal, this time louder. Maddock managed to seize an ankle and pull its owner from her feet. "Zoya, what the hell?"

In reply, she kicked out and caught him in the chin. Maddock hung on. The next kick went wild. "I've got her," Bones hissed. He had a beefy arm in a chokehold about her neck.

Maddock let go, figuring the sheer mass difference would give Bones a few seconds of advantage. Amid the shuffling feet and flailing legs, he groped around in the leaf litter. His hand fell on a familiar smooth staff just as Zoya squirmed free and landed on his back. Like some enraged animal she pounded on him until Bones reached down, grabbed her by one bare ankle, and lifted her thrashing and hissing into the air. "What should I do with this?"

"You caught it, you keep it," Maddock said. "We have to get out of here before all the forces of Christendom come after us."

He climbed toward the road. Bones followed, dangling his wriggling captive at arm's length. At the top, Maddock checked both directions. Light traffic, a few pedestrians passed on the far side. He rubbed his chin and turned to Zoya. "Are you done, or should I have Bones throw you back?"

She made a few half-hearted kicks in his direction. "Tell this overlarge asshat to put me down."

"I want your word."

"Just let me go and I'll give you *something*."

"It's about thirty yards down to the villa, Bones. Think you can fling her that far?"

Bones peered out over the darkened slope. "I've got the wind at my back, want me to try?"

"Okay, you have my word. I won't kill either of you...tonight."

She tucked as Bones dropped her and managed to roll her feet to the ground before she landed. Maddock nodded as she stood. "Nice move. Where did you learn that?"

"My mum was from Sri Lanka. She taught me a few *angampora* moves. What do you care? Give me the staff and we'll be even."

Maddock didn't bother to answer. "You hungry?"

"Oh, here's where I get the fatherly talk from Captain Midnight."

"I just thought you might be hungry. I know your friend Bones is."

Zoya looked up the street. A yellow glow from the taverna lit the sidewalk. She nodded. "We eat outside, if that's okay."

"I wouldn't have it any other way."

Two lamb gyros had disappeared from Zoya's plate before Bones had started on his second or Maddock had even finished his first. She polished off her glass of ouzo and licked her lips. "Now what?"

Maddock took another bite He chewed a moment, savoring the garlicky sauce, before answering. "You wouldn't happen to know where Corey is?"

"Having dinner with the Preacher, last I saw."

Bones jumped up and almost knocked the table over. "He's in there with them and you weren't gonna tell us?"

Maddock managed to rescue their meals as they slid his way. "Sit down, Bones. I already knew. At least I suspected." He put the staff on the table between them. "Corey went in looking for this."

Bones settled back in his chair. "He's an idiot."

"I already knew that too. Just like I know your little friend here is calculating the odds of a snatch and run with this black stick." He kept his hand on the staff. "It's not going to happen."

"Don't be such a tool. I'm not so little I couldn't take you out…if I wanted to. So don't patronize me, bub."

"If you say so," Maddock said with exaggerated patience. "You're still not getting Corey's stick. What else is happening in that villa?"

Zoya crossed her arms and stared off into the night. "What makes you think I'm going to tell you anything?"

"Because otherwise, you would have been gone after the first round of food." He waved for more of ouzo. "Now help us out here, what are they doing?"

When the waiter arrived, she said, "Just leave the bottle."

Zoya poured herself a shot, tipped it back, and poured

another. Maddock poured one for Bones and himself but didn't drink. "Again…what is Prester John doing with Corey?"

"Probably beating the crap out of him. They'll realize the relic is missing by now and figure he swiped it. That's what I'm sure he went in for, you know. And bumbling around like that," she took another sip of ouzo and looked up at Maddock, "didn't you teach him anything? He near screwed me up. I had to hide in the rafters for like, hours while they thrashed all over trying to catch him."

Bones put the half-eaten gyro back on his plate. "What are you thinking, boss? We trade the staff for Corey?"

"No, that puts us back where we started, and they'll still come after us. Worse, they'd probably rat out on the deal."

"Yeah, but if we keep it, they'll come after us anyway."

Maddock ran through a few scenarios in his head. None of them ended well. He considered the young woman. *She's here for a reason, something more than ripping the staff.* He wondered for a moment if she worked for Prester John. It didn't make sense. *Did she still care for Corey?*

Zoya glared back at him. "Well?"

"Well, I think you can help us out."

"Fat chance."

Maddock pushed the staff across the table. "Here, you keep it for now." She cocked her head and squinted at him. Maddock dug into his pocket and pulled out a key on a flat, plastic fob. "And take this. It's for our room. Three packs are in the closet, all done up and ready to go. Take them and disappear. I'm sure you can do that."

"That's it? I take the packs, then *adios, sayonara, ayubowan*…goodbye, that's it?"

"Bottoms up. You can meet us in a couple of hours at the cave of Loizos. I expect you've learned where that is. We'll have Corey with us."

Maddock started to tell her where to find their lodging, but she shook her head. "I already know that too. Well, 'so long, and thanks for all the fish,' as they say." Before Zoya left the Taverna, she turned. "Oh, one more thing, turn off your mobiles and you'll be a lot harder to trace."

Bones watched her disappear up the sidewalk, his mouth slightly open. "Just like that, you give her everything?"

"It'll keep the staff out of the Preacher's hands…and solve the problem of retrieving our gear without being seen."

"I was gonna sleep there, man. It has those nice fluffy beds, that bottle of…"

"…ouzo, yeah, I know. Ain't happening."

"No bed, no bottle—do you even *have* an exit strategy?"

"I'm working on it. Come on, we have a comrade to rescue."

Maddock explained his plan while they crept back to the villa. "Give me your gun, Bones."

His friend stopped midstride and stared. "Ha-ha. I thought I heard you ask for my gun."

"I did. They won't know you don't have it and you can't shoot your way in anyway. But Corey's going to need something when we find him."

Bones unclipped his holster and passed the weapon over. Checking the magazine and chamber, Maddock shoved it in his pocket. "Here, put the holster back on. It'll give you a nice bulge. The ladies like that."

"Screw you, Maddock. If I go down without a shot, I'll come back and whup your ass."

Fifty yards from the patio, they split up. Bones circled around from the hillside while Maddock crept closer to the side door. He worried a moment about Zoya, then remembered her kick to his chin. Somewhere inside, a doorbell rang. Maddock waited a moment, eyeing the side entrance. When nothing moved, he slipped through. Massive kitchen, silent dining room, he heard a commotion from the front. Padding down a carpeted hall, Maddock checked each of the darkened rooms. *Freaking place is enormous.* He passed an open door and glanced out onto a small courtyard or atrium. Bones stood at the entrance, arguing and waving his arms. Three men argued back, one clearly the Preacher.

Maddock continued searching, bathrooms, a gym, changing rooms for the pool, no Corey. *Bones can't bluff it out much longer. What am I missing?* He doubled back. *No towels, no laundry.* A narrow door next to the gym opened onto a darkened stairwell. Maddock took out his mini-light and started down. Shelves, linen, cleaning supplies—he panned the light around—Corey.

Contusions on both cheeks, blood running from his scalp, Corey slumped, bound to a heavy wooden chair. Maddock checked for a pulse. His friend lived, but his breath came in short gasps. A few knife swipes and he collapsed against Maddock's shoulder. "Come on buddy we're getting you out of here."

Corey twitched and vomited. *Head injury*, Maddock knew the drill—lay the patient flat, elevate his feet, protect him from shock. *No time for that now.* "You've got to walk out of here buddy, or we're both dead."

Corey retched again, gasping for air. "I'll be fine. Just need to rest."

"No. No rest. We have to fight our way clear." He shoved the pistol into Corey's hands. "Bones needs us, *now*."

Maddock dragged Corey up the stairs. His friend shuddered in the hall and collapsed to the carpet. "No, just let me rest a moment."

The atrium had gone silent. *They have Bones.* Maddock looked back at Corey shivering and retching on the floor, then dashed down the hall and stepped out into the open. Pete and Repeat had drawn weapons, he recognized them now. Bones stood, arms hanging and met his eye. Maddock drew his Glock. "Guns down or the Preacher dies."

The two spun, eyes flashing between him and Bones. Prester John didn't turn. "They will shoot you both, regardless."

Maddock felt a gun barrel pressed against his back. "Drop your pistol and don't move."

Prester John still didn't turn. "You haven't met my copilot yet. He is an expert in both hand-to-hand fighting and firearms."

Maddock returned his pistol to its holster. *Never give up your weapon*. The man kicked him behind the knee, crippling his left leg. "I said to drop it."

"I can't risk an accidental discharge. Besides, it would damage the finish."

He waited for the next kick, the one that would knock him to the pavement. In its place, a detonation echoed across the atrium. Maddock felt a hammer blow to his back that spun him around. Corey leaned against the doorframe clutching Bones's pistol. "I—I did it. I shot the gun from his hand."

11

Screams. At Maddock's feet, the man writhed, clutching his ruined hand. Prester John yelled, "Stop, for the Lord's sake, all of you stop."

Except for the wounded copilot's quiet gasping, the atrium fell silent. Bones cleared his throat. He brandished a Heckler & Koch machine pistol. "Ain't but just got started, Preach."

Pete and Repeat bent double, clutching their groins. Maddock limped over and grabbed Corey before he fell. "I'll explain later how dumb that was. Right now, I've got a bruise on my back where that gun hit me, and we've still got some cleanup to do." He turned to Prester John. "Get your men together and march them down to the cellar where you held Corey."

"My copilot needs medical attention."

"You can give him the same attention you gave our friend. Now get going."

Bones wedged the cellar door shut with a squat rack from the gym. "It'll take Godzilla to move that thing."

"We've got to scram," Maddock said. "There are more of them out there somewhere and I don't want to be here when they return."

"Or we could stay and fight…"

"Preach will have called them the minute you showed up. They're headed this way and loaded for bear. Besides, do you really want to explain a gunfight to the local police?"

While Bones secured the villa, Maddock had Corey lie flat, staring up at the open sky. "I don't think I can walk."

Bones jingled a set of keys. "Why walk when we can boost their wheels?" He insisted on driving. "I found a back road that stops just above the cave."

Maddock swung into the passenger side and hung on, hoping his friend didn't feel like showing off. Corey sprawled across the back seat. "If I get carsick, it'll be on your neck."

Bones took the hint. He rolled through town and crunched

down the gravel road like an old lady in a new Cadillac. For the last two miles, he killed the lights and cruised by moonlight and instinct. They stopped at a wide spot on the edge of a steep bluff. Maddock got out to inspect the terrain.

"Where you going, big fellow?" Zoya glided out of the shadows. "I figured you might come in this way."

Corey dragged himself from the car. "Zoya? How the hell did you get here?"

"You didn't tell him about me? That was cruel."

Bones shrugged. "I didn't think you'd show."

"I knew she'd show," Maddock said. "But she needs to answer Corey's question. How *did* you get here, on Ithaka I mean?"

"Your girlfriend, the Boomer, she diverted to Athens when you three all went skydiving. How do you think the Preacher's little buddies arrived so soon?"

"They sure found us easy enough," Bones said.

Zoya fidgeted a bit and looked around. "From what I overheard, he claims God is his copilot. Tells him everything that's happening."

"Bullcrap. Who else came to the party?"

"I saw six inside, including the Preacher."

Corey did a doubletake. "You were in there…all that time?"

"Yeah, Gingerbread. Not much I could do. Besides, I needed to swipe this." She brandished Corey's black staff. "Why do you think you're not dead? They needed you to get this, and they needed this before they could off you."

"That Preacher guy, he thought I'd hidden it…"

Maddock said, "Six total means two out looking for us. They will have sprung the Preacher and his men by now. We need to move on."

Corey, Zoya, and Bones all spoke at once. "Where?"

"If I don't tell, then you'll follow me out of curiosity."

"Which means if you *did* tell us," Corey said, "we'd run screaming the other direction."

"I'm in," Bones said. He nodded toward Zoya, "but what about her?"

"She can help Corey. We'll have time to decide later."

"And what about my little darling here?" Bones produced the H&K machine pistol he'd swiped.

"It's got your drool all over it. Wipe everything down and leave it in the trunk. With any luck, the local cops will get hold of it and blame Preacher's goons."

Zoya slipped away and returned with their packs. She had even lugged her own small satchel. "You know, you guys need to travel a little lighter."

Bones slammed the trunk lid and returned. "It broke my heart, but I jammed the barrel full of rocks."

Zoya tossed him a pack. "You could have used some out of your own collection."

"If you lugged all these down here, I'm impressed."

Maddock grabbed his pack and made a few unsteady steps up a goat path that contoured north along the coastline. Bones shouldered his own pack and scooped Corey's from the ground. He took Zoya's satchel as well. She grabbed Corey's arm and half dragged him after. "You got any destination in mind," she said, "or are we just going to stagger around in the bushes all night?"

Maddock glanced back at the moon. Its silvery disk rode high above the Strait of Ithaka. Across the glittering water, the hills of Kefalonia basked in their own shadows. He turned his attention to the trail at his feet. "We've got another three hours before the moon sets. We'll walk north for an hour and then I'll show you."

Bones grumbled something about baggage mules until he looked back at Zoya supporting Corey. Maddock had his own problems. His injured leg hurt like hell and the bruise on his back didn't help matters. It all just compounded his doubts, but if they could carry it out, his plan would certainly throw Prester John off their scent.

The moon had crossed half the strait by the time Maddock felt the path descend toward a small pocket cove. Bones had offered to help Zoya several times, but she refused. They rounded a copse of scrub pines and descended to a tiny beach.

Bones dropped his baggage and gazed out across the sparkling water. "A guy could live here."

Maddock flopped down. "Bull crap. You'd be bored in twenty minutes. Which is a good thing because you're not going to be here that long."

Corey lowered himself next to Maddock and lay back in the sand. "We defeated the boss and passed to the next level. Tell me this is where a portal opens that takes us home."

Zoya squatted a short distance away, her face in the shadows. Maddock knew she was looking at him. Bones sat on one of the packs. "Light 'em if you got 'em. Roll 'em if you don't." He looked out at the moonlit cove, glanced at Zoya, and turned back to Maddock. "Okay, spill."

"Everybody rested?"

Zoya leaped to her feet. "No! No, no, no—you're trying to *freaking* dump me again, but I'm warning you, this time it's not going to work."

Bones leaned closer. "Unless you've got a speedboat coming, we'd have to swim…" He jumped up next to Zoya. "Oh crap no! I'm with Princess Toadstool on this one. No way in *hell.*"

Maddock gestured at the Strait of Ithaka. "It's less than two miles across to Kefalonia. If we go now, we will reach the other side while the moon is still up. From there, we can hoof it to the ferry terminal before the first boat leaves in the morning."

Corey levered himself up on one elbow. "Two miles? I think I could make that."

Zoya snorted. "Yeah, and if not, you're dead, seal-boy. Oh wait, I forgot…"

"You didn't forget," Bones said. "That was you, just being mean."

"That was me, not wanting him drowned, okay?"

Maddock gazed across again. "Our packs float—we push them ahead of us. If we stick together, nobody drowns."

"Yeah, except mine doesn't float, get it?" Zoya poked him in the chest. "If I get tired, I drown."

"I *had* considered that possibility," Maddock paused and

grinned at her expression. "That's why you should take a plane to Thessaloniki and meet us there."

Corey sat up. "So, we drag Zoya all the way out here to the boonies and just ditch her?"

"Looked more like it was her dragging you." Bones said. "Still, seems a little rude."

"Not quite." Maddock passed her a wad of Euros. "That'll get you airfare and a few nights in a decent room. Take care of the staff and watch your back. We'll show up in a couple of days."

Zoya picked up her satchel and looked down at Corey. "I'd give you a kiss for luck, but I'm allergic to stupid." With that, she glided off into the shadows.

Corey yelled back at her. "You gave me a kiss the last time I did something stupid."

The swim didn't seem *that* stupid until a large cruise ship came into view. Maddock led their small flotilla, swimming sidestroke to conserve energy and push his pack in front of him. Corey followed, hugging his pack and kicking frog-style. They'd stuffed most of their clothing inside to give it extra flotation. Bones swam behind, pushing his pack along water polo style.

It was Corey who spotted the ship. "Lights off our starboard quarter, captain."

Halfway across, the waves had grown to a short chop. Maddock gasped and raised himself up. Green and red, with a mast light centered between, the vessel came straight at them. Bones shook the hair from his eyes and stared for a few wave cycles. "What do we do, boss?"

"Swim like hell and pray we're near the channel edge. Come on Corey, you can do this." Maddock took Corey's pack and put it with his own. "Swim for it!"

Maddock's injured leg screamed in pain and every stroke brought a jolt from the bruise on his back. Without the drag of his pack, Corey managed to keep up, but Maddock knew that his friend was near his limits. Bones followed, one eye on the ship and one eye on Corey. They nearly made it.

Maddock heard the hiss of the bow wake before he turned

to see a shadow loom across the sky baring teeth of gleaming phosphorescence. Bones shouted something—then chaos. Thrown high in the air, Maddock caught a glimpse of glowing yellow portlights before he plunged down, buried beneath a mountain of tumbling water. The packs were ripped from his hands and the throbbing rumble of twin screws froze his heart. *Down, swim down!* Maddock frog-kicked his way deeper into the black water. A rush of turbulence, a moment of thunder and blazing green light…then it was gone.

He followed a trail of glowing bubbles to the surface and scanned the sea for his friends. "Bones, Corey…" Maddock paused and listened—nothing but the hiss and slap of passing waves. He called again, spinning about in the water. Only the cruise ship lights, receding in the distance. Overhead, the moon hovered above the darkened island of Kefalonia. *So close.* Maddock shouted again.

"Cool it, bro. We're right here."

He spun about. Bones floated a few yards away, holding Corey's head above water. "I think he got conked on the way down."

Maddock swam over. His friend gasped and gagged as waves washed over his head. "I'll look after him. See if you can find our packs."

A few minutes later, Bones swam back holding a shredded scrap of Kevlar. "I think this was yours. Couldn't find mine."

"Damn. My gun and everything is gone." Twenty yards off, Maddock thought he spotted a small gray shadow bobbing in the chop. "What's that?"

"With our luck, it's a shark." Bones turned to look. "I don't see anything."

"The moon is about to set. You take Corey and start for land. I'm going to search a little longer." He knew Bones was a strong rescue swimmer with plenty of lifesaving creds. He could easily tow Corey the rest of the distance.

For as much as Maddock didn't like being separated, he liked the idea of losing their gear even less. A few strokes took him to where he thought he'd seen the object. Nothing. He began a spiral search pattern. Five strokes east, ten strokes south, fifteen west, he circled outward. Headed north, his hand caught on something, a rag of shredded fabric. A shaving kit floated nearby.

He stopped and looked around. *It's hopeless. We'll have to wander into town half-naked and broke.* Still, Maddock searched until the moon dipped behind the hills of Kefalonia and plunged the waves into darkness. In frustration, he followed the moon west, hoping he would make land somewhere near where Bones and Corey went ashore.

A hundred strokes and he stopped to get his bearings. In the darkness, little could be seen of his destination. He sighted on Polaris, then turned to pick out Venus, trailing the moon into the west. Maddock felt something soft bump him in the back. He recalled Bones's mention of sharks. It hit him again, harder this time. Spinning around, he jammed a fist into whatever it was. Hard and lumpy, Corey's pack put up little resistance.

12

Maddock emerged from the water on a rocky stretch of open coastline. There was no sign of Bones and Corey, but that didn't surprise him. Scrubby pines grew all the way down to the water's edge. He scrambled along the shore until he spotted a glimmer of light shining between the trees. A few hundred yards up the hillside, he reached a road and a small store, closed for the night. A single bulb glowed above the entrance.

Bones emerged from the darkness behind the building. "Glad you could make the party, and hey, looks like you brought a gift."

"Corey?"

"He'll live, but he's not doing so well."

Maddock found his friend slumped against the wall. Although the night was warm, Corey clutched his knees and shivered. A welt stretched from his forehead nearly down to his chin. "I got your pack, buddy. Let's get you into some dry clothes."

He pulled out a yard and a half of blue jeans and threw them to Bones. "Get dressed before you get arrested." Corey's clothing came next, dry and neatly folded.

His own jeans were wrapped around a slender glass bottle. Maddock unscrewed the cap and poured some of the contents on a clean tee-shirt. Inspecting his friend's scalp wound, he said, "Hold still a minute, this might sting."

"Yow!" He shoved Maddock away. "What the hell is that?"

"Ouzo—here, take a swig. Gotta finish the job."

Corey tipped it back, grimaced, then took another swallow. Maddock finished cleaning his injuries, including the ones he'd suffered at the hands of the Preacher's men.

Bones dug around in the pack and found their shirts. "Corey's got shoes in here, but I'm afraid we're barefooting it. Our guns are gone too—makes a guy feel naked."

Maddock checked his pockets, wallet, knife, keys, all good.

The dry clothing and ouzo revived Corey somewhat. He dug into his pack. "Remember, I had your pistol. It's right here with my computer and phone."

Maddock closed the pack and slung it on his shoulder. "How do you feel about walking?"

"As long as it gets me out of here."

Less than two miles up the coast, they entered a small fishing village. Lights had come on in most of the houses as the eastern sky above Ithaka glowed in anticipation of the dawn. Bones cursed and grumbled at the stones in the road, and Maddock's own feet were raw and bruised from the walk. They reached the ferry terminal at first light.

They found a ticket kiosk each bought passage to the village of Vasiliki on the mainland. Maddock watched the approaching hills and rocky cliffs topped by decaying ruins. The town on the horizon grew from a thin line of orange tile roofs to rows of whitewashed walls climbing the hillside. Bones watched with increasing intensity. "I only hope they eat breakfast in this Vasiliki place."

The ferry swung into a snug little harbor and tied off along a concrete quay wall. Maddock surveyed the town and spotted a tiny café tucked into the surrounding hills. Strong black coffee and omelets stuffed with feta cheese made the entire crossing seem worthwhile. Corey slurped his coffee and ordered another. He knocked that one back as well. "Stim packs, they'll hold me over until I can level up my health."

Maddock asked the proprietor about transportation. Despite some language difficulties, he learned that most visitors rented a car. "We might have a look at the car rentals."

"It's a trap," Corey said. "We can't take the obvious exit—we'll lose all our reputation points."

Bones swallowed a mouthful of egg and cheese. "And what do you suggest, Doctor Denarius, another swim?"

Maddock eyed the other patrons, all locals. He lowered his voice. "Car is out of the question. We'd have to use a credit card, and that would leave an obvious trail."

"Ferry?" Corey suggested. "With real seats and food?"

"It would take over a week, including a stop in Athens."

Bones finished his omelet and slammed back the rest of his coffee. "I don't like where this is going."

Maddock stood to pay their check. "First place *I'm* going, is to find some shoes." He spoke a minute with the proprietor before heading out the door.

Tavernas and tourist hotels lined the waterfront, but farther inland, Maddock led them to the *agora,* the market center. Bones picked out a Sasquatch-sized pair of sneakers that must have sat unsold for decades. Maddock found a pair of surplus military boots to replace the ones he'd lost. Corey prowled the stalls and tiny shops. He came away with a used bowler hat that fit reasonably well. "Got to keep up appearances."

The next stop didn't suit Bones at all. "You have *got* to be kidding me—a freaking bus station?"

"Our gateway to the world." Maddock examined the schedule board. "There's a northbound express leaving in thirty minutes."

They didn't roll out of Vasiliki for over an hour. When it finally left, the bus was almost empty. A gaggle of old women sat up front and glared at the three as they slouched on board. Maddock claimed the rear seat for Corey. "Get some rest. We're going to need you showing a solid green health bar when we reach Thessaloniki."

After a half dozen stops, the bus picked up another handful of passengers. Maddock agreed with his friends that it was hardly an express. By midday, Bones had sprawled across three seats and begun to snore. The day passed in a succession of verdant hills and picturesque towns. By early afternoon, the bus groaned to a stop outside an isolated taverna, and everyone filed off for a welcome break.

When they all reboarded, Maddock leaned against the window and thought about their next move. He settled back to run through a few ideas. The next thing he knew, night had fallen, and the valley below blazed with the lights of a large city, Thessaloniki.

As they stepped off the bus, Corey seemed to have truly leveled up his health. His bruises remained, but he no longer wobbled as he walked. Maddock's injured knee still hurt with every step, but he'd dealt with worse. Bones came right to the point. "We're here. What's next?"

Corey said, "Next, I need a place to sit down…"

"Sit down?" Bones interrupted. "You've been sleeping all day."

"Sit down and open my VPN."

"I thought you did that back in the restroom."

"Virtual Private Network, doof. I need to check if Zoya has left us a message."

Maddock mentioned a coffee shop he'd seen as they rolled up. "They might have wi-fi, but won't that give us away?"

"That's the 'Private' in VPN. I've got end-to-end encryption that I doubt even Prester John has the tools to crack."

The coffee shop had wi-fi. Corey wasted no time logging in and checking for messages. He scrolled through his mail. "Mostly junk, look at this one, Nigerian's dilemma. I haven't seen that scam run in years."

Maddock read over his shoulder. Madam Cordova Angampora needed Corey's help to recover her sixty-million-dollar fortune. She was willing to give him ten percent for his troubles. "I guess there's still one born every minute." He stopped and bent closer for another look. "Angampora? That's not a Nigerian name. I've heard the term recently."

Corey reread the message. "Angampora—yes, it's the Sri Lankan fighting style that Zoya uses. What the…?"

"Hotel Cordova," said Bones. "Your Princess Toadstool may be crazy as a one-eyed mongoose, but she's clever too."

Corey pivoted both directions. "Crap, she could be right behind you, Bones. You wanna get us both killed?"

Maddock had gone to find them a cab. Twenty minutes later, they rolled up to the only Hotel Cordova in Thessaloniki. Corey found Zoya in the bar, sipping ouzo. Bones walked in behind him. "Breaking hearts tonight?"

"Break more than that if you're not careful." She looked them over. "Not that it would change much. You three been French-kissing dump trucks or something?"

"Something like that," Maddock said. "I'll see if I can get us all rooms."

"Cool your jets, Captain Midnight. I already booked us a suite."

"Honeymoon?" Bones said. "With that heart-shaped hot tub and the mirrors on the ceiling?"

"Yeah, that's it. Keep on dreaming, Gomer." She rolled her eyes. "Maybe that's why they call it a family suite, huh?"

Maddock sighed and took a stool. "Come on, we're all going to need something strong to get us through this night."

Zoya tossed back her drink. "And I'll need another if I've got to sit downwind of you three."

13

Zoya had scouted out the ideal refuge, out of the way, comfortable rooms, wi-fi, and privacy. Before they crashed that night, Maddock took inventory. They all had cash, he and Bones still had their pocketknives, but their mobile phones had been lost with their packs. Corey dug into his own pack "Still got our bottle."

He pulled out a flashlight, his phone, and the pink notepad computer. "And I've got this." He handed Bones his Glock. "Only used once."

"Yeah, maybe by you." Bones checked the chamber and magazine. "Got sixteen rounds left."

Maddock said, "Let's hope we don't need them. Unfortunately, we lost our maps when my pack was shredded."

"And we'd have had pics if my mobile wasn't at the bottom of the sea."

"Might have 'em still," Corey opened his notepad, "if you can remember your phone password."

"It's ginormous."

"Good, then it'll be plenty secure."

"No, that's my password, 'ginormous'."

Zoya rolled her eyes. "I don't *even* want to know why."

Corey tapped out a few keystrokes. "There…I'm into your cloud account."

Bones jumped up and peered over his shoulder. "You're into what?"

"The cloud, where all your pics and old text messages are stored."

Bones tried to grab the notepad. "Nope, no one's peeking at that."

"Hands off. I'm only opening the most recent folder."

Maddock looked at the screen. Corey had four pictures up, three placemats from the museum, and the fragment Maddock had taken from Lazar. "Can you combine them into a single image?"

"In progress boss. How do you want them?"

Maddock had him overlay a map of the eastern Mediterranean. The parchment fragment aligned with Ithaka's shore. The Maenad it depicted held her lyre by its right arm. Corey zoomed in on the image. "It looks like mine."

Zoya dug Corey's staff from her satchel. "Almost identical. If you had bothered to look at it, you would have seen where it was socketed into the body at the bottom and where it joined the crossbar at the top."

"And the Maenad's eye is centered on the coast," Maddock said, "just about where Loizos's cave is located."

"Got that," Bones said, "but what makes Thessaloniki so special?"

Maddock had Corey enlarge one of the plates. "That's what gave me the idea. Same Maenad, but she's holding her lyre by its left arm, the mirror to Corey's. And there, look at the lines across her face, three distinctive peninsulas like the ones just east of here."

"And the eye is…?" Bones hunched forward to give the image a closer look.

Corey zoomed out to display more of the coastline. "The eye is right at the end of the northern peninsula."

Zoya snorted. "Well, good luck with that. It's Mount Athos, the Holy Mountain. *You* can't go there, and *I* sure as hell can't go there."

Bones leaned back. "I didn't think there was anywhere you wouldn't go."

"Females, women, girls, we're not allowed on the Holy Mountain. Hell, they don't even eat eggs because they're not allowed to have chickens." Zoya turned and glanced at her companions. "Seriously—it's a religious thing, no females—in fact, nobody period, unless they're invited. And you three, you ain't getting no invite, I promise."

Bones rubbed his chin and squinted. "So, what keeps us out?"

"That's about all I know. Get the wiz here to look it up."

"Let him rest," Maddock said. "We should bag it for the

night and pick things up in the morning."

Maddock arose before the others. He arranged for coffee and rolls to be brought up and headed down to the gym to work out a few kinks. On returning to their room, Maddock found all three drinking coffee and arguing about the last roll. "You pigs, that one's mine. Corey, did you find anything?"

"Yeah, Zoya is right. It's an autonomous enclave of the Orthodox Church. Look at these monasteries, they're like fortresses—and the whole mountain is crawling with hermits and priests, and worse."

Bones scanned the pictures Corey had brought up. "Damn, those places look like cities. None of that comes cheap. Where are they getting their dough? Not tourists."

"That's the thing," Corey said. "I checked a few of my unconventional sources. There's Russian, Serbian, and Armenian sects represented. Guess where most of their money is coming from?"

"Russia," Maddock said.

"Yeah, but here's the deal. The Greeks are afraid of too much Russian presence, so they've amped up their own outfit. The place is crawling with quasi-military guys calling themselves monks."

"Crap," Bones said. "We'd be like a three-man invasion force against an entrenched army."

Corey turned back to the computer screen. "It gets worse. Look at the eye on this figure. It covers the entire mountain and down both sides. That's almost thirty square miles."

"We're looking for something pre-Christian, pre-Roman even. Can we zero in on the ancient monuments?"

"The early history has been wiped clean and the old structures have all been demolished." Corey opened a browser page that came up in text. He scrolled down. "Here's an article about an archeological expedition launched in 1952. They were run off at gunpoint."

Maddock finished his breakfast roll and drank the rest of their coffee. "We need a different source of information. Find us the local history museum."

"Thessaloniki Archeology Museum," Corey said, "but I already checked their website. They've got nothing."

Maddock set his coffee cup down. "Anyone care to go touring?"

A fifteen-minute cab ride along the waterfront brought them to the museum. Maddock had already snagged a tourist map at the hotel. When they arrived, he pointed up one of the diagonals. "The university is about a quarter mile that way. Corey, we need you to find us the best maps you can of Mount Athos. Try the geology department."

Zoya stepped in front of Maddock. "That's about the stupidest thing I've heard yet. Last two times you bozos sent him off somewhere, he got snagged by the Preacher. What do you expect this time?"

"She volunteered, Bones." Maddock grinned down at her. "He'll be fine, because you're going to watch his six. Stay where you can see him but don't be too obvious."

"Now you're telling the cat how to lick cream?"

"Just show us the moves."

Zoya glanced back as she crossed the street, shadowing Corey from the other side. Bones laughed and punched Maddock in the arm. "You just caught some serious stink-eye, pal. A lesser man would be writhing on the pavement right now."

"A *smarter* man would have bailed on this whole stupid mess days ago. Come on, we've got a museum to ransack."

Spacious and filled with Greek antiquities, the Thessaloniki Archeological Museum was almost bewildering in its scope. They'd browsed the exhibits, acres of local artifacts. After wandering what seemed like a mile of halls, Bones stopped and stared up at a sign. "Doesn't archaic mean older than old? So how can it be pre-archaic? It all looks the same."

Maddock had to agree. "I thought I knew something of Greek history, but this is an overload."

Fortunately, the signs and labels were plentiful and written in multiple languages. The opposite was true for the docents, or any kind of attendants. A few ancients in frayed uniforms lounged on stools trying to look interested. Eventually, they stopped at the museum café for a midmorning snack. Bones smiled at the waitress and found that she not only spoke English but was a student at the nearby university.

She brought them both coffee and some kind of meat pastry. "Is slow today, yes? I will sit with you and practice English words."

"Get yourself something too," Maddock said. "We would like to talk about the museum."

"Thank you." She poured herself a cup of hot tea. "I am only student, yes? What can I tell you?"

Bones leaned forward. "Mount Athos, are there exhibits?"

"No, we are for *arkhaiología,* old things. There are no *arkhaiología* on Holy Mountain Athos."

"No research into its past, its history?" Maddock said.

"Always Holy Mountain, it belongs to God. Research would be *ierósylos*—sacrilege." She gave Maddock a dark look. "What you say, it is not right."

He dropped the subject and let his friend chat with her while he finished his coffee. A nice tip with the check, and he dragged Bones out into the morning sun. "So much for finding anything here. Maybe Corey has had better luck."

A few blocks north of the museum, Maddock found himself in the middle of a sprawling university campus. Unlike the museum, most of the signs were in Greek characters. Bones looked around. "It's all Greek…"

"Don't say it. It's a stupid joke, so don't say it."

"…to me." Bones grinned back at him. "You don't know how long I've been waiting to use that."

"Just find us the bookstore or something like it."

As he was about to head off in a random direction, Maddock felt a tug on his elbow. "Wrong way, Captain Midnight. We're over here."

Zoya stood behind them. Bones spun around. "Crap. Give a guy some warning, will ya."

"Let me guess, you two crack detectives struck out, and now you're pissed."

"Not quite, but close," Maddock said. "You're looking awfully smug, so lead on."

They crossed between two nondescript buildings in a style best described as seventies-modern. The condition of the grounds along with the accumulation of trash and graffiti did nothing to raise Maddock's hopes. As if she'd read his mind, Zoya said, "The whole place is going broke. Sucks for them, but it might help us out."

They crossed a small plaza to a decaying wooden picnic table where Corey sat with another man. Lean, weathered almost, he stood and held out a hand. "Morning gents, Chaz the name."

Bones introduced himself. "You're not from around here."

"Been for a bit, you know. Fell to the outs with Sir John at the BM and sent straightaway down here."

Noting the look on Bones's face, Corey said, "That's British Museum."

"Right, right, they call me an attaché of sorts. Negotiations and whatnot. The Greeks are all keen on return of some antiquities, you know. Sir John, not so. Been that way for twenty years. A body could retire out here and never be missed."

Maddock introduced himself as well. "So did Corey and Zoya fill you in?"

"Corey, yes. We had a nice chat. I don't think I met your Zoya."

Maddock looked around—she had disappeared. "She came with us."

Chaz looked back at Corey. He shrugged in return. "It doesn't matter. We'll see her when she wants to be seen. Tell my colleagues here what you told me."

Glancing around, Chaz returned to the table. "Sit gentlemen. We can chat here with some privacy." He looked around again. "My advice? Don't go asking just anyone about this Mount Athos. Your chum Corey here is lucky he talked to me first."

Maddock nodded. "That's the gist of what we learned at the museum."

"That place especially. Beautiful right? Half their stuff is fake. Believe me, I know because we Brits nipped the originals last century. What we didn't get, Schliemann and his team had packed out under the nose of the Ottomans a few years previous."

"I thought that guy was just about discovering Troy?" Bones said.

"You might think that, but no. He was obsessed with something—dug like a badger. Demolished whatever there was of Troy, right down to the bedrock. Quite bonkers, really." Chaz tipped his head to one side and looked Maddock in the eye. "You chaps are keen on finding something yourselves, right?"

"We're not digging, if that's what you mean. More like following up on a theory. Settling an argument, wouldn't you say Corey?"

"That's what I told Chaz," Corey said, "There are places we can't go, so we came here, hoping to find old maps, or records...or *something*."

"Right, right. Well, your lot won't make it to Athos, but you might have found *something* if we can reach an agreement, so to speak."

The agreement involved money. "Truth is," Chaz said, "the Greeks are broke, and with the current Parliament in London, the BM isn't too keen on boosting my stipend."

Bones said, "And you can't go back to London...because?"

"The story is long and sordid, but no, I cannot return."

Maddock negotiated hard with his remaining cash. Chaz eventually agreed to supply them with a few maps. "On approval," Maddock said. "Unless it's authentic, we're not interested."

Bones watched the man leave. "By the way he trotted out of here, I'd say you could have held out for a better deal."

Maddock grinned. "I'm not done with him yet."

Corey stood, walked around the table, and sat back down. "I don't see Zoya. Where'd she get to?"

"I hope she's following your Double-oh Nothing," Bones said. "I'd hate to think who he might be calling right now."

"You're paranoid."

"Just because I'm paranoid, it doesn't mean they aren't out to get us."

Maddock watched a few cars pass on the street behind them. He'd seen no one else in the plaza but wasn't sure who might be watching from the buildings. "I'm with Bones on this. We've been lucky so far, but we left a pretty wide swath. The Preacher will watch the raft. I'm sure he's found his car. He's checked our flat, too, and found the gear gone. When we don't show up at the airport, he'll figure it out."

"Bet he's on his way here right now," Bones said.

Maddock spotted a lanky figure striding across the plaza. Chaz arrived with a folded map and a packet of frayed paper. "There was a British expedition to Athos in the eighteen-thirties, just after we kicked the Turks out. This stuff should go back home and all, but tough luck getting it out of the country."

Corey opened the map. Pen and watercolor on vellum, it looked authentic. The notes were in bad condition, but legible. Maddock glanced at both, folded the map back, and said, "Where is the geologic map I asked for?"

Corey said, "I did mention a geologic map."

Chaz sat back, stunned. "I do recall, but I thought this would be more than adequate. That will cost you extra."

"Same deal. We can wait, but don't be too long. I'd hate for the Greek authorities to get wind of this transaction, wouldn't you?"

Chaz strode off, returning shortly with a roll of paper. Maddock thanked him without opening the map. "Here's what we agreed on, plus fifty euros for your trouble."

Chaz stood and looked both directions. "No one needs to know, right?"

Maddock agreed and added, "If I possibly can, I will deliver this to the Bodleian Library in London."

"Done and done then." Chaz shook his hand and departed.

Behind them, a cab honked twice. "I think our chariot has arrived," Bones said.

Zoya called out the passenger window, "Come on—move

your butts."

Maddock jumped in. "Back to town…tell him to follow the waterfront."

Ten minutes later he had them pull over. "Bones, I need you with me. Corey, you and Zoya return to the hotel and see what you can learn from our treasures."

"Big deal," Zoya said, "whatever we find will be out of reach anyway."

"Pretend it's not." Maddock slid out of the cab. "We'll catch you this afternoon."

Bones tumbled out behind him and eyed a sign across the street. "Yacht sales?"

14

Across the median and through a parking lot, Maddock found his way down to a row of slips that fronted the street. High-end cruisers thumped and squeaked against their fenders. He followed the margin of a paved quay. A few yards from the street front, the cruisers gave way to row after row of sailing yachts. Tall aluminum masts, glowing mahogany, and chromed bronze fittings stood on review for the length of the pier.

Bones examined a gleaming white yawl tied to the dock. "Thirteen meters, four staterooms, auxiliary power, diesel generator, yeah, I could handle something like this." He skipped down to the price and whistled. "Whoa, I think they got the decimal in the wrong place."

"Dream on, Rockefeller. There's nothing in this row for us."

Maddock crossed to a small office that faced the water. As he approached, a man with dark hair and olive skin stepped out and smiled. "So many, so beautiful, yes?"

Maddock shook his hand. "Beautiful yes, but we are looking for something smaller."

It didn't deter the salesman. He gestured toward the docks. "He has good taste, your friend. I see him look at our *Corretta*. She is luxury. A few hours, try her. Is a beautiful woman, eager, responsive."

Maddock shook his head. "What else?"

The salesman led them down the quay, extolling the virtues of each yacht. None of them looked like anything they could afford. Near the end, rows of smaller boats sat high and dry in wooden cradles. Maddock nodded in their direction. "And these?"

"You do not want. Is all wrecks, abandoned. Auction for junk, yes?"

Maddock had found *Thetis* cradled among the wrecks. It had taken some negotiation to reach a deal that included a tank of fuel, sails, and new batteries. "We will come tomorrow with cash."

It had taken the rest of that day to convince the others and most of the next to outfit their voyage. The sun had sunk over the western hills by the time they stocked *Thetis's* tiny galley and topped off her water tanks. Zoya surprised Maddock by volunteering to shop for supplies. "I'll pick up some prepaid mobiles while I'm there."

Maddock thought for a moment. "Good idea, but I doubt we'll find reception. I'll get a marine band handheld to communicate from shore instead."

He had planned to roust them all early and clear the harbor before sunrise. That evening, Bones rediscovered the bottle of ouzo buried in Corey's pack. He filled four shot glasses, eyed the remaining liquid, and said, "Bottoms up, maties—we sail with the tide."

Corey had been prowling the internet news feeds. He took a sip and choked. "Holy crap, take a look at this!"

Maddock leaned over his shoulder and read the headline out loud. "*British Attaché to the Thessaloniki Archeology Museum Found Beaten to Death on University Campus.*"

The others gathered around and read the article. No specifics, no witnesses, but the assault had taken place some time that day. Maddock straightened, tossed back his ouzo, and said, "We sail tonight."

"At least it's not a bus." Bones sprawled across a splintery teak bench.

"And we're not swimming," Corey said, "not yet, that is."

Zoya stared off across the blue Aegean Sea. "Well, I'm used to far better accommodations."

Bones glanced up. "Like what? That tunnel full of freaks under Atlanta?"

Maddock sat at the helm. "Go easy on our host, guys. She owns this fine craft."

Corey glanced up at the telltale and sheeted in the jib a few turns. "Yeah, but it was my crypto account that bought it."

Thetis's bow eased a few degrees closer to the wind as

Maddock adjusted her heading. Rocky beaches and scrubby hillsides passed in review. Sailing too near the land they would lose their wind…too far would require an extra tack.

The southernmost of three peninsulas, Cassandra ended at Cape Seva. He hoped to round the cape before dark and anchor in the lee of Sithonia, the central peninsula. Athos on the north would be less than a day's sail from there. Like a giant claw, the three rocky talons groped eastward from Greece toward the ruins of Troy on the Turkish mainland.

Zoya had tired of pestering Bones and found a bunk below. For his own part, Bones seemed happy enough to snore away on the cockpit bench. Corey checked the set of their sails once more before wandering back to sit near the helm. "How much do you think the Preacher learned from Chaz?"

"I'd been asking myself the same question," Maddock said. "He knows about Athos, probably figured that out when he followed us here."

Corey glanced below deck. "I don't know how he could have traced us if he even did."

"Someone murdered Chaz the day after we spoke. Do you believe in coincidences?"

Corey glanced once more into the darkened cabin and lowered his voice. "I just don't think she would have."

"What, kill Chaz or alert the Preacher?"

"Hell no, neither one. I just get this feeling there's more going on here than we can see."

Bones sat up. "Amen to that, brother. What I want to know is, are we chasing this dude, or running from him?"

"Both," Maddock said. "We need to get far enough ahead that he has to come to us. Then we make a deal, an ultimatum, or…"

Bones finished for him. "Or we smack this asshat down so hard he never gets up."

Corey scratched his head. "What I don't get is the prize, the goal. Say we catch the Preacher and make him cry 'Unkle,' what do we get?"

"The name of the entity trapped in the lyre," Maddock said.

"With that, you can abjure it and renounce your connection to the staff. You'll be free and we'll all go home to drink beer and tell lies."

"Then we should use game strategy," Corey said. "We should think like a game designer. What are the players likely to do? What are their strengths, and how do we counter them? Preacher has men and a lot of money. He'll have weapons too, but we have knowledge. We have the notes and maps that he doesn't."

Corey paused and grinned at them. "And one other thing, you have me. I've played Dragon Apocalypse for years—I know all its secrets. For instance, I'm left-handed, and you know what? All the best moves are to your left."

Bones nodded toward the open hatch. "And don't forget our secret elf-under-the-shelf. She counts for something."

"At least *she's* smart enough to sleep when she can," Maddock said. "Corey, take the helm. Bones, spell him when he needs it. Point her southeast, about a hundred and thirty degrees magnetic. I'm going below to get some shuteye—wake me in four."

It seemed like only minutes before Bones rousted him. The sun hung low over their wake and the wind had shifted to the southeast. Maddock took in the rocky cliffs about two miles distant. "What's our heading?"

"Almost due east." Bones seated himself at the helm and released the tiller rope. "You can see Cape Seva off our port bow. We should reach it in about an hour."

"How long have I been out?"

"Corey went down two hours ago. You've slept at least six."

Maddock nodded his thanks. "I'll take it from here if you want to go crash."

"Kind of getting into this—I'll sleep when we anchor up."

A chartbook had come with the boat. Creased and water-stained, most pages were still legible. Maddock thumbed through until he located the Athos Peninsula. "I'd planned on arriving from the north, but Corey got me thinking. Preacher will figure we're coming by boat, but he can't patrol the entire shoreline. He'll try to intercept us when we leave. Maybe we should land on the southern shore but depart on the north."

Bones glanced at the chart. "How far is it across?"

"Say about five miles of tough terrain."

Hand on the tiller, one eye on the little tell-tale streaming from the windward shroud, Bones held their course until the Sithonia Peninsula hove into view. "Where away, Captain?"

Maddock had Bones turn *Thetis's* bow north. As they settled into a different tack, Zoya poked her head above deck. "What's all the racket up here?"

Bones looked at Maddock. "I thought you said they only came out at night?"

"Twilight is upon us, old buddy." He slacked the main sheet a little farther. "And good evening to you, Madam Zoya. I trust you slept well."

She nodded without meeting his eyes and looked back at Cape Seva. "Where the hell are we?"

"Dead ahead," Maddock pointed north, "our anchorage for tonight. We've got four more hours, so grab a beer and chill."

Zoya hopped out of the cabin, beer bottle in hand. "Way ahead of you, Popeye."

Right behind her, Corey peeked out on deck. "How do you like your steaks?"

It didn't surprise Maddock that Zoya liked hers seared and running blood. They watched the sun creep down on the horizon as the cliffs and little coves grew out of the sea before them. He finally relaxed when their anchor slid off the bow davit and found purchase on the rocky bottom.

As *Thetis* swung on her anchor line, they gathered around a tiny dinette table. Corey had coffee boiling on the galley stove while Maddock brought out their maps and notes. He folded the geologic map so that only Mt. Athos showed. "It looks like the mountain is a granite bump," he said, "poking up from beneath limestone carbonates east and west. The map shows contours, which will help identify major features."

Bones ran a finger across the paper. "Along with roads, and a butt-load of monasteries. The place is paved with them."

"Churches, dormitories, and hermit cells. I'm sure they did all they could to cover up the old temples and shrines," Maddock said. "The natural caves all have chapels built over them."

Corey unfolded the nineteenth-century map they had bought from Chaz. "The scale is different, and the proportions are way off, but I think we can correlate temple locations based on landmarks."

Six of the ancient Greek temples corresponded to monasteries. Maddock plotted four others high on the mountain itself. "I'm worried that the site we're looking for is buried under some huge warren of priests and monks."

Bones held the old map up to the dim cabin light. "You mean like this big one here?"

"Yeah, Monastery of Saint Cosmas. Even if we could get inside, it's huge. We could search for days without finding anything."

Corey glanced at the archeological map. "Cosmas is shown at location D-23." He opened the notes. "That's strange— there's nothing in here about it."

Maddock paged through the descriptions. Nothing had been removed, yet he found no entry for that site. A few small references had been scribbled in the back. Someone had written, *D-23 Temple of Dionysus? Verify.*

He compared the old map with the modern geologic survey of the island. The site seemed to correspond to the monastery. More to himself than the others, Maddock said, "What if the old temple is not where they plotted it?"

Zoya took another experimental sip of her coffee. "Is the drowning man grasping at straws here?"

"No look, Saint Cosmas is located on the lower slopes of the mountain, below the limestone outcroppings. If we are looking for a cave, and I think we are, then it must be higher up." He studied the geologic map again, "There—an old fault line crosses the band of carbonates right through here."

"And when you find nothing but a bunch of scorpions and angry monks," Zoya said, "what then?"

"We'll deal with it. Don't forget Prester John. He'll be out there too. Who knows, maybe we can lure him into a scorpion nest."

They left the anchorage early the next morning and rounded the cape by noon. Maddock kept them well offshore, cruising north, with Mount Athos crouched in a bank of clouds. Corey didn't like the plan. "I'm part of this quest. I want to go there."

"You and Zoya have to be our extraction team. Bones and I will swim in after dark and do some recon. You pick us up the following night and we'll plan our next move."

"But I go on the next one, you have to promise."

"The only thing I know right now is that you two need to drop us off and then take *Thetis* well offshore during the day. If they see this boat loitering around, they'll know what we're up to."

15

Even if he hadn't thoroughly explained it, Maddock had planned this operation from the moment he saw *Thetis* standing on the quay in Thessaloniki. He and Bones traveled light. Headlamps and spares, water, energy bars, rope and radio, all stuffed in Corey's waterproof pack. Bones pushed the ouzo bottle in. "I don't want us to come back and find a tipsy Tinkerbell."

Maddock hated using the diesel, but it was the only safe way to approach the shore. Even then, he and Bones swam the last hundred yards. When he reached their landing site, Maddock flashed a quick signal to Corey. He was rewarded by the low sputter of the engine starting, and then dwindling in the distance. "Come on Bones, let's get out of here before anyone comes to investigate."

"It's just a bunch of monks. What are they going to do, pray us to death?"

"Yeah, Russian and NATO monks that know this place better than you know Toni's beer cooler."

Bones grumbled as he shouldered the pack and followed Maddock through a tangle of brush and rocks. They didn't dare use lights, but the waning moon had climbed above Mount Athos and painted the terrain in shades of gray. After an hour of hiking, they reached a dirt track that contoured the steep hillside. "Looks like an army expeditionary road," Bones said.

"It's recent. Makes a guy wonder what all is going on out here."

Bones grimaced. "Never liked it when religion got armies and armies got religion."

Maddock allowed the luxury of following the road until they spotted headlights moving off to the west. "Time to do a little more climbing, brother Bones."

A small vineyard bordered the road. Maddock picked his way between the staked vines. "There will be a hut or something nearby," he whispered.

Bones pointed to a dim light between the stakes. Maddock led them the opposite direction. Another half mile found them both standing on the edge of a deep ravine. "We bag it here until we get some daylight."

Flat on the ground, Bones crossed his arms beneath his head and dozed. Maddock knew his friend slept like a jungle animal, ready to spring up at the slightest sound. Wishing he could do the same, he sat with his back to a rock and waited. *Crazy?* He went over his plan once more. It seemed crazier to do nothing, to wait for trouble to find them.

He awoke to the sound of dogs barking in the distance. Bones had rolled up on one elbow. "Think they're looking for us?"

"It doesn't matter. We've got a bit of daylight. Let's get going."

Angling up the western slope kept them in the mountain's shadow. Maddock hoped the darkness hid their movements long enough to climb above the network of roads and cottages. He pointed toward a gray cliff face higher on the mountainside. "We head up there. I want to take a look at those rocks."

The patchy vineyards and cultivated fields gave way to a steep climb through scrub brush and boulders. As they worked their way upward, the sky lightened and one by one, the hills below appeared out of the morning mist. Bones stopped to look back. "I still hear dogs and they sound louder. What do you figure?"

Maddock glanced up at the cliff and pulled out their geologic map. Risking a little light, he pointed to an area where the contour lines converged. "I think we're just below here. If we can climb that, it will buy us some time."

He chose a direct route up the hillside, scrambling over boulders and scree. When he stopped to look back, Maddock realized they had already scaled the lower part of the cliff. "It looks like there are some fissures over here we can climb."

He didn't wait for Bones's reply but began chimneying up a rocky crevice. As the slot narrowed, he struggled to jam his feet and fists into the crack. Higher, the crevice disappeared entirely, and Maddock groped in the gray dawn light for any handhold he could find. Swinging his right leg out, he found a narrow ledge. Stretching his left hand above his head, he gripped a tiny lump. For a moment, he feared he was stuck, until his right hand landed in a deep horizontal notch.

Pulling himself up, he could see the sunlit clifftop just above. His foot slipped. He slid back, hanging from his right arm. He slapped the smooth rocky face hoping to find a purchase. His hand began to slip. An arm and outstretched hand snaked down from above. "Next time, let me pick the route," Bones said.

Dragged over the top, Maddock lay flat, willing his heart to stop pounding. Bones crouched next to him, keeping his profile below the line of stunted bushes. "You're wetter than when we came ashore—I hope it's only sweat."

"I must be getting old, Bones. That should have been an easy climb."

"So, did you learn anything?"

"Yeah, it's limestone alright. Hard as your head, almost marble."

"Bro, my hard head has gotten us out of a few tight spots."

"And into a lot more." Maddock glanced up at the mountainside, then back at the map. "Faults create water channels—water channels create caves. We're well above the Monastery of Saint Cosmas. So, if something is hidden, this is as good a place as any to start looking."

"By that logic, so was our room in Thessaloniki, and the bed was a lot comfier."

Maddock had already started searching the ground. Any kind of structure would have left an imprint. He angled up the mountain hoping to at least find some evidence of a fault in the rock. Thirty yards south, Bones started his own search. As the sun climbed, they worked their way back and forth up the mountain. By noon, Maddock called a break.

Bones dug a couple of energy bars from his pack and tossed one to Maddock. "You know, archeological teams can take years to find something like this."

"Yeah, but they aren't desperate like we are. Besides, I've got a hunch on this one. We're close."

"That's just great," Bones said. "A stolen map, some pictures of souvenir placemats, and now a hunch. Well...that clinches it then, we're almost home."

Maddock grinned at his friend. "We're reversing roles again, buddy. You're supposed to be the optimist with me the skeptic."

After two more hours of searching, Maddock was ready to concede to Bones's doubts. They'd found evidence of a fault line, displaced strata, zones of broken rock, but nothing that looked like a cavern and no evidence of an ancient temple. Bones handed him a large cobble. "I'd say this looks more like granite than limestone."

"Yeah, we're well into the igneous strata here. The transition zone is about a hundred yards back. I just don't see what we could have missed."

"How about a temple way down there under that monastery, where the map shows it?"

"Nope, and here's why, D-23. Remember? They flagged it but said nothing. A temple of Dionysus would have been a big deal."

"But why?"

Maddock sat a moment watching an eagle patrolling the valley below. "The messenger of Zeus," he said, "avatar of Hermes. That eagle is telling us we're on the right track."

"Hey, only room for one Indian on this team."

"Well, technically Zoya..."

"Forget it. What next, oh great shaman?"

Maddock leaned against his hand, then jerked it back when he felt the sting. "What the crap?"

Bones jumped up. "Scorpion?"

Palm up, Maddock saw a small drop of blood form just below his thumb. He scooted away and searched the area where his hand had rested. "I don't think so."

He looked closer and dug a thin metal wire from the ground. "A nail, it's a bronze nail."

Bones held up a tiny fragment of broken pottery. "Well, I'll be double-dipped."

"It washed down from somewhere up there." Maddock pointed up a narrow draw.

Climbing higher, they found more pottery and a few shards of marble. Maddock scrambled up between the rocks and emerged on a broad shelf. Bones followed. "You'd think there would be columns, or at least some old foundations."

Maddock poked around. "Nothing, not even pieces."

He sighted down the draw at the valley far below. In the distance, he saw the orange roof of Saint Cosmas Monastery. The eagle flew closer now, climbing toward them. "I just know this is the place, Bones."

"Problem is, this place is no place. What's your solution?"

Maddock bent double, scanning the ground. *Solution?* Something from an advanced geography class, geomorphology, the professor had called it. *What was it?* Suddenly, he straightened. "It's my fault, because the solution is no solution."

"Sometimes I worry about you buddy."

"Come on, we've got to hurry." Maddock leaped back down into the shadows of the draw. "Help me move these rocks."

Between the two of them, they rolled boulders and cobbles away from a narrow crevice. "Can't be," Bones said, "but I feel a draft."

"This is it. I should have figured, it's a fault cave, not a solution cave. They're rare, but some of them go incredibly deep."

Bones helped him roll aside another boulder and wiped his brow. "And we're digging like rabid woodchucks because?"

"Because that's no eagle out there, it's a drone."

As he spoke, Maddock saw a shadow cross the sky. Bones drew his pistol and waited. A moment later, he fired, and a tumbling mass of arms and propellers bounced off the rocks and spun rattling into the valley below. He looked back. "Guess they knew we were here anyway, huh?"

"Doesn't matter, they know now." Maddock dragged another boulder from the hole and panned his light around inside. "It was a lot bigger once. Someone had rocked it up and did their best to cover any sign of the place."

Bones scanned the interior with his own light. "Snakes, spiders, scorpions?"

"Didn't see any—rodents maybe." Maddock caught Bones's look. "Nothing of unusual size, so don't say it."

He turned sideways and pushed his way in. "Got columns in here and a portico."

Beyond the entrance, Maddock found enough headroom to stand. He focused his light on the crumbling marble façade. Bones jammed inside. "Place looks like it was crushed in a giant vice."

"Fault cave, remember. They aren't all that stable."

"Wonderful. Damned if we stay here and damned if we go inside."

Maddock stepped over a pile of broken marble and entered the portico. It led to a columned passage that burrowed straight into the mountainside. In places, mounds of fallen rock blocked their way. Maddock wormed through the wreckage and stepped into a huge circular chamber. Bones shouldered in behind him and panned the walls. "Holy crap. They didn't have *that* in history class."

"Eleusinian mysteries. Their rituals were uninhibited," Maddock said. "No wonder the archeologists hid this place."

Twelve columns ringed the outer wall framing mosaics of various couples in contorted poses. Bones stopped at one. "Never tried that position, never even thought of it."

Maddock shined his light up at the domed ceiling. Broken and crumbling, it still retained much of its lapis veneer. Golden stars glittered in the lamplight. Searching the floor, he picked one up and hefted it. "Take a look at this. I think it's solid."

Bones found another. "Gold, a small fortune."

Maddock searched farther and stopped at a pit in the center of the floor. "I believe we are in the chamber of Persephone."

"And that would be the entrance to hades. Mom always said I would wind up there."

"If you were going to dispose of something, where better to

stash it?"

The pit was little more than two feet across. Bones flopped on his belly and looked down the hole. "It goes straight down, no steps or anything. Phew, the air stinks."

"Could we chimney it?"

"Could. Think you're up to climbing back out, old man?"

Maddock had already gripped the rim and lowered himself into the hole. His feet against one wall and his back against the other, he tested the friction of the rock. "Should be okay, as long as we take it slow."

"Wait a minute," Bones said, "my pack."

He tied it to a length of cord and lowered it past Maddock. The cord buzzed against the rock lip for a few minutes before going slack.

Bones thumped it up and down a few times and dropped the cord. "About a hundred and twenty feet. Okay, you next."

Inching his way, Maddock concentrated on placing each foot, gripping the walls, sliding his back. Ten yards down, he called up to Bones, "Come on, there's no loose rock."

For the next ten minutes, they worked their way down the shaft. Maddock found his rhythm and watched the rough crystalline walls sparkle in his lamplight. He was composing a remark when the walls shook, and a blast of air punched him in the belly. Bones yelled and slid down the pit, crashing into Maddock. The impact knocked him down a dozen yards. He tried to hold on, jammed his feet against the wall, slid, broke loose, and fell.

16

Maddock awoke in darkness. Stretched across a pile of debris, his head rested on Bones's pack. *Bones!* The weight across his legs shifted and groaned. "You alive, buddy?"

"Regretfully," Bones grumbled. "What do you figure? Earthquake?"

Maddock thought on it. "Someone dynamited the entrance on us."

A moment later, Bones flicked on his light. "Why would the Preacher seal us in if he's looking for the other parts of the lyre?"

"It wasn't the Preacher. Someone from the monastery down below launched that drone. They had a team up here looking for us."

Maddock spotted something sparkling in the debris. His headlamp had smashed when he landed. *Could have been my skull.* He moved his legs. His left hip hurt like hell and his chest felt like he'd cracked a rib. "How are you doing, Bones?"

"Little skinned up, but okay. You look like crap, by the way."

Something ran down his cheek and dripped off his chin. Maddock put a hand to his face and pulled it back covered with blood. Bones knelt beside him. "Got a nasty gash on your forehead. You may not feel it now…"

"But I will," Maddock finished for him. "There's bandages and your bottle of ouzo antiseptic in the pack. I'll patch myself up."

They had a spare light as well. Bones volunteered to climb up and inspect the damage. Maddock boosted him high enough to find a purchase in the shaft. He figured fifteen minutes at least to the top, even if his friend hustled. "Holler if we can get out that way. I'm going to do a little scouting."

The shaft had ended in another chamber. Smaller than the one above, its walls and ceiling had been hewn from the raw granite. It took Maddock some time to realize that the gravel underfoot was something different altogether. Bone fragments, fist-sized and smaller, they paved the floor in a thick dusty blanket. Circling the perimeter, he found row upon row of skulls, both animal and human.

Halfway around, Maddock discovered a narrow vertical crevice that pierced the wall. He aligned it with the shaft. A patter of small stones announced his friend's pending arrival. Bones hung for a moment above the floor. "Be a pal and flop down there again so I don't have to land on the rocks."

"Don't worry, they're not rocks."

Bones dropped with a thud and bent to inspect the floor. "Human?"

"Not all of them. I think this was a sacrificial pit. A nasty one. Worse than your kitchen sink."

"If that's the case, we're screwed, because half the chamber above is collapsed and we'd need mining equipment to dig our way out." Bones kicked some of the fragments around. "Say, they might have tossed some coins down here too. Figure we ought to search around?"

"Yeah, we could run downtown and spend them on groceries. I've got a better idea."

He showed Bones the crevice. "It's part of the original fault cave. I think we can squeeze through."

"Great, deeper into Mount Doom."

"Another Tolkien reference, but you say you're not a nerd." Maddock shook his head. "And we're not going deeper. The fault strikes that direction. It leads back toward the cliff."

Bones panned his light around inside. "Look at the walls. Something else has been slithering around in here."

On closer inspection, the rock had been worn smooth and mats of hair still clung to the cracks. Maddock turned sideways and jammed himself in. "Only one way to find out."

His injured ribs burned with every twist of the passage and true to Bones's prediction, Maddock's head began to pound. A hundred feet in, the crevice widened. He inspected the walls and found the granite had given way to slaty layers that crunched beneath his feet. Behind him, Bones grumbled something about

Quasimodo. Maddock stepped into a bell-shaped chamber and stopped. "Not Quasimodo, more like Gollum."

Across from him, a wizened figure crouched against the wall. Its skeletal torso was coated with lime. From within its skull, two sightless eyes glared in silent malevolence. Maddock crossed the chamber and picked something from the figure's lap. It looked like an arm bone, but straight and covered with crystalline white rime. "He won't be needing this anymore."

"Is that what I think it is?"

With a little rubbing, the white coating fell off in flakes. Stained and mottled, the smooth oryx horn gleamed in their lamplight. "I think this is what we came for."

"It's not going to do us much good—it sure as hell didn't do him any good."

"Think of it Bones, this guy must have lived here. He ate whatever or whoever they tossed down the pit. Now and again, someone would survive the fall. They would eventually kill the current resident and take his place."

Bones shook his head. "If they had teamed up, they both could have escaped."

Maddock held up the staff. "Except for this, the golden apple of discord. It would only allow one master."

"Truly hell then." Bones shuddered. "Put it in the pack—I don't want to even touch it."

After a moment's reluctance, Maddock pushed the staff into their pack and reclosed the top. "How about I carry this thing for a while?"

"Suit yourself, pal. Where to now?"

Maddock had already investigated a few irregularities in the chamber floor. He heard the trickle of water and followed the sound. In the shadows behind the mummified figure, he discovered a low passage angling deeper into the rock. A tiny stream ran down one wall and tumbled into the darkness below. "We're into limestone here and the cave continues."

Maddock pushed the pack ahead of him as he crawled into the tiny opening. Typical of solution caves, the walls were smooth, and the floor was wet. He had to break through curtains of soda-straw stalactites that dripped from the low ceiling. Bones crawled after him, grumbling about vandalism. "I mean, it's bad enough we have to damage this cave, but think of the cultural heritage that was just destroyed in the name of religion."

"It's happened before. The Crusaders ransacked Constantinople and the Levant. The Ottomans came back and returned the favor."

Maddock slid into an elliptical chamber decorated on all sides by curtains of flowstone. He handed Bones an energy bar. "Take five?"

"I'd eat a whole case right now." Bones glanced at his watch. "Still early afternoon. We've got another six hours before Corey returns and it's time's up for us."

"Six hours before Corey picks us up at the beach, you mean."

"Yeah, that's it. But what if this cave just peters out in a pit of wet gravel and broken rock?"

"Then we're no worse off than we were an hour ago. It'll be tougher if our lights go out. How much time do you figure we've got?"

Bones tapped the back of his headlamp. It showed two bars out of three. "Maybe a couple of hours. You lead. I'll turn mine off for a while."

Beyond the chamber, the passage turned into a vertical crevice. Despite his injured ribs, Maddock wormed his way around to descend feet-first. They spent over an hour wriggling between rough limestone walls. Often, they had to reascend when the route Maddock had chosen pinched down to a narrow slot. Somehow, just knowing the hell that his predecessor in the halls above must have endured, made the burning pain in his chest more bearable.

Bones was first to land his feet on the soft mud floor. "We've reached rock bottom, but I'm not seeing the light."

Maddock slid down next to him, glad for the respite. Something...something about the dirt under his feet and clinging to the walls, Maddock held his light up closer and pinched some between his fingers. "I'm seeing the light, buddy. Bat guano, if they can get out, we can get out."

"Bats are tiny and squeaky, and they fly. Not sure I fit that description."

Maddock had already ducked and started crawling along the floor, following the horizontal crevice. Above, his light picked out clusters of furry bodies, clinging to the rocks. Bones followed for a few hundred feet, then tugged his pant leg. "Stop a minute and listen."

Nothing. Maddock heard nothing more than the slow drip of water somewhere in the darkness. A minute passed before a distant rumble grew and then faded. "I hear it. Got any ideas?"

"Smaug? The minotaur? Thought it was my stomach at first."

As Maddock continued to work his way down the passage, it diminished to a low tunnel. The rumble grew louder and against the far wall, he noticed a wan yellow glow. "We got something up ahead."

The glow came through a narrow opening. Maddock killed his light as he approached and peered out into a huge echoing chamber. Bones sidled up and looked out as well. "An underground warehouse and I think I recognize some of those crates but what is this place?"

Maddock studied the concrete floor and the rough limestone walls. "It's a cavern that was converted into an underground warehouse. Look at the back—somebody built a wall across the natural entrance."

"Saint Cosmas," Bones said. "I'll bet they built that big freaking monastery right on top of this place."

A distant rumble grew to a prolonged growl. Moments later Maddock saw a forklift swing into view and stack its load on a row of similar boxes. "Kind of closes the loop with Atlanta."

"What are the chances that chasing this lyre thing would lead us right to one of the Preacher's nasty little customers?"

Maddock thought for a moment. "Pretty good if someone else has been stage managing all this. Preach thinks he's in charge, but I'm beginning to think he's as big a pawn as we are."

"He's bigger than you are maybe, not me."

"Okay, big guy. Think you can squeeze through this hole?"

"I'm big, not fat." Bones poked his head out and looked around. "The floor is about fifteen feet down. Feel like dropping that far?"

Maddock heard the forklift returning. "Just get ready to jump. I've got a better idea."

A large plywood crate swung into view. He waited a moment, then said, "Now!"

They both wormed through the low slot and leaped for the crate. Maddock landed dead center, but Bones missed. He grabbed the side as he fell and clung on. Maddock took him by the wrist and dragged him up. Moments later the hydraulics hissed, and the crate settled to the ground.

Bones hopped off and waved thanks to the driver. Maddock tossed him a salute. "Don't run, don't run. We're supposed to be here.'"

Bones glanced back. "He's talking on the radio. I think we ought to run."

Dodging behind a row of boxes, Maddock pointed to the far wall. "That way."

They made it half the distance before an alarm started blaring, the lights went out, and flashing red beacons came on all around the perimeter. "Screw it," Maddock said. He flicked on his headlamp. "Follow me."

Bullets whined off the stone floor. Maddock dodged left and put a row of equipment between him and the shooters. Behind them, a row of lights advanced up the aisle. A few more shots rang out as they crossed an open space. Maddock crouched behind a crate and Bones joined him, pistol drawn.

"These monk dudes get too close, I'm ready to make them plenty holey alright."

"Hold your fire, Bones. I'd rather they not know we're armed." Maddock switched off his light. "Leave your light on and set it on that box. There's an exit right over there."

Maddock flitted across the intervening distance and tried the door. Locked. Bones slipped up behind him. "Another fine mess you've gotten me into."

Behind them, sporadic gunfire targeted Bones's lamp. Maddock tried the door again. Steel plate, brushed aluminum hardware, nothing budged. Bones wrenched on it to no avail. "Better think of something quick."

"This is a longshot." Maddock drew the staff from his pack, touched it to the door handle, and said, "Open."

With a soft click, the door swung inward.

"Oh crap," Bones muttered. "I'd rather you hadn't done that."

Once through, Maddock closed and locked the door. "Come on."

He flicked on his light to reveal stone walls all around them. A circular iron staircase nearly filled the chamber. Bones looked up just as a thunderous pounding began on the door. "That way, then?"

Maddock began the climb. Once, twice, five times around before they emerged into a silent gallery. Robes hung against one wall and a row of beds lined the other. "Barracks," Bones said.

"Or dormitory. It doesn't matter. Those guys are gonna find a key any moment. Grab a robe and put the hood up. Let's try to blend in."

Light streamed in through an open door at the far end. They stopped just inside and scoped their surroundings. Vines, fruit trees, a few monks stooped, tending rows of vegetables. Maddock checked behind him. No one followed. "We walk out through the vineyard and keep going until we reach the sea."

They crossed a small patio and passed three robed figures discussing something at a table. A few paces farther, Maddock heard the rattle of a weapon being racked and a familiar voice. "You can stop there, gentlemen."

17

Maddock turned to face Prester John. Repeat sauntered up, holding a familiar Heckler and Koch machine pistol. His partner, Pete reached down and placed a short-barreled assault rifle on the table. Bones scanned the three of them. "Can't say I'm happy to see you again but can't say I'm surprised either."

Prester John stood and glowered at them. "Did you two just think you could walk out of here dressed like that? Your pant legs show beneath the robes and those shoes…they're an abomination. You mock these holy men with your arrogance."

Maddock noticed movement at the door they had just exited. He slipped off his robe and waved. "Oh look, our friends have arrived."

Pete jumped up from the table and raised his weapon. Repeat just grinned and kept his machine pistol trained on them. Prester John shook his head. "They're not…"

Before he could finish, three men in camo burst from the monastery. They took one look at Maddock and opened fire. Maddock and Bones both hit the deck as Pete returned fire. Repeat snarled something, pointed his machine pistol at them, and squeezed the trigger. The resulting blast knocked him backward. Prester John lurched backward, cursing and clutching his face. Pete leaped to his boss's assistance, crouching nearby and returning fire at the men pouring through the doorway. Maddock grabbed Bones by the shoulder and yelled, "Let's go."

They scrambled over a low berm and followed an irrigation ditch into the orchard. Maddock stood and ran, Bones right behind him. Shots smacked into the tree trunks and hissed through the leaves, but Pete's confusion and Prester John's shouts deterred any pursuit. Maddock's head and ribs screamed in pain. He slowed and turned. Bones caught up. "We're going the wrong way, man."

Maddock leaned on his knees and puffed a moment. "We'll head south toward our old landing site." He began an easy jog through the trees and brush. "We need them to follow until dark. If they realize Corey's coming in on the north side, we're screwed."

The sun had crossed well into the west by the time they stopped to gaze once more over the sparkling blue Aegean. "Another mile or so," Bones said, "then what?"

Off in the distance, Maddock heard what he had been fearing, dogs. Bones heard it too. "Oh crap, you better have a plan, because they're not coming on foot."

He didn't answer but took off running. *Stay away from the roads.* He wondered about another drone. *Or aircraft even.* Maddock followed a shallow ravine leaping over rocks and fallen limbs. He could hear Bones padding behind him. They halted in the shadow of a boulder. Just ahead a gravel road crossed their path.

Maddock stilled his breath and listened. Tires rumbled on the stones and potholes. He pulled Bones back just as a truckload of armed soldiers growled by. "Monks my ass," Bones said, "those dudes are going to war."

The growl faded. Maddock signaled to his friend. They slipped across the road and down the embankment. Dogs barked at the top of the ravine. Through the pines, Maddock spotted the bluff he'd seen earlier. "Follow me—I've got a plan."

He halted on a rocky ledge looking down on the surging blue water. Bones said, "Great, you go first."

Maddock shrugged out of his pack and kicked off his boots. "Shoes and gun in here, no time for anything else."

As soon as the pack was secure, they both leaped off the ledge and plunged into the churning water. Maddock swam west along the shore, listening for gunshots. They crossed behind a row of rocky islets, and he paused to check for movement. Bones grabbed his shoulder. "Over there."

On the hillside above, the truck they'd seen stood empty. Maddock nodded. "I'm hoping they'll be looking for a boat." He heard the dogs again, yapping in confusion. "We keep swimming. I want to be gone before they figure it out."

He'd seen Bones swim ten miles. *I've done it too.* After some thought Maddock reminded himself that he'd been younger then and didn't have a broken rib. *Or an injured leg, or a mild concussion.* He slowed his stroke. The sun had fallen further toward the western horizon when they reached an isolated cove at the foot of a cliff.

Maddock splashed ashore and rested in the sand. Bones trudged up beside him and sat. "Your bandage is gone, and your head is bleeding again."

"Least of my worries. Remind me not to fall down any more holes today." He turned to catch some of the dying sunlight. "That water gets cold after a while."

Bones glanced up at the low bluff behind them. "Think they've left?"

"Would you have?"

Bones made a face and flopped back in the sand. "We've really pissed him off this time, you know."

"The Preacher and Repeat are both going to need some stitches."

"Bet they've got ol' Machinegun Pete down in the cellar doing *Mea Culpas* or whatever it is the Greek guys say."

Maddock thought about it a minute. "I wonder if they were Greek, or Russian. Regardless, none of them were happy to see us."

He unsealed the pack and pulled out the geologic map. "I think we're here and I'm assuming we showed up under the Saint Cosmas like you guessed. I didn't have a chance to ask."

Bones used his thumb to estimate distance. "We're about six miles from our pickup point, say eight to ten with detours, maybe four hours."

A skein of high clouds had formed across the eastern sky, blowing west. Maddock squinted at the setting sun. "The moon won't rise 'til later tonight and I don't feel like stumbling blind across those hills."

"If we stay on the roads, they'll bag us for sure."

Maddock brushed a lock of hair from his face and winced. He eyed the blood on his fingers and dabbed his forehead with some of the ouzo. "Enough of running, I've got an idea."

A steep draw ended at the west side of the cove. Maddock scrambled to the bluff top. Bones followed him up and whispered, "The truck is still there. What do you figure, ten guys?"

Maddock nodded. "Looks like they're mostly spread out east of us."

Movement off to their right caught his eye. "Oh, crap!" He pulled Bones down. "Two of them—three o'clock."

Brush crackled as the searchers drew closer. Low voices, one of them laughed. Maddock held rock-still. Boots clattered on the bare ground. Hard breathing, then Bones jumped straight up and pistol-whipped the nearest soldier. He pointed his Glock at the other. "Looking for someone?"

They relieved both men of weapons, hats, and shirts. After twitching and vomiting for a few minutes, the one Bones had hit tried to sit up. "Nope," Bones shook his head and gestured with his pistol, "both of you, on the ground."

Maddock tied them with their own shoelaces and tossed their shoes off the bluff. Bones pawed through their gear. "Russian then, old stuff. These guys look like mercs."

Maddock buttoned a camo shirt as far as it would go and pulled a beret down over his head. "Just wiggle into one of those shirts. Time to split."

Twisting and squirming, Bones managed to get both arms into a shirt without ripping the shoulders out. Buttoning it was out of the question. He jammed a hat down over his forehead and tucked the rest of his hair under his collar. "Next time we mug a couple of dudes, they better be big ol' Cossacks or something."

Rifle on his shoulder, pistol and ammo belted around his waist, Maddock trudged up toward the road. Bones followed, glancing back at the two men they'd trussed and hidden in the ravine. "I feel a little exposed."

Maddock eyed a squad combing the brush on the opposite hillside. One man waved, and he waved back. "We're two guys searching this hill. Just head back to the road. They're all tired of the wild goose chase, not paying us any attention."

They angled across a shallow gulley and up the embankment. On the road, Maddock spotted a familiar silhouette. "U.S. Army deuce-and-a-half, six-wheel drive, damn near unstoppable, I haven't driven one of those in a decade."

"They're gonna be pissed."

"They're already pissed. Come on." Maddock hopped in the cab, hit the fuel cutoff, and toggled the starter. Nothing. "Crap!"

Shouts from nearby, three guys ran up to the road. Bones spun around in his seat. "Think of something, quick."

I'm thinking, I'm thinking. Maddock checked the dash panel. *Fuel cutoff, disengaged—air pressure, good.* He scanned the gauges. *No power, no...* He switched on the electric and toggled the starter again. The engine roared and he jammed it in gear. A soldier jumped to the running board and jammed a pistol in his face. Maddock swerved, throwing the man to one side. They wrestled for the pistol as the truck veered off the road and tried to climb an embankment. Tipping, tipping, the engine raced, and the tires spun. Maddock released the pistol and yanked the wheel over. He had one last look at the angry mustached face as the tires slammed back down on the road. Three shots zipped through the canvas cover and smashed the windshield.

Bones knocked out the broken glass as they sped away. "We're just not making friends here."

Maddock slowed as they approached an intersection and turned north, away from the coast. The road cut between two hills, then entered a series of switchbacks that climbed toward the monastery. They negotiated two hairpin turns. Rounding the third, they found the road blocked by a half-dozen men waving their arms.

Maddock jammed on the brakes. He drew his stolen pistol and held it just out of sight. The group came running at them. Bones tensed, but Maddock shook his head. All six ran past the cab and climbed in the back. Someone yelled, "*Aditiya*," and slapped the fender. Bones shrugged. Maddock slipped it in gear and took off.

By the fourth turn, the men had started singing. Bones glanced back. "They haven't got a clue, have they?"

Maddock shook his head. "Someone hasn't worked up the guts to call it in. We'd better lose these guys before that happens."

He steered for the potholes and swerved to one side, rolling down into the ditch and then back up and across the road. Veering from side to side, Maddock skirted the cliff edge, with nothing but a sheer drop visible beyond the truck bed. Bones dug the bottle of ouzo from their pack and waved it out the window.

The singing stopped. Maddock took the bottle and made a show of tipping it back. Shouts and curses followed. At the next turn, they slowed. All six passengers bailed out the tailgate. Bones laughed as the men picked themselves up and threw rocks at the truck.

The big deuce-and-a-half growled over a long series of hills, passing vineyards and small huts along the way. A mile farther, they dipped into a valley, already cloaked in evening darkness. Maddock slowed. "They'll be after us soon, with vehicles and guns. We need to disappear."

A shallow gully crossed the road. Maddock stopped, pulled the shifter into low range, and crawled off the road. The tires spun, then caught as they lurched through the brush. He wrenched the wheel around and powered the bulky vehicle behind a copse of trees. "Now what?" Bones said.

Maddock cut the engine. "Now we wait to see who's following us."

In the sudden quiet, he heard the sound of approaching vehicles. They hopped from the cab and crept to the road as a small convoy hove into view. Bones watched it rumble toward them. "I'm sick of being chased."

Maddock thought for a moment. "Two can play this game."

He ran back to the cab and fired up the engine. As the last of their pursuers roared past, he jammed the old truck in gear and smashed through the trees. Bones clung to the grab bar as they lurched back to the road. Maddock banged the shifter into high range and took off. "With any luck, they'll think we're just part of the posse."

The convoy rumbled through two checkpoints. Maddock waved at the guards as they passed. A long climb brought them to an intersection where the lead truck turned off toward the monastery. Bones checked their map and pointed the other direction. Maddock swung them north to a dirt track that skirted the coast. He glanced in the rear-view mirror. "How long before he figures it out?"

"Who, the Preach? You think he's still in play?"

"Someone is stirring up the hornets. A couple of lost tourists wouldn't rate this kind of manhunt."

Bones stuck his head out the window and looked around. "We need to get lost—permanently, this time." They rounded a turn, a little close to the edge. "Whoa, I didn't mean *that* permanently."

In the shadow of the hills, the road had faded to a pale, gray band. Maddock slowed through the next curve. "Not sure how much longer I'll be able to see where I'm driving, and I don't dare use the lights."

Bones pulled his head back in. "Bad news boss, the guys behind us got their brights on."

"Call Corey then. It's pickup point three...and tell him to hustle."

Bones dug out their handheld marine radio and extended its antenna. He looked over at Maddock. "As soon as I light this up, they'll know exactly where we are."

"Light 'em up, Bones. It's too late to worry about that now."

The road wound down toward the shore. With every passing turn their pursuers closed the gap and Maddock could see headlights sweeping the hillsides behind them. "This will be close."

"Yeah, and we'll be sitting ducks waiting for Corey to show."

And outgunned on every front. Maddock kept that thought to himself. A lot would depend on where *Thetis* was cruising when their message came through. *If it came through.* He hoped that Corey was monitoring the radio, that he and Zoya hadn't started squabbling again. *Or doing something else.*

Bones craned his head out the window again. "Crap, another fifteen minutes and we'd have been home eating beans. Doesn't this heap go any faster?"

"Yeah, I figure a free-fall terminal velocity of over two hundred miles an hour. Want to try it?"

Bones straightened and dropped back in his seat. "I just saw muzzle flashes. The dumb bastards are shooting at us."

As he spoke, a bullet smacked into the driver's side doorpost and spun sizzling out through the vacant windshield frame. Bones glanced back. "Lucky shot."

Another round smacked into the truck bed. Maddock switched on the lights. "They've got night vision scopes. We need a smokescreen—hang on, buddy."

Downshifting as they roared up on the next turn, he pulled the wheel over and let the eight big rear tires slide. Steering into the slide, he jammed on the throttle and heard the front axle cut in. They slewed across the dirt road entering the next turn. Maddock let the truck's momentum carry it around. Bones clung to the grab bar. "I think I'd rather be shot at."

Maddock wrenched the wheel back and braked, sliding across the road. He hit the throttle at the next turn and let the truck bounce and skid over ruts and potholes. The front tires lost traction for a moment. They careened into the ditch, riding halfway up the hillside before slamming back on the road. "Look behind us, Bones. See anything?"

"Dust. Dust and lights. I think they've backed off." He watched for a moment. "Oh crap! Look at that."

Maddock glanced back. A pair of headlights bounced and spun toward the water below. They flew over a bluff and disappeared. He concentrated on the road. *Corey—be there, be there, be there.* Their momentum carried them around a long curve down to a gravelly beach. No Corey, no *Thetis*, nothing but open water ahead.

18

Maddock shifted into high gear and pushed the throttle down. "Pack your kit and get ready to bail. We're going amphibious."

The old truck hit the water like a bull elephant on a field of corn. It fought for a moment, trying to float, engine still roaring, trying to find traction. Both Maddock and Bones braced against the dash as a small tsunami blasted through the open windshield and filled the cab. Maddock wriggled out a side window, dragging the pack with him as their ride finally gave up and sank.

Headlights on the beach, then a spotlight panned the water. Shots. Maddock swam north, away from the shore. Bones joined him. "Where are we headed?"

"Istanbul, if we have to."

The star Polaris hung about twenty degrees above the northern horizon. Little else was visible in the evening sky. Maddock pushed the pack ahead of him as he swam. *Not giving this up—no way.* He concentrated on the north star and waited for a bullet to find its mark. Shouts…shouts from a concrete mole at the east end of the beach. "Bones, Maddock, they're shooting. Head this way."

Corey Dean stood on the mole waving a flashlight until a fusillade of bullets peppered the concrete seawall and drove him back. Bones swam that way and Maddock followed. Perhaps it was the low angle, or perhaps their only night-vision scopes had plunged into the Aegean, but Maddock rounded the mole without taking a hit. *Thetis's* bow swung north as he climbed the boarding ladder and flopped to the deck.

They all lay flat as rounds peppered their stern transom and ricocheted off the water on either side. Bones crouched behind the tiller and returned fire with his Glock. More for effect than any hope of hitting something, it did manage to discourage the shooters on the beach.

Maddock lay on his side and clutched the pack. *It's mine. It's safe.* Polaris hovered just above their port bow and smiled down on him. He dozed until Bones shook him awake. "You still alive?"

Startled, he sat upright. His injured ribs reminded him not to do it so quickly next time. "Yeah. Something just like, sucked the life out of me."

"Nothing a little grub won't cure. Corey's hustling up some cheese sandwiches. Sea Witch is at the helm…"

"Watch it, jerkwad."

"…so why don't you help me get the mainsail up?"

Maddock shook the cobwebs out. "Damn. I must be losing it. Where are we headed?"

"Second star to the right, and straight on 'til morning."

"Northeast it is then." He stood and checked *Thetis* for damage. Their stern transom had taken the worst of it. Bullets had torn into the heavy fiberglass and plywood. Some had lodged in the stern locker but most never made it past the hull. He turned his attention to the rigging, shining his flashlight up the varnished spruce mast. Save for age and general neglect, it looked sound.

Maddock turned and caught Zoya eyeing his pack. *Corey's pack*, he corrected himself. It went below with him when he scrambled down to check on his friend.

"Ham and cheese, Skipper?" Corey handed him a bread roll dripping in melted cheese.

"Thanks, you may have just saved my life."

"Well, they were shooting at you. What else could I do?"

"No, I mean right now." He tossed the pack into one of the bunks and took a bite. "This is a miracle drug."

"Bones has already eaten two. What did you guys do all that time?"

"Let me help get the sails up before Bones capsizes us. Then we'll huddle."

Zoya held to the northeast course until Bones took the helm. "You are relieved."

Zoya stood and headed for the cabin. "It's about time. She turned a frown in Maddock's direction. "All that and you found nothing?"

"You peeked. Bones, tell her what we found."

"Well, we found Prester John waiting for us. Almost had him, too."

"Yeah, he's full of shrapnel," Maddock said. "It didn't look fatal though."

"You should have been there…our Captain Midnight, he waves at these merc guys and Pete—you remember Pete, don't you? Sketcher with a tommy gun? Anyway, he opened fire on the mercs and they returned the favor. It wasn't pretty."

Zoya rolled her eyes. "And you two just walk away."

"Kind of crawled."

Maddock nodded. "Yes, crawled and ran too. We ran. A lot."

"And swam. Remember? We swam."

"Yes, we did—and drove around a little."

"And Repeat, was he there?" Corey asked.

Bones grinned. "That was good—he was about to dust us with that H&K." Bones held up a finger. "Learn this, children, always check your barrel for rocks and crap before you fire your weapon. I'm afraid his youthful good looks were spoilt when the breech exploded."

"So, you managed to piss off the most powerful man on this end of the Mediterranean," Zoya said, "along with his army of mercenaries *plus* the entire Greek Orthodox Church, and you came away with *nothing*?"

Maddock pulled the length of oryx horn from behind his back. "I wouldn't say nothing."

Corey's expression was almost worth the trip. When the goggling and gasping subsided, Bones told the whole story, from their landing at the south of Mount Athos to their escape and extraction on the north. "And look what else I found." He held up a double handful of stars. "Solid gold, they fell when the ceiling collapsed."

"Is that what you were doing up there? You weren't looking for a way out, you were scrounging for loot."

"Hey, we came all this way, and I couldn't let it go to waste. Believe me, if there had been a way out, I'd have found it."

Maddock pulled four more stars from beneath his shirt. "Here, add these to your collection."

All through the narrative, Zoya had watched Maddock. She hunched lower and grabbed her knees when Bones told of opening the warehouse door. "You used it, you damn fool. You know what you did?"

"I did what I had to. We would never have escaped alive if I hadn't. Besides, I think it had bonded the moment I touched it."

"And strengthens that bond every time you use it." She shook her head. "This is unique, unprecedented. Never has the lyre answered to more than one master."

"You mean before Orpheus there were…"

Corey broke in. "That's right. This proves there's something to the story." He stood and began pacing. "We've passed another level. The dream of maidens, the sacred scrolls, and now the holy mountain. We've won a powerful heirloom and increased our lore. What's next, oh dungeon master?"

Bones leaned forward. His face took on a ghostly glow in the orange light of their compass. "Aren't we forgetting something? These guys must have a navy—won't they be looking for us?"

"Fiberglass hull, wooden spars," Maddock said, "We're invisible to radar. No moon, running lights off, they could pass within a quarter mile and never know we were here."

Corey pointed off to the west where a cluster of tiny yellow dots moved across the dark horizon. "That's probably them now."

Maddock nodded. "Most of them would have figured we'd head back toward the mainland. Preacher will have others waiting out at the cape. He'll probably fly the coastline tomorrow morning. We better be gone by then."

Bones straightened and adjusted the tiller. "Do you have a bearing, or do you need to stop and ask somebody for directions?"

"Another two hours on this heading should put us about fifteen miles offshore. After that, due east toward Turkey…and just don't say it, Bones."

"What, Turkey, Greece? At least we're not going Hungary," Bones deadpanned.

"For that, you're taking first watch. The moon should be up in a few hours, wake me when it clears the horizon. I'm going to sack out here on the deck." He looked at Corey. "You, Zoya, both of you scram below and get some rest. We'll regroup in the morning."

Maddock curled up on a settee pad he'd dragged from the cabin. It seemed like moments later that Bones nudged him with the toe of his shoe. "The moon's over the masthead."

"I thought you were going to wake me when it came up."

"Yeah, well you were snoring so hard, the whales were singing back."

Maddock sat up and checked their heading. "How far do you figure?"

"We're just ghosting along—twenty miles, maybe."

"Far enough then. We've got a northwest breeze. Haul her around due east. I'll sheet in the main and cross the jib over."

The sails flapped briefly, then caught as he cleated them home. Bones said nothing more, but flopped face down on the pad and began his own night music.

Maddock sat listening to the water hiss past their bow. Next to him in the cockpit, he'd kept the staff, the oryx horn. *Left arm of the lyre, if I can believe a three-thousand-year-old legend.* Hefting it, he sighted down its whorled surface. *The Preacher will eventually hear about the drone on the mountainside. He will know I opened a locked door. He may even have known about the cave.* Maddock puzzled it over and concluded that his possession of the second lyre arm was no longer a secret. *So how soon before they find us again and how do we gain an edge?*

The moon had paled and faded by the time the eastern horizon began to glow. A disheveled Zoya climbed from the cabin. She crouched on the seat next to Maddock and whispered, "Can I at least touch it?"

Bones still lay face down on the deck. He mumbled back, "I

heard that."

With some reluctance, Maddock handed the staff to Zoya and watched her inspect it. She held it up to the compass light and ran her fingers over the smooth bumps. "You know, you're totally screwed."

"Bones has been telling me that for years."

"Funny man—got me in stitches. I wish he'd sleep more."

"I heard that."

"Go back to drooling on the deck planks, okay?" She handed the staff back to Maddock. "Corey has the right arm and already you can sense the difference in him. You have bonded to the left. Consider that."

"You know more about this than you let on. Tell me, how can I unbind it? That is, without dying."

"Lazar spoke the truth. There's an entity, a djinn, a god, something bonded to the lyre. You must learn its name and renounce it. I can't tell you anything else."

Zoya climbed to the portside coaming and watched the sun rise. The little boat heeled and pitched, but she stood as if on gimbals and let it ride beneath her. Without looking down, she said, "Where are you taking us now?"

"Schliemann would have called it the island of *Scheria*, Odysseus's last refuge before sailing home. It's known today as Samothrace, legendary home of the Gods."

"Schliemann was an idiot." Bones still lay on his belly, hugging the settee pad. "Which doesn't say much for the four of us."

Zoya continued to balance on the coaming. Maddock figured she was showing off. "If you want to climb down and take the tiller for a while, I'll go see about some coffee."

She hopped to the cockpit deck. "Doctor Denarius is brewing some now."

Corey emerged a moment later. "Tea for the tillerman…uh, *tiller-woman*. I'll have coffee in a minute."

Bones raised his head. "Got any breakfast down there?"

Maddock climbed down into the cabin where Corey bent over a tiny propane stove. "You lose a bet or something?"

"No, no…well yes, sort of. We worked some things out the last couple of nights. I agreed to cook."

"And the staff—you're keeping that?"

"That was part of it. Yeah, I kind of have to, don't you think?"

Maddock helped himself to a mug of coffee and poured one for Bones. "And the other part?"

"Well…you know." Corey looked away. "Stuff…like stuff we do. You know…"

"Yeah, I know. Just watch your back. She's got secrets."

Corey nodded and cracked a handful of eggs into a pan of sizzling butter. Maddock climbed back on deck to find Bones sitting upright and talking to Zoya. He handed off the mug and climbed forward to sit just behind the forestay. The sun had cleared the horizon and the northwest breeze had freshened. Maddock had just taken his first sip when he heard the plane.

Coffee forgotten, he scrambled back to the cockpit. "Where is it, Bones?"

His friend knelt on the bench and shaded his eyes. "There." He pointed aft. "It's flying right up our scuttlebutt."

The low drone had risen to a multi-engine growl when Corey came on deck bearing an ancient pair of binoculars. "I found this in one of the cabinets."

Maddock wiped the lenses on his tee-shirt and panned the western horizon. "It's the Preacher's C-130. I guess June forgot to tell us something."

The plane grew in his field of vision. He handed the glasses back to Corey. "Everyone get below. Zoya, you stay at the helm and don't look up until they've passed."

"Oh, sure. Leave me the sitting duck."

"That plane isn't armed. Besides, they won't shoot until they know who we are."

"You're so reassuring."

Maddock pushed Bones ahead of him and clambered down the cabin steps. A few minutes later the growl grew into a roar that rattled Corey's frying pan. Zoya yelled, "Maddock, get your lying ass up here."

Scrambling on deck, he watched the plane pass. Its tail ramp had lowered, and a mounted machine gun poked out from the interior. Still holding its altitude, the plane banked and turned. Bones raised the binoculars as it circled to the west. "Crap! They've got a fifty-caliber M2 mounted on that tail ramp and they're making another pass." He turned to Corey. "We wouldn't happen to have an old stinger missile down in one of those cabinets?"

Maddock knelt and opened a locker beneath the helm bench. "We just might at that."

He scrounged through a tangle of mildewed lifejackets and found a rusted steel ammo box. Slamming it against the deck, the lid popped open and a clunky bronze pistol the size of an impact wrench flopped out. Two fat cardboard cylinders rolled across the deck.

The roar of propellers grew to a thunderous pitch.

Maddock yelled, "Get down. Everyone into the cabin and lie on the floor"

Bones dove for the deck and grabbed the cylinders. "This is insane. That thing's got to be fifty years old."

Maddock didn't answer, but broke the flare-gun open and dropped a cartridge in. The shooting started before the C-130 had even passed. He tore his eyes away from the churning splashes that zipped toward them like a miniature tornado of death.

Thetis heeled over on her starboard beam under the prop-wash hurricane. Maddock knelt on her upturned side and braced against the coaming. An open cargo ramp, a bandaged face behind a machine gun, Maddock took it all in. He estimated the lead and squeezed the trigger.

The old pistol slammed into his hand as a brilliant white star screamed toward the cargo bay. Muzzle flashes from the M2 scattered in six different directions as the flare ricocheted about the aircraft interior and burst into a blinding white glare. The plane banked hard and climbed. Maddock clung to the coaming as *Thetis* slowly rolled back to an even keel.

Bones watched—his mouth open. "*Freaking-a!* Magnesium

no less."

Maddock could only stare in disbelief at the retreating aircraft. "That's not the June I thought I knew."

A trail of smoke followed the plane west. Bones watched as it disappeared over the horizon. "I guess we all have our price. I hope it was worth it to her."

19

They'd found a berth for *Thetis* at a little marina on the west end of the island and spent that afternoon repairing her hull. Corey bought a tube of white caulk and managed to fill the bullet holes in her transom. Bones and Zoya had spent most of the afternoon arguing over their next move. Maddock came between them. "You two sound like an old married couple. Do something useful while you argue. Go check out the ruins or something. Corey and I will finish cleaning up here."

Bones glared down at Zoya. "I am not thinking my happy thoughts, and I'm guessing you're clean out of pixie dust, so I suppose we have to find us a cab."

That evening, they linked up at a seaside taverna not far from the ruins. Zoya described their visit. "We didn't see much. A bunch of broken marble. They've got a museum, but it was closed by the time we got there."

"Then that's your target for tomorrow." Maddock cleared a space on the table. "Corey, break out your mystery machine and bring up maenad number three."

As the image came up, Maddock continued. "At first it seemed a slam-dunk. The ancient Temple of the Gods predates the Iliad, it predates the Trojan War, it may even predate the founding of Athens. Schliemann was all over this place. He was convinced that here on this island Odysseus had dragged himself from the water and knelt before the king to weave his tale of sirens and witches, of the great Cyclops and the wrath of Poseidon."

He paused a moment and took a swallow of the local red wine. "What place could be more appropriate to hide something like a piece of the Orpheus lyre? Take a look at the picture. The seated woman's eye is centered on this very spot, the Temple of the Great Gods."

Bones had been staring intently at the image. He sat back with a puzzled look on his face. "Same problem. Her eye could be covering a thousand acres. What do you want to bet our old buddy, Preach, is getting ready to rain some serious brimstone on our asses if we stay here too long."

Maddock nodded. "There's another problem as well. This maenad isn't holding the lyre—it's sitting on the floor next to her."

"That means something," Corey said. "What's she pointing at?"

"And that's what we're here to find out."

The next morning, Maddock rousted Corey before daybreak. "Grab a. We need to go."

"Crap it's still dark. We'll never find a cab this early."

"Who said anything about cabs?"

The night before, Maddock had bought a tourist map at the taverna and located the *Paleopolis* site. He checked their route. "We're only about three miles west of there. A nice morning walk will do us both good."

While Corey stumbled around pulling on his boots, Maddock slurped his lukewarm coffee and stuffed a granola bar in his pocket. "The sun will be up in an hour. I want us scouting the hills above the ruins before then."

Bones continued to snore where he lay on the deck. Corey stepped around him. "What about them?"

"They survived yesterday. They'll survive today. We'll meet for lunch and exchange notes.

Two hours later, with the sun glittering between branches, and the distant sea turning from black to turquoise, he and Corey stood and scanned the valley below. "It really wasn't a city," Corey said. "I mean, there's no market, no residences, no center of commerce, only temples and those..." he paused, "...those round things. What *are* they anyway?"

"Most people think they're amphitheaters, but they're not—at least not all of them. That circular structure up against the hillside is called the '*Arsenoeion*.' Its foundations predate the Greek civilization, maybe five thousand years old. Schliemann thought it was where Odysseus stood to tell his stories, but I doubt it."

Corey didn't look convinced. "Like you said, they dug the

crap out of this place looking for artifacts. What could we discover that your Schliemann didn't already run off with?"

Maddock just stood and took in the view, the big picture. Something he learned in the Navy SEALS, know the situation, the terrain, before you go in. *Grunts on the ground face the fog of war—that's expected, but knowing your surroundings is what wins the battles.* Something from Sun Tzu, he couldn't quite remember. *It doesn't matter.* He studied the geometry of the buildings, the two rivers that crossed the site, and the surrounding hills.

"What I don't get," Corey said, "is why here?"

"Exactly. You nailed the fundamental question of this place. Of all the fabulous sites in Mycenaean Greece, why this little goat turd of an island?"

"Yeah, well I meant in this valley. Look at the size of those blocks. Transportation would be a pain, they had to contend with flooding, earthquakes, landslides. Why this particular spot?"

"That too. They picked the worst possible building spot on the island."

Corey took another moment to survey the landscape below. "There's got to be a pattern to it all. The ancient Greeks weren't random, they weren't stupid. They had their reasons. Has anyone figured that out?"

"I don't think anyone has stopped to ask the question. The academics, the excavators, even Schliemann, they've all had their noses in the dirt scrounging for artifacts."

Corey nodded. "And that's why you brought me up here. I get it now, but what about Zoya and Bones? What can they accomplish?"

"The museum for starters. Bones might act the clown, but he misses nothing. If there are other maps or diagrams, he'll ferret them out."

Corey kicked a few pebbles down the hillside. "I think Zoya might know more about this than she lets on."

"I know she does. All the more reason to include her on the

team."

"I've got other reasons to include her, you know." Corey kicked another pebble down the hill. "That's okay, isn't it?"

"Wouldn't be the first time—won't be the last. Just watch your back. I think she cares about you, but she's got her own agenda."

"Yeah, I know that too. So, what next?"

"I want to talk to Bones and Zoya first. Let's continue circling west until we reach the taverna. We should make it there before lunch."

They arrived shortly after eleven. Corey had picked out a few more crumbling foundations. Maddock wasn't sure if they were ancient, or merely old. The cool morning breeze had warmed as the sun crested a rocky shoulder. He followed the sound of voices to a wooden deck facing the blue Aegean. Bones and Zoya sat on either side of a round table, arguing about something. Maddock cleared his throat.

Bones raised an eyebrow. Maddock sat down. "Got snacks and local brew on their way. You guys want to eat, or are you going to fight some more?"

"Up to her, man."

Corey sat down. "Did this go on all morning?"

"No. He was too busy farting and watching our tour guide's ass."

Maddock almost told them both to grow up but figured it wouldn't help things. Their beer arrived in a pitcher along with four glasses. Dark brown with a moderate head, Maddock poured it around and raised his glass. "To LARPing with live ammo. May we all survive."

Corey raised his glass. "I want to know what you guys found, besides ways to irritate each other."

"We hit the museum first," Bones said. "Bunch of statues, not much else. But I did find us some more maenads."

"Dancers," Corey said. "They were just dancers."

"Yeah, *the museum* says they're dancers." Bones gave an exaggerated wink. "But *we know*, don't we."

Maddock caught Zoya's look and raised his glass. "Peace of

the waterhole. Drink your beer everyone."

Corey leaned forward. "I'd kind of like to see what you guys found."

At least Zoya didn't roll her eyes—Maddock gave her credit for that much. She unfolded a wide photomontage and pressed it flat on the table. "It was a frieze that once ran around the top of a building. There's not much left of it. What the Byzantines didn't bust up, the Ottomans did. I think the Americans found this chunk but couldn't fit it in their luggage."

The detailed photos showed a chain of female dancers in high relief. Maddock bent closer to compare them. "Is that some kind of symbol on their gowns?"

"Yeah, I asked," Bones said, "no one knows what it means…if anything."

Zoya mumbled something. When Corey nudged her, she repeated, "Musical notes…I think."

"Yeah, if they were just dancers," Bones said, "but if they are *maenads*…"

Maddock interrupted. "For now, let's say they are. Did you get a map of the site?"

Zoya opened a brochure with a map on the back. "Came with the tour."

Bones pointed out a square box set at an angle to the other buildings. "That one"

Maddock nodded and sat back. "Show and tell is over. I see our lunch coming."

Their server arrived with platters of roasted meat and fried pastries. Maddock pointed to the empty pitcher and held up a finger, *one more*. A few minutes passed in quiet munching. Corey was first to break the silence. "I'm curious to hear what you guys saw on the tour."

"For one, the building with the maenads," Bones began.

"The dancers."

"…the *dancing* maenads. There's not much left of it, just foundation stones and a few columns, but it's set weird. I mean, if they'd turned it about forty-five degrees, it would have fit the site better and been easier to build."

"Did your tour guide know?" Maddock said. "Because I'm sure you asked."

"Yeah, I asked. The alignment had something to do with that giant firepit."

"We saw that," Corey said. "The Arseno building...what did you call it?"

"The *Arsenoeion*, at least Schliemann called it that. He was convinced it was where Odysseus hung out. Poseidon too, they didn't get along. Did you guys get a look at it?"

Zoya said, "I did, anyway. It does look like a giant firepit. There's some kind of structure at the bottom." She flipped the tour brochure over. "Here's a picture of the reconstruction. I think it's stupid. No one would build something like that."

The drawing showed a round tower that looked like a water tank. Maddock read a short blurb on it. "I think you're right. Corey made a point earlier about the Greeks being anything but stupid. Can we go get another look?"

Bones poured the remaining beer into their glasses. "First, everyone hydrate."

The site was no more than a twenty-minute walk from the taverna. Bones led the way. Zoya took Corey's arm and slapped a shiny gold sticker on his shirt. "Here you go, Gingerbread, souvenir of the Samothrace Archeological Museum. What else did you see?"

"There's a lot of stuff they haven't dug up yet. Tell her, Maddock."

"Corey's right. From above, it looks like more went on here than you read about. I've got a theory. We should find out in a few minutes if it means anything."

They passed beneath a stand of trees and followed a stone path to a broad opening. Like an aging city park, weeds and vines decorated a scatter of broken marble. They approached a circular wall of gigantic stones. At least eight feet thick, it enclosed a cellar almost sixty feet in diameter. Bones leaned over the edge and whistled. "Barbeque pit of the gods. What's that in the bottom?"

"Let me guess—a line of stones crossing from left to right."

"You peeked."

"Nope, hunch. Zoya, let me see that site map again."

Maddock oriented it with the buildings and held it over the pit. "It's an east-west latitude line. I don't care what they say, this thing was an observatory. Too bad it's been trashed."

"I could hop down there," Zoya said, "but how will it help us find anything?"

"No need. Nothing's down there anyway. Nope, it's your tiny dancers in the sand that will tell the story."

"What were you two smoking up there on the hill," Bones said, "and can I have some?"

"Turn around. That's the Hall of Dancing Maidens…"

"*Maenads.*"

"…behind us. I'll bet it's aligned about forty-five degrees from the east-west line. Those dancing figures were pointing at something. We need to get a bigger picture—what's northeast of here?"

"If I had my computer," Corey said, "we could check out the satellite images."

Bones looked around. "Yeah, you could plug it into the Zeus-juice wi-fi network if we could just find a bronze-age USB cable."

"Zoya has a mobile hotspot."

Bones waggled his eyebrows. "Oh, I'll bet she…"

"Shut your hole, Bones. I meant her phone."

Maddock eyed them both and said, "Are we done here?"

"Well, I've heard enough," Zoya said. "It's a wonder that any of you survived puberty…or maybe you didn't. What you should be asking yourselves is, where's Prester John right now and what's he planning."

"I thought we stuck it to him pretty good back there," Bones said. "His stooges are all busted up, his shiny toy got a white-hot enema, and the man himself has some awesome new tats on his face.

Maddock shook his head. "Zoya is right. It will not stop him, only anger him. There's nothing more for us here. Time to move on."

They picked up more provisions at the marina. Bones topped off the fresh water tank while Corey booted his notepad and pulled up the satellite image app. Maddock pointed to Samothrace. "We're here. Now stretch a line east and bring it up about forty-five degrees."

Corey drew a line through the island and dragged it northeast, into the Turkish mainland. "How much farther do we go?"

"That'll do. Now take the other end and pull it back toward Athens."

Corey adjusted the image, moving the line around and rotating it slightly. "Doesn't tell us anything."

Maddock stepped back and scratched his chin. "I know it's there somewhere."

Bones leaned in to watch. "You solve the mystery of the missing maenad yet?"

"That's it, you're a genius! Overlay that third image, the picture you downloaded from Bones's phone."

Corey brought it up, adjusted the transparency, and wiggled it in until the island outline matched the satellite image. Maddock inspected the results. "Her left arm is pointing down forty-five degrees, aligned with the building foundation. Follow her right arm."

Again, Corey stretched a line east. He centered it on the maenad's eye and dragged it through her right index finger. The line extended past the Dardanelle Strait, across the Sea of Marmara, and into the Black Sea. "Far enough?"

"Yeah, now drag the other end back, but not to Athens, rather to Olympus."

Corey looked and then did a double-take. "It crosses right over Mount Athos where we found the other staff."

He adjusted the line so it crossed exactly at the *Paleopolis*. Maddock followed it east and dropped his head when he saw where it fell. "I was afraid of that—the maenads are sending us to Istanbul."

20

The Hagia Sophia, the Basilica of Holy Wisdom, now the Mosque of Holy Wisdom, broods over the Bosporus Strait like a dowager empress surveying her lost realm. Almost fifteen hundred years old, she has survived earthquake and war, riot and fire. But those who know her well, know that time eats at her bones and not even the Holy Wisdom can outlive time.

Maddock sat across the street from the ancient structure and sipped strong Turkish coffee from a small bowl. The British archives they'd bought in Thessaloniki outlined a few other sites in the region, but the Hagia Sophia was by far the most prominent. He gazed down the street and wondered where else the maenads may have been pointing.

They'd had two days of sailing to discuss their options. Zoya hadn't thought much of Maddock's plan. "I hear Turkish prisons are the model of luxury."

Corey had been silent most of the trip. He'd helped with the sails and done most of the cooking, but much of the time, he sat and held his piece of the lyre, watching the shore go by. On the morning of the second day, they'd passed the Dardanelles and entered the Sea of Marmara. Maddock turned the helm over to Zoya and brought Corey a cup of coffee. "So why does a wizard tote his wand when he's off duty?"

"Yeah, these things need holsters or something. I can't bring myself to leave it just lying around. It's like, I don't know…maybe like it calls to me?"

Maddock nodded. "Same here. We worked too hard getting them. I'm not going to lose mine or risk having it stolen."

"I must have been nuts walking around Atlanta with this thing. So where did you hide yours?"

"Taped to my leg. Seriously, it's out of sight, but I always know where it is."

"Good idea. Zoya will laugh at me, but it won't be the first time." Corey watched a passing freighter heading outbound.

"So just like that, we're going to Turkey? No passports, no visas?"

"We'll stay in stealth mode," Maddock said. "This shabby little rig isn't going to attract much attention."

The next morning, they rounded the fabled Golden Horn, site of Byzantium's heart, ancient Constantinople. They had to pay a month in advance, but a little negotiation bought them a snug mooring among a fleet of small boats, all equally shabby. Maddock pulled a final check on their mooring and said, "Let's head to the old city and look for a place to flop."

The others agreed. They grabbed their gear and headed toward the towering minarets of the Blue Mosque. Passing the Topkapi Palace and the Hagia Sofia, Maddock spotted a street-front restaurant. Bones grinned as they pushed their way through the door. "Strategy session everyone."

After the beer and the platter of kebabs arrived, Zoya brought up the problem on everyone's mind. "How in hell do you expect to find anything in this warren?"

Bones nodded. "It's not a needle in a haystack we're looking for—it's a needle in Kansas and half of Nebraska. So really, what do we know?"

Maddock poured himself a glass of beer. "Not a lot. Schliemann had considered Istanbul as a possible location for Troy, but no one was going to let him dig the place up. The journals we bought in Thessaloniki also describe Istanbul, and more specifically, the Golden Horn area and the Hagia Sophia in particular. There are some intriguing notes about underground cisterns and storage rooms."

"All of them looted out a thousand years ago," Zoya said. "What do you hope to find that the Vikings, the Crusaders, and the Ottomans didn't carry off?"

"They were looking for gold. We're looking for pieces of wood. Besides, our treasure was hidden a thousand years before any of this was even built."

Bones belched and wiped his mouth. "And now that ancient basilica is a mosque. I'm sure the Turks would be delighted to have us poking about in its cellars."

"You know I was here once," Zoya said. She looked at the three of them. "No, seriously. My…um, cousin plays the harp—she did a concert at this old church next door, the Hagia Irene. Older than the Hagia Sofia, she told me. It's been converted into a cultural center and museum."

Bones leaned forward. "And you were going to tell us this—when?"

"It was a long time ago. I was a kid."

Maddock squinted at her. "You say this Hagia Irene is older than Constantine's Basilica? Why is it not in our papers, or in Schliemann's notes?"

"Maybe because it's boring," Zoya said. "Nobody goes there unless they want to hear a bunch of amateur musicians butcher the classics."

"As good a reason as any to see the place," Maddock said. "Eat up everyone."

Zoya led them past the towering minarets of the Hagia Sophia, past its enormous central dome, and down a side street to a smaller structure. Ancient stone and high windows, it once must have been an impressive basilica itself. Maddock stepped through a modern glass door to a well-lit lobby and bought tickets for all of them. "Look around. Ask questions. I think this place has stories to tell us."

Corey found a rack of literature and began thumbing through publications. Bones wandered out into the echoing nave and stared up at the dome high above. Maddock followed.

Inside the ancient church, the very air whispered like a thousand ghosts. At the far end, a string ensemble rustled in their chairs and tuned their instruments. The conductor was a young woman in tan slacks and a white blouse. Maddock walked past rows of chairs to sit near the front. The woman smiled at him. "Music aficionado?"

"You speak English…"

"Canadian, actually." She grinned. "But we should understand each other."

Waving a short baton, she pointed to the musicians on stage. "Now that lot is a different story. They're all brilliant performers but they do nothing but argue."

Maddock took a second look at the group. It could have been a band of high school dropouts. Not one musician looked a day over eighteen. "Where are they from?"

She found a seat next to Maddock and pointed to a girl adjusting her violin. "That one is from East Brooklyn and the kid over there came off a farm in some barbaric place called Fresno. I've got two sisters from Toronto that fight all the time. God knows where the rest came from."

"Music camp?"

"Something like that, it's a scholarship program for gifted kids that need a boost."

Maddock listened a moment to the cacophony on stage. "Sounds like they need more than a boost. Does it help? I mean, do any of them go on to a career in music?"

She cocked her head to one side. "I think so. In fact, I might have just seen a former student prowling around. Maybe she'll be in the audience tonight."

"Let me guess, goth, intense, antisocial?"

"Yes, that's the one—played some kind of zither, if I remember." The woman held out a hand. "My name is Elain, by the way. You should come by tomorrow and catch our program."

Maddock rose and tipped an imaginary hat. "Thank you, I might just do that."

He headed back to check on Corey. Passing a row of columns, someone grabbed his shirt and yanked him into the shadows. Zoya glared at him. "What were you talking to *her* about?"

"Who, Elain? She was telling me about her students." He gestured toward the stage. "I might come by tonight and listen to them play."

"That would be stupid. If the Preacher pays her a visit, she could identify you. What do we need with *her*, anyway?"

"Well, she fills a blouse nicely…" Maddock held up a hand. "Kidding, just kidding."

Bones wandered out of the museum shop and strolled over.

"Probs?"

"Nope," Maddock said. "Just discussing Elain over there. She's kind of nice, maybe your type?"

Zoya's glare turned into a scowl of disdain. "You two goons are even stupider than I thought."

Bones winked. "Jealous?"

"How could I be jealous of some arctic blonde that probably doesn't know a lyre from a zither."

"Not sure I know either," Bones said. "What does it matter?"

Zoya's eyes flashed between the two of them. "It matters because I think somehow this may be the place."

Maddock studied her face a moment, then turned to Bones. "Get Corey—I want him in on this."

They stood in a small niche that could once have been a baptistry. Maddock retreated deeper into the shadows as Bones returned with Corey in tow. "Now spill it. What do you know?"

"Well, I know that I've been doing my work, instead of hitting on the staff or random blonde music teachers." When no one spoke, she continued. "Above us, just below the dome, there is a walkway beneath that circle of windows. If you three weren't such enormous klutzes, I'd take you up there and show you."

Bones squinted at her. "I think I just heard a challenge, lady."

Corey drew his breath. "A quest—I'm in."

"Before we risk proving you right," Maddock said, "what did you find?"

"Rows of carvings, etched into the stone, and they definitely aren't Christian."

Bones made a curt bow. "Then lead on, Sir Edmund."

"Ha, Hillary wasn't the first up Everest. You know it was Norgay the Sherpa who summited first. Just Hillary gets all the credit because he wasn't short and brown."

"Trust me, tall and brown doesn't get much better treatment." Bones nodded knowingly. "Lead on."

Zoya took them through an iron gate. She stepped over the

broken remains of a rusted chain and shrugged. Maddock followed up a narrow stairway to the second level. Stacks of ancient military equipment and broken display cases littered the floor. He longed to investigate, but Zoya shook her head and kept climbing. Third and fourth levels were the same, but less stuff, and more piles of dust and crumbling mortar.

Passing through a steel door, Maddock found himself outside, high on a narrow ledge. Across the street, Hagia Sophia's towering minarets frowned down on his small group. Beyond the plazas and lawns, the lumpy domes of Topkapi Palace emerged from a garden of trees and fountains.

Bones was first to spot the handholds. Like a ladder cut into the ancient stonework, they led up the outside wall to a tiny opening high above. "Easier than taking money from Maddock in poker." He flashed a side-eyed grin at Maddock.

Bones tensed to spring for the first slot, but Zoya caught his pant leg.

"Hold it there, Spidey. Once inside, any noise you make they'll hear it down below. You so much as *fart* and we're screwed."

"Noted," Maddock said. "Wait here. Bones and I will go up and check it out."

He followed his friend up the wall and paused at the top. From below, the sound of violins echoed through the opening. Maddock touched his lips and nodded. He followed Bones inside.

Windows around the base opened to the sky every eight feet or so. Half of them had been filled with masonry, he couldn't tell when. What struck him was the frieze of naked dancing women that circled the dome. *So much like the fragments we saw on Samothrace*, he thought, *but with one significant difference.*

Maddock put his hand on the wall and let his fingers trace the outline of a seven-pointed star. Indented into the white marble facia, it bore a close resemblance to something he'd seen recently. Between each pair of dancing maidens, a star. He counted around the circle, *fourteen maidens, fourteen stars*.

They climbed back down and found Corey and Zoya perched on a scatter of crates inside. Zoya eyed them as they slipped back inside. "Well?"

"You were right," Maddock said. "Hagia Irene is the spot. Look at the orientation. A medieval basilica would be facing west, but Hagia Irene is canted at a forty-five-degree angle, just like the temple of dancing maidens…"

"*Maenads*."

"…in the Paleopolis."

"That's something," Corey said, "but is it enough to go tearing up the floor?"

"Not sure we'll have to. Bones, you must have noticed."

"Besides all the naked chicks? The walls, they were smooth and polished, not just rough-cut stone like the lower levels."

Maddock nodded. "Not all the lower levels, just the newer additions. Look at the columns—look at their bases and capitals, Hagia Irene wasn't built *on top* of an ancient Greek temple. It was converted from one."

Zoya wasn't convinced. "Maybe some part of the lyre was here—maybe it still is. Who knows, maybe you've found the right haystack in all of Kansas and Nebraska or whatever…it's still a freaking haystack."

"Bones knows the answer, but he won't say it."

"I want my lawyer."

"Give them up, Bones."

It took some arm-twisting and snide remarks from Zoya, but Bones finally dug through Corey's pack and pulled out a heavy envelope. "I'm assuming you mean these and not like…something else."

Maddock found a large plywood box and wiped the dust and grit from its top. Bones shook a stack of glittering yellow stars from the envelope. "Happy now?"

Maddock examined them. Bigger than his outstretched hand, each star flashed in the reflected light. Bones had obviously spent some time polishing his collection. Only a few millimeters thick, each star was slightly dished in the middle.

He looked for any symbols or distinguishing marks. Bones shook his head. "Nothing there, bro. I already looked, top, bottom, and edges."

Maddock counted thirteen stars. "We're one short. Whatever they are supposed to do, it's got to happen with a missing piece."

"Oh, this is just so rich." Zoya's smirking face appeared between Corey and Bones. "You three are going to climb all the way up there, totally clueless about what will happen. I'd give you all a gold star but…"

"…but you pawned it." Maddock said. "Truth now, you've been here before. What happened?"

"I told you, my cousin…"

"Bull crap—it was you, not your cousin. Elain spotted you earlier today. She said you played a zither. That wouldn't be something like a *kithara*, would it?"

Corey moved away from her. "What the hell, Zoya?"

"Yeah, so your little Zoya isn't the sweetie pie you thought. Grow *up*, Gingerbread. Mister bigshot here is right—I played for Elain, she's a nasty piece of work. But I needed to get out of West Philly."

"Then you *did* find a star," Bones said, "and you sold it to Lazar in Atlanta."

"Yeah, three of them, but back then the man was nosing around Jerusalem. We played there too, you know." She pushed closer to the packing crate and its golden pile. "He'd crap his pants if he saw all these."

Maddock edged closer to the crate as well. "You found the remaining stars under the dome. That's how you knew how to get up there."

"Lady is afraid of heights. I'd go up and dance around the ledge—made her crazy."

"I thought you were in the circus," Corey said, "worked a magic act or something."

"Mom was in the circus. A contortionist, until she got too old and they dumped her. I stayed on a bit—magician's assistant. The assclown couldn't keep his hands off me. One night I broke his fingers. Had to run after that."

Bones chuckled. "So, you're the first kid to run away *from* the circus?"

"Not the first. Let me tell you, that bit about carnies sticking together? It's a pile of crap. Plenty run away."

"To West Philly?" Corey said. "Why?"

"If you had to disappear, you'd go to like, Silicon Valley or something. Me? I just faded into the bad part of town. Lived with a rap group for a while. Drove their van because I was the only one not stoned stupid all the time. Never had a license— no one gave a rat's red ass."

"Let me guess," Bones said, "you also played the lyre, because…what's a rapper without some ancient Greek backup."

"Yeah, smartass…*not*. I played the lyre and the zither at the big Methodist church nearby. They actually paid me to play for Sunday services. It was all good until I picked some guy's pocket. Turns out, he wasn't just any guy. Freaking gangster dude—came for me. No peace after that." Zoya shrugged. "So, there was like, Elain, and what the hell."

Maddock turned one of the stars until it reflected daylight from outside and lit her face with a pale, yellow glow. "So why the confession? Why now?"

"Because we're all gonna die."

21

The applause long over. The murmuring shuffle of the departing audience gone. The chairs folded and put away. Even the whisper of brooms that had echoed up from the nave to the lofty vaults above, now silent. Darkness and the subaudible hiss of empty space pervaded the Hagia Irene.

Maddock was first to scale the outer wall. He crept along the ledge, moonlight his only guide. Corey followed, prodded by Bones, taunted by Zoya. In the comforting darkness, he dared venture farther under the dome. Maddock stopped him. "Here, hold this a minute."

Corey took the star while Maddock applied an adhesive dot to a recess between two dancing figures. "I have no idea what it means, but this particular star fits this opening."

Corey turned it until the rays aligned with the seven rays of the opening and pushed it in. "You think all those stars from Mount Athos will fit the openings here in Istanbul?"

"I'm counting on it. Bones and Zoya should be working their way around the other side. We'll meet in the middle, exchange whatever doesn't fit, and work our way back."

"Yeah, easy-peasy until Zoya pushes Bones off the ledge."

"I heard that you know," echoed across from the opposite side.

Maddock whispered back, "How many you got?"

"Three, so far. You?"

"Two fit, two didn't."

By the time they met, Maddock had found four matches for the six stars in his collection. They swapped. Maddock passed two golden stars to Bones and Bones passed two back. "Looks like the missing star is on your side. I found five matches over here."

Zoya peeked from behind Bones's elbow. "Damn, Corey. I'd have lost money on that bet."

"Yeah, me too. I never would have thought our stars would have been even close to a fit."

"No, I mean you, making it this far without going splatter down below."

"Not funny," Maddock said. "No one is dying today."

For some reason, her remark rattled him. *Perhaps the sudden confession,* he thought, *she still knows more than she's telling.* He and Corey worked their way back, fitting two more stars as they went. Halfway around, one opening remained. Maddock aimed his penlight at the empty recess. "Crap. We're so freaking close."

Corey peeled something off his shirt. "I probably don't need this anymore."

He held up a shiny gold sticker, the one Zoya had given him on Samothrace. Maddock worked it into the center of the vacant cavity. "Like a spare tire, it'll do in a pinch."

Zoya's whisper reached them from the other side of the dome. "Nothing's happening. What now?"

Maddock dredged a black aluminum cylinder from his pocket, a tight-beam, LED spotlight. He aimed it at the dome over her head, careful not to blind her. "Look at these window openings. Half of them have been bricked up, but they must have had a purpose."

He panned his light across the array of polished stars. The beam scattered, reflected, and flashed about like bolts of golden lightning. Bones grunted in surprise. "I thought I saw a shape or something."

Maddock and Corey worked their way back to the others. Zoya said, "Impressive, too bad the ancient Greeks didn't have Maglites."

"But they had the sun," Maddock said. "Think, this church has been reconstructed many times since Constantine. The Hagia Sophia basilica was built almost next door, twice as grand and four times the size of the Hagia Irene. It's been looted and burned. Yet still, the Patriarchy ordered it restored, to include these pagan dancing figures. Why?"

Corey said, "If it was destroyed and rebuilt, wouldn't they have found our lyre part?"

Maddock nodded. "No doubt they did, and that's the point.

Someone must have found it, perhaps Constantine himself, and recognized its power."

"He hid it then," Bones said, "and left this as what, a puzzle?"

"That he left it at all, and his successors left it, is what's important. Likely the Ottomans crawled up here, ripped most of the stars, and bricked up the windows. The most important thing is that they never defaced the dancers and never turned this structure into a mosque."

"You almost had me convinced." Zoya waved her arm at the shadowy dome. "But this, how does this help us?"

Corey panned his own penlight about the interior. For an instant, the reflected beams blazed across the open space. "We need to think like game designers. Bones is right, it's a puzzle and we need to solve it before we can advance to the next level."

Maddock passed his Maglite to Zoya. "Take this and walk it around the dome, shining it on the opposite stars."

The beam flickered from star to star, crossing in the middle. Maddock could just make out a vague shape forming and dissolving in the emptiness below the dome. "Faster Zoya, run if you can."

She sprinted around, leaping past them and orbiting like a tiny comet. The light beams coalesced into a moving figure. Bones caught his breath. "A golden maenad—playing a lyre."

Corey flattened himself against the wall and watched the strange apparition of light dance in mid-air. Maddock was equally spellbound. "An ancient zoetrope, but what does it mean?"

Zoya circled one last time and stopped. Barely out of breath, she held the flashlight beneath her grinning face. "I know."

Half a minute of silence passed before Bones said, "You want to share that with us?"

"Yeah, yeah…but I just needed a moment to savor your blank looks."

"C'mon Zoya," Corey said, "you've had days to savor our blank looks. Are you bluffing or just showing off?"

"Well *now* I'm inclined not to play anymore."

"It doesn't matter," Maddock said. "You just told me all I needed to know."

Zoya handed him back his Maglite. "Then you go running around that ledge for a while."

"Don't have to. I just saw what you saw and asked myself, 'What does Zoya know that we don't.' Now I'm not a musician, but you are. Tell me, what notes did the maenad play?"

She gave him a look—Maddock wasn't sure what it meant. "I'll explain," she said, "but let's go back down before Corey soils himself."

Maddock made Zoya descend first. He sent Bones after and stayed behind to help Corey find the footholds. The change in Zoya, her attitude toward Corey, he wasn't sure what had happened, but it was disturbing. *Just another part of the puzzle.*

Bones had wanted to retrieve his stars, but Maddock nixed that. "We'll get them later. For right now, you need to dog her six. Figure out what else she knows."

Once again among the abandoned display cases and dusty crates of the fourth level, Maddock paused to listen for voices or movement in the ancient nave below. Hearing nothing, he put on his flashlight and signaled the others to huddle close. "We all saw it, a projection, or an illusion, but the image, maenad if that's what she is, played some kind of ancient instrument—a lyre or a lyre. It means something and I think Zoya knows what."

Zoya shook her head. "I think I know what notes she played…that's all."

"So, do they spell something?" Corey said. "Like 'Every Good Boy Does Fine' but maybe in Greek?"

"Can you possibly be that stupid? Three thousand years ago and you think they had letter notation?"

Corey just closed his eyes and hung his head. Maddock pushed between them. "Ease up. If you know what it means, then tell us."

"Not sure I'm going to, not now. Maybe you could beg."

Hunched over, his back toward them, Corey descended the

stairs. Bones started after, but Maddock held him back. "Let him go." He turned to Zoya. "Do what you want. This partnership is over."

"It never was a partnership, fanboy—I should have split when you gave me that wad of cash and the staff."

"And I should have left you back in Atlanta, so maybe we're even."

Without a word, Zoya stepped back and vanished into the shadows. Bones glanced at the ceiling. "I'll bet she's up there right now, swiping my stars."

"Let it go. I don't want either of you getting into it sixty feet above the floor. We need to collect Corey and get the hell out of here."

With visible reluctance, Bones followed Maddock down to the first level. Corey stood in the center of the nave. Still hunched over, he cupped a small glowing object in his hands. Maddock stepped near him. "Your mobile, Corey? You sure that's smart?"

"Yeah, to hell with her—to hell with what she says. Look at this."

On the screen, a video played of a woman holding a singular musical instrument. She plucked the strings one at a time and Maddock heard her read off the notes. Bones peered over his shoulder. "That's one of those lyre things."

"It is," Corey said. "That's an authentic replica of an ancient Greek lyre. She says the originals had seven strings and came from the Middle East." He slid his finger across the bottom of the screen. "Here, watch it again. She's naming each string."

Maddock watched for a few moments longer. "Interesting, but I think we've probably stayed here too long. Let's talk about it back at the boat."

"I want to try one more thing. That image we saw, I can remember every detail." Corey tapped the screen and brought up a keyboard. "I know the notes now, I can play the actual music that the maenad was playing."

Hesitant at first, Corey tapped out a few dissonant notes. "No, that isn't it." He tried again, six notes and a clunker.

"Something's not right."

Bones said, "Weren't we missing a star? You stuck some tacky bit of tinfoil in its place."

"That's right," Maddock said. "There were fourteen figures, but we only had thirteen stars. They each must have represented different notes."

Corey pinched his eyes shut and stood motionless for almost a minute. When he opened them again, he grinned. "I got it. She would have re-tensioned the strings and played the second round in a minor key. I can reconstruct the missing note."

He played a few notes and stopped. "Still not how it should sound."

"Sort of tinny and electronic," Bones said. "Can you make it more *echoey* or something?"

"Yeah, reverb would help." Corey fussed with his mobile phone. "But I can also adjust this app to use a harmonic scale like maybe the ancient Greeks used."

Again, he tapped the screen. A musical pattering, a hint of melody, Corey upped the tempo. The notes melded together. Like a rising cloud of incense, a glissade of harmony whispered from the phone's tiny speaker. It echoed from the galleries far above and permeated the nave, echoing off the shadowy columns lining either side.

A counterpoint melody answered from the apse at the far end of the ancient basilica. The fine hairs on the back of Maddock's neck prickled against his collar. Haunting, lyrical, yet somehow utterly alien, the music drew him to one spot, the center of a circular chamber, almost an arena. It thrummed against the walls. He felt it in the soles of his feet—something close, something powerful. Almost against his will, Maddock drew up his pant leg and tore the oryx horn staff from the tape binding it to his calf.

He aimed it downward at the origin. The nexus, invisible yet so bound to the music, so burned into his consciousness, it had to be there. Maddock gave the simple command. "Open."

At once, the echoing notes vanished. Only Corey's mobile

phone remained—squeaking out its melody alone in the hollow silence of the basilica. At Maddock's feet, a circle of tile sank into the floor. Bones stood at his side and shined his flashlight into the well of darkness. "When the going gets weird…"

"Yeah, the weird get going." Maddock sat on the edge and lowered himself into the hole.

He hung for a moment, then found a ledge several feet below the floor. A few experimental steps took him lower. Bones followed, flashlight in hand. Arched passageways, rotten crates, a glitter, Bones redirected his light. A jeweled icon slumped in crumbling disarray against one wall. Maddock flicked on his own light and swept the passageway. Books, paintings, statues, fifteen hundred years of Christianity lay in decaying heaps against the walls. Bones gave a low whistle. "There's more here than they taught us in Sunday school…" He panned his light across a niche at the far end. "…And I don't think that's the Virgin Mary."

A marble statue leaned against the back wall. Naked, smiling, inviting almost, she stood unabashed among the other relics. Maddock investigated further. He illuminated another statue nearby. "This would be Aphrodite—and here's her friend with obvious benefits, Priapus."

"Holy crap," Bones said, "will you look at the weapon on that guy."

"A lot of this stuff must predate Constantine." Maddock continued to sweep his light about the chamber. "Some of it's pretty old, maybe pre-Hellenic."

Muffled cries from above, the scuffling of feet, Bones shut off his light and drew back. "Someone's got Corey."

Maddock dashed for the circular opening, only to be driven back by three uniformed figures wielding batons. He parried the first blow with his staff, driving a fist into the man's face. Bones waded in, swinging a wooden crucifix. It shattered against his opponent's helmet. A wild baton blow numbed Maddock's arm and knocked his flashlight spinning to the floor. He retaliated with the butt of his oryx horn. The uniformed man fell, twitching and shaking.

Bones returned holding the remains of the crucifix. The crossbar seemed to shimmer in the faint light. He jammed it into the remaining assailant. The man grunted and fell. Maddock clambered up to the Basilica floor. Corey struggled in the darkness with two large figures. A third man stepped forward. In the reflected moonlight, Maddock caught the glint of blued steel.

"*Durmak!* Halt, I shoot...I shoot now."

Bones sprang up and pointed his broken crucifix at the man. "Drop."

The man quivered, staring, almost frozen. His arm lowered.

"*Drop.*"

The gun clattered to the tiles.

Maddock glanced back at his friend—a moment too late. "Bones!"

A baton felled Bones where he stood. Strong arms caught Maddock from behind and wrestled him to the floor. A flash of light, then nothing.

22

Maddock awoke on a wet stone floor to the stink of urine, vomit, and unwashed bodies. He tried to lift his face from the shallow pool that bubbled and spattered with every breath. His head throbbed at the slightest movement. His wrists, shackled before him, burned and chafed as he shifted his arms. *Remember, remember…where the hell am I?* He bent his knees and rolled to one side.

"Don't fight it, man." Bones's voice came from somewhere nearby. "They'll just come in and beat the crap out of you…again."

A fleeting memory, a fight, uniformed men, Bones and… "Corey—is Corey okay?"

"Still out…no, don't try to look, he's behind me."

"And you?" Maddock tried to roll over.

"Been better. They were waiting for us, weren't they—someone tipped them off."

"Zoya? Doesn't make sense."

"None of this makes sense," Bones said. "Why didn't they take us out back at the Hagia Irene?"

Maddock said. "I wondered about that too. Someone wants us alive, and I've got an idea…"

Before Maddock could finish, a steel door clanged open to the clatter of boots and cacophony of shouts. Seized by both arms he was wrenched to his feet. Starched uniform, short hair, florid face, a beefy man looked him in the eye and screamed invectives. Before Maddock could respond, he was punched in the abdomen and dragged to the cell door.

Behind him, he heard Bones yelling, and the sound of several bodies hitting the floor. Maddock tried to turn, but they jammed him in the kidneys with a baton. *Bones will have to watch his own six.*

A tall man in a gray suit stepped from the hall. Scowling, he pressed a finger into Maddock's chest. "Looter, vandal, you commit serious crimes against the Turkish people. You violate our national heritage. You assault a Turkish official. What do you say?"

"I need to speak to the American Consulate."

"You are not American. You have no papers. I think you are Greek," he spat on the floor, "or Bulgarian."

"What about my friends?"

"They are criminals. We do not allow criminals to conspire. We execute them."

"That's a little harsh. Don't we get a trial?"

"Where do you think you are, United Nations? In this place you are nothing, nobody. You never were."

A secret prison then. Maddock tried to keep him talking. "You say Turkey is so ashamed of its justice system that you hide your prisoners?"

The man paced back and forth, then smiled at Maddock. "He is the clever one. This one thinks I must defend what I do, maybe show mercy and prove something."

Lighting a cigarette, he exhaled through his nose. "Do your crusaders show mercy to the sons of Islam? Do your British or your Russians show mercy in 1918?" The man shook his head and kept pacing. "It is in this place your crusaders build notorious Bodrum Castle for torment of the faithful. Castle is now a museum for archeology. Ironic, yes? But dungeon is reserved for faithless sons of crusaders who spit on our Turkish culture."

Maddock stood listening to the tirade. His head felt like a bucket of broken glass. The muscles in his back twitched and spasmed. He'd managed to remain standing, but knew he had no chance if it came to a fight. "So why am I here and not already dead?"

"You are to be seen. Yes, before you die, there is one who pays to see you."

With that, the man snapped his fingers and left. Maddock had the brief impulse to dash through the door. It lasted only until he tried to move a leg. One foot shuffled painfully forward before he was thrown to the floor and kicked in the face. Maddock tried to curl, to protect himself, but with his arms still shackled behind him, there was little he could do. When he resumed consciousness, he found himself face down on the floor. A door clanged behind him.

"You look like crap."

"Well, you should have seen the other guy."

"Seriously, you're gonna have a tough time getting chicks with a face like that. Anything broken?"

"No, I'll be okay. What about Corey."

"I'm here, boss. I got respawned like you guys."

Maddock pushed himself upright against a wall, his eyes swollen half shut. The chamber seemed a blurry jumble of gray shapes. One of them wriggled toward him. "Jeez man, you should be in a hospital or something."

"I don't think that's on our tour. You still cuffed?"

"Yeah, right arm is pretty messed up too. Good thing I'm left-handed." Corey scanned their cell. "If I had my wand, I could free us all."

Maddock sighed. *That's what it was.* "They took our relics, our staffs. I could sense something wrong, but couldn't figure out what." He remembered the night before, the Hagia Irene and its hidden chamber, the fight…something else? "Bones, what the hell were you doing? The guy had a gun, and you just had this broken stick or something."

Another gray blob crawled toward him, larger. Maddock blinked some of the blood from his eyes. Bones crouched next to him. "I don't know. The thing spoke to me, that's why I grabbed it."

"You mean spoke like Corey's wand?"

Bones fell silent for a two-count, then pushed himself upright. "Yeah. *Crap!* Crap, crap, crap. It was there. We had it…so close, so freaking close. What do we do now?"

Maddock leaned back against the wall and closed his eyes. "We wait them out. Someone will make a mistake and we'll take our shot. For now, you guys rest—get strong."

Corey leaned against the opposite wall, puffing an imaginary cigarette. "We need some theme music. Say— remember *Good, Bad, and the Ugly,* there at the end where…"

"Shut *up* Tuco, or I'll come over and *personally* fix you up just like me and Maddock, broken ribs and all. Besides…"

Whatever Bones was about to say died on his lips as the steel door whisked open. A towering figure in white robes filled the entrance. "Now I will proclaim that the Lord *does* move in his own mysterious ways."

Maddock didn't blink. "Preacher. I thought the shrapnel took you out, back there on Mt. Athos."

"I was raised from the dead, son, raised from the dead and sent by God to save you three from eternal perdition." Prester John threw open the robe and revealed a strip of bandages across his chest. "Mine was a blood sacrifice as is demanded of all who believe." He stepped into the chamber. "You must come follow me, and I will show you the way."

Bones said, "I think I'd rather stay here and trade punches with the Turks."

"And look where that's gotten you—standing at the brink of the fiery pit. Gaze upward son…and take the outstretched hand."

"Say we take…a hand," Maddock said. "What then?"

"What indeed? Why, we all ascend into the light and depart this later-day Gehenna."

Bones closed on the Preacher. "Your men tried to kill us. More than once. How do we know they won't try it again?"

"Had you only put aside your fears and walked with me from the beginning, none of this would have happened. As it is, you have injured several of my followers. You can understand their righteous anger. Still, they broke covenant with me and disobeyed my commands. Rest assured, they will be chastised for their transgressions."

Corey closed in from the other side. "And your pilot, did she make it back to Thessaloniki?"

The Preacher squinted and looked him up and down. "She…? Yes, pilot and crew returned to the airport. They will have the aircraft flying again soon." He turned to Maddock. "My people only fired warning shots to get your attention. I don't understand why you had to answer with a missile."

"Flare gun. We sent a flare to tell them we'd received their message."

"Ah—miscommunication. Thus, it has been since the time of Moses. Our glorious Lord sends a clear warning and Pharoh in his arrogance refuses to hear it."

"Speaking of Exodus," Maddock said. "Why don't we just saddle our asses and ride on out of here."

"Hallelujah, I have been waiting for you to accept me as your…*benefactor*." The Preacher shot a glance at Bones and Corey. "You are more worthy than you can possibly know. As my Apostles and trusted surrogates, you will find true deliverance."

Maddock didn't expect their deliverance to come without a cost, so he was surprised when the man simply stepped away from the entrance and gestured toward the hall. "There is an elevator on your right."

"That's it? We just leave?"

"Under my stewardship." Prester John pulled out a key. "You must still wear handcuffs, but if you promise to behave, they will come off when we reach my Holy City."

Various scenarios ran through Maddock's head—they all ended badly. Despite his misgivings, he saw no better option. When Corey began to sidle away, Maddock shook his head. "Take point and wait at the elevator."

Bones made a brief gesture. Maddock nodded in response and followed Corey. Simply walking up the corridor was painful. Footsteps echoed behind him. He hoped that Bones was in better condition than he looked. He hoped too, that whatever nasty surprise the Preacher had in store could somehow be managed. *Brute force and ignorance only get a guy so far.*

Corey gave him an inquisitive look when he reached the elevator. Maddock shrugged. "Push the button."

The elevator bell rang, and the doors rumbled open. At the top, four guards waited with leveled submachine guns. The Preacher held up his hands until the tall man in the gray suit shouldered his way between them. Signatures, papers exchanged, Maddock saw a fat envelope disappear into the man's pocket. "You understand," the Preacher said, "not many walk out of here alive."

Pete and Repeat waited on the street outside. Neither looked happy to see them. The right side of Repeat's face sported several lines of stitches, still bearing red daubs of antiseptic. He wore a white patch over his right eye. Maddock bit off the sarcastic remark that sprang to his lips and prayed that Bones would do likewise.

Prester John waved a black van over and signaled that they get in. Pete and Repeat crawled to the rear. Maddock let Corey get in before he followed. With the two men glowering at their backs, and the Preacher sitting in the front, Maddock felt more like a captured specimen than a freed prisoner. Bones pressed his face to the side window. "Where are we, Preach?"

Their host took a few moments to answer. "Understand, you are unwanted visitors to this land. Had they kept you in Istanbul, you might have found an advocate, perhaps an audience—better you simply disappear."

Bones leaned forward. "So, they shipped us off to some private little hell?"

"Bodrum Prison is about four hundred kilometers south along the coast. Naturally, you were unconscious for the trip. When I heard what had happened, I offered to compensate them for their trouble...and to dispose of you discreetly. You may thank me later."

"And how are we to be *disposed?*" Maddock said.

"Oh, nothing so terrible as you might think. After all, our mighty Lord has a wonderful destiny for each of you." He glanced back at Maddock. "In case you're curious, I have recovered your pack and other belongings. For now, they will remain in the Lord's capable hands."

Maddock sat back. *Their wallets had been confiscated, as had Corey's phone.* He wasn't sure about the relics they'd carried, but his staff felt close by. *Bones had that chunk of wood.* Whatever it was, none of them had had a chance to get a close look at it. *But the dancing maenad...her music led us to it.*

Maddock also considered that his friend used it to disarm one of the guards.

The van rumbled along a major thoroughfare, past a succession of little towns. Corey unglued himself from the window and said, "Where are you taking us?"

"The airport, lad. Thence we fly to ancient Makuria on the southern Nile, better known as the Kingdom of Prester John."

Down a back road, the van passed through a service gate with a wave to the guard and rolled out on the tarmac between rows of private planes. Maddock recognized Prester John's Gulfstream parked at the end of the apron. "June tells me that you pilot this thing yourself."

"Ah yes, Judith. You should know that your friend has fallen from my favor over that little antic of yours. I've left Ms. Moon in charge of repairing our cargo ship…if that's at all possible." He waved out the van window. "You've met Margo— she pilots for me now."

Margo did not seem terribly pleased to see Maddock and the others as they shuffled on board. He smiled at her and held up his cuffed wrists. "What goes around, comes around, I guess."

Once seated, Maddock shot the Preacher a questioning look. The man shook his head. "No, the restraints must stay on. You and your people have abused my followers to the point where they are no longer comfortable in your presence. It will be some time before you can regain their trust."

The three shared a dinette-style table near the front of the plane. As its twin jet engines purred to life, Margo strolled up and settled into the vacant seat next to Maddock. "You know, I'd sure like to see you do that bail-out stunt again, this time without stealing a parachute and a life raft."

Bones sat across from her. He nodded and said, "We didn't exactly steal them, ma'am. We just sort of borrowed them. I expect right now they're being packed up and trucked back to Thessaloniki."

"And I suppose you didn't shoot the Preacher's copilot either? Poor Reznik is stuck helping your Ms. June with repairs to our C-130." She leaned back and smiled. "Oh, I guess I should thank you for that. I get to help fly this cute little toy now, instead of that noisy tin boxcar."

The engines wound up to a sonorous drone, and Maddock felt the seat press against his back. The blacktop rumbled beneath their wheels for a thousand yards before disappearing with a soft bump. Margo sat in silence as they gained altitude, only standing when the jet leveled off and the engine noise dropped to a low hum. "It's certainly nice to see you all looking…um…like you do, but I need to go help with navigation."

"Before you go," Bones said, "could you get us some of those little snack bags? I like the trail mix myself, and my friend here would appreciate some cashews. What about you, Corey?"

"I need to use the lavatory. Is it up here, or in the back?"

"Oh yeah, me too, can you help me?" Bones held up his manacled wrists. "It's so awkward with these…and 'it takes two hands' as they say."

Margo just snorted and left. Corey craned around in his seat. "I really meant it—I have to go."

Maddock said, "I don't think we're getting any help from her."

Bones smirked at him. "Yeah, she's gonna give the Preach a hand."

Corey pushed his shoulder. "Just let me out. I'll go find it myself."

Bones slid into the aisle and Corey wormed out behind him. They both froze. Bones grunted, "Whoa, whoa…easy guys."

23

Maddock turned in his seat. Pete and Repeat came striding up. Repeat led the way, a nine-millimeter in his outstretched hand. His ruined face a rictus of hate, he centered the pistol on Bones's chest. Hammer back, finger on the trigger, Maddock knew it could go off with only a twitch. For a few seconds, nobody moved. He held his breath. Then, a brief rumble…and another. They flew into a pocket of turbulence. The pistol wavered as Repeat struggled for balance. Maddock reached up with both hands and wrenched the slide back, locking the trigger.

They struggled until Bones stepped forward and slammed both fists into Repeat's injured face. The man howled in pain and fell to the deck. Pistol in hand, Maddock rested one knee on the seat and drew down on the one they called Pete. "Just try something."

Repeat scuttled back. Hands on his bleeding face he staggered to his feet, cursing in Russian. Bones said, "Take a break, Corey. We got this."

Maddock didn't take his eyes off the Preacher's two thugs. Pete helped his comrade find a seat and held out his hands. "*Puzhal'sta…prostit'iya moi druge…*"

Whatever the man was trying to say was cut off by the clatter of the cockpit door and a roar of indignation. "In God's Holy Name, what is it with you treacherous Philistines that I cannot leave you alone for one moment without your attacking my followers?"

Prester John stood glancing back and forth between Maddock and his injured minion. Bones didn't turn, but stood facing the two thugs, manacled fists at ready. Maddock glanced back and said, "I believe your followers attacked us."

He took a second look as Corey emerged from the lavatory and crept toward the Preacher's back. *How good is Corey in a brawl?* He played the scenario out. Injured and cuffed as they all were, it didn't work. Maddock squinted at Corey and gave him a small head shake.

"I hope that meant to stand down," the Preacher said. "I'd hate to see any more unnecessary violence on this trip."

"It meant I'm not going to shoot these two idiots...right this moment." Maddock lowered the hammer with his thumb but left the safety off. "Corey, Bones, you can sit. Nothing good will come from taking this any further."

The Preacher settled into a single seat on the other side of the plane. "You know open water isn't the best place to make an emergency landing."

"Nine-millimeter, I figure the slug won't emerge with enough energy to damage the fuselage."

"We do not need to find out." The Preacher growled a few Russian phrases and his two minions retreated to the back of the plane. "Now tell me son, what do you intend to do with that gun?"

"Give it to you." Maddock unlatched the trigger guard and removed the slide. He handed the frame assembly across the aisle. "I'll keep the other half. Feel better?"

The man snorted, dropped the pistol on the floor, and kicked it aft. "My people have other weapons, you know."

"Yeah, but I'll bet those two don't, or we'd have more problems than hurt feelings and a busted face."

Prester John glared at the two men. "I am surrounded by fools, incompetents, and rebels." He bent forward and poked a finger in Maddock's chest. "You three are uniquely suited to my mission. You answer to a higher power, to the Lord's Holy Instrument."

"Yeah, sticks and bits of wood," Bones said. "You didn't happen to see them lately, did you?"

"By God's witness, your relics are safe in my hands. They only need proper conjoining...and they need you to wield them."

Bones looked as if he was about to jump up and throttle the man. Corey went into a crouch. Maddock said, "Both of you, sit back and relax. This flight will be long enough as it is."

He could think of no better option. *Overpower Prester John? Coerce Margo into diverting. Where...Egypt, Israel, back to Greece?* All Maddock could envision was an army of security police waiting wherever they landed. "Let's go visit this *Wakanda* of his—we may learn something from our new...*benefactor.*"

Prester John rose from the seat. "The name is *Makuria*. It is an ancient Holy enclave, not some blasphemous comic-book fantasy."

Bones turned to watch the Preacher stride back to the cockpit. "Way to get on his good side."

Corey rejoined them. "I could have taken him."

Bones moved over to let him sit. "And then what? We fly back to Turkey? We kill a man and hijack his plane? Our collective ass is toast." He turned to Maddock. "What's our endgame here, besides getting cut up and fed to the chickens?"

"The Preacher needs us for something," Maddock said, "otherwise he'd have just scooped our stuff and left us to rot in that Turkish dungeon."

Bones eyed the two characters sitting in the back. "I don't *comprende* amigo, not any of it. He's got the dough, why does he surround himself with idiots?"

"Maybe because they do what he says...most of the time. What gets me is June. How did she get mixed up in this circus?"

Bones nodded. "I got a feeling we're going to find out."

Maddock leaned his seat back. "In the meantime, we have a chance to rest...recover some strength. Stop bleeding, at least."

Maddock's eyes flickered open when he felt the plane begin its descent. Banking slightly, Prester John's Gulfstream circled low over Makuria. Bones grumbled, "Now he's just showing off."

Maddock let out a low whistle. "Pretty impressive, nonetheless."

His mouth hanging slightly open, Corey stared from the airplane window at the forest of gleaming spires and waving pennants. "I know this place. It's...it's Dragonfire Hall."

Bones squinted and jerked his thumb at the towering

structure. "You're telling me you've been here?"

"Yeah—well sort of—in the game. You know, Dragon Apocalypse…"

They leveled out, crested a low hill, and touched down on a narrow asphalt strip. Smooth, practiced, the plane seemed to land itself. Maddock wondered whether it was Margo or the Preacher at the controls. Sitting across from him, Corey remained glued to the window, but Bones crossed his arms and watched the two men in the back. Maddock caught his eye. "What do you figure they'll do next?"

"Stay put, if they want to keep their teeth."

As the plane rumbled and bumped toward a row of white cinderblock buildings, it looked like the two were taking Bones's advice. They continued to sit in stoic silence while the engines whined down and Margo came aft to open the cabin door. Four young women in matching blue pantsuits climbed on board. Dark curly hair cropped short, smooth black skin, large expressive eyes, they could have been sisters. One of them gestured to Bones. He raised an eyebrow and said, "I think we have a welcoming committee."

Maddock had the same impression. Corey stared at the women, back out the window, and then up at Margo who just stood, her face an impassive frown. Maddock made a shooing motion with his hands. "We're here, we're here. Everybody off."

He filed out after Corey and Bones. As he passed Margo, she hissed, "You're all dead men, you know."

His cuffs removed, Maddock was given food, water, and fresh white coveralls to replace his torn and bloodied clothing. He just finished washing himself in a spartan shower stall when one of the young women burst in, took him by the elbow, and marched him naked and dripping into an adjoining room. Surprised and somewhat confused, he sat where she pointed on a low examination table. A moment later, the door opened, and an older woman stepped in. Same build, same profile, she could have been mother to the other four. The stethoscope around her neck lent her a measure of authority. Maddock lay back where she indicated.

Her examination was short, thorough, and painful. The doctor, if that's what she was, poked and palpitated every wound, bruise, and broken rib. She worked her way up to his face and prodded the contusions. Maddock kept his eyes closed, tried not to flinch. Her fingers swept through his scalp, explored the lumps and gashes. He heard her click her tongue in disapproval.

A rumbling sound. Maddock rolled his eyes to watch the two women wrestle an unwieldy X-ray machine over and position it next to his head. A brief hum, he held still. Moments later the women sat him upright. One held his arm, while the other gave him an injection and stepped back. Maddock sat and stared at her…one, two, three…

Fighting, running, crazy dreams flashed by like headlights on a midnight highway. He awoke in a darkened room. His left arm hurt. He reached over and touched four needle marks. Antibiotics…he hoped. That, and something else, his head no longer throbbed. Maddock felt the smooth sheet and mattress beneath him—he was still naked, but the room felt pleasantly warm.

The next time he awoke, the opposite wall held an orange glowing rectangle. It took him a minute to recognize it as a window covered by a blackout curtain. Maddock eased himself from the bed and lurched across the cool tile floor. *Walking is a little easier this morning.* He raised the curtain.

Sunrise on the desert, all purple and gold, Maddock looked down five stories at the neatly raked gravel below. *No friends out there. Where the hell are Bones and Corey?* He wondered about the ibex-horn staff that lay somewhere…somewhere close. *Did Corey have it? Was he hiding it…keeping it for himself?* Maddock shook off the thought and scanned the room.

The opposite wall held a flat, metal door. He expected it to be locked but tried it anyway. The door swung open in silence, revealing an empty hall. *Naked—not good.* He closed the door and looked around for his shirt and jeans. Maddock considered wrapping himself in a bedsheet when he spotted the white coveralls just behind his pillow.

No socks, no shoes, no tighty-whities—just coveralls, he slipped them on and tightened the belt. Shoes were a problem. Without shoes, he was as good as shackled to the building. And he had to leave—no, *they* had to leave. Maddock wondered again about Bones and Corey. *Had Bones really found another part of the lyre? The cross-piece perhaps?* He wondered if his friend missed it as much as he missed the dark, smooth feel of ibex horn. *And Corey, he'd had a piece of the lyre longest, used it the most. Corey must be going nuts by now.*

He prowled the room, ceiling ventilator, recessed lights, window, door, light switch, bed. Maddock checked underneath, steel frame, clean floor, nothing. He flipped the light switch a few times, and it worked. *The door then.* He slipped out into the darkened hall. Pitch black with the door shut, he opened it again and let golden morning sunlight drive the shadows back.

Other doors, he tried a few, all locked. All except one door at the end of the hall. The light switch inside revealed a gleaming white bathroom, the kind you find in college dorms...or military barracks. Maddock took advantage of the facilities. Rushing water grumbled and hissed in the pipes. He took a moment to glance in the mirror. *Crap!*

Butterfly tape decorated several lacerations crossing his cheek. Various contusions burned red beneath a coating of orange disinfectant. Just above his hairline, a swath of scalp had been shaved to the skin. He reached up and touched the neat row of stitches that crossed the stubbled patch. Maddock had to admit that they'd done a pretty good job of putting him back together.

He slipped out into the hall and waited to see if any of the other doors would open. Silence reigned. Nothing happened. He walked the length of the hall and stopped at a double-swinging door. It opened onto a dark empty space. He searched for a light switch but found none.

Stay here? Stumble around in the dark? Maddock glanced back at the empty hall, then pushed through the door. A light flickered on. He stood on a narrow landing. Stairs zig-zagged up, out of sight above and down into the darkness below. He examined the light fixture. Infrared switch—he nodded in approval.

Up or down? He figured there'd be more to see on the lower levels and began descending. *My staff is down there too.* One, two, three landings lower, the lights flickered to life as he approached and died away above. Maddock had peeked through each set of swinging doors at the dark empty hallways beyond. He tried the bottom floor and found it locked tight. *Odd...*

He looked down at the basement. *There has to be something. Bones would have found breakfast by now, but he's probably still sleeping.* He started down.

The basement was nothing but a single open gallery. Morning light filled a row of high windows. In the cool gleam, arrays of columns marched the length of the building. Maddock explored the interior. Bare cinderblock, open wiring, and a tall wooden box stood against the wall. Without much else to see, he padded over, wincing at the bits of concrete and gravel underfoot.

The dark hardwood case was burnished and oiled. It stood over six feet tall with two doors shut tight across the front. Maddock ran his fingers along the seams and felt the rough lines of hinges set into the wood. No sign of a handle, a latch, or even a keyhole. He lay his hand flat against the wood and pressed. With a click, both doors popped open. He swung them wide and gasped.

24

Behind the inner glass doors, he recognized Corey's wand. His own hung just below it and below that, an odd stick, inlaid with ivory and studded with pegs. Maddock felt the glass, pushed it pried it. The edges were embedded in the thick hardwood frame.

"You couldn't open it, even if you knew how."

Maddock spun to face Prester John standing a mere arm length behind him. "How in hell did you sneak up on me like that?"

"Makuria is the *Lord's* place—it is *my* place. I know its silence and I know its voice. I followed you from your room all the way down here and you had no idea. What do you think of God's desert refuge?"

"Where are my friends? Where are Corey and Bones?"

"Ah, yes, your Doctor Denarius has been difficult. He's under sedation now, but you should be able to see him soon. As for Mr. Bonebrake, he is currently prowling the roof above us. Stark naked I fear, he didn't have the patience to find his uniform. Mr. Bonebrake will return when he gets bored."

Prester John stepped up and pressed his hand against the glass. "Open."

The doors swung wide. He reached up and removed Corey's staff before closing the doors again. "This item is of some interest to your friend. Do you think he would be willing to use it in service of his Lord?"

"I doubt Corey would serve you, if that's what you mean." Maddock turned back and tapped on the glass. "You went to a lot of trouble to build this, to bring us here." He noticed a bare shelf beneath the other objects. "Something still missing from your collection?"

"So many questions, my son. Such doubt, such lack of faith. Did the followers of Joshua hold back when he crushed the idolators of Jerico? Did the Christian armies of Europe hesitate to drive the Saracen devils from the Holy Land?" He leaned forward and stared Maddock in the eye. "Before you can know, before you can understand *anything* of these sacred artifacts, you *must* understand Makuria."

The Preacher turned and walked away. "Come."

Maddock shrugged and followed him across the littered floor. He glanced down, the Preacher walked barefoot, despite the construction litter and occasional shard of broken glass. *Bones was right, hoot-owl crazy.*

Back up the stairs, Prester John waved Corey's staff. "Perhaps this will change his mind."

"How about me?" Maddock said. "Give me my staff and let's see if it won't change my mind as well."

"I have other plans for your conversion, Mr. Maddock."

Prester John led him out into the daylight. Rising tall in the morning sun, a great basilica of spires and flags stood before them. He stopped short. "There…there is where you will gain your wisdom. There before you is the heart of ancient Makuria. That holy edifice is where your enlightenment begins."

Maddock looked around at some of the other structures. A low building nearby seemed to have people moving about. "What's that over there?"

"Reception and infirmary. It's where you first arrived yesterday. They also have a dining hall. Perhaps you are hungry?"

"Bones will be hungry too. Why has he been left on the roof?"

"I'll see that your friend is brought over."

With that, Prester John cut across an open plaza. Maddock followed, feeling every stone and splinter beneath his feet. If the Preacher noticed, he never showed it. A smiling woman met them at the entrance. Tall, slender and mature, she was younger than the doctor who had attended him the night before. Prester John handed her Corey's staff. "I must now go attend to the Lord's work, but Halima will explain our community to you."

With a flick of his robes, he turned his back and glided off. The woman held out a hand and said, "Greetings Dane Maddock. How are you today?"

Somewhat nonplussed, he took her hand and gave it a gentle shake. "I am much better this morning," he made a short bow and grinned, "although I may not look it."

Halima wore a dress of bright yellow and orange that fell to her ankles. A tall matching headscarf wrapped her hair like a pharaoh's crown and like a pharaoh's wife, she glowed with an almost regal beauty. The woman returned his bow and opened a door. "Come, you must be hungry."

Past an official-looking foyer, Halima led him to a small cafeteria. "Sit where you wish." She glided off and returned a few minutes later. "We make buckwheat porridge with honey and fruit. Also coffee. Good?"

Maddock nodded. *Eat when you get the chance. You never know when you'll get another.* He smiled at her. "That would be just fine."

The woman brought over two small cups and sat. "Food comes soon." She took a sip. "Ethiopian coffee. You like it?"

Maddock tried his. Smooth, dark, strong, and very sweet—he nodded again "Good."

They made small talk while Maddock ate. Halima sipped her coffee but ate nothing. He tried to draw her out about the Preacher, about Makuria, about what she'd done with Corey's staff, but she avoided his questions. Maddock took another tack. "My friend, Bones, he should be here eating too."

Halima hid behind her cup and said, "Mr. Bonebrake is being attended somewhere else."

"And Corey Dean? He's here. When can I see him?"

"Your Mr. Dean is very ill. He is being treated, but visitors are not allowed." She lowered her coffee cup and smiled. "Do you wish to tour our Tabernacle of Light? It is very beautiful in the morning."

Maddock stood. "I wish to see my friends."

Halima stood as well—two meters tall in her elaborate headdress. "That is not an option, Mr. Maddock. You can tour the Tabernacle, or you will be returned to your room. Those are your choices."

Save for the two of them, the cafeteria was empty. Maddock

didn't doubt that enforcers waited somewhere out of sight. He smiled and cocked his head. "You're very persuasive. Tell me more about this Tabernacle of Light."

Once more the gracious hostess, Halima led him back across the plaza and up a smooth stone pathway. Maddock noted her long, brown toes flicking from beneath her skirt as she walked. "Does no one wear shoes in this place?"

"We go shoeless that we remain in contact with our God. Only…" she hesitated a moment, "…only *certain* people wear shoes in Makuria."

"The pavement must get hot."

"You will eventually become used to it."

Maddock didn't plan to stay that long. A few people passed as they walked. More were out on errands or business than had been earlier. He recognized several different ethnic groups, mostly women. Only Maddock wore white coveralls. None stared, few even glanced his way. Halima set a challenging pace. Maddock stretched it out in response and felt his injured knee scream in protest. Still, he pushed past it. No time to show weakness. They climbed a steep flight of stairs and stood within a towering arched entrance.

"Welcome to the Tabernacle of Light." The woman beckoned him inside.

Maddock turned and faced back the way they'd come. "Give me a minute to appreciate the view."

Halima stood next to him and pointed to a cluster of buildings farther out in the valley. "Village dwellers, the *chandalan*, they live in that place. Chandalan are those who work here but have not been touched by the light."

"Village dwellers? You mean like a lower class?"

"You could say such a thing. They accept payment for labor, but do not follow the God that we do. They live outside the wall…and they hate us."

Maddock saw it then, a low stone wall that encircled the inner complex of Makuria. "And those within the wall," he asked. "What of them?"

"We are the devoted ones, the *latreftés*, the acolytes of our

Lord."

"Not me."

"No, no, not you. But you will learn. Come inside." She took him by the arm and tugged him through the portal.

Caught slightly off-balance, Maddock stumbled after her. He tried to look back, but something she did prevented him from placing his feet straight, kept him moving the direction she led. He wondered how Halima would have handled both him and Bones together. *She doesn't have to,* he realized. *We've been separated for a reason. Divide and conquer.* He tried to put the pieces together.

Halima led him farther inside, as one friend might lead another—almost. He thought back on his earlier encounters with Prester John while she explained something about a fresco on the adjacent wall. Maddock was working out the connections when she stopped talking and stared at him. "You hear nothing I say."

"I'm just overwhelmed by the magnificence of this place."

"You have not yet been to the central atrium. You see nothing. Your mind is a lost goat." She narrowed her eyes. "You dream of escaping. You think how you might overpower a mere woman and run."

Maddock pointed to his bare feet. "I assure you, running is the last thing on my mind."

"Then if you cannot learn from the Tabernacle, do you wish to go back?"

"No, please show me this atrium."

"First you attend my fresco and listen."

He looked up at the wall. The worn marble carving had been mounted and hung like a museum exhibit. Egyptian-looking figures, bas relief, elongated eyes, stylized poses—he started in surprise. They each held some kind of lyre. Halima nodded when his expression changed. "Do you listen now?"

"Is that a genuine Egyptian artifact?"

"Genuine, yes, but it is Kushite, a thousand years before Egyptian Pyramids. Even before pharaohs, ancient Kush had science, astronomy, writing, and great cities." She sighed. "All are gone."

"And this building, this Tabernacle?"

"My Lord arises once more in the desert. He builds anew."

A zealous glitter sparkled in her large brown eyes. Maddock changed the subject. "What else can I learn here?"

Halima blinked, but the glitter remained. "So much more Dane Maddock. So much above, so much below. Come."

She led Maddock through a high-arched gallery lined with inscriptions he couldn't read. At the far end, they stepped into an enormous courtyard. Halima fell silent as he tipped his head back. Tall spires rose on all sides, almost obscuring the sky.

"Welcome to our Tabernacle of Light."

Maddock turned. Prester John stood at his side staring upward. "Welcome to the house where God himself abides."

"God lives…*here?*"

"Walk with me. I will show you his ancient throne."

Maddock did his best to match stride for stride with the Preacher. His soles had become numb to the rough stone floor, but his knee still protested with every step. Halima walked three paces behind them. He'd have preferred that she stay where he could see her. They approached a large black stone. The Preacher raised his arms, "*Behold!* The ancient altar of King Solomon, the center of his Temple, the Holy of holies."

Black basalt, almost six feet long and three feet wide, it dominated the entire space with a dark presence that Maddock couldn't quite define. "May I touch it?"

"Certainly, my son. I have clung to it many a time. It gives me strength and inspiration."

Maddock ran a hand over the smooth stone. He recognized the *horns of the altar* that projected like stone tusks from each corner. At some time, iron rings had been embedded in each side. The treasure hunter in him grew envious. "Where did you find something like this?"

"You should ask, 'Where did Solomon find it?' The Altar of God is older than the kings of Judea. It's older than the ark of Moses. Some say the Altar of God had been on Temple Mount before the flood, perhaps even before the Fall of Man."

"I doubt you looted it from present-day Jerusalem."

"Hardly. It was incorporated in the Second Temple only to be carried off by the Romans." He paused and looked Maddock up and down. "Like you, I enjoy a good chase. Lore had it that the Romans plundered God's Holy Altar and buried it in one of their pagan shrines. As a young man, I explored the caverns deep beneath Rome's Aventine hill and lo, here it is."

Maddock had to nod in appreciation. "That would likely have been below the water table."

"You know the caverns then? Yes, I had help of course. We dove for nearly a week to retrieve it. As God has willed, there was construction nearby. It gave us an excuse for removing such a large block of stone. Fortunately, the ancient Romans had provided us with lifting rings, or we might still be trying to retrieve it. The Lord guided my hands. He wanted me to bring his Altar to this sacred place."

"This place, not Jerusalem?"

"The Holy Mount has been forever desecrated by the Babylonians, the Romans and the Saracen hordes. This place *is* the new Jerusalem." Prester John lowered his head and gazed at Maddock with the same zealous glitter as in Halima's eyes. "When God descends on Makuria, all the world will tremble."

25

"**That sounds ominous**." Maddock gazed up at the towers that rose above the open atrium. "But why here…"

"Enough," Prester John interrupted. "I must attend to other matters, but Halima will show you more."

The woman took Maddock's elbow. "Come. You will find your truth soon enough."

Her grip was gentle, yet firm. Her tug on his elbow once more threw him slightly off balance. Surprised, he took two steps away from the altar before he realized that was where she wanted him to go. *Jujitsu hold?* Maddock tried to think of where he'd seen a similar move.

"…seven spires for the seven laws of devotion…" He suddenly realized Halima was speaking again and looked up where she pointed. "…seven banners for the seven peoples."

Maddock tried to pretend he'd been listening. "Seven peoples? Who are they?"

"You are not one of them." She gave him a hard look and then continued. "Seven paths, for the seven ways of righteousness."

Maddock shook his head. "You've lost me."

She pointed north, south, east, and west at the tall gateways penetrating the atrium walls. "We walk the paths. We enter from the west and depart the east."

Devoid of windows, the walls rose in lofty terraces. He looked for other entrances but saw none. "I see only four pathways from here."

Halima pointed up. "You miss the sky above and the dark chambers below." She gave him a pinched smile and said no more.

Maddock decided to play along. "Then there is a seventh path that I cannot see."

"The path of God, yes. Only the blood of the lamb will open that path. Only the holy music will bring our God and his wife to the altar."

"God has a *wife?*"

She led him through the eastern portal but didn't reply. They walked the length of a high gallery, identical to the one where they'd entered. He paused at a large painting of contorted figures. When he felt her hand on his elbow, Maddock braced his feet. Halima tugged, but he didn't move. She dropped her hand. "Very well, I will explain this painting. It is a Picasso, one of his early ones. He called it *Subjugation.*"

"Why is it here?"

"Our Temple of Light holds many treasures."

"That is not an answer."

She sighed. "Look with your heart if you would know."

Maddock stepped closer and examined the figures. Contorted, agonized, he realized that they were all female. Halima nodded. "You see it now. We walk the path of liberation. Come, you will know more."

He followed her outside. Morning had passed and Maddock found himself emerging into the merciless desert sun. Before them, hundreds of women danced in rhythmic patterns. Row upon row performing identical movements, they wore a broad array of clothing from jeans to abayas, from trousers to floral dresses. Different ages, different skin tones, their stylized movements mesmerized the eye. Maddock knew the moment he saw them. "Refugees."

Halima nodded without smiling. "I am one, a fugitive from persecution. Prester John gives us a sanctuary."

"At what cost?"

"Only gratitude, only loyalty, these we give willingly."

"And only women…or do men practice elsewhere?"

"In my world, it is women who are enslaved by oppressive laws." She gave him a sly look. "We have men—some follow wives, and some like you are brought for other purposes."

Maddock let that one pass. He watched the women move. *It's not dance. It's martial arts.* "You are not all from Sudan, or even Africa."

"We are the seven ancient peoples, Kushite, Sabaean, Phoenician, Thamudi, Parsian, Sindu, and Sinhalese."

"Thamudi, I think is an old term for the Arabian tribes, Kushite is North African, but the Sabaean, who are they?"

"Yemen, Eritrea, and Ethiopia…you would know it as *Sheba*, the land of Solomon's treasure. I am descended from Queen Makeda herself." Halima stood a little straighter. "Yet here I am educating the *chandala*…when he listens."

Maddock didn't rise to the bait. He watched the women a little longer. "I know the Sinhalese are from Sri Lanka. Is that…*dance* Sinhalese?"

"When I show you women, you *do* pay attention, yes?" She grinned at him. "Of course, we dance the *angampora*. We are the Army of God, and this is our dance of liberation. It is all that defends us from the chandalan rabble. Even now, they mass at our gates."

The women kept spinning, kicking, jumping. Maddock's thoughts turned to Zoya and her fierce martial skills. "I met someone recently who practiced your angampora. Do many of your acolytes leave Makuria?"

"One, a troubled girl. Prester John speaks of her sometimes. He calls her his lamb, but I do not know why."

Maddock nodded and filed that bit away. He turned back toward the Tabernacle. "How do you actually go inside the building?"

"We will go by the Apostles' path. It is on the south wall— come."

She strode along the featureless eastern wall. The walkway on that side was strewn with tiny rocks. Maddock winced and limped every time he found one under his foot. By the time they'd rounded the southern corner, the pavement shimmered in the morning sun. Despite the light fabric and loose fit of his jumpsuit, Maddock felt rivulets of perspiration running down his back. He stepped as lightly as he could across the hot pavement and gladly joined Halima in the shaded corridor of the southern entrance.

She waited just inside, a tiny smirk on her lips. "Few *chandalan*, few outsiders have walked our Apostles' Path. A small price, your discomfort."

"I thought the Preacher would save my soles, not make them a burnt offering."

The woman's momentary look of concern faded. She glanced at his feet and shook her head. "So close to the truth, it is not funny. Come, there is more to see."

Maddock scanned the walls for clues as to what an *apostle* might be. He found only bare stone until the midpoint of the corridor where Halima stopped him. "You look only with your eyes, Dane Maddock. Close them now and open your *ruah*, your Holy Spirit that is within."

Maddock looked around. The interior was shadowy, but not dark. He checked behind him. Nothing moved against the outside glare. "I close my eyes and you do—what?"

Halima gave the barest shake of her head. "I wait."

Nothing overhead, he looked past her at the inner atrium and the black stone at its center. *Crap, they could have offed me a dozen times if that was their plan.* He stood still and closed his eyes. Nothing. He felt the cool stone beneath his feet—smelt the dry acrid desert air—something else, not perfume, but the clean womanly scent of Halima standing at his side. Maddock waited but felt nothing more. occurred to him that he wanted her respect. *Come on, Maddock. You've done things plenty of things like this before.* Like a sniper, he stilled his breath, relaxed his body. A tiny movement, cool air against his cheek. Maddock waited. Behind closed lids, a shadow moved. He turned toward it. Another tiny whiff of air. He stepped in that direction.

"You feel it now, the breath of God. Follow." Halima's voice held a note of satisfaction.

Two steps, hand outstretched, Maddock stopped and opened his eyes. He stared at a blank wall. On second look, he spotted the illusion. A row of blocks, set back from the others, hid a narrow opening. Slightly larger and lighter in color, they blended with the surrounding wall. Moving his head from side to side, the illusion was almost perfect. He turned and slipped through.

Gray shadows and little else filled the chamber beyond. Maddock paused to let his eyes adjust. Stairs climbed the far wall and wound their way upward. He tipped his head back and watched shimmering dust motes glide through narrow beams of sunlight far above.

"We stand within Dragon Song Tower." Halima had slipped through after him. He felt the warmth of her body press against his back. "You wish to see?"

Maddock followed the winding staircase with his eyes and thought of his injured knee. *Education is always painful, and this is gonna hurt.* He looked up and started to climb. "I can think of no other reason for being here."

He climbed slowly. After thirty steps they reached a landing. No handrail, just empty space, He paused to look down. Aside from the woman, no one had followed. A heavy wooden door filled an opening in the near wall. Without asking, Maddock tried it. No handle, no keyhole, it didn't budge when he pushed. He felt a twinge, almost an ache. *If I had my staff, I could open it.* He put the thought out of his head. Another thirty steps, another door, he tried that one too with the same result.

Six landings, six doors, Maddock had babied his knee, favoring his strong right leg, but now he felt every blow he'd suffered over the past week. Halima stepped up beside him. "Are you well?"

At least she didn't smirk. He leaned against the immovable door. "I have been better, but you can see that. Your Preacher's flock has been a little rough on my friends and me these past few days."

"It is for your good. With pain comes wisdom."

"Yeah, I was telling myself the same thing a while ago. It didn't make my knee feel any better." He looked up. The stairway narrowed to a tight spiral, disappearing into the tower above. He placed one foot on the bottom step. "I hope this is worth it."

As they climbed, the ambient light grew brighter. Maddock counted one hundred and twenty steps before he emerged onto a broad platform, open to the sky. In the center, a heavy pylon rose another twenty feet. There, an enormous banner streamed and cracked in the dry desert wind.

No parapet, no handrail, flat and featureless, the high platform seemed to float hundreds of feet above the Nile River valley. Maddock stood at the western edge and gazed across the river, green with palms and lush foliage. Beyond that narrow band, the orange Sahara Desert spread like an infinite sea of rock and sand. A dust storm raged on the far horizon.

"You have no fear?" Halima stood with one hand on the pylon.

"I'm cautious, but there's a difference between caution and fear."

"I could have pushed you."

"You could have done that a long time ago and saved yourself the climb."

Maddock walked to the southern edge and looked out at the buildings that surrounded Makuria. Below stood the dormitory. He could still sense his staff...waiting. "I see farms and settlements all up and down the river. Mosques too, if I'm not mistaken. One down there and two on the other side. How does your Preacher maintain this little Christian enclave here of all places?"

"You assume much, Dane Maddock. Do you see icons? Do you see pulpits or hymnals? Do you even see a cross, Dane Maddock? Do you think it is Yahweh we worship, or perhaps his father, Baal?"

"Well, the Preach sure talks the talk."

"Prester John has been a force in this world for centuries. He is an Apostle of the Light, the latest of an ancient order. He does not bow to Rome, or any of the upstart sects that call themselves Christian."

"He is a cult leader then, a proselytizer."

Halima stepped away from the pylon and raised her arms. "Our Lord is so much more than that. follow him now, and he will give you the world."

"I think I'd rather go see to my friends." Maddock returned

to the spiral stairs and turned. "You can stay up here, if you prefer."

26

Maddock didn't look behind as he descended. His knee hurt with every step. *Was it worth it?* He ran through some of the things he'd learned and made a mental map of Makuria and the surrounding countryside. On the bottom landing, Maddock noticed the door slightly ajar.

Damned curiosity just won't let me leave well enough alone. He pushed it open and entered a carpeted chamber. Bookshelves along the walls, modern ceiling lamp, black oak desk—Prester John rose and crossed the room to meet him. "I trust you enjoyed your tour of our Holy City?"

"Enough of the tour. Where are you keeping my friends?"

"Close the door please and we will talk."

Maddock felt another twinge, a compulsion, almost as if Halima had tugged him by the elbow. He planted his feet and shook his head. "We can talk with the door open. Where are my friends?"

"Very well." The Preacher raised his hand. Maddock heard the door click shut behind him. "I see that you have not yet learned to fear the Lord. Come with me then."

He gestured and a bookshelf slid to one side. With a flourish of white robes, he spun and stepped through the opening. The adjoining chamber was little more than a featureless cylinder. Maddock followed him in and gazed up at the pale blue illumination above. The smooth metal beneath his feet began to vibrate as the entrance sank below the floor. The Preacher said, "You are about to enter the Eye of God, a vision shared by very few."

The blue glow brightened, and Maddock realized that the chamber floor was rising like the head of a piston, lifting them to another level. Moments later, they emerged into a large hemispherical space. Like a flattened dome, it reminded him of a 360-degree theater. Images swirled and spun about him, not on individual panels, but as if the whole interior surface was one, gigantic monitor. Prester John swept his arm before them.

"Behold."

It took Maddock a few moments to orient himself and follow the images. They formed a collage of battle scenes. Prester John let him watch. "War, Mr. Maddock. Our world loves war. Even our games consist mostly of battles." He paused while a battered mob of retreating soldiers crawled across the screen. Seconds later, a flash and cloud of debris obliterated the scene. "Unfortunately, these images are real, happening as we stand here."

"That looks like Kherson."

"Northern Ethiopia, if I am not mistaken. It's Tigray fighting the Afar—someone else's war." The Preacher waved a hand and the view faded. The scene shifted, focusing on a small group. "My faithful followers, Mr. Maddock. Obviously, they are discussing something of great importance."

Maddock recognized Beardo and Twitch. Reznik held forth on some topic. "Where are your Russian brothers?"

"Turn around Mr. Maddock."

He spun. Pete and Repeat huddled with others behind him. Prester John waved a hand and the view zoomed back. "They gather near our perimeter wall where the Lord's ears do not reach."

"Do you trust them?" Maddock said.

"I trust no one." Prester John shook his head. "I believe you asked about your Mr. Bonebrake."

Another wave, and the room was filled with Bones, sitting at a table and chatting with an attractive young African woman. "The cafeteria. He's just sitting there eating lunch while I'm…" Maddock paused and squinted. "The image, it's too perfect. It's got to be a fake."

"The Eye of God sees only truth." Prester John glowered down at him. "It is not what you call *fake*. What you see is a composite of tiny cameras embedded throughout this complex—tens of thousands of them."

Maddock watched while Bones shoveled another forkful into his mouth. "And he doesn't know?"

"Neither did you."

Inwardly, he shuddered. "That could get a little intrusive."

"God sees all, knows all. There is no hiding from Him."

It suddenly occurred to Maddock. "Your god must be part of a machine. It controls the doors and everything else in this place."

"My Lord is all-knowing and all-powerful, yet he needs you, Mr. Maddock. Accept the conversion. Join us and feel his power."

"If this god machine is that powerful, then have him show me what has become of my friend Corey."

The image of Bones looked directly at Maddock and winked. An instant later, it expanded to fill the entire room, faded, then coalesced to form a new image, one of Corey sitting up in a hospital bed, eating from a tray. A nurse stood nearby, smiling, attentive, she could have been one of the four young women who had met them on the tarmac.

The video filled the room as if he were sitting at the foot of Corey's bed. Maddock looked more carefully—something didn't seem right. The EKG equipment scrolled an even heartbeat across its screen. The image was so sharp he could read the numbers. Corey raised a spoon to his mouth. It looked...*Corey is left-handed.* Another spoonful, no hesitation, he wielded the spoon in his right hand. *Busted! The Eye of God is bogus.*

Still watching his friend eat, Maddock nodded. "It's amazing how your god shares so much with you. Did you ever wonder why?"

"I am the Chosen One. I am the Apostle of Light, a star player in this vast game called *Apocalypse.*" Prester John eyed Maddock and rubbed his chin. "I read doubt in your heart. You don't believe. Have you never considered that the macrocosm is but a reflection of the microcosm? That our world of strife and pain simply mirrors my online world of Dragon Apocalypse?"

"Are you saying that all of this is nothing but a giant video game, *a machine?*" Maddock gestured around the chamber.

"Because if you are, then your game has a bug in it. My friend Corey eats with his left hand."

The image froze. Prester John stepped away from the metal platform, his face filled with astonished rage. He clenched his fists. "Heretic, I pronounce Anathema on you and curse you to eternal darkness!"

The floor dropped beneath Maddock's feet. He leaped for the edge as the platform fell away. His fingertips clung for a moment, then slipped and dropped him into the void. His feet slapped down on the descending floor. Like a passenger in a runaway elevator, he rebounded, his stomach churning. A brush with the wall sent him spinning away and slammed him again to the floor. He clutched the smooth metal waiting for impact. Instead, he felt the crush of rapid deceleration before the platform stopped.

Silence. Maddock froze, his heart pounding. Nothing. Cautiously, he turned his head and looked up. Darkness so profound it was as if he'd never had eyes. Counting the seconds, he remained in place, waiting to see if the platform would rise once more. He could picture the Preacher, standing in the darkened Eye of God. *Pissed as hell, I'll bet.* At three hundred seconds, he stopped counting. *How long would the Preacher do nothing?*

He thought of just waiting it out. Waiting for the Preacher to raise the platform again. *Or start dropping bricks down the hole.* Waiting didn't seem like an option. Maddock stood and explored his surroundings. Smooth, curved wall, he ran his hand along it until he felt the edge of another opening. *Not someplace I want to linger if the platform goes back up.* He groped around past the edge. Clear.

Maddock jumped through. Something behind him whirred and clicked. He spun and slapped his hand against the steel door that had just shut. A hydraulic pump hummed someplace nearby. *So much for my free ride.* A little exploration found walls on both sides. He moved forward along the narrow corridor, hoping his eyes would adjust, hoping to find some tiny light source. He found nothing but absolute darkness.

A dozen paces in, Maddock reached a junction. *Crap, what now?* He forced himself to stop and get his bearings. The drop, the darkness, he had no idea which way he faced. Corey had said, *'There's always a way out if you find the right loot.'* Loot, the staff, he felt it off to his left. Maddock turned. *Facing west now, but which way is out?* He shook his head. Playing the game. Not something he liked. This God-machine, whatever it was, it lied to him…*and to the Preacher,* he realized.

Closing, opening, locking doors, the Preacher wasn't in charge, the machine was. And it cheats. He wondered if even now, it didn't watch him with thermal imaging. There had to be a reason for these chambers. *Rat maze?* He doubted it. *I was dumped here in what, panic? Because I spotted a bug in the game?*

The door to the elevator had almost gotten him, would have, if he hadn't stepped so quickly. His mind raced. *So, the thing doesn't see that well down here, and this place isn't part of the game,* he thought, *or maybe it is now, but wasn't meant to be.*

Maddock stood at the intersection. *There might be doors…or not.* Turning left every time wouldn't work. *The machine cheats.* He thought on that a moment. *Screw the game.* He felt around the corridor. Two doorways, going left would lead him west toward his staff. The pull was almost irresistible.

The machine cheats—screw the game. He repeated his new mantra as he touched the doorframe. Rough stone, twenty-four inches wide, *I can climb this.* He set his back to one side and pushed his left foot against the other. His ribs and collarbone protested. Maddock adjusted his back and inched upward. *Something the damned Apocalypse game won't anticipate.* A little higher, he shifted pressure to his right foot and kept climbing.

The doorway was taller than he thought. Maddock estimated he was ten feet above the floor when his head hit something cold and hard. He reached up…*pipes? No, conduit and electrical trays.* His right foot started to shake with fatigue. Maddock inched higher, crouching beneath the row of conduits until he could reach around and drag himself up. Rising to his knees, he cracked his head on the ceiling above.

Low-crawling along the conduits, he passed above a doorway. A soft metallic *thunk* sounded below. Maddock grinned. *Screw the game.* He wondered whether the Apocalypse machine would figure it out. *The thermal image must be only two-dimensional.* Ten yards farther, he heard another metal door whisk shut. Judging from the direction of his staff, he had crawled somewhere under the Tabernacle's central atrium.

From off to his right, another cluster of conduits and rectangular steel cable trays joined his group. Maddock now crawled along a regular freeway of electrical connections. Below, a third door slid shut, slamming into its frame hard enough to shake dirt and mortar down from the overhead. *I'm getting somewhere it doesn't want me to be.*

He noted that the Apocalypse machine had upped its game, throwing extra power into the door mechanisms. *It's learning every time it fails.* Maddock paused to consider the machine's next move. *It has only one option left—turn on some lights.* He squeezed his eyes shut just as rows of bright LED bulbs flared to life.

The lights remained on for a count of twenty, then died. He froze perfectly still, waiting. They flashed on again, then off. *It's comparing the thermal image against the visuals.* The lights were directly below him, aimed down. Maddock had no idea how the cameras were positioned. *I might even be above their field of view.* The lights cycled once more. *It's confused. It sees me as an infra-red blob in the darkness, but I'm invisible in the light.* He knew what would come next, minions, human searchers.

He'd let his eyes become reaccustomed to the light. The LED bulbs stayed on, but all the doors slid shut. Maddock scrambled amidst the conduits and cable trays. They packed the overhead, forcing him to squeeze through ever smaller holes above each door. Something was close, he could hear it humming and whirring in the passageways.

Below him, a door slid open. He kept perfectly still as two figures dashed through. Acolytes, probably ones he'd seen earlier. Maddock waited until they disappeared behind him. He continued along the cable tray as far as the next wall, then stopped. Above the door, the opening was crammed with conduit. *No way I'll squeeze through there.* The door below remained open. The ever-present background noise felt like the purr of a large cat. *Apocalypse awaits my next move.*

Maddock didn't dare let himself stop to think. He hung for a moment, swung forward, and dropped. The instant his feet hit the stone floor he sprang through the doorway. It smacked closed, inches behind him. Maddock rolled when he landed and looked up. Halima stood blocking the passage.

27

Halima didn't blink. "You are caught."

"And you should have stayed up there on your Tower, princess."

She smiled down at him as he scrambled to his feet. "Why is that, my chandala?"

"Because then you would never need to know the truth about your precious *Lord.*"

"You outsider, you think to tell me of my God?"

Maddock looked up at the bundles of conduit and wiring channels that ran along the overhead. "I can show you."

"And the chandala thinks again to elude me, to run."

He looked Halima in the eye. There was no derision in her voice, no mocking tone. She simply spoke her mind. He replied, "I respect you too much for that."

"Then show me where is this truth, that I may see it."

Maddock glanced at the overhead once more. "This way."

He walked with her another twenty yards to a closed door on the side of the corridor. The conduits bent left and disappeared through the wall above. "Can you open this?"

"I am forbidden."

Maddock examined the door. Different from the others, it didn't slide, it swung inward on hinges. Heavy steel frame, brushed metal facing, it was clearly meant to keep people out. He bent to examine the latch. Where most of the doors he'd seen in the Tabernacle had no visible knobs, this one had a mechanical combination lock and deadbolt latch. "You wouldn't know the combination, would you?"

She shook her head. "Do not try it. He knows if you break covenant, you will die."

"I've made no covenants with your god or your Preacher."

Maddock recalled the other searchers that had passed earlier. *Right now, running back this way.* He looked at the lock—three random numbers. *Get it wrong, the thing's gonna bolt itself up tight.* He wondered if it had other defenses.

"Stand back."

"It will kill you."

"Just stand back."

He closed his eyes. *What is the code? What would be a magic number for the Apocalypse machine?* Maddock opened his eyes, grinned, and punched the number six, three times. A twist of the latch and the door swung inward.

Shouts from the far end of the corridor. He turned to Halima. "In, in...quick." She didn't move. Maddock knew better than to grab her. He stepped through the doorway. "Come. Now or never."

More shouts, she stepped through and shut the door. "We are both dead."

They stood in a shadowy chamber lit only by a golden nimbus that played across its high ceiling. A sonorous *whirr* filled the room. Just inside the door, a tall partition separated them from whatever the chamber had been created to house. Maddock turned left and followed the partition to its end, to what he knew he would find. "Here is your god, Halima. Here is your truth."

She moved out of the shadows and stood beside him. "No. It cannot be."

Before them stood row upon row of skeletal towers. Clusters of silvery pods climbed their golden frameworks, connected by bundles of slender filaments. Cautious, checking above and behind him, Maddock approached the nearest tower. Halima followed. "This *thing* is not my Lord."

"This thing...these things...form a massive quantum computer. My friend Corey could tell you more about it, but from what I can see, this machine is more advanced than anyone has ever dreamed."

"It is a golden idol, a blasphemous thing best buried and forgotten. My Lord sings to me, speaks to me, guides me in all I do. This is not him."

"How do you know?"

"If any look upon the Lord's face, they will die. Yet we live.

This is not him."

"I don't think your Lord can see within this chamber any more than you can see your own brain. It doesn't know we are here. This machine doesn't even know it's a machine—it thinks it's *God*. Come, I will show you."

Halima followed Maddock past rows of golden towers. He stepped over giant conduits snaking along the floor. Above, more conduits and cables crossed the ceiling, feeding a black panel set against the far wall. Maddock stopped when he reached the panel.

"Lord means *master*. What if this machine was your master?"

"It is not."

"Then you won't mind if I shut it off?" Before she could answer, he ran his hand down an array of switches on the panel's face. Individual towers wavered and flickered out. Halima shrieked, clutching her head. Klaxons echoed her cries and red lights flared all about the room. Maddock had thrown most of the switches when he caught movement out of the corner of his eye. Half crouched, her colorful headdress crumpled on the floor, a different Halima growled and sprang at his throat.

Her attack was so primitive, so visceral it took him entirely by surprise. He barely had time to raise an arm before she bore him to the concrete floor. None of the fluid grace he'd seen in the dancers, Halima came at him like an enraged tiger. Maddock fended her off with a simple jiu-jitsu move. He spun her around, her arm behind her back, and pushed her away. Before she could recover, he reached up and swept a hand across the remaining switches.

Not all the quantum units went down. Four remained, pulsing and glowing at the four corners of the chamber. Maddock had expected some degree of emergency backup. *It doesn't matter, I've peed in the punchbowl, now it's time to bail.*

Halima remained on the floor, convulsing with sobs. He knelt at her side and took her hand. She seemed unhurt, but he could only imagine the emptiness. The woman turned her head and looked up at him. "The silence, oh my God the *silence*."

He helped Halima to her feet amidst the cacophony of alarms and flashing lights. Maddock thought of smashing the towers, of doing some real damage, when he looked up and saw the descending cloud. "Gas…we've got to get out of here!"

Still weeping in despair, she leaned on his shoulder. Maddock half dragged her to the exit. He held his breath, praying it wasn't a nerve agent, praying the door wasn't sealed shut. A simple knob, no lock, he wrenched it open and shoved Halima through. She collapsed in the corridor as Maddock yanked the door shut.

He checked her pulse, her breathing, the woman lived. Her eyelids flickered, but he saw no sign of tremor that would indicate a nerve agent. Maddock waited–leaving her just felt wrong. Two others shared the corridor with them. Crouched against the far wall, they hadn't moved when Halima and Maddock burst through the door. He recognized them as the two acolytes who had passed earlier. Halima's eyes opened. "I have died. You should have left me."

"No, you have only just now awakened. I need you to stand up and live."

"Why?"

"Because your Preacher is a fraud, and your God is an illusion." He extended his hand. "Come. We have work to do."

Halima clung to Maddock as they staggered along the winding corridors. She pointed the way but said little. Lights flickered in the overhead, sometimes going dark for minutes at a time. They'd stop and wait. Doors opened at random, revealing caches of materials and supplies. *I wonder what fresh hell is erupting in the rest of Makuria.* Maddock kept his thoughts to himself. Getting Halima out was problem enough. *How do I find Bones and Corey?*

A hundred yards farther, the corridor bent left and ended. Halima had seemed to recover enough to walk unsupported— still, she clung to Maddock's arm. They faced yet another sliding door. Solid, unmoving, it blocked their way.

"I…I don't know how to open this one."

"How did you get through the first time?"

"I just touched it and…"

As she spoke, the door shuddered, then slid aside. Margo stood grinning at them, a compact Beretta pistol in her hand. "I see you finally caught him, Halima dear. Too bad you didn't kill him when you had the chance."

Maddock felt the woman at his side stiffen. "I was sent to find him, not kill him."

"And look what happened." Margo centered the pistol on Maddock's chest. "Now I'll have to kill you both."

Another figure moved into view…Reznik. He put a hand on her shoulder. "Not yet, sweetheart. We need Maddock to lure his friends from hiding."

"Then I'll only kill her."

Margo extended her arm toward Halima. As she did, Maddock sprang through the doorway and smacked her pistol aside. He landed a left cross on the woman's chin and struggled for the gun. The door whisked shut as they both stumbled into Reznik. Margo fell to her knees and her Beretta discharged with a sharp *pop*. The bullet buried itself in the far wall. Stepping back, Reznik said, "Both of you can stop now."

Maddock looked up into the barrel of a forty-five-caliber automatic. "Kind of old school, isn't it?"

Margo pushed herself to her feet and planted the little Beretta against Maddock's temple. "Preacher's bootlick got away. I say we kill this one now and be done with it."

"Put the gun down, Margo. We'll bag the others. After that…"

Margo rubbed her chin. "I hope it'll be slow."

"I've got my own beef with them." He held up a bandaged right hand. "This and a damaged aircraft."

Maddock tried to ignore the gun at his head. "I thought June was flying the C-130."

"Not after that little stunt over Greece."

"The Preacher grounded her for something I did?"

"Our intrepid leader has too much on his mind for such mundane administrative tasks. I grounded her."

"So where is she now?"

"Let's go find out." Reznik twitched his head toward the corridor. "Margo, put that damned toy gun away and lead us out of here."

The woman shook her head. "I prefer to keep my men where I can see them. You go on. I'll watch your back."

With a little prodding, Maddock followed Reznik to a long iron stairway. The man's black jogging shoes clunked on each tread as he climbed. A door at the top opened just beyond Makuria's walls. "Things are somewhat chaotic lately thanks to your little stunt back there. I'll say it was a ballsy move. The Preacher is going out of his mind right now. Margo and me, we've got our own concerns…"

"Can it Reznik." Maddock felt a shove to his back. Margo stormed by, still holding her Beretta. "This guy doesn't need to know jack-squat about our plans." She turned to Maddock. "Not that he's gonna live long enough to tell anyone."

Reznik glared at her a moment, then nodded. "Let's just get this over with."

In the midday sun, Makuria's paving stones felt like walking on a hot griddle. They circled behind the Preacher's towering stone edifice and descended toward the building complex. People, mostly young women, walked about aimlessly or stood in groups, staring at each other. They wore the same dazed look Maddock had seen in Halima's eyes down among the corridors.

He was not happy to find Pete and Repeat waiting for them at the cafeteria. Repeat spat on the ground and cursed in Russian. Reznik said something terse in return. He turned back to Maddock. "You seem to make enemies wherever you go."

"Yeah, and it seems the enemies of my enemies are also my enemies. How inconvenient."

Margo narrowed her eyes. "And what do you mean by that?"

"Does Prester John know anything about this? Or is it the

four of you with some private agenda?"

Reznik drew his pistol and centered it on Maddock. "Just get inside."

The dining hall was empty. The tables had all been pushed to the walls. A single wooden stool occupied the center of the room. Resnick waved his pistol. "Sit."

They zip-tied his ankles to the legs. Margo jammed a stick behind his elbows. "I found this. It ought to hold him."

Reznik lashed Maddock's wrists together across his stomach. Ten feet away, a video camera stood on its tripod. Margo smirked at him. "Comfy? I hope so, because my friend has a little present for you."

Reznik crouched next to him and held out a small metal sphere with a familiar curved steel spoon on its side. "I'm sure you know about fragmentation grenades, Mr. Navy SEAL. The special thing about this one is that it is missing its pin. Here, I'd like you to hang on to it for a while. You see, as long as the spoon stays in place, it won't go off."

He placed the grenade in Maddock's lap, just within reach of his fingers. "Hold your hands steady and your fingers stretched out, and maybe, just maybe you can keep it from rolling on the floor and going...*boom*."

Margo adjusted the camera. "Smile for your friends." She switched on a monitor and spun it to face him. "This video is on a direct feed to all the rooms in the complex. The Preacher's little tin god has nothing to do with it."

Maddock stared at an image of his own face, sweat and dirt staining his once-white jumpsuit. Perspiration from his brow mixed with blood from the reopened scalp wound and ran down one side of his cheek. Reznik knelt by the stool and spoke to the camera. "Make no mistake, I have the pin in my hand and that is a live M67 grenade. I don't think Mr. Maddock here can hold out for more than ten minutes."

Straining against the staff behind his arms, stomach drawn in as far as he could hold it, Maddock pressed the steel spoon against the grenade body. If it slipped, even a fraction, the spoon would fly off and the striker would ignite the fuse.

Margo and Reznik both backed out the door and left him alone with the camera and the grenade. Maddock tried not to think of what could happen. He looked away from the monitor and concentrated on holding his stomach in, on remaining perfectly still. Every tiny breath he drew slid the grenade a few millimeters lower.

If anyone comes to help, they'll get jumped before they ever reach the door. His diaphragm ached. He closed his eyes and felt the muscles in his arms and wrists begin to quiver. Maddock's outstretched fingers burned. He waited.

A small commotion at the entrance. He opened his eyes to see Corey walk in. Hands cuffed behind him, he looked back. Maddock didn't have to see the guns pointed at his friend to know they were there. He closed his eyes again and said, "You shouldn't have come. Now we're both dead."

28

Corey crouched at his side. "Quiet! Wait for it."

"Where's Bones?"

"Just wait." He sidled a little closer to Maddock's stool.

Without moving a muscle, Maddock rolled his eyes toward Corey. "In less than two minutes, I will have to drop this grenade. When I do, get behind me, open your mouth, and cover your ears. After the detonation, run for the kitchen."

"Not gonna happen, skipper." Corey leaned against his side and said, "Open."

Maddock heard the cuffs clatter to the floor. His friend reached over, grabbed the grenade, and lobbed it through the entrance doorway. Five seconds later, the blast knocked them both backward. Corey pulled out a scalpel. "Snitched it from the infirmary." He cut Maddock's bonds.

The camera and monitor seemed to have absorbed most of the shrapnel, but the burning on Maddock's left shoulder meant he hadn't escaped uninjured. "You okay?"

Corey held a black stick in his hand. "Good to go. Which way?"

"Behind us, the kitchen door." Maddock made his legs move despite their protests. Corey followed, ducking low.

A few shots buried themselves in the back wall. Maddock burst through the kitchen door. "What the hell, man?"

"My staff." Corey brandished the stick that had been jammed behind Maddock's elbows. "The idiots used my staff when they tied you up."

Daylight from the swinging door outlined counters and cabinets in the darkened kitchen. Maddock yanked open a few drawers. *There's got to be a knife here somewhere.* Muffled footsteps in the dining hall, he looked up. "Screw it—let's bail."

He found a pantry door past the stove and large commercial freezer. Stumbling over a mop bucket, he felt his way through. Corey waited just inside, peeking out at the shadowy kitchen. Past a row of shelves Maddock found what he'd been looking for, a glimmer of daylight shining under a back door. He eased it open and stepped out just as Pete and Repeat came running around the corner.

Bullets smacked into the steel door as he yanked it shut and flipped the deadbolt. Nothing penetrated, but he didn't feel like standing too close. He heard hammering on the other door. "Corey, what's happening?"

"Jammed a mop under the doorknob, but I don't know how long it'll hold." Corey did a double-take. "Jeez, boss...your arm."

"Shrapnel from the grenade. I'll worry about it later." Three more bullets peppered into the back door. "Damn. We got Machine Gun Pete on the other side."

More hammering. "Dane Maddock, you and your friend would be well advised to open this door."

Silence, then another voice called out. "For crap's sake, Maddock, open the freaking door."

"Bones?"

"Yeah, standing here with the High Holiness himself. Open up."

Somewhere, a motor started. The overhead lights flickered on. Corey looked back and raised an eyebrow. Maddock nodded—it seemed the better option. Corey kicked the mop away.

Prester John stood in the open doorway, holding a battered wooden box. Behind him stood Bones, grimace on his face, shaking his head furiously. "Mr. Maddock, must you always bring chaos to whatever you touch? I name you *Havoc*, the bane of social order."

"Uh, I think you were the one who dumped me in the pit."

"*The Pit*, you call it? You must know that you were allowed to witness the holiest of holy sanctuaries. The seat of God Almighty—and what? What did you do? You desecrated God's sacred image. You should be scourged, and you shall be...just not yet."

"What about your friends. They tried..."

The Preacher's voice went up an octave as well as a few

decibels. "My *friends?* You call them my friends? They walk shod through my Tabernacle as if it were a stable. They disobey their Lord and rebel against his kingdom. I renounce and condemn them."

"Two of them are trying to shoot their way through the back door."

A powerful blast shook the building and threw Maddock to the floor. When he looked up, the entire rear wall of the pantry had been blown open. Prester John stood much as before. "God's Tabernacle of Light has its own defensive system. The Lord smote them for their wickedness…as he will soon destroy all that is wicked in this world."

Maddock helped Corey stand and waved to Bones. "I think we're gonna leave now. Which way is the bus station?"

"You will not go, for I have this." Prester John held up a length of black horn.

Maddock knew it for what it was, his staff. The one he had recovered from Mt. Athos. Stolen from him, kept apart from him. He felt the rage building inside. Maddock clenched his fists. "Draw your sword, Preacher. We end this now."

With a single deft motion, Prester John raised the wooden box and inserted the staff into one side. "You will stand where you are, *Havoc*, and not move."

Like he had been welded to the floor, Maddock struggled against a compulsion ten times stronger than the nudging he had received from Halima. Corey raised his staff. "Back!"

The Preacher simply reached forward and snatched it away. "Thank you. I had been hoping you would give me that."

With two staffs attached, Maddock recognized the box. "The body, you've had it all the time."

"Yes. Even though it is not bonded to me, its influence is still quite powerful. You might be wondering why your muscular friend here has been so docile. Why don't you tell him, Mr. Bonebrake?"

Bones just shook his head. "Nothing I can say. He knows."

"Nothing you can say that I don't *tell* you to say." The Preacher reached beneath his robe and drew out an irregular wooden bar. "You see, I don't need a sword when I have this."

He fitted it between the two staffs. "The lyre is complete. It need only be strung to gain its full strength."

"I don't understand," Maddock said, "why you want anything to do with the instrument of Orpheus, a pagan."

"Orpheus?" Prester John looked taken aback. He examined the instrument, then smiled. "Ah, yes. The idolator Orpheus, he was last to use it wasn't he? Poor fool had no idea of its power." He turned to Corey. "Drove him mad along with his followers. Do you feel a little of that Doctor Denarious, the divine madness?"

He looked back at Bones. "And you, just a touch of confusion perhaps?"

"Yeah, you got me all confused, boss. If this Orpheus guy wasn't the first to use that thing, who was?"

"Who indeed!" Prester John hugged the lyre to his chest. His eyes glittered. "I know that a hundred years before your Orpheus was even born it rested in the hands of Makeda, queen of Sheba. Do you have any idea where she might have gotten it?"

It all clicked for Maddock. "Solomon, who inherited it from his father. What you hold is the magic lyre of King David."

Near ecstasy, Prester John closed his eyes. "*Hallelujah*, you do understand. With this instrument, David led armies, controlled birds and animals—he raised thunderstorms and smote his enemies. With this instrument, King David ruled Palestine until it drove him mad. Solomon as well, it brought him immeasurable wealth, but once Queen Makeda stole it from his temple, Solomon lost his mind. All of Judea collapsed in ruin. Torn by war and dissent, the entire world fell into corruption."

Corey broke in. "So, you ripped our loot. Now what do you want from us?"

"He needs us," Maddock said. "Am I right, Preacher? Queen Makeda couldn't use the lyre, while it was still bonded to Solomon. You can't use it because the parts are bonded to us."

"Makeda didn't use it because she was wiser than Solomon

and knew that God would steal her wits if she tried. I will heed the wisdom of Makeda and make you my surrogates to wield the lyre." Prester John backed into the empty cafeteria. "Come, it is time."

As if in a trance, Maddock found his legs moving. He swung his arms to maintain balance. Bones said, "Go with it, man. Not much use fighting."

Corey cursed and slammed into a wall. He fell at Maddock's feet, pulled himself back upright, and staggered toward the Preacher. "Give me back my staff, you bastard."

"Your staff?" Prester John stopped. "This artifact is over three thousand years old, yet you presume to claim it as yours? The Lord gave it to David the Shepherd that he might become King. So, he has given it to me, that I might become King of the World. You are but an infant challenging a lion. For this, I name you *Hubris*." The Preacher turned and marched to the entrance. "Come, *Hubris*."

"Told ya," Bones said.

Corey leaned against Bones, trying to keep his balance. "So, what does he call you? *Sloth*?"

"I have declared him *Strife*," Prester John said. "Brother of *Havoc*."

"He gets a brother," Corey said, "how come I don't have one too?"

The Preacher led them through the shattered entrance hall. Once outside, Prester John didn't look back, but climbed the stone path to his soaring Tabernacle of Light. "You have a sister, Hubris. At least you do for now. Her name is *Treachery*."

"Ow, crap. These rocks are hot." Corey swung his arms, still struggling to keep his balance. "If I've got a sister, how come I've never met her?"

"Oh, but you have not only met her, you have *known* her, Hubris. Does that shock you?"

"Nothing shocks me right now...*ouch, ouch, ouch*...why doesn't anybody wear shoes around here?"

"You must be grounded to the earth of Makuria in order to

hear the sound of God's Holy voice."

Maddock had stopped fighting the compulsion and simply let his legs carry him forward. Walking behind the others, he said, "I think you just don't want us leaving."

Prester John stopped and turned. "Close your eyes and listen. Listen with your heart, your holy *ruah*."

Corey danced in place. "Can't, can't…can't we do this in the shade?"

The Preacher's face darkened. "Halt!"

His arms extended, one foot in the air, Corey froze where he stood. The Preacher glared at the three of them. "Must I paralyze the lot of you?" On hearing no response, he continued. "Now close your eyes and open your hearts to the Voice."

Mostly to get it over and get them moving again, Maddock complied. "The blinding sunlight, the pain radiating from the soles of his feet, even his injuries seemed to fade away. He heard faint chanting, almost subliminal. The words sounded like nonsense, but their effect was calming, reassuring. He opened his eyes. "Subsonics, either that or electromagnetic waves."

"Think what you wish, Havoc, it is the Voice of God, guiding our lives. If you are to stay among us, you must hear it every breathing moment. The Voice will be as a mother's heartbeat, a comforting divine presence."

"You're all addicted to this thing," Maddock said. "I freed everyone for a while, but now you've rebooted the computer and it's back."

"You blaspheme against our Lord. You desecrated the Holy Sanctum and drove Him into the darkness. I had to relight His golden fire lest we all perish." In three strides, Prester John closed the distance between them. He glowered down at Maddock. "Just be thankful *your* Lord has shown you mercy…for now."

"How about a little mercy from you, Preacher? My friend Corey is in pain. All of us are."

Bones rocked from one foot to another. "Holy crap, man. You're bleeding!"

Maddock raised his left hand. Fresh blood glittered in red

streaks down his arm and dripped to the scalding pavement at his feet. "Yeah, that too."

Prester John closed his eyes. "If you cannot cease your blasphemy *Strife*, I will have to mute you. Is that what you wish?"

"All I wish is for us to get out of this sun."

"We understand your power," Maddock said. "We'll do what you want—we will be your surrogates, whatever that is. Let us all climb this hill together and discuss things in the shade."

"Your faith is weak if it cannot bear the sun." Prester John rolled his face to the sky. "But I will permit it." After a moment, he straightened. "Halima, tend this man's wounds."

His feet once again free, Maddock turned to see the tall woman standing close behind him. Her long colorful dress rippled in the wind. She whispered beneath her breath. "I followed, I see your truth, and now I know."

"You told the Preacher about Reznik and Margo?"

"I cannot. If he knew, there would be war. Then your life is worth nothing, not to him, not to them." Halima nodded toward the Preacher's retreating form. "If you are free and is war...it is on your terms, yes?"

She examined Maddock's arm. "You will live until we reach the top. Come."

Hand in hand, they resumed their climb. Maddock shook his head. "I don't feel terribly free. Only somewhat alive."

"You earn your freedom, Mr. Dane Maddock. You fight for it—you *will* fight for it." She glanced up ahead at the Preacher. "And you *must* win this fight...for all of us."

29

When they reached the cool entry hall, Halima took off to find a medical kit. Maddock found Corey crouched against one wall, examining his feet. "I'd rather walk barefoot through Legoland than do that again."

Bones wandered about, seemingly unfazed by the heat. His white jumpsuit hung about his midriff but clung in splotches of dark perspiration across his chest and back. He pointed at the frieze Maddock had seen earlier. "Look, more maenads playing lyres. We have got to be on to something."

"It's not that simple, but yeah, I get the connection. Where's our buddy, the Preach?"

"He said something about preparing the lamb, and then split. Good thing too, 'cause I'm getting hungry."

Maddock didn't think that was quite what the Preacher meant. Glancing around, he saw no other listeners. He gestured to Corey and said, "So this place isn't quite what it seems..."

Maddock related everything he'd seen since awakening in the pre-dawn hours. He told of the Apocalypse game, the quantum computer, and the bug he'd discovered in the system. "I don't think the Preacher himself understands that his God is nothing more than a rogue collection of qubits."

Corey sucked in his breath. "No, it's much more than that. Think of the millions of online players, solving problems the machine creates. Think of the combined computing power of all that hardware and all those users." He waved his arms. "This whole place, the buildings, everything is identical on a large scale to what we play on Dragon Apocalypse. If a god does live here, it is the god of artificial intelligence."

Maddock explained Halima's role and told them about Margo and Reznik. "What happened with you?"

"Got me a nice shower," Bones said. "Then this nurse comes busting in. I'm all naked and thinking my day is improving. But no, she drags me off to see the doc. Little bitty thing, she just grabs my elbow and I stumble after. Doc gives me a quick once over, then, before I can say boo, she shoots me up with something."

"And you woke up in some kind of dorm, right?"

"Yeah, all the doors are locked except the crapper, so I climbed out the window and headed up to the roof. Bet they never dreamed I could do that."

"You climbed the building?"

"I was on the top floor. I didn't really feel like climbing down…too far, ya know, and I was like, naked. So, I wandered around for a while. There was this access hatch, so I scrambled down a ladder and presto, a stairwell. Back on my floor, I found these spiffy dress whites."

"How did you find Corey?"

"Yeah, that's the thing. I walk down a bunch of levels and the lights go out. I'm thinking, *what the freaking hell?* There's this door right below me. Someone comes flying out and goes clomping down the stairs. So, I grab the door before it shuts and slip inside. It looks kind of like a hospital in there, but the only patient is Corey and…"

Corey interrupted. "…like, I was strapped to this bunk with all these wires stuck to my head."

"You were freaking out man…"

"Was not. I'm cool, it's just that it all went down so weird."

"You were yelling about that damned staff thing."

"Well so what? It was right below me. I could feel it, but nobody listened."

"So, there's this video monitor, and all of a sudden it comes on, and well, guess who's the star…"

"Is everyone all good here?" Halima had returned carrying a bulky medical pack.

"They're good," Maddock said, "but I'm still hemorrhaging. Got any band-aids?"

She grabbed Bones and slung the pack at him. "Put this on."

He no sooner had it on his back than she spun him around and opened the pack. "There, walking infirmary," she smiled at Maddock, "and so much more. In here is freedom."

Halima zipped a scalpel up Maddock's bloody sleeve and

ripped it off. Before he could flinch, she jammed a wad of gauze into the wound. "Your hurt is deep. Hold this for me."

Maddock reached across and pressed the gauze tight. In the few seconds that his attention was diverted, the woman whipped out a suture kit. She looked him straight in the eye and said, "Forgive me. This is necessary."

Maddock nodded. "Do it. If I'm going to be hurt, it may as well be by a woman."

He gritted his teeth while she stitched the wound closed. Like shoelaces, the sutures crossed and recrossed his open laceration, drawing the skin together. Once the bleeding had stopped, she wiped his arm with a rag soaked in alcohol.

Halima kissed his cheek and whispered, "Now you are ready to fight." She held up three small syringes. "This is soma. It lets you control your *ruah*—it frees you from the machine. I will give you this when it is time."

Bones had turned to watch the operation. He glanced from Maddock to Halima and said, "Wait, what am I missing?"

"I think our guide has just had an epiphany."

"Ooh, does that mean she's gonna go smoke a cigarette?"

Corey grabbed his arm. "Shut it, Bones—Preacher's coming and he's not alone."

Maddock pushed past his friends to get a better look. Prester John came striding through the entrance hall flanked by a swarm of followers. In his white robes, he loomed above the others. Bones sucked in his breath. "Holy Dragon Con, it's Beardo and Twitch."

Maddock had picked them out. It was the faces hovering behind the Preacher that drew his attention. "Yeah, along with our good friends Margo and Reznik. Looks like they've still got the Preacher fooled."

Bones handed the medical pack back to Halima. "You better hang on to that, we may need your services again soon."

She muttered, "It is not time, but almost."

Halima faded back as the Preacher and his entourage arrived. Maddock stood firm. "You brought reinforcements?"

"Margo you already know, and I think you've met our Mr.

Reznik." The woman smirked at him. Preacher continued. "I wish to introduce…"

Corey marched up, pointing at the two. "I know them. These two bastards tried to kidnap me in Atlanta."

Prester John stared down at him. "Fool! They rescued you. Beset as you were by Jezebel, the false Lilith, they tore you from her clutches. Do you not realize? They suffered concussion and dislocation for your sake. You should fall on your knees in thanks to them."

As the Preacher spoke, six others circled them from behind. Maddock recognized a few of the women he'd seen exercising that morning. Bones stepped up and put a hand on Corey's shoulder. "He's not bowing to anyone—and neither am I."

Prester John closed his eyes and raised the lyre above his head. "You will all now do as you are told. No more rebellion, do you hear?"

The paralyzing compulsion never came. In its place, Maddock felt a joyous singing arise through his feet. The same soothing voice he'd heard earlier, now amplified a thousandfold. Here, within the Tabernacle entrance, it had become irresistible. *How much more so must it be within the inner atrium.* His senses on edge, he put one foot forward, then another, each step an act of bliss. Bones and Corey followed without a word.

The bright daylight should have blinded him. The hot atrium pavement should have seared his feet. Drawn to the black stone at its center, Maddock felt none of that. He could not tear his eyes from the small naked figure, writhing between the altar horns.

The lamb of sacrifice, Zoya.

Prester John brandished King David's lyre above his head as he led the procession to the black altar. "Behold! The great Whore. Jezebel, I name you *Treachery*."

He spun about and addressed the gathered throng. "I now present our four horsemen. *Hubris*, *Havoc*, *Strife*, and *Treachery*." He held his pose, tall, menacing, powerful. The crowd grew silent, even Zoya ceased her hissing and cursing. The Preacher continued. "Each of the four is bonded to one element of this holy instrument, Hubris and Havoc to the arms, Strife to the head-bar, and Treachery long ago took the body and made it her own.

"Hear me my people, today will be a new beginning. Today your Lord will ascend the Tower of New Dawn and sound the call to Armageddon. Today David's holy instrument will speak, and all nations will rise up in war." Prester John panned the audience with his gaze. "*Nuclear war!*"

Maddock fought the lassitude that gripped him. He tried to make sense of the preacher's words. Bones stood at his side, blinking and jerking as if trying to escape a nightmare. Corey could only stare at Zoya, his face a mask of horror.

The Preacher droned on about releasing the inhibitions that had staved off nuclear conflict for over seventy years. "And lo, the weapon stockpiles have grown in the past decades. You know we have done our own small part to ensure that the world is well-equipped to destroy itself. When our Lord reveals himself, all of humanity will know. Now, only one step remains. We must play the Lyre of God and call him to us."

Prester John approached Maddock. He clutched the lyre to his breast and put a hand on Maddock's head. "Will you be my surrogate, *Havoc*? Can you be my left arm?" He repeated the question with Corey and Bones. "Can you be my right arm? Can you be my head?" He paused and looked them each in the eye. Maddock tried to speak but could say nothing.

"I take your silence to be assent." Turning, he stepped to the altar and glared down at the naked young woman bound between its horns. "And you, *Treachery*, I know your answer. You gave it in our last encounter, I needn't hear it again."

Beads of sweat streamed down Zoya's dark skin. She thrashed and spit at him. The Preacher stepped back. "You choose your own fate, *Treachery*. Your bowels will provide the gut with which to string our holy instrument."

Prester John once more raised the lyre above his head. "I

call upon Sister Margo to take the place of *Treachery* and bond herself to the body of God's Lyre."

Grinning, Margo stepped forward. "I hear the call and accept, my Lord."

"Then I name thee *Glory*." He drew a bronze dagger from beneath his robe. "Take this blade of Abraham, blooded in sacrifice to his God. Take it now, and bring me the gut with which to string this holy instrument."

Her face a mask of elation, Margo accepted the dagger and held it up. "With this blade, I pledge myself to God's work."

"Then together, let *Havoc*, *Strife*, *Hubris*, and *Glory* ride forth, let them wield the holy instrument of God in My Name. Let the Apocalypse begin."

Margo leaped to the altar and spread her arms. "Let it begin with me."

Shouting, Prester John turned to the gathered crowd. "Let it begin now."

Knife in hand, Margo straddled Zoya's writhing torso and knelt, pinning her to the stone. She raised the blade. Maddock caught movement in the corner of his eye. Syringe in hand, Halima stepped up and whispered, "It is time, my warrior."

She jammed the needle into his neck. A flash, like an electric arc coursed through his body. Freed from the subliminal compulsion, he leaped to the altar and tackled Margo, slamming her to the ground. She rolled with the impact and leaped up, knife in hand. Maddock circled and backed away, drawing her further from Zoya.

In a flurry of red hair and white coveralls, Corey sprang to Zoya's side. His purloined scalpel made short work of her bonds. Maddock didn't see much of what happened next. Margo stalked him, her face a rictus of hatred. Someone grabbed him from behind. He threw them off, only to have his arm twisted back and his legs kicked from beneath him.

On his knees, it took both of the Preacher's minions to hold him down. A hand in Maddock's hair wrenched his head up. Margo gazed down and grinned. "I alone will wield the Lyre of

God," she whispered. "Only those who follow *me* will be rewarded."

A flash of movement, the woman stumbled forward. A dark screaming fury of feet and fists clung to her back. Before Margo hit the ground, Zoya had climbed to her shoulders and torn the knife from her grip. The two caromed into Maddock where he knelt, knocking him back into his captors. He wrestled free and rolled to his feet in time to see Zoya plunge the bronze dagger into Margo's belly. She reached in and pulled out a bloody fist. Coils of intestine hung between her fingers.

The horrified crowd fell back as Margo shrieked and thrashed in agony. Zoya crouched at her side. Another swipe cut the bloody mass free. She spun about, waving the knife. Corey stood a few yards away, frozen in shock. Zoya growled and sprinted for the building. She took one look back, clenched the trailing wad of entrails in her teeth, and began climbing the sheer stone wall like a spider with its prey.

30

Maddock shook Corey from his trance. "Follow her."

The atrium erupted in chaos. Bones wrestled with Prester John while Twitch lit off after Corey and Zoya. Maddock scooped the bronze knife from the pavement and turned on Beardo. "Now where did we leave off?"

The big man dodged away, glancing desperately at the crowd. Maddock risked a quick scan. Bones had Prester John on the ground, a knee on his chest. The man had one hand on Bones's face trying to push him off. Maddock backed toward them, keeping an eye on Beardo. *If we can neutralize the Preacher, it'll be game over.* Movement, he looked again. Reznik stood, a pistol aimed at the struggling pair. "Call off your dog, Maddock, or I'll have to put him down."

Maddock grabbed his friend's shoulder and tugged. Bones rolled away, only to come back with a right hook to the Preacher's face. He drew back to swing again and glanced up. Reznik had the pistol centered on his forehead.

Bones shoved the Preacher down and squatted on the pavement, glaring at the man. "You gonna shoot, or what?"

Prester John stood and slammed a fist into Bones's face. He sprawled backward, then looked up. "Hey, what about turning the other cheek and all?"

Maddock put the knife down and helped his friend stand. Reznik held the gun on both of them. "Just give me a reason."

"Put that thing away," Maddock said. "It wouldn't look good if you shot Prester John's holy horsemen."

Reznik seemed to consider his options before tucking the pistol into his belt. Firm hands gripped Maddock's wrist and bent the arm behind his back. He didn't resist. Bones received the same treatment from two burqa-clad women. He turned to Maddock. "Next time you say we'll have ladies crawling all over us remind me to ignore you."

A circle had formed around Margo's convulsing body. Reznik and Beardo lifted Margo between them, still gasping in agony. Prester John stood aside as they laid her on the altar. Halima appeared as if from nowhere, carrying the medical kit. After a brief conversation, she emptied a large syringe into the woman's arm. Two others stepped up, unwound the hijabs from their heads, and gently wrapped Margo's gaping torso. Bones watched in stoic fascination. "What now?"

Maddock chanced a look at his captors. *Not much to read beneath all that fabric.* What he could see, didn't look happy. "It's not good. The Preacher will want to blame someone and we're all he's got."

"Did you recognize that blade? Freaking bronze knife from Lazar's emporium of death."

Maddock scanned the ground. "Our *own* freaking bronze knife. Bastard Lazar seems to be turning a fine profit." He craned his neck around. "I laid it here somewhere…wonder where the hell it went."

Bones lowered his voice. "What about the l, y, r, e…you know? I don't see it anywhere."

None of their minders reacted. Maddock wasn't sure if any of them spoke English but had to assume they did. "Haven't seen it since Zoya stole the show. Preacher got it maybe?"

"Nope. Beardo neither. Everything went crazy, you know…then poof, gone."

A series of gunshots echoed across the atrium. Maddock followed the sound. Out beyond the crowd, Twitch knelt, pistol in his good hand. On the wall, a dark shape worked its way toward the roof. Two more shots rang out as tiny dust clouds appeared against the white wall. Bones shook his head. "Burning bullets just to make noise."

Twitch quit firing when the figure reached a low parapet and wriggled over. The man stood and looked around. Maddock scanned the same area. *Where the bloody hell did Corey get to?* Twitch seemed to have the same question in mind. He trotted back across the stone courtyard. Bones eyed him a moment. "Crap, here comes trouble."

The man didn't slow as he approached. He slammed into

Maddock. "Where is he, the little guy? Don't play stupid either."

"Uh, pardon me a moment," Bones interrupted. "But before you go beat on my friend here, would you ask these nice ladies to loosen up on us a bit?"

Twitch spit on the pavement and turned back to Maddock. A moment later, he hit the ground. Two of the burqa-clad women had him twisted in knots while a third wiped the stones clean with his face. His pistol had spun away and fetched up against the altar. Prester John didn't seem to notice. He stood, hands clasped, and watched Margo in her agony.

Bones eyed the pistol and said, "Something's weird. Did you notice? Margo is wearing shoes." He glanced down. "So's our buddy, Twitch—that Beardo guy too."

"Also, Reznik and the others," Maddock said. "Halima had a name for them. Still, Zoya didn't wear shoes and she's like us, on the outs."

"Corey can sure pick 'em. Wonder where he went?"

Before he could answer, Maddock felt the grip on his arm tighten. Prester John had turned away from the altar. He took in Twitch, supine on the pavement, then directed his glare in their direction. Bones grunted and struggled a moment. "Our pal, Preach, looks like he's about to flip his lid."

Three strides brought him face to face. "Havoc and Strife, the Great Lord needed you." He looked each of them in the eye. "He needed you, yet you let your base instincts destroy any chance you ever had."

The Preacher raised his arms to the sky and roared, "Where is my Lamb of Sacrifice? Where is my Holy Instrument? *Treachery. Treachery* has stolen it all."

Twitch rose and tried to stand. Prester John threw him back to the pavement. "You…you, all of you are worse than useless. Where were *you* when your Lord needed help?"

The man knelt and bowed. "It happened too quickly Lord. We thought they were controlled."

"Stop groveling, you fool. Where is Halima?" The Preacher spun about, searching the crowd. "Halima! I need you now."

Like a ghostly djinn, summoned to its master, the woman

appeared from the crowd. "I am here." She trotted up and stood next to Maddock, slightly out of breath. "I give Margo all of the morphine. She passes over now."

"Margo?" Prester John glanced at the stricken figure sprawled across the altar. "My copilot, yes, very sad." His eyes wandered across the crowd of acolytes that stood in whispering groups around the atrium. "Rid me of these fools. Send them all back to their cells. There is nothing here for them anymore."

Halima bowed. "Yes, my Lord. Do you need something else?"

"Manacles," He grabbed her arm, "and quickly,"

The woman bowed once more and glided away. Prester John reached down and dragged Twitch to his feet. "Idiots, all of you. Reznik, get him out of here. Go find the girl—find me my lyre."

The Preacher turned to the women holding Maddock and Bones captive. "I want these *chandala* men chained to God's holy altar. Perhaps *then* He will arise and show them his wrath."

Bones watched the Preacher's departing form. "It could have gone worse."

"You've forgotten the manacles."

Bones smiled at the four women surrounding them. "Maybe someone will get us a drink of water while we wait?" He held his smile and looked from cowled face to cowled face. "This is confusing. I can't tell if you're all mad at me or what."

One of the figures shifted slightly. Bones gasped and rose to his toes. "Okay, okay. I get the picture."

"You're not getting a drink, buddy."

Bones continued to gasp and dance for another minute before they let him relax. Maddock tested the hold his own captor maintained. She'd locked an elbow behind his arm and bent his hand up behind his back. Even a slight change of posture put excruciating pressure on his wrist. *No use picking a fight I'm not going to win.* He relaxed his stance and concentrated on finding another angle.

Makuria's Tower of the New Dawn cast a long shadow

across the atrium. It had moved several degrees before Maddock felt his captors' grip loosen once more. Halima had returned, followed by two large men in coveralls. She spoke a few words and nodded toward the altar. Maddock found himself frog-marched alongside Bones to Margo's sprawling corpse. Just below her flaccid hand, a corroded metal ring protruded from the black stone.

Forced to his knees, an iron shackle encircled Maddock's wrist. Chain rattled through the ring. He heard Bones curse and twisted his head in that direction. His friend struggled with one of the mechanics. Maddock yanked the chain free of the loop and swung it against the back of the man's neck. A flurry of muslin cloth and a kick to Maddock's chin. His head slammed into the altar and the world went gray.

He came to with his face pressed against the smooth black stone. Margo's lifeless hand hung above his ear. He tried to move away but felt a sharp tug on his wrist. Bones grunted out, "Stop wiggling around, dammit. You're only making it worse."

Maddock rolled his head toward the voice. Bones lay in the same position, belly to the ground, arm above his head, and face pressed against the stone. A short chain and a pair of manacles joined their wrists through the iron lifting ring. He caught a glimpse of yellow and orange passing behind his shoulder. Halima knelt between them. "If you behaved, we would secure you facing the other way."

His jaw burning, Maddock pushed himself up with his free hand. "We are Havoc and Strife, remember? Did you really expect us to behave?"

"No, I would be disappointed.

Bones inched himself up. "All my friends call me Bones." Maddock saw him put on his best smile. "If we promise to behave, you could like, turn us around."

"Forget it Bones. She's not gonna do that. Not with the Eye of God watching us."

"I would not anyway. You amuse me this way. Besides, it may motivate Mr. Maddock to use his *ruah*."

Halima smiled at the two of them and glided off on an

errand of her own. Bones watched her go. "That woman does have an enticing sway about her. No wonder you're so entranced."

"I am not entranced."

"You are. I can see it in your eyes, buddy. The eyes don't lie."

"Okay, maybe I am a little intrigued."

Bones tilted his head back and crooned, "When the moon's in the sky like a big piece 'a pie…"

"It's 'hits your eye like a big pizza pie'." Maddock yanked on the chain. "Now, shut up and let me think."

Bones inspected the manacle on his wrist. "You wearing a hairpin or something?"

"White coveralls, just like you. That's it."

"Brother commandos, we are. Maybe there's some wire or something on the ground."

"There isn't. Already checked."

"Crap." Bones took another look at the manacle. "These need a pretty fancy key anyway. So, what did your sweetie say about that *roof* thing?"

"It's *roo*…I think. She's not my sweetie."

"She's telling you something, buddy."

"It's just some mystic crystal bullcrap. The breath of God…who knows."

"Well, your breath is starting to smell like the ass end of a forty-year-old school bus. So, if we don't do something, we're just gonna dry out and shrivel up here."

"Yeah, good thing is, we don't have to pee."

"Or crap…I haven't eaten or drank in so long I've forgotten how to use a toilet."

Maddock relaxed, his arm in the air, his face against the stone. "Looks like we're stuck here for a while. What do you think Corey is doing?"

"Looking for a key, I hope."

"We're a trap, set for him." Maddock thought a moment. "And Zoya, she can't stay away."

"All undressed and no place to go?"

"Yeah, that's weird, isn't it? Comfy though, in this heat maybe."

"I don't think that was the idea. Preach said she was the lamb."

"Sheep gut is the traditional instrument string material. But human sacrifice?" Despite the heat, Maddock shivered a moment, remembering the feral look on the young woman's face. "Zoya didn't handle that very well."

"Yeah, what was that all about…Zoya bonded to the lyre body? I thought it was the Preacher bonded to it."

"Nope. He as much as said so. I've wondered why she was here, why she stayed with us. The Preach knew who she was from the beginning. He wanted us here so she would follow."

"That's what drove Zoya crazy," Bones said. "I'm hurting about that piece of crap—whatever—they ripped from me. I can't imagine how she feels. You figure she's making her own lyre strings? From like, Margo's nasty innards?"

Maddock thought about that for a moment. "It's hot enough and dry enough. She could, maybe stretch them out on the roof somewhere." He paused. "Oh crap! I know where she went."

31

Maddock watched the shadows creep across the atrium floor. His head pounded, more from the heat and dehydration than from the blow he'd taken earlier that day. Blessed night would fall eventually. *The Eye of God sees all, but it sucks at infrared.*

Bones stirred. He rattled the chain and growled. "Still haven't figured out that *roof* thing, huh?"

"It's *ruah*, and no, I told you it's meaningless. Now, quiet down for a minute."

Bones shifted around. The chain tugged Maddock's wrist and rattled against the iron ring. "I don't get it—the Preacher's minions seem to have their own agenda. Think he brought them here to sort it out?"

"I thought so at first," Maddock said. "Now I'm not really sure."

Bones slumped back. "Well crap, I'm confused. I think you need to do that *roo* thing, whatever it is. Your girlfriend was trying to help us out here."

"She's not my girlfriend."

"Then do it for the great Lord Prester John."

"Okay, but you need to hold still for a while. This takes some concentration."

Bones grumbled and curled up next to the altar. Maddock relaxed as much as anyone could, chained to a stone block. He closed his eyes. Halima had said it was a breath, a tangible breath of God. Maddock wondered for a moment which *god* she meant. He tried to concentrate on his senses, his breathing. *Ten, nine eight... No crosses, no icons, which* god *then?* The thought came thundering back. His eyes flew open. "We've got this all wrong, Bones."

His friend grunted and yanked on the chain. "Screw you, Maddock. I thought you were getting us out of here."

"Listen. We've looked at this Prester John guy as your standard evangelical Christian missionary, maybe a little more whacked out than most. But he isn't praying to the same God my Aunt Hazel prays to. He's calling himself *Lord*. He's got a machine in his basement that's running this operation…and the thing is lying about it to boot. Hell, the damned machine was giving *us* instructions until Halima did something."

"She spritzed us with some reality juice is what she did. I just hope it doesn't wear off."

"Maybe with the lyre gone, it's not as effective." Maddock settled back. "I don't know what Halima was trying to tell me. Last time she mentioned that *roo* thing, the answer was right in front of my face. I'll try again." He relaxed—counted backward from one hundred. The chain jerked and Maddock opened his eyes.

"You bastard," Bones said. "You were snoring."

Above, the evening had immersed the entire atrium in shadows. Maddock looked around. "How long?"

"Couple of hours. The drink cart came by, but I told them not to disturb you."

"Yeah, in *my* dreams too." He'd dreamed something about Halima as well. *What the hell was it?* Once more, Maddock stilled his breathing, emptied his mind. He tried to stay in the moment, ignore distractions. *Something…Halima had tried to tell me something.* He waited. The growing scent of blood, decomposition, and decay wafted down from Margo's stiffening corpse. He looked up at the rigid hand, clasped in final agony. It hovered over his head like some malignant spirit. *Freaking impossible—Halima must have meant something else.* He leaned on one elbow. "Give me some slack."

"I've been cutting you a butt-load of slack this whole stupid…"

"No, the chain! Feed a little more through."

Bones sighed and raised his manacled hand up to the iron ring. "You start snoring again, I'll bust your head."

Up against the stone, one knee on the ground, Maddock reached up and touched the cool fingers. Stiff, he pried them open. Something dropped on his face and fell to the shadows beneath his chest. Maddock scrabbled about the rocks and came up with a small metal key. "Bingo."

"What do you mean, *bingo*?"

He lowered his voice. "I mean, we're out of here as soon as it gets a little darker." Maddock unlocked them both but convinced Bones to stay put. "The damned thing watches us, but its night vision sucks."

Bones grumbled and rolled over. "Just glad to get my butt under me where it belongs. Do you think it's watching Corey?"

"Likely. But it's a game and Corey knows it. He's played it before. I'm hoping he knows the moves."

Bones squirmed impatiently. "I can't just do nothing. We've got to find the Preach and beat the crap out of him."

Maddock shook his head. "He's watching. Sitting in his Eye of God and watching the feed. I just wonder if this Apocalypse Game is giving him the straight poop."

"Which means he knows where Corey is."

"Maybe, maybe not. The machine lies—makes stuff up—doctors the feed." Maddock sat up straight. "It's treating Prester John like another player, pitting him against us, or Corey, or any of the others. That's why there are so many little cabals and conspiracy groups. They're all being manipulated by this machine."

"Nice theory, bro, but I'm not buying it. Who benefits?"

Maddock leaned back. "Yeah, I wish I knew. For now, we've got to reconnect with Corey, form a team again, find the lyre. It's a game we've got to play."

"And Spider Lady?"

Lips pursed, Maddock pictured his last image of Zoya, feral, bathed in Margo's gore, a nightmare creature. "Yeah, the girl too. No one left behind."

"Then I'm ready to move out."

Shadows enveloped most of the atrium. Maddock looked up at the purple sky and picked out silvery Venus following the sun into the west. "Now's good. The warm pavement should mask our heat signature for a while yet."

Bones glanced over his shoulder. "Which way then?"

Maddock took in the darkened atrium. "We came in the

west gate. I've been through the east and the south earlier today." He checked for movement and saw none. "Corey went south. We go north."

Ducking low, they ran for the shadows of the north wall. Maddock sidled along the rough stone until he reached a dark archway. Bones peered past him. "Tabernacle of Light, huh? You'd think they might have spared a little for us."

"Be glad they didn't." Maddock slipped through the opening and padded toward a blue glow that marked the passage entrance. He moved slowly, stopping every few steps.

A dozen yards in, Bones ran into his back. "What the hell, man? Let's go."

"Hold up. It's here—I can feel it."

"Nothing's here. Let's split before they know we're gone."

"Just shut up a minute and hold still." Maddock paused. "There, you feel that draft?" He moved to the wall and felt his way along the stones. Nothing.

Bones began to fidget. "You're going whacko, boss."

"No, it's got to be here. My staff, my piece of the lyre, I feel it nearby."

"I think that last crack on the head knocked something loose. There's nothing around except a butt-load of dark."

"Okay, smartass. Stand right here and think about that thing, that ugly stick you smacked the guards with back at the Hagia Irene."

Bones shuffled up and stood next to Maddock. "Okay, I don't…" He paused a moment. "Yeah, I feel air or something."

"That's the *roo* Halima was talking about. Just concentrate—I know you can do it."

"Screw you, Maddock."

"Do you feel anything?"

"Besides punching your…Wait, kind of…something. It's above us somewhere."

"The south entrance had a hidden doorway. There must be one here, too."

"Trap door the ceiling maybe?"

Maddock thought about that for a moment. "If there is,

there's got to be a ladder. Check to the right. I'll go left."

He heard Bones's bare feet pad away. Hands outstretched, Maddock shuffled the other direction. He touched the wall, feeling the smooth-cut stone laid in regular rows. Running his hand high, low, he felt nothing but…*wait, what was that?* Maddock reached up again. *There, a missing stone.* He felt lower, *another.* "Bones," he hissed, "over here."

"Well, make up your mind…"

"Stop crying. I found a way." Maddock put a hand in one of the empty cavities. He raised a foot until his toe felt another. "Come on follow me."

About twelve feet up, the wall began to arch over, but the handholds climbed straight and true, disappearing through a hole in the overhead. A few feet farther and Maddock reached a floor set above the passageway. He climbed up and scrambled out of the way as Bones followed. "Great, like it wasn't dark enough down below."

As he spoke, lights flickered on. Maddock froze. "Crap, now it knows we're here."

They stood in an empty chamber, surrounded by doors. Bones spun around. "Okay Monty, I'll take door number three." He pressed an ear to the nearest panel. "Don't hear anything. Does it matter? I mean the computer…what's it gonna do?"

In sequence, all the doors clicked and stood slightly open. Bones jumped back. Maddock crouched, waiting. Nothing else happened. "It's going to mess with us. That's what."

Eight doors, eight different directions. Maddock tried to orient himself. Straight ahead, would be north, the airfield where they arrived, and downriver, Cairo. Left would be back toward the west entrance, the way they'd come in. His staff, he could feel them somewhere in that direction. Bones reached for the nearest door and pulled it open. At once, the other seven clicked shut. Maddock heard the rattle of locks slamming home. "Let's hope you chose wisely."

"It's here, I can feel it." Bones glanced at the adjoining doors. "Or maybe that one on the right."

"Great, you get to go first."

Bones peered inside. "Hallway, I knew it. Come on."

The two of them shouldered their way through. A split second later, the door slammed shut. The lock clicked. Bones glanced back and raised an eyebrow. "That sounded final."

"Just go—but be careful."

He ignored the snarky reply and followed his friend down the shadowy hall. It ended in another featureless door. Bones ran his hands over the steel panel and cursed. "You don't happen to have that *roo* thing handy again, do you?"

Maddock checked the blank surface. He felt along the doorframe and adjacent walls. Nothing. "It's a game. We've got to look for clues."

"Screw the clues." Bones slammed his fists against the unyielding surface and yelled, "Open up, dammit."

A shout from the other side, scrabbling sounds, and the door swung wide. "You!"

32

"June?" Maddock stepped into the next chamber. "What in bloody hell are you doing here?"

"You know, big fella, I was wondering that myself." She eyed Bones as he pushed in behind Maddock. "I see you brought backup. I hope you're both armed."

Bones grinned. "Only dangerous, Ms. Junie Moon, only dangerous."

"Seriously," Maddock said, "how did you get here?"

"Reznik, that bastard. Him and Margo, they got the drop on me. I'm blindfolded, run up and down stairs and crap, then dumped in here." She looked around. "You wouldn't happen to have a bunch of keys or something?"

Thumb over his shoulder, Bones said, "You opened the door. Can't you just let yourself out?"

"Right now, is the first time that dam' thing would open. So, what do I get? You two galoots. Can we escape the same way you got in?"

Maddock shook his head. "A machine operates these doors. It thinks we're playing a game."

"It *thinks*? And I figured it was the Preach who was all hoot-owls."

"We've got a whole barn full running around and I think the machine may be the sanest of the lot." Maddock went on to recap their journey since bailing out of June's C-130.

"The three of you are all whacked out about this musical instrument," June said, "and Reznik is playing Judas. What about Margo?"

Bones grimaced. "You don't want to know."

Maddock prowled June's cell. A cot, a few empty water bottles, two other doors, he tried them both—locked. He felt for his wand. It seemed farther away now, a different direction. *Crap, stupid Bones took us the wrong way.* He glanced over at June and felt a moment of guilt. *Okay, maybe not totally wrong.*

Bones had given up explaining and started sniffing around

the room himself. He grabbed the door nearest to Maddock and yanked on the handle, yelling, "It's here, I know it's right here someplace."

"No, you took us completely the wrong direction." Maddock pointed off to his left. "Our gear is way over there."

"It's here I tell you." Bones kicked the door. "Dammit. *Open.*"

With a soft click, the door swung toward them. A wooden bar studded with knobs fell to the floor at Bones's feet. He stared at it a moment. "Shazam! That's it, my stick." Cradling it in his hands, he looked it up and down. "Just leaning against that door, waiting for me."

Maddock grabbed the door and swung it all the way open. "Where the hell is the rest of it?"

June looked back and forth between the two of them. "When you said hoot-owls, I thought you meant present company excluded. Now I'm not so sure."

"I'm fine," Bones said, "he's the one that's losing it."

Maddock set his jaw. *He got his way, but I'm not going to let Bones goad me into something I'll regret.* Still, it irked him. *I found my staff first, and now it's gone, but Bones, he just kicks the door...* He took a deep breath and swallowed his ire. "Well, we better find the rest of the parts. "No more opening doors at random, Bones."

"*Jawohl, herr kommandant.*"

"And no more smartass, either. I'm sick of it."

June stepped between them. "Boys, boys, what am I missing here?"

"You're missing a lot..." Maddock stopped himself. *This is June. The same June who pulled our chestnuts out of the fire more than once.* "It's that lyre, the lyre, whatever the hell it is, it can make a guy crazy."

"We've each connected with a part of the lyre," Bones said. He held out the stick. "This is the crossbar. It's got some kind of juju—helps you do stuff. After a while, it sort of owns you."

"Like oxy."

Maddock nodded. "Exactly like oxy. That stick that Corey was carrying, I've got one too…somewhere. I can feel it, like the sun, shining through clouds."

June thought for a moment. "Then Corey can feel it as well. He will be headed to the same place."

"Maybe not," Maddock said. "Someone dismantled the thing. It could be scattered all over the building."

Bones clutched the wooden bar to his chest. "Oh, and what about Zoya?"

"The girl?" June said. "Petite, dark complexion? I think I saw her loitering around the tarmac in Thessaloniki. She's not here, is she?"

For once Maddock grinned. "Chances are, she rode here in your cargo bay."

June shook her head. "I knew it, I knew it. There was this little dude with the ground crew, flitted around, then disappeared. Reznik wouldn't listen, but I knew he…or she, was up to something."

"Preacher wanted her here," Maddock said. "He had plans…they worked out differently."

"So, what's the little sneak doing now?"

Bones said, "That's another thing you don't really want to know."

"But I do, I need to know everything."

"She's stretching Margo's guts across the roof somewhere. We think she's trying to make strings for the lyre."

In the wan overhead light, June turned several shades paler. She shivered and said, "Okay, so you warned me—too much information—I don't want any part of this. Let's just figure a way out of here."

Bones held up his wooden bar. "I believe I may have found the keys Ms. June was asking about. Which way shall we try?"

Maddock looked past the door Bones's kick had opened. "This seems like some kind of storeroom." He dragged a box of toilet paper from beneath a shelf and propped it in the doorway. "Should hold while I check it out."

The room had another door. It opened slightly at

Maddock's push. Hushed feminine voices whispered through the darkness beyond. Soft laughter, banter in an unknown language. He pulled the door shut and backed out. "Women's dorm. And no, Bones, you won't sweet-talk your way through that lot."

Bones didn't reply, but turned his attention to a second door, further to his left. He tried it—locked. Extending the crossbar, he touched it to the door and said, "Open."

With a soft click, it swung toward him. Maddock pulled it open and stepped out. A pale blue light flicked on, illuminating a steel landing. Circular stairs disappeared into the darkness below. He looked up. They spiraled past his head and faded into the soft, blue haze that filled the chamber. June eyed the stairs. "Yeah, figure that's the way they dragged me up here." She paused, turning between Bones and Maddock. "I'm not much for climbing you know."

Bones smirked. "Want me to carry you?"

"In your dreams, Superman. But I'm packing too much kryptonite in my butt for that to work."

"Not a problem," Maddock said. "We'll climb slow, but we've got to go up another level."

"Anything to get out of this place."

Maddock started up the steps. *One at a time, up, up, up.* His staff was at least one level above and off to the left. The rib, the leg, they all reminded him of earlier insult. He took another step, then another. Maddock reached the next platform and faced another featureless door. Bones joined him. "Shall we?"

"No, give June a break before we go in."

The person in question arrived, puffing at the exertion. "I'm just not built to keep up with you boys."

Bones put a hand on her shoulder. "Not a problem, Junie Moon. Take five before we go inside."

June looked down, then up. "Breadcrumbs. Someone is leaving you guys breadcrumbs. Are you sure you want to follow?"

Maddock grinned. "Yeah, and I think I know who. Ready?"

June hitched her pants up. "I'll guard the landing while you two go stomp the spiders."

A touch of the wooden bar, a brief word, the latch clicked, and the door swung inward. Maddock expected to see an office like Prester John's, instead the door opened on a small infirmary. Lights glowed along the baseboard. Otherwise, the space seemed deserted. Bones followed him in. Two alcoves on either wall held examination tables—Maddock couldn't see much. A faint rustle froze him where he stood. A shadow flicked from the corner and sprinted for the door.

Maddock heard June cursing followed by a brief scuffle. He dashed to the platform to find her sitting on Corey's back. "Little bugger thought to get away." She looked a second time and gasped. "It's your buddy. I'm so sorry."

"Just let me up, already. What are you guys doing here?" Corey got to his feet and brushed himself off.

Bones shrugged at Maddock and said, "We're looking for his, uh, stick…you know, the big one."

Maddock glanced back at the room. "How did you even get in there?"

"I've spent the last four hours replaying this level until I could convince the stupid game to open the door. How did *you* get in?"

Bones waved his wooden bar in the air. "I've got admin access."

"No crap? So the lyre is here?" Corey said.

"I think parts of it are…my staff for certain." Maddock looked around. "I just haven't found it yet."

Behind him, the door swung shut. It slammed into June's foot. Maddock caught it and wrenched it open again. "Nice save."

June replied with a creative string of curses and leaned on Bones's arm. "I knew I should have just stayed put and let you idiots take all the grief."

Corey slipped back through. Maddock followed. Bones said, "Thanks for holding the door, Ms. June—we'll only be a minute," and ducked through after them.

Shelves filled with medical supplies lined the walls.

Maddock began poking through boxes of gloves and linens. *It's here, right here. I'm just too damn close.* Across the room, Corey ransacked a row of cabinets, muttering to himself. Bones stood in the middle of the room, his arms crossed. "You guys recognize any of this stuff?"

Maddock straightened. "Why should we? There's nothing here we've seen…" He followed Bones's gaze. Eye-level, just inside the door, a portable med-kit hung on a brass hook. *Halima, of course.* Maddock wrenched it open and pulled out two polished horn staffs.

Bones rummaged through the pack and shook his head. "We're still missing a vital piece. What do you figure?"

"Halima must have scooped the lyre. Your crossbar drew us to June. The staff's connected us with Corey. I'll bet she hid the lyre body too."

"Zoya's got it," Corey said. "If it's out there, she'll have…"

He was interrupted by a scuffle out on the landing. June yelped and backed through the door. She was followed by a tall, disheveled woman smeared in blood. Maddock jumped back. "Halima, what the hell?"

"She wants the other parts."

A small figure stood in the doorway brandishing Prester John's bronze knife. She hissed and shoved into the room. Halima shook the hair from her eyes. "She comes to me for the lyre body. I think I have her, and then no."

Corey inched forward. "Zoya, no. Put the knife down. We're friends."

Like a desert cobra, she struck. Corey leaped back as the knife sliced through his coveralls. Maddock pulled Halima aside and grabbed Zoya's hand. Spinning, kicking, she danced up the wall and connected with Maddock's face. She broke free of his grip. In an instant, she had Corey's arm behind his back and her knife at his throat. "I…I think we should give her what she wants," he croaked.

June had glued herself against the back wall. Maddock glanced at Bones. The look on his friend's face was not reassuring. "No sudden moves, guys." He returned his attention to Zoya. "Join us. We can help you reassemble the lyre."

The knife pressed harder against Corey's throat and a thin stream of blood trickled into his collar. He gasped and dropped his staff. "Here, here, take it."

Zoya never broke eye contact with Maddock. "Give," she said. "Give now or die."

Bones pointed his crossbar at Zoya and snarled, "*Drop it!*"

Zoya let go of the knife. Slamming Corey to the floor, she sprang at Bones. He batted her aside, but not before she'd grabbed one end of the crossbar. She twisted like a gigged eel, wrenching the bar from his hand.

Corey grabbed for his staff. Zoya dove under Bones's return swing and collided with Corey on the floor. They struggled for a moment, then Zoya sprang to her feet, leaped up on an examination table, and pointed both lyre parts at Maddock. Her voice dropped an octave and lost its hoarse, animal growl. "By the Lyre of David and the Stone of Abraham, I command you…" She bared her teeth and chuckled. "You will now give me what is mine."

Maddock bent his will to holding fast against the power of her words. He concentrated on the staff, extending it as a shield. A frozen eternity passed. Then slowly, one foot behind the other, he inched away from the hypnotic voice. Zoya wavered. For a moment, she seemed to lose concentration. Then, gritting her teeth, she refocused on Halima. "I steal your breath, your holy *ruah*."

Halima clutched her chest and heaved. Her face reddened, and she collapsed to the floor. Maddock sprang forward and made a grab at Zoya's legs. Laughing, she danced away. "The woman dies in your place."

Maddock risked a glance at Halima. She trembled with convulsions. Her back contorted into a bone-breaking curve. Her eyes bulged, yet she made no sound. Maddock turned back. "No. You don't have to do this, Zoya. Make it stop."

"Give me what is mine."

Maddock shoved the staff across the examination table. "Take it. Now let her go."

She hopped off the table and stepped to the entrance. "I think not."

She glided through as the door whisked shut. Maddock dropped to Halima's side and held her off the floor. "She's seizing! Check the shelves, someone."

"Got Diazepam spray," Corey yelled back. "*Incoming.*"

Maddock snagged the flying package as it sailed across the room, tore it open, and administered a dose in each nostril. Bones knelt next to them and listened to Halima's chest. "She's not breathing…"

The woman's contortions seemed to relax—her shuddering tremors subsided. June huddled next to Bones and took his arm. "Is she dying?"

"Not on my watch," Maddock said. He held Halima's face to his own and began rescue breathing.

Bones checked her pulse. "Still got a heartbeat."

Minutes passed, perhaps half an hour. Maddock couldn't tell. Bones offered to spell him, but Maddock shook his head. The ache in his knees, in his back, he knew it was nothing compared to the pain he would feel if they lost her.

Another dark eternity. Maddock breathed in, exhaled gently into Halima's mouth, then paused. A thousand repetitions before he lost count, lost track of time…before she twitched and gasped. Like a distance runner crossing the finish, Halima took great gulps of air and opened her eyes. "I live."

33

Corey stared at the door. "That wasn't Zoya."

"I don't know what it was," Bones said, "but it sounded like something from *The Exorcist*."

Halima pushed herself upright. "It is God's wife, Ashera, who lives in the lyre."

"God has a *wife?*" Bones slapped Corey on the back. "You've been messing around with the wrong woman dude…I'm impressed!"

Maddock helped Halima stand. "I've studied a lot of ancient lore, but I've never heard that God had a wife."

"It is old, before King David, perhaps before even Moses. Many conflicts in those stories—you must have noticed, yes?"

"But in all the stories Yahweh acted alone."

Halima put on a face "It is not your Yahweh that lives in this place. It is *Baal* that we worship."

Corey turned and glared at Halima. "I've played this level…I mean, online. It's tricky and the final boss, it's this god-monster thing named Baal, almost impossible to beat. Are you telling us that your Preacher worships this character from a *video game?*"

Halima grabbed Maddock's arm for support. "He has seen it. I have seen it. Baal rules Makuria as it must soon rule our world."

June signaled time out with her hands. "You're losing me, boys. This game, this machine—you say it's running the place— what else is it about to do?"

"I don't want to stay and find out," Maddock said. "You've played this level, Corey. How do we get out of here?"

"This building…it's like a giant maze. You must run it in the right order."

"Then lead on, wizard."

A trapdoor beneath the examination table led to the level below. Corey showed them a narrow passage that opened into a dark compartment. "Quiet everyone." He cracked open a door. "There are others in here."

Halima hissed and drew back. "The acolytes, they will tear you to shreds."

"I know, but it's the only way."

"Then maybe I can help you."

Halima pushed past them and slipped through. A sliver of light from the next room illuminated shelves of bedding and towels. Maddock glanced past the door. Halima stood talking with several other women. A laugh, a few nods, and they wandered off in the other direction. She waved. Maddock padded across the room. "What's the fastest way out of here?"

"Come." She led them to the back. "Wait while I get something."

Maddock fidgeted as Bones and the others huddled around. June followed. "Do you trust her?"

He nodded. "I think she was trying to bring Zoya in with that lyre body. It might have worked with anyone else."

"Yeah, and here we are, back to square one," Bones said. "I want to go have it out with Preach and blow this cow-town."

June nodded. "Works for me. I'll go get my forty-four and start putting holes where folks don't want them."

Halima glided into their midst. "Does that mean you have a plan?"

"Bones has one we can try." Maddock nodded at his friend. "Let's get out of here and I'll explain."

Halima grabbed Corey's elbow. "First, I bring you something."

She handed him a large bundle of straps. "My pack!" Corey slipped it over his shoulders. "Where?"

"I removed it…" she hung her head, "I know it is wrong to do, but this is yours, not his. So, I keep it here for you."

Maddock led them through a door that Halima had opened. Corey dug his phone from the side pocket of his pack and handed it to Maddock. "No reception here, but it makes a good flashlight."

The light from Corey's phone illuminated a steep set of descending stairs. "Where does this take us?"

Halima started down. "There is a hidden door to the atrium. You risk being seen if you pass through."

"That's what I'm hoping." Maddock forced a weary grin. "We've run long enough, waited long enough. It's time we turn and fight."

Without another word, he started down. Maddock thought on Halima's words, her *roo*…whatever that was. *I'm going to need a weapon*—he thought again—*that, and a whole lot of luck.* His bare feet made a dull thump with every step. In the darkness, June's shoes clattering above let him know the others followed. Before they reached the bottom. Maddock killed the light. "The machine knows we're down here, but it can't see worth crap in the dark."

They completed the descent, testing every step as they went down. Maddock reached the bottom and looked out through a narrow slot at the broad starlit atrium. He told the others to wait and slipped through. Warm paving stones beneath his feet, silent gray walls, the black stone altar loomed—a hole in the night—nothing moved.

Halima followed. "Be careful. The chandalan mass for attack—they come any time. Our acolytes patrol." She smiled at him. "As you know, they are not gentle."

Maddock smiled back and slid inside. "We need a diversion. Bones, circle the perimeter, be obvious, be seen, then disappear."

"Yeah, sounds like a great plan—for you."

Corey said, "I could do that. I know this place better than you guys."

"No, I'm counting on you to go catch your pet tarantula," Maddock clapped him on the shoulder. "I'll bet you know where she went."

"Yeah, Dragon Song Tower, that's her favorite hangout in the game. I've been up there before, online at least."

Bones snorted. "And she'll filet you like a mackerel with that big bloody knife of hers."

"I don't think so. I might have bagged it while you were all fighting." Polished bronze glinted in the starlight. Like the conjurer that he was, Corey revealed the ancient dagger. "We lost our wands, but I ripped us a legendary weapon."

Maddock said, "Well played. I will need a legendary weapon for what's coming."

With obvious reluctance, Corey handed him the dagger. "

Slender, unadorned, it balanced well in his hand. Maddock held the blade in the wan starlight. "This is exactly what I need."

Halima stepped back inside and glanced at the knife. "I do not hear a plan."

"You gave me the idea. The seventh path—it is the altar, the path of your god. I want to confront him and the Preacher. They have lied to you, both of them. It's time for a change."

"And you think to use that little knife when the others have guns?"

"If this is truly the Blade of Abraham, it will be enough."

June peered out at the atrium. "Well, I've had my fill of bloody knives and hoot-owls tonight. So, if y'all don't mind, I think I'll just wander back to my plane and polish the hubcaps or something."

Maddock grinned. "You do that. Gas her up for us too…you can put it on my tab."

Bones added, "Grab us some grub and water while you're at it. I think Brother Maddock may be considering a quick exit."

Corey spread his hands. "Yeah, cool, but what about—you know—Zoya with our wands and all?"

"Now more than ever," Maddock said, "we need our *Doctor Denarius* to come through. Whatever is driving her, whatever she needs, tell her that we can work it out, but we must get out of here first."

"I'm all for that," June said. "When's Chief Big Hunk going go cavorting around the arena? 'Cause I wanna be slipping out the back, Jack, while they all got their eyes on him."

"June, get that bird ready to fly. Take the north portal, go past the garages, your landing strip is about a quarter mile away." Maddock thought for a moment. "Halima I'd like you to go with Corey. The two of you get Zoya down here. We need the lyre as well. Get her to the plane any way you can…I don't care how. Bones, you'll be the distraction, but I'll be the target. Cover my six as soon as the crowd shows up."

Maddock checked outside once more. The night sky had lightened with the first pink tendrils of dawn. He turned to the others, "Go, go, go!"

Bones sprinted for the north wall, arms waving, legs pumping. June peeked out, shook her head, and crept after him, hugging the dark perimeter. Corey left next, with Halima a silent shadow in his wake. Maddock watched her receding figure, filled with regal grace. *Solomon didn't stand a chance.*

He waited for his friends to disappear before stepping into the open. *Now for it.* Across the open atrium, Bones cavorted along the east wall. Nothing else moved. No armies of acolytes, no mob of chandalan, no sign of Beardo and Twitch.

The bronze knife tucked in his belt, Maddock strode toward the black rectangle. It waited, a patient shadow. He glanced at Bones, just turning west along the south wall. Margo's supine corpse hung across the altar top. Maddock circled, looking for others. The empty atrium echoed with Bones's footfalls. Eyes, he felt them watching from the dark corners and unseen doorways. Shrugging off his unease, Maddock inspected the stone. *The key to the seventh way, but how?*

He panned Corey's phone along the sides, looking for symbols, for clues, **anything dammit**. The smooth, mottled surface had been polished once, but if it had ever borne markings, they had long since vanished beneath the hand of time. Maddock knelt at the altar's foot. Eyes closed, he silenced his fear of the encircling army. *Bones better be headed north by now.* Suppressing even that thought, Maddock opened his mind to Halima's *ruah*, the sacred breath. And it came.

Clear sweet chords echoed from the walls. Harmony and melody danced in counterpoint, filling the air with music of the gods. The rising sun glowed above the parapets and painted the Tower of New Dawn in gold. Maddock watched the silent shadows flee, replaced by a tall figure striding toward him—the

Preacher. He fingered the bronze blade and waited.

Shadows flickered around him. Maddock turned to the altar in time to see Margo's bloody corpse lurch upright and stand. Growing like a plume of gray smoke, she spread her arms and laughed. Prester John halted mid-stride and gazed up at her. "Ashera, my goddess, you have come to me at last."

Margo's form, swathed in smoke and flame, turned its eyes on him. "I know you Lord of the desert. *Baal*, you were called. Mighty kings once trembled at your name. I call on you again to rise. Come, and we will build an empire for our children."

As the sacred lyre sang from above, smoke and flames wreathed Prester John's robed figure. Growing, rising above the stone floor, he drew an enormous glittering sword. "I have come, my Ashera. We will cleanse this land and return the old gods to their rightful place."

"Then let the Apocalypse begin here—and spread throughout the nations."

Prester John raised his sword and shouted to the sky, "Let it begin now!"

From shadowy corners and hidden portals, a throng of milling figures crept into the light. White-robed acolytes massed at the east while a *chandalan* mob poured in through the west portal. Cries of rage, of raw hatred echoed across the atrium and gunfire erupted as the two sides clashed. For all the pandemonium, none dared approach the altar.

Beardo burst into view, wielding a pistol and firing at random into the charging acolytes. He swung toward Maddock and squeezed the trigger. At that moment, Bones sprang from the shadows and tackled him to the ground. The bullet whined off the black stone and smacked into something behind Maddock. A roar of anger shook the Tabernacle to its foundation.

A being of fire and smoke advanced on Maddock. No longer the Preacher, this was Baal incarnate. Maddock drew his bronze blade and held it before him. "We still control the lyre. You are powerless without every one of us."

From the altar, Ashera gazed down and laughed. "Shall I

crush this tiny worm for you, my Lord?"

"No, he is mine." The figure turned a withering gaze on Maddock. "David's sacred instrument has done its part. You are now meaningless and your tiny weapons but toys."

Maddock ducked as the gleaming blade passed over his head. Gouts of fire sprang from the stone floor where it struck.

A return slash, Maddock leaned into it with everything he had. The ancient blade sang as it passed through Baal's flaming robes, but the figure only snarled and swung again. A frantic dive put Maddock behind the altar. Baal's sword smashed down on the hard basalt, shearing off the near corner. "Stand and face me now, Havoc—or I shall let Ashera draw the soul from your worthless body."

In desperation, Maddock leaped to the altar's surface. "She stands on the stone of sacrifice, and I hold the sword of Abraham."

With that, he thrust the blade as high as he could into Ashera's body. The music from above fell into a dissonant cacophony of shrieks and wails. The goddess reached for him, stretching down, down—she almost touched him before collapsing back into Margo's bloody corpse. A moment of near silence passed before Prester John howled in rage. No longer wearing the form of Baal, he still wielded his glittering steel sword. Advancing on the altar, he raised it before him. "You will not live to see the dawn."

"Back off Preacher." Bones held Beardo's pistol. Its former owner lay facedown on the stone pavement.

Maddock heard footsteps behind him and spun. A familiar figure approached, brandishing a submachine pistol. "Put the gun down, Mr. Bonebrake, nice and easy."

Prester John glanced away from Bones. "Reznik, thank the Lord. Have you found the lyre?"

"Easy Preacher man. You and Mr. Maddock still have some business to attend." He grinned. "I want to see you fight."

Prester John took a few steps closer. "Child, that is not how you should speak to me."

"I'll speak any way I want, old man. Who do you think

programs your equipment? Who looks after your little Dragon Apocalypse game? Your Russian stooges were just stupid, and poor Margo, she could never accept the truth…now look at her." Reznik glanced around the atrium. "And the rest of your fools? It looks like my chandalan host is keeping them busy."

Twitch pushed his way through the fighting crowd and retrieved the pistol Bones had dropped. "Preacher man, don't you have a score to settle with these two? Because if you don't, I do."

Prester John cocked his head to one side. "I'm not sure I understand what you are trying to tell me."

Maddock heard the first hint of doubt in the Preacher's voice. He scanned the situation and turned to Reznik. "So, this was your show all along."

"Yeah, crazy huh? Are you going to fight this guy, or do I need to kneecap your buddy here to prove I'm serious?"

Blade raised to guard position, Maddock faced the Preacher. "You wanted to see Armageddon—well here it comes."

Tall and powerfully built, Prester John was a formidable opponent. He slashed the sword back and forth before advancing on Maddock. "I do not lightly forgive betrayal."

The lunge came a split-second late. Maddock saw the eyes move and deflected the deadly blade. *Bronze is no match for steel.* He stepped back, holding his guard. A second thrust—he knew it was a feint. Maddock slashed at his opponent's sword arm. The Preacher drew away and returned a riposte that tore through Maddock's loose coveralls but didn't draw blood.

Maddock held his guard but disengaged. *Damn, the man's got the reach of an orangutan.* He looked for an opening, a weakness, but Prester John had proven himself an expert swordsman. *Two guns and a sword against a bronze knife—not good.* Maddock remembered the man's words, *'I do not lightly forgive betrayal'.* He backed toward Reznik and Twitch. "Come, Preacher. You know what you have to do."

"Yeah, Preach," Twitch jeered and waved his pistol, "show

us your stuff."

Howling, slashing, Prester John rushed up. Maddock sprang away, batting aside his sword. He ducked the next swing and jumped back, landing less than an arm's length from Reznik.

The man didn't seem to notice. "Is that all you got, Preach? My money's on the little guy."

The Preacher lunged, his face burning in rage. His sword moved faster than the eye could follow. Reznik froze—two feet of glittering steel protruded from his chest. Before Twitch could recover, Maddock spun and slashed the man's throat, nearly beheading him. Bones lunged for Reznik's gun, but the Preacher stepped in, his sword at ready. "No guns. We finish this with righteous weapons."

Maddock backed away and began circling. *He can't take his eyes off Bones, and he can't leave the guns.* Prester John spun, sword in hand. Bones stepped closer, then sprang back. The Preacher's slash passed inches from his chest. Maddock lunged, nicking the back of his opponent's arm. Prester John roared, "Face me coward—sword to sword."

Maddock stepped forward and parried the slash. He let the deflected blade pass over his shoulder and spun, locking his elbow around the Preacher's sword arm. The man reacted with surprising strength, swinging Maddock around and slamming him to the ground. The gleaming sword descended. Maddock waited, waited. At the last instant, he rolled to the Preacher's feet and stabbed upward, into the man's knee. Prester John tottered, howling, then toppled like a mountain of bricks.

Bones had already scooped a pistol from the ground. A single shot silenced the howls. "That didn't go so well for any of them."

34

A handful of stray shots spattered off the stone paving and whined past Maddock's ear. He ducked behind the altar and dragged his friend with him. "It won't go so well with us either if we don't move."

Bones peeked over Prester John's bloody corpse. "Not looking good boss. Where to?"

"South Entrance, we've got to grab Corey and Zoya."

Maddock broke cover and scooped up Reznik's submachine gun. He glanced back, then dashed across the atrium with Bones hard on his heels. A scattering of bullets followed them into the darkened portal. Maddock flattened himself against the wall.

Bones arrived a moment later. "I don't know what this gained us. I thought he was in some dragon tower or something."

"Yeah, Dragon Song Tower, I've been there." Maddock felt his way along the wall until he reached a narrow opening. "In here—we've got some climbing to do."

Maybe it was the adrenaline, but the second time up the spiral stairs didn't feel quite as painful as the first. Maddock didn't pause at the landings but pushed himself to keep climbing. Bones followed, his bare feet thumping on the steel treads. "You know it's going to be totally FUBAR out there before we get down."

The screaming started before they reached the top. Maddock paused just below the platform and held up a fist. Bones nodded in silence. They heard Corey's voice, then Zoya began to shriek, "I'll drop him, I will. Let me go, damn you. I have to…I have to."

Maddock rushed to the platform. Corey hung from one arm, dangling off the western edge. Zoya crouched next to him, gripping his collar. Halima had her other arm in some kind of hold. She looked up at Maddock. "I could not stop her."

Zoya twisted around, pure animal hatred in her eyes. She

released Corey and turned her fury on Halima. Corey's head fell below the platform. His hand slipped. Maddock dove for the edge and gripped his arm. Hanging, his friend looked up. "I got it! I got it!"

With his other hand, Corey clutched the lyre against his chest. "I did it. I completed the quest."

Someone thumped down at Maddock's side and clutched his shoulder. *Crap, it's Zoya.* He tried to shake it off until a slender brown hand snaked down and grabbed Corey's collar. Halima murmured in his ear, "He will not die today."

Together they hoisted him, lyre and all up on the platform. Corey just lay back and stared at the morning sky. "It's so beautiful from up here."

"Not from where I'm looking." Bones stood, dangling Zoya by the ankle. "We've got to stop seeing each other this way, sweetheart."

She thrashed and hissed but could do nothing. Corey sat upright. "Be careful…you're going to hurt her."

Halima circled behind them, crooked an elbow around Zoya's neck, and punched her hard behind the left shoulder blade. Like a marionette with its strings cut, Zoya hung lifeless. Halima managed a tiny smile. "You can set her down now."

Covered in blood and dirt, Zoya looked like nothing more than a disinterred corpse. Cory crawled over. "What have you done? You killed her."

"Her *chakras*, her vital energies, I blocked them. She will recover."

Bones carried Zoya down. Maddock had Halima carry the lyre. Corey followed, still wobbly after hanging hundreds of feet above the Nile Valley.

As they approached the south portal, Maddock heard the ongoing battle within the atrium. He lingered at the bottom of the stairs while the others made their way down. Bones peeked out through the narrow entrance. "Clear outside, but things don't sound good."

Maddock slipped through and checked the far entrance. Halima met him on the way back. "Chandalan hold the west side. They will hate us. We go east along the outer wall and find my acolyte sisters."

"I doubt they'll welcome us either."

Bones had joined them. "Are you saying we're trapped?"

"I'm saying we have to cross the atrium and head north to the airstrip."

Maddock sidled along the inner wall and kept to the shadows. The fight seemed to have moved to the east. Corey and Halima crowded up behind him. Bones slid past and poked his head out. "Oh crap, looks like they're bringing in some serious artillery."

Maddock risked a glance. From the west, a column of uniformed men trotted up carrying RPG launch tubes. Most of the white-robed acolytes had disappeared through the east entrance. Moments later, a barrage of grenades exploded against the wall above their heads. Bones said, "I don't think that angampora stuff is gonna help much."

Halima leaned in. "The atrium is not safe. It is a trap for the chandalan."

"Well, we're not staying here." Maddock grabbed Bones's arm. "While they're all occupied…"

He didn't get a chance to finish before his friend stood and dashed across the atrium, Zoya's limp form flopping against his back. Maddock turned to Halima and Corey. "Run! Run now while they're shooting at each other."

He checked their six, then ran like hell after him. Stray shots rattled off the pavement, but most of the fighting had moved east. On reaching the north portal, Maddock spun and scanned the atrium. Halima and Corey hugged the wall just inside.

Two men charged up. One crouched and lowered an RPG at the entrance. Maddock squeezed off a three-round burst and dropped him in a heap. His partner flopped behind the body and opened fire.

Maddock flattened himself against one wall, fully aware that his friends huddled in the darkness behind him. He returned covering fire and yelled back, "Out, out! Everyone get out."

Bullets whined and sizzled about the open passageway. His magazine nearly empty, Maddock did what he could to keep the shooter down. In desperation, he switched to single fire and knelt, taking careful aim at the tan RPG tube. One shot, it erupted in flames. Maddock ran.

At the far portal, he found Bones crouching behind a boulder. "I've got Tinkerbell from hell, but where's the lyre?"

"Still with me." Halima glided out of the shadows. "You must all go quickly. Many will die here before the sun rises."

Bones said, "The atrium, this whole place, it looks like a giant kill chamber."

Maddock glanced back. A heavy door slammed down across the tunnel interior. "Crap, it's happening now. Run, run for the airstrip."

They almost made it before the world exploded. The blast knocked them face down across the rocky hillside. Maddock blacked out for a moment. When the ground stopped spinning, he spotted Halima slumped across a large boulder.

The woman breathed, she had a pulse, but would not respond when he touched her. Maddock looked back at the Tabernacle of Light, now a towering beacon of flame. Debris began to peel off the walls and rain down around them. Bones crawled to his knees. "Let's get out of here, man."

Corey raced over and crouched next to Zoya's huddled form. "I'll carry her then."

"No," Maddock said, "you take the pack. Keep the lyre safe until we get to the plane."

Bones helped sling Halima across Maddock's back. "That's a lot of woman you got there. Sure you can handle it?"

"Shut up and break trail. We have daylight now. Let's use it."

Bones lifted Zoya in his arms and draped her over one shoulder. Maddock let his friend lead and concentrated on the steep path beneath his feet. When he reached the landing strip, it looked deserted. June's C-130 crouched in the shadows next to a small shed. Bones crossed the tarmac and headed for the loading ramp. He waved Corey past and waited at the foot.

As Maddock approached, a figure stepped from behind the shed. "Thought you'd left me for dead, didn't you." Beardo moved closer, brandishing a pistol. "You and your friends will look a whole lot worse, full of nine-millimeter slugs. Now where's this magic box the Preach was all hot about?"

"I don't have it," Maddock said. He gestured back at the flaming ruin they'd just left."

"Bull crap. It's here, or you'd still be looking for it."

"I have it." June moved from behind the nose wheel. "You want it? I'll give it to you."

"Dam' straight I want it."

She fired two shots from her Ruger forty-four magnum. Beardo dropped like a sack of dirty laundry. June blew across the barrel and holstered the huge revolver. "He asked for it."

Halima started to kick and struggle. Maddock bent and helped her sit. The woman began to mumble in a language he hadn't heard before. She clutched her head and rocked. Maddock knelt next to her and held her in his arms. "We're all safe. In a few minutes we'll fly out of here."

Halima shook her head and began to sob. "No, my poor *Latreftés,* my sisters, they are not safe."

Maddock helped her to her feet. He didn't think a woman with so much strength and courage could cry like she did, but Halima just held him and wept against his shoulder. "Everything I live for is a lie. My city, my people, even my God, all lost, all broken."

Maddock returned her embrace and tried to comfort her. "What is lost can be found. Broken things can be mended."

The woman straightened her back. "Then for that, I must stay."

Once more, every bit the proud Makeda, queen of ancient Sheba, she looked him in the eye. "I love you, Dane Maddock. I love you like my forebearer loved King Solomon. But like them, we come from different worlds. Go now."

With that, she threw her arms around his neck, kissed him on the lips, and fled.

35

While the auxiliary power unit began its spin-up, June shooed them all on board and began her instrument check. "I called ahead to Mek'ele airport. "It's in the Tigray region of Ethiopia and we've got just enough fuel to get us there."

Maddock shook his head. "I thought you were going to put gas in this baby."

"Couldn't—place was locked tight. You'll be happy to know I found some shoes though. Clothing too, including shirt and shorts for Corey's little pet spider."

Zoya had started to regain consciousness as they boarded the plane. Corey explained that she'd freaked when Maddock stabbed Ashera. "I just climbed up behind her…didn't know what to do…and then yow! The music goes crazy and I grab the lyre. Then Halima and Zoya had this kickass fight. I think she tried to jump and take me with her but then you guys arrived and saved my ass."

Maddock nodded. "I think Zoya will recover eventually. You take care of her, but I'm going to have to keep the lyre. She cannot ever touch it again."

Fully assembled and strung, the instrument was over three feet tall. Maddock kept it next to him, wedged between the copilot's chair and the starboard cabin wall. June ran up all four engines and then pulled pitch on the propellers. Beneath them, the wheels grumbled to a roar. Maddock felt a lurch in his stomach as the big plane leaped from the tarmac and howled into the night sky. Between his knees, the yoke moved and turned as if by invisible hands.

"I've set our course for Mek'ele Airport," June said. "The autopilot will do the rest."

Maddock watched the burning hulk of Prester John's Tabernacle pass beneath their wings. "You've got a lot of confidence in that hardware. How does it avoid other aircraft?"

"*Ha*, between here and Mek'ele? Nothing but sputniks and flying saucers. We've got radar and ADS-B transponders to track other planes. The course computer monitors all that—but hell, with the conflict going on in Ethiopia, only a bunch of damn fools would wanna fly there."

"Present company excepted, I assume." Maddock looked over his shoulder at the flight deck's open door. "What if I watch the flashing lights for a minute while you go back and check on our crew?"

"You can't check them yourself?"

He glanced down at the lyre. "I'd rather not take this back there."

"And you can't just leave it up here? Brother, you *are* in a bad way."

"Zoya, Bones, Corey, we're all screwed and it's going to get worse unless I can figure a way to deal with this thing."

June grunted something and heaved herself out of the pilot's chair. "Don't go playing with any of the shinies while I'm gone."

"Yes, Mom." Maddock scanned the row of digital displays. The dash didn't have as many switches and controls as he'd been used to seeing. In the center, a digital map scrolled slowly from right to left. He checked their heading, southeast at 125 degrees.

June returned and wedged herself into the lefthand seat. "All's quiet. Your little tiger princess is sacked out in one of the bunks. Corey is sitting guard over her—I've got some concerns for that guy."

"What about Bones?"

"Pretending to sleep, but he's not."

"That's kind of what I figured. None of us are going to get much rest with this thing around." Maddock didn't have to look down at the lyre to feel it hum in response.

"Why don't I just crack open the cargo bay and let you chuck it out?"

"Wouldn't solve anything. It would still be down there, and we'd still feel it. I might as well chuck myself out after it."

"None of that talk mister. We'll figure something out." She paused and stared at the flight map. "Say, about eighty miles east of Mek'ele there's this active volcano. You could go there and pitch it in."

"No crap? You mean like Mt. Doom? Corey would go nuts, but I worry about what would happen to Zoya."

"I worry about all of you. Look, I got this—we're still a few hours from Mek'ele. Why don't you lean back like your friends and pretend to sleep."

Eyes closed, relaxed as well as he could, Maddock tried. He still heard Margo's screams. The thing she became, it still lived behind his eyelids.

He might have dozed—it didn't seem like hours. June's muttering and tapping roused him. "What's up, we landing?"

"Damn thing's messed up or something."

Maddock straightened and rubbed his eyes. June tapped the instrument panel and scowled. He looked out the windscreen. In the afternoon light, all he could see was a chain of rocky hilltops glowing orange. "Beautiful down there, but where's the airport?"

"Now that's one helluva question." June thumped the panel harder, trying various buttons and digital displays. "Damn thing won't let go."

"Won't let go of what?"

June leaned back and cast a worried glance out the side window. "I tried the transponder. The freaking screen won't show me the beacons. Mek'ele airport isn't answering. And look, this stupid map is just bullcrap."

The screen still showed their heading as southwest, 125 degrees. Maddock checked the landmarks and then looked at the passing terrain. An orange glow pulsed among the hills below. "Doesn't seem to match up."

"No crap. We ain't in Kansas anymore, Dorothy. We're flying over the Danakil Desert and that's a freaking volcano up ahead."

"Can't you just turn us around and fly by…"

"The seat of my pants? Not even these size nineteens are gonna help." She pounded on the yoke and stamped her feet. "The autopilot won't release control."

Maddock tried moving the yoke in front of him. It vibrated and twitched in his hands but wouldn't budge. He braced himself against the seat. Muscles bulging, he pressed. It gave slightly, slammed into the instrument panel, and flopped to one side. "Sorry, I think I broke it."

"Wouldn't matter, this thing is all fly-by-wire. If the autopilot doesn't disengage, we're screwed."

Maddock climbed out of his seat and began searching the cockpit. "There has got to be a switchbox or breakers that control this thing."

He opened a panel on the overhead. Seeing nothing of use, he was about to open a second when Corey stepped onto the flight deck. "How much longer to Mek'ele?"

"If we can't find some way to disengage the autopilot, we won't get there at all."

June tapped the instrument panel again. "Wouldn't matter. It's been lying to us about our fuel as well. We'd never make it back."

"Lying?" Corey stared at the array of digital instruments. "You mean your airplane lies to you?"

Maddock straightened. "Oh crap! It's the machine. The Apocalypse machine was not destroyed by the fire. It's still down there, pulling our strings."

"Why—what does it want with us?"

"We've got the lyre. We know too much. The damned thing is a game, remember? It's trying to eliminate the competition. We're about to fly into a volcano."

June twisted in her seat. "I thought it was that Reznik guy controlling everything."

"He thought he was too, but it's been the machine all along. The damned thing's gone sentient. It thinks it's God because of all the crap Prester John fed it."

June reached alongside her pilot's seat and drew out a huge black revolver. She stood and backed away from the instrument panel. "Then I'm just gonna take this and blow its freaking brains out."

Maddock grabbed her arm. "No, not yet anyway. Let me try

something." He glanced around. "You wouldn't happen to have a microwave oven on board?"

"You mean like for heating coffee and stuff? Yeah, right behind that bulkhead."

Bones chose that moment to stick his head through the door. "Is there a party I'm missing, and what's right behind the bulkhead?"

"Microwave oven. Bring it in here, will you…"

Maddock heard a grunt. The aluminum wall buckled, and Bones reappeared clutching a large metal box. "It must have been bolted down or something."

"Thank God it has a long cord, or you'd have ripped that out too." Maddock turned to June. "Put that cannon away and find me a screwdriver."

"Will a pocketknife do?"

He wrenched open the microwave door until it tore out of the frame. Bones twitched. "Mind helping me out here? This thing's getting heavy."

Maddock jammed the blade into the latch mechanism and took one end of the bulky oven. "June, crank five minutes into it. Bones, when she hits start, we hold it face-up against the overhead."

June ran her fingers along the plastic headliner. "I think the antenna array is a little farther aft."

They sidled back until she nodded and punched *start*. In a single movement, they rolled the oven on its back and slammed it against the ceiling. The magnetron inside hummed to life and Corey stepped away. "You're gonna fry your brains with that thing."

"Gonna fry somebody's brains," Maddock said.

Minutes passed, but nothing happened. June watched the instrument panel. "Maybe a little further aft."

Maddock and Bones slid the oven through the flight deck door and held it against the crew compartment ceiling. Zoya looked up from her bunk. "What the hell?"

A moment later, June whooped and shouted back. "*Toasted the sucker.*"

The C-130 pitched nose-up. Maddock fell against a bunk and the microwave spun clattering to the deck. Bones and Corey tumbled after it. June cursed as she struggled to regain control of the aircraft. Hand over hand, Maddock climbed back to the flight deck and vaulted into the right-hand seat. June jammed the control yoke forward and stabbed madly at the panel switches. "See if you can do something with the flaps, or we're gonna stall out."

Maddock found what looked like a flap control lever near the back of the center console. He eased it down to twenty degrees and checked the tell-tale gauge on the panel. It barely moved. "What gives with our controls?"

"Main hydraulics shut down and the auxiliary power unit won't start. We're working off the batteries."

Maddock jammed the flaps lever all the way back. On the panel, the gauge twitched lower. June somehow managed to horse their attitude nearer to level flight. "We ain't gonna fall out of the sky just yet, but we ain't gonna make it much farther either." She throttled back the two outboard engines. "I'm setting us down."

Bones leaned over Maddock's shoulder and scanned the dusky landscape below. "I don't think they got a first-class lounge down there." He craned forward. "Hell, it looks like the whole airport is on fire."

"It's not an airport, Bones. Our geologist pilot lady found us a volcano."

"Holy crap! Can we pick someplace a little better to land?"

"We can if the terrain-mapping radar still works," June tapped the screen, "I hope…" She was interrupted by a shuddering roar. "Damn, the prop pitch control is gone whacked—get your ass back there and strap in. Lash down your little friends while you're at it."

The big cargo plane shook like a wet Labrador. The lyre hummed and rattled at his side—Maddock snatched it up and cradled it in his lap. *Not gonna lose it…not gonna lose it after all this.* He considered picking a few notes, calling for help from…something. It didn't seem like a wise move, even under the circumstances. Distracted for the moment, he looked up to see a craggy ridge just off their nose. He glanced at June. "You got this?"

"There's a four-point harness draped over the back of your seat. You might think about wearing it."

He looked again. She hadn't even fastened her lap belt. "Junie, what's going on?"

"I ain't never lost a plane, never lost a passenger. If we all don't walk away from this, I don't want to either."

"Bloody hell!" He put the lyre aside, reached over, and fastened her in. "We're all going to walk away from this one, and I'll be damned if you think I'm about to carry you."

"Sweet, now buckle yourself in. We're riding the updraft over the next hill and then land wherever we can—short of that lava pit."

The plane rumbled and shuddered as Maddock secured his shoulder harness. He felt it lift, pressing him into the seat. The serrated ridgeline swept so close he could make out individual rocks, then whisked beneath their fuselage, disappearing like a mirage. June fought the controls, but Maddock felt the aircraft drop. She banged on the yoke in frustration. "Give me more flaps, dammit. The props have reversed and we're stalling out."

She cut all four engines. Maddock tried cycling the flap control up and down. The panel indicator twitched and wavered, then froze at thirty degrees. "Looks like the best we're gonna get."

Under her breath, June whispered, *"c'mon girl...c'mon girl..."*

Maddock wondered if she was talking to the plane or to herself. Ahead lay nothing but a flat reddish haze that rose to meet them.

June horsed the yoke back and forth, her eyes on the terrain map. "Goin' in gear up—gonna be rough." She glanced out the side window. "That better be sand down there. We've got enough battery power for about three more minutes and then it's all over."

Maddock clutched the lyre to his chest and ducked his

head. The initial impact came like a punch in the gut. They bounced and spun. One wing dug in and crumpled. The entire plane lifted up, then plunged nose-first into the dirt. Maddock lost track of the tumbling and jarring as sand and dust blasted through the shattered cockpit.

36

As suddenly as it had started, everything stopped. Maddock found himself hanging upside down, still clutching the lyre. The reddish glow of emergency lights barely penetrated the choking dust. Oily smoke filled the air. He punched the release on his harness. It didn't budge. The smoke grew thicker. Maddock tried to locate June, but trash and dirt filled the cabin. He craned around. "Bones, you back there somewhere?"

He heard someone grunt and curse, the words muffled. Maddock hunted around and finally located a brown trouser leg that looked like June's. He yanked the twisted debris away. *Her belt, left-hand side near the back, she always carries a knife.* He found it.

Straps cut, he tumbled to the loose earth filling the cabin. June didn't move. He dug away more of the twisted metal and found her harness straps. Cutting, tugging, Maddock dragged her from the pilot seat. *She's got a pulse. Got to get out.* The forward windows had blown inward and buried themselves in the dirt. The side windows were gone. Maddock found a long tear in the aluminum skin behind his seatback. He pushed. The metal gave and he glimpsed the dusky orange sky outside. Another shove and he could squeeze through. *No way I'll get June through that hole.*

With strength borne of desperation, he wrenched the crumpled metal aside, crawled out, and pulled June's unconscious form after him. Flames licked among the debris and smoke swirled through the murky darkness. Maddock looked around for his friends. "Bones, Corey, where are you guys?"

An enormous, twisted propeller stood sentinel over the flickering remains of a shattered engine. Nothing moved. He started to drag June farther from the wreckage, but something felt wrong—he needed to stay. *Crap! The lyre...* Maddock crawled back into the wreckage and groped about until he found the battered wooden box, still bearing sticks and strings.

Lyre clutched in his arms, he sat, choking on oily fumes. *Something else?* It took a moment of thought. *June.* Maddock backed out of the broken fuselage. Yellow flames flickered around the wreckage. *I left her here somewhere.* Rocks, sand, mounds of twisted aluminum, they all wavered about in the glimmering light.

He staggered to his feet—the world swam in a yellow haze. Choking and gagging, he bent double. The ground flew up and slammed his face. Maddock rolled to one side and struggled to his knees. "June…" His voice little more than a soft croak, he tried again. "June?"

"Bones, he's over here." Corey, his white coveralls now black with soot and dirt, grabbed him beneath his arm and heaved.

Maddock stumbled and stood. "Where's June?"

"She's safe. C'mon, you need to get out of here."

A wave of heat struck the back of his head. Maddock turned to see flames engulf the ruined fuselage. Corey half led, half dragged him up a low hill. A tall figure stood at the top, outlined against the evening sky. "Where the hell were you?"

"I was…" Maddock looked down at the lyre under his arm, then back up at Bones. "I was getting something."

"Well, you look like crap, as usual."

Maddock tried to answer but fell into another fit of coughing. He choked on something and spat out a black wad of phlegm. His head spun. *Corey, Bones…aren't there four of us? There's someone else…* "June, where is June?"

"Flat on my back in hades, that's where."

"Then we're all alive? That's…"

"Did you forget Zoya?" Corey said.

The previous day came back into focus, the girl, the lyre, and the horror she had invoked with it. *Hell and damnation, I'm losing it.* Maddock shook his head. "Did…did you get her out?"

"She's here, next to June," Bones said, "but she's not doing too good."

In the debris field below, a fragment of wing burst into

flame. Corey eyed it and said, "Shouldn't we move?"

June sat up. "No need. There's barely enough fuel left in there to make smores."

Maddock eased himself down next to the dark figure curled up beside June. She breathed in ragged gasps, jerking and twitching as if locked in a nightmare. Corey crouched on the other side. "I can't wake her. She's been this way since...since..."

"Since you dragged both of our sorry asses out of that pile of wreckage." Bones said.

He explained how Corey had managed to cut them all free of the ruined crew compartment and pull them to safety. "I was out cold and his girlfriend there is still zonked."

Corey ducked his head. "We were just lucky. When the plane busted up, our section stayed mostly intact."

June groaned and covered her face. "Worst landing I've ever pulled. I think I gotta go back to rock-hounding, if anyone will have me."

"Volcano wrangling," Maddock said. "You were one of the best. Get back to your roots."

"Then, I guess this is as good a place as any to start. Smell that sulfurous stink? It ain't coming from my poor old aircraft."

"Well, it's not coming from me," Bones said.

"Nope, we've managed to set ourselves down in the Danakil Desert—the original Abaddon, a place so godforsaken hot even Ol' Scratch himself avoids it. A hundred and thirty degrees, daytime temp." As she spoke, the ground trembled and a nearby hilltop spat hunks of incandescent rock into the air. The glowing plume lit the slope before it fell back into the crater.

Bones stared at the desolate landscape. "And a volcano."

"Yup, more than one. You find 'em, I'll wrangle 'em."

Bones sat on a rock next to June. "In the meantime, I don't suppose you could wrangle up some water? I don't think this hotel has a mini-bar."

"Not unless your friend rescued that too."

Corey slipped something off his back. "I might have. Grabbed my pack when I carried Zoya out." He rummaged through it. "Got four bottles left. It's not enough, is it?"

Bones grabbed the pack and reached inside. "You carried Zoya? You *dragged* me. I've got the bruises to prove it." He pulled out a handful of energy bars. "You got food too. Holding out on us, huh?"

"I wasn't…I just…it just…"

Bones dug a little deeper. "A towel—what the hell?"

"Never leave without a towel. It's massively useful…"

Maddock stood. "Give him a break, Bones. He saved your ass, didn't he?"

June pulled herself to her feet. "Am I going to have to send you boys to your rooms—what's gotten into you?"

Bones lurched to his feet, towering over them both. "It's him, all high and mighty as long as he carries that, that *thing* under his arm."

"Oh, and like I'd trust you with it. Maybe let you toss it in that bonfire down there."

Bones stepped forward. "I just might. Think you can stop me?"

"The hell you say." Corey pushed in between them. "That's my staff he's got, and I had it first."

Bones shoved Corey out of the way. "I've had it with both of you."

June pushed between them. "Now listen all of you, there's water, a whole river of it, just twenty-five miles west of here. Think you can keep it together that long?"

Bones backed away and sat on his rock, but Corey remained standing. "I want my staff back."

"No way," Maddock said. "We don't divvy this thing up again. It stays intact."

"Yeah," Corey said, "like it isn't messing with you any more than it's messing with us."

"There's only one person here this thing hasn't managed to infect." Maddock handed the lyre to June. "Keep it safe until we figure out how to deal with it."

Zoya chose that moment to sit up and burst into a fit of hysterical laughter. By the time Corey reached her side, the hysterics had devolved into jerking convulsions. Maddock knelt and held her head. "She's going into convulsions. Come on, Zoya, breathe!"

Zoya arched her back. Her eyes rolled open, and blood ran from her mouth. "Get her on her side," Maddock said, "and Bones, put Corey's towel under her head."

Two minutes passed before her tremors subsided and she inhaled great shrieking gulps of air. Maddock held a finger to Zoya's throat. "Her pulse is off the chart. Another seizure like that will kill her."

"Oh Lordy," June said. "It's a head injury, isn't it…"

Corey sat and held her in his arms. "I don't think so. She looked fine when I brought her out, no bruising, no contusions. It was lighter and I would have known."

"Stay with her," Maddock said. "June, keep an eye on them for us. Bones and I will go see if there's anything left to salvage."

The fire had died back to a few guttering pockets, leaving the crash site in darkness. Bones produced Corey's pack and pulled out a small flashlight. "Something else I found."

"Yeah, that's what we need to discuss."

"The pack? No, you mean that other stuff."

"That *other stuff*, Bones. I know it wasn't you talking…not really. Wasn't me either."

"No, it's that damned thing we found. What in blazing hell did Corey drag us into?"

"He didn't mean to do it." Maddock looked around as if someone might be listening. "I think we've been manipulated, all of us. I just don't know how."

"You're getting paranoid, ol' buddy. What I don't understand is how you could just hand that thing off…it's making me crazy just thinking about it."

"Like pulling a tooth with a pair of vice grips." Maddock glanced back up the hill. "I'll be wanting it back. Can't help it. Come on, let's see if there's anything left we can use."

The tail section lay on its side, mostly intact. Bones ducked through a hole and panned the light around the interior. Maddock followed, looking for emergency gear or water rations. "Nothing much here."

"Gutted," Bones said. "That flare you fired up her ass did a real number on it."

The crew quarters were in worse shape—a burned-out, crumpled shell, little more. Maddock took one peek inside and shook his head. "I don't see how any of you survived that."

"Almost didn't. If there'd been more than a few snorts of fuel left in the wings, we'd have been toast."

They made their way through a twisted mass of wings, engines, and bent propellers. Maddock avoided the small fires that guttered and fumed among the debris. "Shine that light this way. Let's see if there's anything left up front."

The forward end of the fuselage had broken free just behind the flight deck and dug into the ground, throwing up piles of dirt and rock before coming to rest. Coated with soot and oil, the flight deck hadn't suffered as much fire damage as the crew compartment. Bones circled the far side. "With all this liquid crud, I'm surprised you didn't get barbequed."

"Hydraulic fluid, toxic as hell, but it's not flammable." Maddock poked his head through the crushed aluminum shell. "Bring that light over. There's some stuff in here we might want."

While Bones illuminated the interior, Maddock searched through the debris. "Found four more water bottles and June's hand cannon." He rummaged up her knife as well and stuck it in his belt.

The lingering smoke and dust caught in his throat as he backed out. "We might find more tomorrow, but I doubt it."

Bones's flashlight beam picked out the gun belt and holstered revolver. "Are you sure we want that in camp with all of us going half squirrelly?"

Maddock had similar thoughts. *Maybe if I keep it myself, the others will stay in line.* He couldn't see Bones's face. *Probably thinking the same thing.* The heavy belt felt wrong somehow. "Trust me for a few more minutes? Just while we walk back."

The flashlight clicked off. "Guess I have to."

37

In the volcano's orange glow, they climbed the rocky knoll. Near the top, Maddock picked out June's silhouette against the night sky. She came to meet him. "Find anything?"

"More water—Bones has it." He paused a moment. "And this…"

She stepped closer and stumbled back when she saw what he held. "The hell you say. I can't believe you were dumb enough to bring that here—not now—not with the hoot-owls so thick you could…you could…"

"Shoot them in the dark? Not my intention, June."

Bones muttered at his side, "What are your intentions, ol' buddy? I'm running a little low on trust right now."

"I want to trade. June returns the lyre to me. I give her the revolver."

June snorted. "What's the catch?"

"You've got to play sheriff. Any one of us gets too crazy, you shoot."

"Even you, Sundance?"

"Especially me. I guard the lyre. You keep the peace."

"I want my knife back too. I don't see it, but I know you got it."

Bones shoved him away. "You didn't say anything about a knife…*buddy*."

It was all Maddock could do to choke back the wad of anger that rose in his throat. *It's not him. it's that damned thing.* He handed June the gun and the belt. "Peace offering."

"Prisoner exchange." She passed him the lyre. "Now the knife."

Maddock drew the combat knife and offered it to Bones. "Hold this for a minute. See how it feels."

His friend stood motionless, knife in hand. June said nothing—just watched. After a long pause, Bones passed it to her. "Something just kept whispering stuff in my ear, bad stuff. Crap, I'm going psycho."

"Welcome to the club." Maddock let out an audible sigh. "Let's get back and figure out what we do next."

Corey didn't look up as they approached. "She doesn't respond." He held her wrist. Her head lolled to one side. "I can hardly feel a pulse. She's barely breathing. What can I do?"

"There is something…" Maddock began tightening the lyre strings.

Bones crossed his arms and shook his head. "Not a good idea, Man—it could kill us all."

"It will kill us if we do nothing. We need all of us whole. No one left behind, remember? Not even Zoya. If the lyre can raise Margo from the dead…"

June loosened the revolver in her holster. "Not sure I like where this is going."

Corey stood. "Wait, wait—It's that *thing*, the *djinn* trapped in the lyre that's killing her. We need more power, something to use against it."

Bones glowered at him. "We're fresh out of freaking turtle shells Mario. What do you suggest?"

"Let me play it, the same music I played back in the Hagia Irene. I know the notes, the chords. I can do this."

Maddock drew back. "I'm not handing it to you. It's…it's dangerous."

Corey lowered his voice. "You can't give it up, can you? Even to save Zoya, you can't."

Arms still crossed, Bones stood, a silent shadow in the darkness. June stepped closer. "You did it once, old friend. Remember, Corey here is the infamous Doctor Denarious, a wizard."

The thing clung like glue, it stuck to his fingers. Giving it away felt like tearing off a limb. Maddock shivered in the sultry night as Corey twisted the tuning pegs. A few notes, off key, they jarred like tearing metal. Corey made another adjustment. Zoya jerked and gasped. Wrapped in concertina wire, scorched by jet exhaust, Maddock's knees buckled. He bent double, hands over his ears.

Then a tone, a chord, a harmony, ice cream on a summer

day—Corey picked out a few bars of *the song*. The maenad's revel, Orpheus's dream, King David's mystic notes floated in the air. Maddock felt the pain of the past few weeks vanish like a morning mist. Zoya gasped and jerked. A shadow at their feet, her eyes glowed with their own pale radiance.

With a sinuous motion, she rose from the ground. "Give me the lyre and I will play you music for the gods."

Corey stood transfixed. Zoya seemed to grow, to loom over them all. "Give it to me. I command you."

June drew her gun and fired at the towering figure. The apparition laughed—its voice a rich contralto. "You insult me with your feeble weapon."

June's revolver shattered in her hand. The thing extended an arm of smoke and shadow. Its smallest finger touched June's forehead and she collapsed to the ground. "One worshipper more or less makes no difference to me. Now, on your bellies, all of you."

Bones grunted but didn't move. Corey crossed his arms over the lyre. Maddock planted his feet. "No—kill us, but we will not bow to you."

A hand filled his vision and extended its slender claw. Dissonance, a clash of detuned strings wrenched his skull. He staggered back. The apparition shrieked and vanished into the night. When Maddock looked up, Zoya swayed in its place.

With a cry, Corey dropped the lyre and ran to Zoya. "You're alive—you're alive!"

"No, no, no. I warned you." On his knees in the sand, Bones cried out, "That damned thing—*it killed June*."

When Maddock knelt beside him, Bones roared, "Don't touch me! Get away from me, all of you." He fell over June's body, shaking with anger.

Corey pulled Zoya back. She wept on his shoulder. "She…she…that thing, it's inside of me."

"Ashera," Corey said. "The goddess Ashera. She's still here?"

"Here? She is a part of me. I have carried her ever since I found that wretched wooden box." Zoya looked down at June's body. "That should have been me."

"No," Maddock said. "It shouldn't have been any of us. Ashera was using you to trick us into playing that thing. She wants control."

Zoya straightened and grinned at him. "Oh, and I *have* control. Play my music one more time and maybe I can return your friend from hell. She screams for you even now."

Bones rose like a thundercloud. "You need to shut up."

Maddock grabbed him by the arm. "For god's sake Bones, she's half your size."

"The damned thing killed our friend." He shook free. "I'm not going to let it kill any more of us."

Zoya smiled up at him, closed her eyes, and fell backward into the rocks. Corey knelt beside her crumpled form. "She's unconscious. It looks like a head injury. Are we just going to fight until we're all dead?"

Maddock scooped up the lyre "It's this thing—we can't keep it and we don't dare destroy it." He gazed out at the darkened landscape. "We should leave, now. There's nothing to hold us here."

"I think I can handle Zoya," Corey said. "What do we do about June?"

"I will carry her," Bones looked up at the glowing hills on the near horizon. "She needs to go back to her roots, to the volcano."

Corey grunted as he hoisted the unconscious young woman across his back. Bones picked June's body from the ground like a father lifting his sleeping child. "She once said I couldn't carry her." He shook his head. "She's not too heavy, not today, not for me."

Maddock shoved the water and everything else into Corey's pack. He rearranged a few items and pulled out a half-filled ouzo bottle. *What the everlasting hell?* He considered dumping it, then paused, the germ of an idea forming in his head. Wrapping it in Corey's towel, he tucked the bottle in a side pocket.

A little room remained. Maddock eyed the lyre, then

shoved it above the water bottles. It made a bulky load—the flap wouldn't close. *Screw it.* He slung the pack over one shoulder. "Let's move out."

Bones led, declining all offers to help carry June. Corey struggled after, climbing the rocky slope. Heat radiated from the ground. Even with the sun hidden behind the western hills, Maddock still felt sweat running down his back. He could only imagine how Bones felt, trudging ahead in stoic silence.

They marched about a half mile, weaving between the enormous boulders. Maddock guessed that they'd climbed several hundred feet. Corey was the first to go. Stumbling on the loose rocks, he sprawled face down and rolled to protect his head. Maddock scrambled up and knelt at his side. "Let's trade for a while."

When Corey grunted something like assent, Maddock slung one arm over his shoulder and rolled Zoya's limp body into a fireman's carry. She couldn't have weighed more than a hundred pounds. He straightened and steadied his legs beneath him. Bones had disappeared over the rise. Maddock followed, with Corey trailing a few yards behind.

Rounding a jagged lava outcrop, Maddock spotted Bones standing on the edge of a glowing crater. June's body rested in his arms like a sleeping child. He didn't look back as Maddock climbed the slope behind him. "We're not going to survive this, you know." Bones looked down. "The sun will rise in a few hours and will die fighting over the last sip of water."

"What do you intend?"

"I will return our friend to her mother earth…then decide."

"Just wait until Corey joins us. We all should have a chance to say our goodbyes."

It wasn't much longer before the crunch of footsteps on broken rock announced Corey's arrival. Bones turned to him and nodded. "You go first."

Corey looked down into the pit of fire at their feet and startled back. "No! Not…" He glanced at June and exhaled. "Oh, yeah. Well…June, I didn't know you…not like I wish I had, may you respawn in a better game than this one."

Maddock managed half a smile and said, "June, you pulled our asses out of a jam more times than I could ever thank you for. May the Goddess Pele welcome you to her domain."

The ground beneath their feet trembled in anticipation. Bones bowed his head. "Judith Moon, you deserved better friends than us, a better end than this. Fly now and never fall." With a grunt, he raised her above his head and flung her body far out over the seething pool of molten rock.

The glowing lava bubbled up. A lick of flame, and June was gone. Corey knelt and ripped the pack from his shoulder. Brandishing the lyre in one hand, and Zoya's knife in the other, he rose to his feet. "I'm sick of this thing ruining our lives."

With a single stroke, he slashed all seven strings. As each string parted, the instrument screamed in unholy dissonance. As if attuned to the sound, Zoya thrashed and shrieked in response. She kicked her way free of Maddock and rolled on the ground. Corey didn't pause—he ripped the lyre apart. "The arms, the crossbar, they're ours. But this damned box, it killed June, it is killing Zoya, it will kill all of us."

Too late, Maddock yelled, "No, Corey don't…"

His friend wheeled about and flung the lyre body into the glowing pit. A gust of hot wind swept the hilltop. On the southern horizon, a line of clouds flickered with distant lightning. Zoya arched her back and sprang laughing to her feet. "I am free. Three thousand years I have waited and now I am *free!*"

A dark nimbus swirled about her. Dust, smoke, and fumes from the volcano all merged into the cloud, rising, spinning. She raised her arms, and the whirling maelstrom clothed her body in night. From above, the dark goddess shook the air with her laughter. Rocks crumbled and roared into the bubbling hell below. Still the figure grew until the stars themselves vanished behind a cloud of smothering chaos.

Like hammer blows, the peals of laughter knocked Maddock to his knees. Then flat on his belly, he groped among the quivering stones. *Something, anything even remotely stable.* His right hand found a smooth staff, it warmed at his touch. His left gripped the rough Kevlar pack Corey had thrown down.

From above, the laughter stopped. A voice boomed out, "Who dares move in the presence of Ashera the Almighty? Who would disturb me in my hour of *triumph*?"

Silence, save for the rushing and keening of the whirling cloud. Maddock eased the bottle of ouzo from the pack. "Me, oh Great Goddess. I have a small sacrifice to offer. Let me be first to make libation to your everlasting strength."

"And so it will be your last, mortal. Give me of your blood, that I may consign your flesh to the fires. The smoke of your burning will please my nostrils."

"You shall have it, Goddess." Maddock poured a generous splash of liquor on the stony ground. "Come, drink, as you would drink of my lifeblood."

The fiery lava below boiled crimson, then white, illuminating a tendril of smoke that drifted down from the swirling monstrosity above. It hovered above the puddle of ouzo, drawing it from the ground. Maddock tipped the bottle again. "I have more, Goddess. It is yours to take."

He felt a cold malevolence radiate from the coiling smoke as it quested toward the bottle. Clad in darkness, Zoya strode toward him and reached down. The tendril, an extension of her finger, thickened as it flowed into the glass neck. Maddock reached up with his staff and thrust it into the goddess. "In! Into the bottle. By the Lyre of David and the Stone of Abraham, I command you."

The smooth horn blazed white-hot in his hand. He felt Ashera's rage envelope him. Maddock forced his mind to quiet. He sought his *ruah,* his inner strength as Halima had taught him. Ashera in her fury bombarded him with rocks. Amidst the chaos, he heard another voice call out, "By the Lyre of David and the Stone of Abraham, I command you."

Corey. Just knowing that Doctor Denarious had seized his wand and joined the battle gave him strength. From the other side, Bones's voice roared. "By the Lyre of David and the Stone of Abraham, I command you!"

Maddock pushed himself to his feet and thrust harder into

the swirling mass. This time all three of them chanted the command. A hail of rocks pounded Maddock to his knees. Still, he rose, tall and straight, with the King of Israel with the Queen of Sheba at his back. Ashera wailed, moaned, and diminished. Her shadow wrapped Zoya one more time, then fled to the depths of the ouzo bottle.

Maddock dropped his staff and jammed in the cork. Zoya collapsed to the ground taking Corey with her. Bones stood at the lip of hell and said, "Slick move, dude."

38

High above the Danakil Desert, a vulture looked down at the singular white rectangle stretched across a cluster of rocks. It circled lower, testing the air for the distinctive odor of decaying meat. Movement. Legs. Some animals lay beneath the rectangle. The enormous bird landed on a rock and fluttered its wings.

"Crap!" Bones sat up. "It's a big freaking buzzard giving us the eye."

Maddock rolled onto one elbow and looked out from under Corey's towel. "You must smell like a porkchop or something."

Bones waved an arm. "Go on…beat it…shoo."

The vulture cocked its head to one side and hopped to another rock.

Corey didn't bother sitting up. "I'm not dead yet."

Zoya chimed in, "Really, I'm feeling much better."

"It pines for the fjords." Maddock flopped back down.

Corey lifted his head. "What? That's the best you could do?"

"It's all I could remember."

Bones locked eyes with the bird. "If it gets much closer, I'm gonna have it for lunch."

The vulture decided its prospects were better elsewhere. It ruffled its feathers, defecated on the rock, and flapped into the air. Bones watched it go. "I wasn't that hungry anyway."

They had spent the rest of the previous night on the crater's rim. Nearly naked once more, Zoya had suffered most from the pummeling debris. She lay unconscious among the rocks until the sun had cleared the eastern horizon. Corey fussed about her, but there was little he could do except spread the shredded remains of her shirt across her chest and dab her forehead with water.

"She'll survive," Maddock said. "We've got other problems tonight."

Bones held up his crossbar. "Yeah, like these damned

things."

Corey looked up. "I didn't just walk through hell to give mine away."

"We won't be seeing hell until tomorrow, pal." Bones picked up his crossbar. "But I'm not going through life worrying about this thing."

"We know the entity's name now." Maddock drew the ibex horn from his belt. "We can free ourselves."

With that, he reached down and touched it to the ouzo bottle at his feet. "I renounce you, Ashera. I renounce and abjure you. As you are bound, so am I free."

He flung the lyre arm far out over the crater's rim. It spun in the air, catching the first golden rays of the morning sun. Bones followed, touching the bottle, renouncing the goddess, and hurling the crossbar up into the sunlight. Corey cradled his length of black horn and watched. "A real wizard's wand, not cosplay, but the *real deal*."

Maddock picked up the ouzo bottle. He held it out and lowered his voice. "Just remember, what you own, owns you."

Corey looked down at Zoya's unconscious form. "I remember what brought us here. That's enough."

As the last vestige of David's sacred lyre touched the bottle, Corey shouted, "I renounce you Ashera. I abjure you and regret ever hearing your name. As you are bound, so am I freed."

The horn glittered in the morning sun as it arced past the crater's rim. "That was easier than I thought," Corey said. "What do we do with the bottle?"

Maddock shook his head. "Protect it. As long as the glass is intact and the cork stays in, we should be safe."

"I'd say give it a concrete overcoat and dump it in the ocean."

Zoya chose that moment to twitch her head and moan. Corey knelt and held her hand. She screamed and jumped to her feet. Bones managed to tackle her as she ran for the crater's edge. Corey looped a bit of gut string around her ankles and bound them together. "You can let her go now."

Zoya thrashed and cursed. She bent double and tore at the

string. "That burns—it burns me. Why, why? Dammit, let me go."

She eventually wore herself out and collapsed. Corey sat at her side, just out of reach. "She's not free, she's not free at all."

"Give her a little time." Maddock wrapped the bottle and nestled it in Corey's pack. "We need to move as soon as she's ready."

Zoya gasped and tried to sit up. "I'm okay, I'm okay. That thing, it had me…it had me…" She looked at her hands, "…and now it doesn't. What happened?"

"We destroyed the lyre." Corey watched her face. "All of it, including the sound box."

"And that thing?"

"Ashera," Maddock said. "She's owned you for a long time, hasn't she?"

Zoya nodded but said nothing more. Corey used his knife to cut her free. Bones did a double take. "That's gut from the lyre…that's a piece of Margo's intestine."

Corey nodded and flung it into the crater. "I found it there on the ledge."

Maddock hefted the pack. "We ready then?"

"No, no…" Corey draped the scrap of shirt over Zoya's shoulders. "Don't we have something she can wear?"

The young woman laughed. "My people dressed like this for thousands of years. Does it bother you?"

Corey turned red and started to unbutton his own shirt. "Here, here, at least…"

"Don't be so stupid. With your skin, an hour of sun and you'd look like bacon."

Bones just grinned. "She has a couple of good points there."

"Shut it, before I relieve you of a few inconvenient body parts."

Maddock had to admit, her tattered shorts would be street-legal in Key West. As for a top, they'd have to figure out something later. He let Bones lead them down—Corey and Zoya followed. Maddock took rearguard, *better to enjoy the view.* By late morning he called a halt. The sun had started taking its toll and even Zoya's dark shoulders had turned red.

Now flat on his back, Maddock heard the vulture flap off into the sky. *Would Bones actually have eaten it?* It started to seem likely. They huddled together in what little shade the rocks afforded. Corey's useful towel now seemed like a stroke of genius. Even so, the heat had become oppressive. June had mentioned water, just twenty-five miles west of the crash site. Maddock did a little figuring. *Say, ten to fifteen miles each?* He wasn't sure they had enough water. *By daylight, we might find more in the wreckage…*He let that circle around in his head while he listened to Zoya talk.

"…we were playing Athens and this asshole tries to rip my lyre…grab and run, you know. I messed him up pretty good for that. Bastard broke the soundbox and I'm like scant. Without an instrument, they would send me back to the States and I'm *sure* not ready for that…"

Corey mumbled something and Zoya continued. "No, seriously not fixable…so I went looking for a replacement. Found one too."

"Pawn shop?"

"Hell no, university museum. They didn't even know what it was…had it upside down on a stand…label said some kind of weird mask or something."

"So how…" Corey paused. "You ripped it. You ripped it from a *museum?*"

"Hell yeah, how else was I going to get it?"

Bones rolled to one side. "Seriously, you looted that thing and no one saw you?"

Maddock heard Zoya snort and grumble. Corey spoke a few reassuring words and asked something. Zoya sniffed. "Give me a drink of water and I'll tell you."

Maddock pulled a bottle from the pack and handed it to Corey. "Everyone drink their share. Leave me some."

After Zoya took her swallow, she passed the bottle to Bones and continued. "…yeah, I fitted the arms and crossbar from my instrument to this beat-up carcass I had rescued and it worked—real good too—sounded great in fact. Teacher-lady thought I was a genius."

Maddock nodded "The gal at Hagia Irene. I figured she was talking about you."

"That's the one. She flew us to Istanbul, then Jerusalem. I picked up a fanboy along the way."

"Let me guess," Bones said, "the Preacher man."

"Nope…Lazar. He gave me ten thousand bucks for my piece of crap lyre, and I split back to the States."

"And…and you didn't feel anything?" Corey said.

"Rich, I felt richer than I ever had. It didn't start to bother me for a few months, then I got the heebie-jeebies—I don't have to explain—looked up Lazar, but he'd already sold it."

"But you said you worked for him…"

"I did. Ten thousand bucks doesn't buy as much steak as I thought it would. Ouzo is expensive as hell in the States…didn't know that either. He wouldn't tell me who bought the sound box, but I finally tracked it to the Preach."

"Crap, my feet are hot." Bones flopped on his back. "You tried to rip it again?"

"No. Well, not then anyway. I started playing Dragon Apocalypse and went to Dragon Con and just kind of stalked him…you know the rest."

Corey sat up. "No, no I don't. How did it involve me?"

Maddock sat up as well. "Coincidences like that don't happen."

"No, well yeah, kind of…" Zoya gave Corey a peck on his cheek. "See, I didn't know who you were, but Lazar found out from someone at Humpty Dumpty's auction or whatever it was. I overheard him talking about it with a customer."

"Bet it was Prester John, his smuggling bud."

"Bingo…Figured I'd step in and preempt the whole transaction. Didn't work out. Funny thing, I already knew Doctor Denarious here, but I didn't realize I'd actually like him."

"Oh great." Corey flopped back down. "I was being used."

"Yeah, well you were." Zoya dropped her voice and

murmured something in his ear.

"You have got to say that again, because I don't believe I heard right."

"I said *I'm sorry*, okay?" She glared at Maddock and Bones. "You two shut up. This is private."

She muttered something else in Corey's ear. He grunted and said, "I had fun too, but then you were a total witch."

Maddock heard her say something about *that freaking box* before he fell into a restless doze. A few hours later, he awoke, dizzy, nauseated, and running with sweat. Bones poked his arm. "Hey man, wake up."

Low in the western sky, the sun cast long shadows across the desert terrain. Maddock tried to clear his head. "What's happening?"

"Brother Corey's not doing too good."

"It's the heat," Zoya said. Legs crossed, she sat with his head in her lap.

Corey's eyes fluttered. He mumbled and twitched but didn't respond to Maddock's hand on his forehead. "We're all dehydrated. Bones, how much water do we have left?"

His friend rummaged through the pack and found four bottles. Maddock poured half a bottle on Corey's head and rubbed it into his hair. "We need to get the rest of this into him as well."

Bones handed him another bottle. "You look like crap. Drink some yourself."

Maddock drank half and passed it to Zoya. "You too." He turned to Bones. "Drink some as well—I'm not going to carry you."

His friend took a swallow from the third bottle and recapped it. "We won't make it out of here on what we've got."

Corey stirred and opened his eyes. Zoya gave him a few sips and poured more in his hair. He tried to sit up. "What...what...the hell?"

"You were delirious, lover boy. Drink the rest of this." Zoya handed him the bottle.

Maddock looked at their remaining water. "We drink it all

now and head for the crash site. If there's more water, we may live. If not, we're screwed."

The sun hovered just over the western horizon as they reached the lower slopes. Something seemed wrong. Maddock held up a fist and ducked behind a boulder. Bones drew up behind him and whispered, "Crap, do you hear that?"

"Someone is at the plane."

Zoya said, "Afar raiders. They will kill us."

"How do you know that?"

She pulled a grim face. "The filthy Afar will kill you for your boots. They will kill me because my father was Tigray."

Bones peered over the rock. "We should go around them. Ten hours of night march and we'll hit the river."

Zoya shook her head. "Too late. They already know we're here."

_____

39

"**Not possible,**" **Corey** said. "I barely know we're here."

"In the Danakil, you either know your surroundings, or you die."

Maddock looked again. A piece of burnt wing jutted into the air. He couldn't make out much else. "We bluff our way through. We're tourists, you were our guide, but we got lost."

Corey raised a finger. "Are you forgetting something? She's not quite uh…modest enough for that kind of company."

"Bones, give her your shirt. She can cover her head with our towel. It will have to do."

Bones's shirt hung almost to Zoya's knees. She rolled up the sleeves and glared at the three men. "No one is fooled. A single woman with three strange men? One of them half naked? This is ridiculous."

"It's all we got, lady." Bones hitched up his pants and tightened his belt. "Let's get this over with."

Maddock led the way, hands at his side, clearly unarmed. Zoya and Corey followed, with Bones bringing up the rear like some enormous servant. Two men stood near the wrecked fuselage. Two others crouched nearby. None of them seemed surprised when Maddock rounded a low hill and stepped into the open. He noted that all four carried ancient Kalashnikov rifles.

"Hello!" He called out. "Thank God we've found you. We've been lost for days."

None of the men moved. They didn't speak, but merely watched as Zoya, Corey, and finally Bones emerged from behind the hill. Maddock stopped. Zoya stepped up behind him and muttered, "Now we die."

A gust of desert air blew down from the north and hissed among the scattered boulders. Maddock caught the stink of burnt jet fuel before the wind shifted to the west. Zoya stood perfectly still, Bones's shirt flapping about her legs. Corey whispered, "Aren't they going to say something?"

One of the men, perhaps their leader, made a remark to his comrades. The other nodded and grunted something back. Zoya pushed past Maddock and shouted at the four. They all waved their rifles and shouted back. She yelled and gestured. They all shook their heads.

One knelt and aimed his rifle at Maddock. "Whoa, whoa, whoa…" he raised his hands, "what's happening?"

"These idiots are Tigray, *my* people. They think this is a trap."

"Tell them we were on the plane, that we overshot Mek'ele. Tell them we need medical attention."

A little more shouting, the leader beckoned them over. Shortly after, they were bouncing around in the back of an aging Land Rover. A weathered canvas flapped and rattled overhead. It gave some relief from the sun but left them open to clouds of blowing sand and grit. Maddock pulled his t-shirt over his nose. Bones had fallen asleep behind the front seats, oblivious to the jouncing and heat. Two of the men followed in another vehicle, seemingly inured to the dust.

Maddock asked how these men had found them in the first place. Zoya explained. "When we didn't land in Mek'ele, they tracked us on radar. Everyone figured us for military from Addis Ababa. The provisional government sent these poor guys out to see what we were up to."

"*Provisional* government?" Corey said.

"Yeah, the Tigray region broke away a few years ago. Addis wants control, but they're dominated by the Afar majority. The place is gone all to hell. I think the Preach had been selling weapons to both sides."

Corey gestured at the dusty barren hills unrolling behind them. "They're fighting over *this?*"

Zoya nodded toward the mountains ahead. "Any water to be found in this region comes from up there. They have fields and herds. They even have hydroelectric power. Addis wants it all. They pit Tigray against Afar, Christian against Muslim, children against parents." She spit over the tailgate. "When I leave, I'm never coming back."

"If any of us *can* leave."

"Oh, believe me. These guys don't want a beef with the Americans—especially the CIA. They'll dump us at the embassy and haul ass."

Bones awoke about halfway up a long winding set of switchbacks that climbed from the desert floor. He gazed over a particularly sheer cliff and said, "Where the hell are we?"

Maddock grinned. "Climbing the stairway to heaven, as Zoya tells it."

They crossed a deep gorge. Far beneath the narrow bridge, a cataract plunged from rock to rock on its way to oblivion in the desert sands below. Their small caravan reached Mek'ele late that afternoon. Clusters of neat white houses and shops nestled beneath terraced mountainsides.

Past the airport and the University, a nondescript brown office crouched behind a gravel parking lot. The Land Rover pulled up in front with a squeal of dusty brakes. Their driver pointed to the building and shouted, "Out...out...*out*."

Bones vaulted over the back. "Well, I can take a hint."

Maddock shouldered their pack and climbed after. He lowered the tailgate for Corey and Zoya. "You heard the man. He even speaks English."

While Corey crawled out, Zoya hopped over the side. She scowled back at the two men. "That, and 'money' are probably the only words they know."

Bones refastened the tailgate while Maddock checked out the entrance. No flagpole, no sign, nothing about the place suggested an American presence. Corey hesitated. "Doesn't seem much like an embassy to me."

Maddock looked around the corner. A dusty Escalade lurked in the building's shadow. "Oh, there's gringos inside alright—just not sure what kind."

He heard gears clunk, a motor growl, and the clatter of tires on gravel as their rescuers fled. Maddock pushed open the mirrored glass door. A small man waited on the other side, hands behind his back.

Maddock stopped dead. "You!"

Corey pushed his way in. "Hey, you're the guy that gave me the Sally's laptop."

"One and the same, my dear Corey Dean…or should I call you Doctor Denarious?"

Bones shoved his way between them, fists at ready. "What new hell? I'm gonna…"

Maddock caught his arm. "Wait a minute. Something weird is going on."

"I know him." Zoya had slipped behind Bones. "He works for Lazar."

Maddock spat. "Uzi."

"Aren't you glad to see me, petal?"

"Are you freaking kidding me?" Bones clenched his fists and towered over the little man. "I know you too…you slimy bastard, you killed our friend Sally, and now you went and killed June."

Uzi's shock looked genuine. "Sister Judith is dead?"

"Like you didn't know you little creep. You messed up her nav system so we'd overshoot the airport."

"That wasn't my doing. She was bringing the lyre directly to me."

"Well, she sure as hell didn't. That Ashera got loose. It killed June—almost killed all of us."

Maddock stepped between them. "Back off, Bones. I think he's telling the truth…for once."

"It doesn't matter now." Uzi looked down and shook his head. "With Ashera free, we're all dead. May I assume the lyre was destroyed?"

"Yeah, chucked it into a volcano, but…"

"Nothing can save us then."

Maddock pulled the bottle from his pack. "…but first, we trapped her in here."

Uzi stiffened. He stared at the bottle for a long moment, then said, "Not one of you move."

Like graveyard ghosts, six men appeared, gliding into the room from behind desks, from open doors, from hiding places Maddock hadn't even realized were there. Bones shifted, crouching slightly, arms apart. Uzi twitched his head. "Don't, Mr. Bonebrake. You will all die, and we will risk releasing that creature again."

Maddock glanced around at the array of submachine guns pointed at them. "Stand down, Bones." He directed his gaze back at Uzi. "You don't want me to drop this, and I don't want any more of my people killed. What's your plan?"

"What it's been all along. I am going to lock Ashera in a titanium cylinder and lower her into the ground. In preparation, we have bored a well ten kilometers deep and have the cement on hand to seal it forever."

Corey said. "Bullcrap. It's all magma down there."

"A hundred clicks west of here it's all granite…over six hundred million years old, and it's deep." He inched toward them. "Now give me the bottle, Mr. Maddock."

"Show me something I can believe, Uzi. I want to see this titanium cylinder first."

The man glanced at his crew and made a sign. Two of them hustled out. "A little faith, petal…a little patience."

Maddock backed away and waited. Five minutes passed before a heavy wooden dolly trundled into the room, a gray metallic cylinder cradled between its wheels. Uzi gave the lid a half-turn and lifted it away. "We made it large enough to take an entire lyre. Pity—we could have saved so much work drilling that shaft."

Ignoring the guns, Zoya shoved her way forward. "You mean you were going to bury that thing with me still bonded to it?"

"Relax, sweetums—but of course—you and your friends too. Greater good, you know." He smirked. "Besides, I'm not a very nice man."

"You manipulated us." Maddock clenched his fists. "You made us do your dirty work and didn't even ask."

Corey glared at the little man. "You gave me Sally's computer. You set me up."

"You *are* the clever one, petal. How else would I track your sordid peregrinations?"

Bones had stood silent for the entire exchange. He pushed Corey aside. "I want to know what June had to do with all of this."

"No secrets, my muscular friend. Sister Judith was with us for many years. Who would suspect, yes? Did you never wonder why she was always there when you most needed her? Judith was a woman of many talents. She will be sorely missed." Uzi turned and fixed his eyes on Maddock. "We are wasting time."

The empty cylinder had a foam liner. Maddock reached in and placed the bottle on the bottom. "Now what?"

"Get back, everyone." Uzi made a hand signal. "You four, call in the helicopter and secure our perimeter."

As four of the men dashed out, two others poured a thick liquid into the cylinder. The mass hissed and bubbled, cresting the lip and running down the sides.

"Pour-foam," Corey eyed the cylinder. "Won't it get too hot?"

"Aeronautic grade…exothermic, yes, but all has been calculated, Doctor Denarius. All the nerdy little science bits have been resolved for you."

The foam soon crusted over. Uzi peeled it off the sides and trimmed the surface. He replaced the lid and turned it until Maddock heard a sequence of loud clicks. Uzi heaved a sigh and stepped back. "The bolts have locked. It is done."

Bones had been prowling the room—little to see besides gray filing cabinets, aging Steelcase desks, and a linoleum floor. He circled back to the titanium cylinder and gave the top a perfunctory heave. "Done for you, maybe. What about us? You're no ambassador. This place looks like the DMV, not some kind of fancy embassy."

"Oh, but I am…attaché that is. Unofficial you know, provisional government and all, but I do have clout in Washington." He waved his arms. "Interim passports for everyone, open tickets and chartered flights, anywhere you wish, how about that?"

Maddock shook his head. "Bones and I, we're going to see this thing through. We'll ride that chopper out to your well-site.

I want to watch it go down. I want to see the cement go in. Then maybe we'll talk about passports and tickets…and a few other things."

Zoya nudged Corey. He looked up from the metal cylinder. "We'll take the tickets and stuff, Mr. Uzi."

"Yeah?" Bones said. "What are you two planning?"

"First, there's that Apocalypse machine back at Makuria. It killed June. We're going to pull its plug…permanently."

Zoya grinned and grabbed his arm. "And after that, there's this luxury yacht I own. We'll take her on a Mediterranean cruise, all the way to the Atlantic."

Corey nodded. "All the way to England and up the Thames. I want to keep that promise we made to Chaz and deliver his documents to the Bodleian Library."

Bones looked him in the eye. "That's a pretty ambitious side quest. Think you're up to it, *Doctor Denarius?*"

"After what we just went through? Hell yeah!"

The End

ABOUT THE AUTHOR

David Wood is the USA Today bestselling author of the Dane Maddock Adventures and many other popular titles. He writes science fiction under the name Finn Gray and fantasy as David Debord. He is a member of International Thriller Writers and the Horror Writers Association. David lives with his family in Santa Fe, New Mexico.

Made in United States
Troutdale, OR
09/21/2023

13099124R00195